Letters to my Daughters is the twelfth novel from beloved and bestselling author Emma Hannigan.

Letters to my Daughters spent four weeks at Number One in the Original Fiction bestseller chart in Ireland on publication in 2018. Emma's novels *The Perfect Gift* and *The Wedding Promise* were also Number One bestsellers in Ireland. *The Secrets We Share* won the Romantic Novelists' Association's Epic Romantic Novel award. Emma won Woman of the Year in the literature category of the Irish Tatler Women of the Year Awards and was shortlisted twice for an Irish Book Award. Emma published her bestselling memoir *Talk to the Headscarf* in 2011, which was updated and extended in 2017 as *All to Live For: Fighting Cancer. Finding Hope* and was a top ten bestseller in Ireland.

In 2005, Emma discovered that she had the BRCA1 gene mutation which carries an 85 per cent risk of developing breast cancer and a 50 per cent risk of developing ovarian cancer. In 2007 she was diagnosed with breast cancer for the first time and her eleven-year battle with cancer began. As an ambassador for Breast Cancer Ireland Emma worked hard to dispel the fears around cancer and spread hope about new treatments. In February 2018 Emma shared with her readers that her dedicated team of doctors had exhausted all avenues in terms of her treatment. In Emma's final days, she launched a social media campaign #HelpEmmaHelpOthers to raise €100,000 for Breast Cancer Ireland. Two weeks later, shortly before her death, Emma revealed that her target had been reached.

Praise for Emma Hannigan's uplifting novels

'Wise, warm and full of joy. Uplifting and magical,
like Emma herself'
Cathy Kelly

'Warm, intelligent and brilliant'
Marian Keyes

'A beautiful book by an exceptional author. Lose
yourself in her wonderful writing'
Sinéad Moriarty

'Hannigan's novel, much like the vivacious
author herself, is brimming with hope, joy
and inspiration'
Sunday Independent

'A moving tale celebrating the bonds
between women, Emma Hannigan beautifully
captures the difficult and wondrous thing
that is loving and learning to let go . . .
just a little. An excellent read'
Irish Tatler

'Emotional and heartbreaking . . . A fast-paced
story with endearingly warm characters – you'll
savour this touching tale'
Candis magazine, Book of the Month

'This fast-paced and endearing novel is about
friendship between women, accepting yourself
and trusting your own judgement'
Belfast Telegraph

More praise for Emma Hannigan

'Restores our faith in human nature
and makes us feel warm inside'
Writing Magazine

'Moving, imaginative and believable, this emotional
novel is the perfect read for a rainy day'
Reveal magazine

'This is her best novel yet. Her heart and soul was
poured into every word of this story and it just radiates
from the pages . . . a wonderful, heartfelt, emotive book'
Shaz's Book Blog

'Savour a novel from an author who knows what
makes people tick'
Irish Independent

'I didn't just like it, I really LOVED it . . .
Grab this book, curl up on the couch and
prepare to have a few lump in your throat
moments too'
Celeste Loves Books

'The author deals with some hard-hitting and sensitive
issues, giving the story a depth that I really did not
expect . . . Emma Hannigan is a gifted storyteller'
Random Things Through My Letterbox

'An inspirational novel . . . Warm, lovingly written
and full of hope'
Bleach House Library

'This was a feel-good read great for the cold winter
nights ahead . . . This is yet another winner for me
from Emma Hannigan . . . She has become a firm
favourite of mine'
Rea Book Reviews

Emma Hannigan

Letters

to my

Daughters

HACHETTE
BOOKS
IRELAND

First published in Ireland in 2018
by Hachette Books Ireland

First published in paperback in Ireland in 2018
by Hachette Books Ireland

1

Cataloguing in Publication Data is available from the British Library

ISBN 978 1 4736 6004 5

Envelope motif © Aleksandr Piven/Shutterstock

Typeset in Palatino by Palimpsest Book Production Ltd, Falkirk, Stirlingshire

Printed and bound in Great Britain by Clays Ltd, St Ives plc

Hachette Books Ireland's policy is to use papers that are natural, renewable and
recyclable products and made from wood grown in well-managed forests and
other controlled sources. The logging and manufacturing processes are expected
to conform to the environmental regulations of the country of origin.

Hachette Books Ireland
8 Castlecourt Centre
Castleknock, Dublin 15
An Hachette UK company
Carmelite House,
50 Victoria Embankment
London EC4Y 0DZ

www.hachettebooksireland.ie

For Sheila Crowley with love, light and
so much admiration.

Prologue

MARTHA BRADY WASN'T THE TYPE OF WOMAN who liked waiting around. She glanced at her watch for the umpteenth time and clicked her tongue against the roof of her mouth in disgust.

'Why don't you go on ahead, Grandma? I'm sure Nanny May will be here soon. It's not like her to be late. Besides, I'm not going to die if I'm left here on my own for a few minutes.'

Looking at Ali's anxious face, Martha softened. It wasn't her granddaughter's fault the other woman was choosing today, of all days, to be tardy.

'If I don't leave soon, I'll miss Marissa's communion mass. The Reilly family have been so good to me over the years. They're of impeccable breeding so they certainly wouldn't make me feel bad for turning up at the last minute, but I'd really rather not do it all the same.'

'Right,' said Ali, rolling her eyes.

'What's with the attitude?' Martha asked as she dialled Nanny May's mobile for the second time. She'd noticed this cheeky sort of carry-on creeping in with Ali over the last while. Martha thought she was spoilt rotten and, being an only child, that she got away with murder.

When she'd mentioned it to her daughter, Rose had scoffed and said it was typical teenage behaviour and to ignore it. But Martha wasn't the ignoring sort and never had been.

'I wasn't aware I had an attitude,' Ali said. 'Sorry,' she mumbled. 'I suppose I'm a bit baffled why you're so eager to rush off to Mrs Reilly.' She did an exaggerated shudder. 'She's rude and obnoxious. Any time she goes into the shop, she finds fault with something. I asked Mum why she doesn't just go someplace else.'

'I can't imagine her being that way,' Martha said with a sniff, 'but I have such a special bond with my mothers . . .'

Being a community midwife meant Martha got to know her mothers and their children better than most. All the same, Ali was family and there was no way she was leaving her.

'I'm not happy about abandoning ship. Hop in the car and I'll drop you over to Nanny May's. That way I'll know you're in safe hands and I can do this trip without worrying. The Reillys are holding the communion mass in the grandparents' estate and it's at least an hour's drive away. So I can't rush back if you need something.'

'Okay,' said Ali. 'It's ages since I've visited Nanny May's, so it'll be lovely. She got new curtains in her lounge, she told me. I'm dying to see them. Apparently they make a statement.'

'Can you remember where your mother keeps the spare key to Nanny May's house?' Martha asked. 'Just in case she's had a fall or something and we need to let ourselves in.'

Ali grabbed it from a drawer in the kitchen and they made their way to the car.

'I bet she's caught up with one of her sewing circle friends and has forgotten she said she'd come,' Ali said.

'Yes, I expect you're right,' said Martha. All of a sudden she had a bad feeling. It crept over her like a slow shiver.

Martha pulled up at the house. The front-room curtains were drawn shut and there was no sign of life. Martha and Ali got out of the car and went up the garden path. Ali rang the doorbell but there was no answer.

Using the key, Martha opened the door and they walked into the tiny hallway.

'Nanny May?' Martha called out. 'It's just us. We were wondering if you've forgotten about minding Ali today?'

Silence. They looked at one another. Walking into the kitchen, they could see no remnants of breakfast. The modern, bright interior surprised Martha. The last time she'd stood in this room must have been twenty years ago, when Nanny May had first bought the place. Back then it was poky and dark, with Formica cupboards and patterned linoleum on the floors. Now it was bedecked with cream high-shine units complete with a neat yet smart breakfast bar, and plush-looking high leather stools with chrome legs to match the cupboard doors.

The wall to the once dark and poky dining room had been knocked through, creating a large space with lots of natural light. The curtains were surprisingly cheery, boasting bold stripes of rose pink against cream and acid green. Clearly green-fingered, Nanny May had a wonderful selection of plants, from tiny ones on surfaces to the large yuccas that brightened shaded corners. The whole air of the place was not what Martha would've expected her to choose in a million years. She'd always assumed May was a very old-fashioned and traditional type of woman. So this edgy-looking place made her feel quite uneasy.

Ali called her name once more before walking back to the hallway and pushing open the living-room door.

'Nanny May? Nope, no sign of her in here. Oh wow, her curtains *are* divine,' she said.

Without thinking, Martha walked out into the hall and towards the bedroom at the rear of the cottage. As she pushed the door open, she could tell by the strange atmosphere that something had happened. Gasping, she looked across and confirmed what she'd just begun to suspect.

'Any luck?' Ali shouted.

Backing out of the room and closing the door, Martha apprehended her granddaughter.

'She's there,' she said, swallowing. 'I'm so sorry, darling . . . She's . . . she's passed away.'

'No!' Tears instantly rolled down Ali's cheeks. 'She can't . . . Oh no, poor Nanny May, and she was all alone. Oh Grandma, this is terrible.'

As Ali launched herself into her arms, Martha wasn't quite sure what to do. They'd never had a physical relationship. Not the way Ali and Rose did. They were always hugging and doing that foreign-style cheek-kissing thing. Martha wasn't comfortable with it, and Rose certainly hadn't been raised to public displays of affection. These were mitigating circumstances, however, and besides, Ali had left her with no choice as she wrapped her arms around her like a koala.

'We need to call people,' Martha said after a few minutes as she led Ali back into the kitchen. 'There's Dr Graham, for a start. He's the first port of call.'

'What about Mum and Aunt Bea and Aunt Jeannie . . . surely they need to know first,' Ali said as she yanked her mobile from her jeans pocket.

'Okay, you call the family and I'll get on to Dr Graham.'

'Mum?' Ali said as tears choked her. 'It's Nanny May . . . Oh Mum, she's dead.'

Within minutes it seemed Ali had called half of Pebble Bay and they were all on their way over.

'Did you want to see her?' Martha asked. Ali nodded, but said she'd wait until Rose arrived. 'Will you be okay for a moment if I go in and make sure she's in the state she'd like to be found? It's the least we owe her after the years she's given to our family.'

'Actually, I don't want to see her,' Ali said, beginning to sob again. 'I want to remember her the way she was.'

'All right, darling,' said Martha. 'You wait here for a few moments and I'll just fix her if she needs it.'

Martha walked back to the bedroom. Her breath caught as she looked over at Nanny May. It was as if she were frozen in time, with the beginnings of a smile on her face. She was sitting perfectly straight in a rather beautiful velvet-covered armchair. Upholstered in a deep sea green, it picked up the kingfishers in the bedroom curtains. The throw on her bed was clearly from the same collection as the curtains and cushions. Martin and Rose must've done the decor, Martha decided. All the same, this wasn't remotely what she'd have thought Nanny May's house would be like. She'd expected it to be gloomy, with old tweed blankets draped over sagging sofas and a tired-looking bedroom with a dark wooden suite. Walking into the en suite, she was further surprised to find a modern and bright room with one of those large round shower heads like they had in the house in Ballyshaden.

She backed out and closed over the door in case anyone suspected she'd been snooping.

She gazed at Nanny May. She was dressed in one of the outfits Martha had seen a hundred times or more: taupe three-quarter-length slacks with a pristine white top and cardigan. Her hair was blow-dried and her carefully applied yet understated make-up looked as if it had just been put on. Doubting herself for a moment, Martha approached her and stooped to take her hand. The cold, hardened skin confirmed she was indeed gone.

Even in death you seem to be able to do things without fanfare and yet manage to make it look easy, Martha mused.

She was about to walk out of the room when a small stack of envelopes caught her eye on the dressing table. She walked over and looked at them. Each envelope bore a single name in May's beautiful script-like handwriting, one each for Beatrice, Rose and Jeannie. Feeling momentarily stung that there wasn't one with her name on it, Martha zoned in on a letter that lay under the others. It had an envelope, but May clearly hadn't got around to folding it and placing it in there.

She knew she shouldn't read it, but seeing it was addressed to her husband, she couldn't resist. She picked it up.

My dearest Jim . . .

The lump in Martha's throat gave way to a sprinkling of tears as she speed-read the words that Nanny May had clearly written from her heart. More than that, these words were from her soul.

Glancing at the woman she'd chosen to help raise her children, she shook her head slowly. So many things made sense now.

Brushing away her tears roughly with the back of her hand, Martha gathered up the letters. Placing the one addressed to her husband in the envelope Nanny May had intended to use, she walked quickly out of the room. Her handbag was still on the hall table where she'd left it a while before. Just as the doorbell sounded, she stuffed the letters inside and snapped shut the clasp.

You reckoned you'd have the final say, Martha thought waspishly, but sometimes even the best-thought-out plans don't come to pass.

Chapter 1

MARTHA GAZED OUT FROM THE FRONT WINDOW of her cottage. She and her husband Jim had made the wonderful decision to retire to the wilds of Connemara, swapping the hustle and bustle of Dublin for trees bending in the breeze and uninterrupted ocean views. A little reminder had just popped up on her tablet, letting her know that it was their first anniversary here at Mariner's Cottage in the rural village of Ballyshaden.

Her old life in Pebble Bay, in Dublin, seemed a lifetime ago. Of course, they still visited their daughters, Beatrice and Rose, and their wonderful granddaughter, Ali, on a regular basis. It was a four-hour drive, but they knew it like the backs of their hands, and the roads were predominantly good once they hit the main motorway. Their other daughter, Jeannie, was living in LA, so they only saw her every now and then, but that suited all round.

The last time they'd seen Jeannie had been in Dublin, for Nanny May's funeral, a month ago. There'd been a huge turnout for her. The girls were still devastated at her loss, a matter that Martha was rather more philosophical about. Now they were talking about organising a month's mind mass.

'She was a wonderful woman,' Martha had said to Beatrice, her eldest daughter. 'But she wasn't family and she was very well paid for the job she did. It's not up to us to organise masses for her. Doesn't she have any relations who could do it? I'm not sure I can make it either way.'

Talk about saying the wrong thing. Well, Beatrice had gone into a complete tailspin, telling her that Nanny May was the linchpin that held their family together and how could she think of her in such a cold manner?

'I'm not trying to be nasty or trite, Beatrice. I am incredibly grateful to her for everything she did with you girls.'

'So you should be,' Beatrice had said in a most uncharacteristically rude way. Normally her eldest daughter wouldn't say boo to a goose. But it was clear that Nanny May was up there with the angels and saints in Beatrice's mind.

'I didn't mean to belittle her. Can we change the subject?' Martha had asked. The letters were safely stashed in the back of her underwear drawer. As she thought of the one addressed to Jim, she smarted once more.

In the end, she'd let Jim go to the mass while she'd stayed in the cottage. He'd said he didn't mind, and Martha wanted to have the place to herself for a few days. She needed to take stock of everything without having Jim breathing down her neck. She'd given it a year and she still wasn't quite sure about this move.

They'd worked hard all their adult lives, she as a midwife while Jim ran a second-generation furniture and design business called Bespoke Design. They'd both juggled their time, energy and funds to ensure their three daughters got the best start in life.

Martha's daughters were adults now, Beatrice turned forty not so long ago and the twins, Jeannie and Rose, thirty-eight. They were settled and, to the best of her knowledge, happy. She tried not to meddle in their lives too much. Jim needed constant reminding that they had to be left to get on with things, without their parents breathing down their necks. But Jim was a softie and found it hard to step away. Especially when there was an upset or a problem. He still felt it was their duty to protect the girls.

They'd made the permanent move to the family holiday home in the country because she and Jim wanted to enjoy the winter of their lives together while they were still healthy and active. In truth, she was genuinely astonished when he'd said he wanted to retire to Ballyshaden. She would have moved anywhere in a heartbeat, but she'd never for a moment thought he'd agree to leave his girls. When he'd put it to her, she'd looked at him in shock.

'You want to move? Really?'

Jim had shrugged and grinned at her. 'It's time we had some time for us, get closer together again after all the years of hard graft. Sure, Dublin is a four-hour drive away. We can see the girls any time it takes our fancy,' he'd reasoned. 'And they'll come and visit. Ali can come on the train and have a little holiday if she feels like it. And Jeannie would see Connemara as paradise in comparison to the madness of LA.'

In the end, it was turning out that Jim was far more at ease with the move than Martha. He spoke to her girls most days and kept up with their granddaughter's life via Facebook. Martha could take or leave the whole social media thing. If it weren't for Ali's insistence, she wouldn't bother at all.

'You'll be brilliant at it once you get used to it, Grandma,' Ali told her. 'This way you can be friends with me, Mum, Auntie Jeannie and Auntie Beatrice and you'll see our posts and know what we're up to.'

Her grandchild was the apple of her eye, and as for Jim . . . well, the silly old fool was utterly besotted! She hadn't thought he could fuss over anyone as much as their three daughters, until Ali came along.

'You didn't give birth to her, Jim. You need to be careful that you don't step on Rose's toes. She's her and Martin's daughter. So perhaps you should back off,' she'd said over and over again. But Martha knew she might as well be talking to the wall. Jim would never be sensible or level-headed when it came to the girls.

All the same, Martha knew that Facebook, FaceTime and Skype weren't the same as being with their daughters and granddaughter. She'd worried that Jim was being too rash and that things would go pear-shaped for them.

How wrong she had been.

A photo of their three daughters, dating back twenty years, caught Martha's eye from the sideboard. They looked so perfect in the picture. In matching clothes, right down to their patent leather shoes, they were nothing short of angelic. When they'd walk into the church or a restaurant in their home town of Pebble Bay, everyone would turn and salute her.

'Here come the Brady girls, and beautiful they are too.'

The girls had reflected so well on her, and she'd loved that. A part of her still missed those precious days. Admonishing herself, she knew she ought to be happy about her retirement, and in truth she was, most of the time.

She and Jim had built a wonderful life here in Connemara.

They were members of the golf club; she played once or twice a week and Jim was out on the course whenever possible. She'd joined a book club, although now that she thought about it, she'd only gone twice.

One thing she hated, though, was the regular 'pot luck' meals Jim's friends loved to host. Jim had returned from Dublin an hour ago and was getting ready to leave for one shortly, and as usual she was dreading it. Everyone brought a dish and they were all put out buffet style, and then people milled around eating off paper plates. Privately, Martha abhorred that idea. She never knew how hygienic other people's kitchens were and she disliked the whole mishmash, slapdash sort of arrangement. She'd mentioned that to Jim a few months ago and he'd laughed at her.

'Oh Martha, you need to learn to let go. People are aiming to have a bit of banter and share an evening or lunchtime having fun rather than pot-walloping or making it all too difficult. That's what retirement is about. It's wonderful if you allow yourself to embrace it.'

She shuddered. If she were totally honest, she didn't actually want to embrace retirement. But she couldn't be totally honest, not with Jim at any rate.

'Are you nearly ready to go, darling?' Jim asked as he walked into the room. 'I know that Clarissa O'Connor doesn't give a fiddler's if people are late. But old habits die hard and I like to keep my standards, no matter where we're going.'

'Yes, and right you are too, dear. Let me get our dishes and I'll meet you in the car.' She walked to her dressing room and shrugged into her navy blazer, then selected a Hermès scarf from her collection. She'd bought them over the years and kept them stacked in their flat orange boxes in a designated drawer in the dressing room. With her crisp white shirt, navy trousers, ballet pumps and pearl earrings, she knew she looked classically smart. While her shoulder-length blonde hair had now turned white, she knew her pale blue eyes still held the same twinkle that had attracted Jim to her so many years ago.

Satisfied that her look was the right balance between smart and casual, she went to the kitchen to pick up her dishes. One was her signature fish pie, which was always greeted with great fanfare, and the other her rocket, pear and blue cheese salad.

The fish pie was neatly wrapped in several layers of tinfoil to keep it hot. None of the hostesses seemed to share her values when it came to hygiene. Some of the ovens were spattered with food so dried in it looked like it had been there for decades. She certainly wasn't going to chance getting food poisoning. The salad was covered in a double layer of cling film, while the dressing was stored in a sterilised jam jar. She always insisted on tossing it herself, telling the hostess she was happy to help. She'd ensure she got the first portion of each of her dishes and nobody noticed that she didn't touch anything else. At least if they did, they never commented.

She joined Jim in the car and smiled. He looked ten years younger than he had this time last year. He was bronzed from the golf course and refreshed from being able to step away from his business.

'You look dashing in your tweed jacket, Mr Brady.'

'And you look very lovely too, Mrs Brady.' They smiled as they headed along the winding coast road towards the O'Connors' house.

Martha had been raised in a home where children should be neither seen nor heard. She was never under any illusion that her parents saw her as anything more than a nuisance. She learned from a young age to keep to herself and ensure she didn't antagonise Agatha, her mother. Sadly, that was easily done. All she had to do was show her face and the irritation would be plain to see in her mother's expression.

'Go on and do your homework, Martha. You must have some arithmetic that needs your attention. Your grades on the last report were nothing shy of disgraceful.'

'I've been doing homework since I got back two hours ago,' she said. 'I thought I'd make a cup of cocoa and take it to bed.'

Her mother's eyes flicked across to the kitchen clock. It was only six thirty in the evening. She'd no television in her room and toys were far too frivolous, so apart from her china doll with the creepy painted-on smile and the neat curly blonde hair that wasn't for brushing or playing with, she had very little to keep her occupied. The books in the library weren't for children either. But she'd read many of them by the time she was ten. One such book was about midwifery. It went into some rather explicit detail and even had sketches to back it up. At first the book terrified her, so she snuck it back and shoved it onto a high shelf. But curiosity got the better of her and she retrieved it. Slowly, over the space of a couple of weeks, she forced her ten-year-old self to read it from cover to cover.

By the end, she understood more about delivering babies than most adults. She longed to discuss the matter with her mother. After all, she'd had babies herself. Figuring it might be a good way for them to make a connection, she broached the subject.

'Did you enjoy being pregnant, Mother?' she asked.

'I beg your pardon?' Agatha asked, looking both disgusted and horrified.

'I was asking whether or not you enjoyed—' She didn't get to ask a second time as a firm clatter hit her across the back of the head. Reeling, she dropped the milk jug, spilling it on the floor.

'You little monster!' Agatha hissed, ensuring nobody else could hear. 'Clean up this mess and don't you dare ask me such a personal question again. I don't know who you think you're talking to. But that sort of subject is not for upstanding ladies and most certainly not for children. I ought to wash your mouth out with soap.'

Martha dropped to the floor to clear away the milk and broken crockery, realising, despite her young age, that she could never have a conversation with her mother without it ending in tears. Moments later she felt herself being dragged backwards as Agatha pulled her to her feet, forced her head against the wall and commanded her to open her mouth. She gagged and spluttered as the revolting flakes of soap powder were shoved roughly into her mouth. They foamed out onto her cheeks and down the front of her school tunic.

'Now look at the mess you've made, you horror. Wash that tunic and make sure it's dry and pressed in time for school tomorrow.'

Martha realised she was staring, with her hand to her cheek. She quashed the bad memory and pulled down the visor in the car to check her lipstick wasn't dotted onto her teeth.

She'd made it her mission not to repeat that sort of upbringing. She knew she'd done a good job of raising her daughters in a loving, disciplined home. She and Jim had made sacrifices to send them to good schools, put them through university and generally prepare them for the big bad world as best they could. They were clever girls. All very different from one another, but they'd always got on quite nicely. There was no denying they were striking-looking, too. Martha wasn't one to brag, but she knew they'd gleaned her and Jim's best features. There was no doubting the two of them made beautiful babies!

When the girls were young, not a day had passed without someone complimenting them.

'Aren't they a picture, the beautiful Brady girls?'

'Your girls got the best of both of you, Martha.'

These comments made Martha smile, especially when she witnessed Jim's chest puff out with pride as he'd reply with something like 'All four of my girls are beautiful.'

With only two years separating Beatrice from the twins, it was more for ease than effect that Martha dressed them the same. The girls were all blessed with blonde curls and her pale blue eyes. She adored fashion and had an eye for colour and style, but in truth, it wasn't difficult to make them look stunning.

She shopped in boutiques for their special occasion clothes. She loved the traditional velvet dresses with white satin collars and matching pea coats for Christmas, and cotton sailor-collared dresses with scalloped-edged cardigans for summer days out.

She knew Nanny May had an issue with it, but then she hadn't paid the woman to have an opinion on how she dressed her girls. When she wasn't around, Nanny May let them mess about in all manner of mismatched casual clothes, but that just wasn't Martha's style.

The thought of Nanny May made Martha think about the funeral. The girls had been beautifully dressed, each in a different style of black. It had given her immense pleasure when they'd filed into the church – it was as if she'd dressed them herself. They were crying terribly, though, which rather ruined the look. As always when she thought of Nanny May, Martha felt a stab of guilt through her chest. But she wasn't going to think about that now.

Martha had needed a live-in nanny because she'd worked full-time. She was a well-known figure in the coastal village of Pebble Bay, so she was used to knowing the ins and outs of all the families she'd helped over the years. A week never passed without someone calling to their door to send a little thank-you gift or to share a special moment.

'I hope you don't mind us knocking, Martha. You were there when she was born, so I wanted you to see Ruby in her dress! Can you believe she's eighteen? You're still welcome to come and join the festivities, you know.'

Martha's work was her lifeline, it was her. It meant everything. That was why this retirement idea was so alien to her.

As they pulled up outside the house, she sighed. They dined out so much and she wasn't running between patients any longer, so she was barely fitting into her clothes.

'Will you take the salad and I'll hold onto the fish?' she said to Jim as the front door was flung open. Cross that she didn't even have a moment to straighten her clothes and gather herself into a plastered-on smile, she forced a jovial delighted-to-be-here sort of greeting.

'There you are! Hello, hello, hello,' bellowed Matthew O'Connor. 'Let me take that from you,' he said, holding his hands out.

'Not at all, it's actually quite hot and I've got asbestos hands. Perhaps you'd take the wine for Jim?'

Seizing Matthew's moment of hesitation, she hotfooted it to the front door, where Clarissa was standing, looking as dishevelled as always. Martha shuddered inwardly. If the woman couldn't get it together to have her hair blow-dried, that led her to believe she wasn't anywhere near reaching her hygiene standards in general.

'Hello, Martha! Look at you, all beautifully turned out. You never fail to look stunning. I love the scarf. Did you get it in the village? Tessa is stocking some lovely ones. They're not too dear either.'

'The scarf is Hermès and it didn't come from Tessa. I don't think she stocks this kind of thing.'

'Ah, right, silly me,' said Clarissa with a shrug. 'Come on in. You're the first to arrive. You're great the way you always turn up on time!'

'It's always lovely to be invited and I actually find it rude when people are too late. It holds up proceedings.'

'Ah, hilarious,' said Clarissa, elbowing her and nearly knocking the fish pie from her grasp.

Rushing towards the kitchen with her heart thudding in her chest, she set it down with a sigh. That was a close one. If the pie had ended up on the floor, she'd be rightly stumped.

Over the course of the next half-hour the others arrived.

So too did their dishes from hell. One was a stew of some kind. It smelled more like dog food than anything she'd ever eat. The rest was a collection of lasagnes with or without meat and an array of salads.

Clarissa announced that lunch was served and they filed across to the groaning table. Martha made sure she was third in the line. That way, she was certain to get her own dish.

'Don't worry if you find a little slug or beastie in my lettuce,' said Erin. 'It's from my greenhouse and I did wash it, but sometimes the little feckers hide!'

There was a roar of laughter as the others enjoyed the thought of eating a slug. Martha forced a noise that was as close to laughter as she could muster and filled her plate with her own food.

Watching the clock, she made sure they stayed a full three hours. That was more than enough in her book. Jim had been knocking back the wine, as she'd offered to be the designated driver, so he wasn't overly aware of what time it was.

'Do we really need to leave now?' he asked. All he was short of was sticking out his bottom lip like a petulant toddler.

'I'm terribly sorry, but I'm expecting a call from Jeannie. I know she has a huge function to attend again tonight. It's all go when you're married to the top plastic surgeon in the hospital!'

She ushered Jim out the door without too much hassle and waved and thanked the host and hostess, saying it was their turn next and she looked forward to seeing them soon.

'I'm going to have a nice boozy snooze in my armchair

when we get back,' said Jim. 'You'll wake me when Jeannie calls, won't you?'

'Of course, dear,' she said, realising she needed to call their daughter and tell her she'd used her as an excuse. Jeannie would be fine with telling a little white lie.

As they sat in the car and hurtled towards home, she played the game and said she'd had a lovely time while smiling like she ought to, but inside, Martha was slowly unravelling.

Chapter 2

ROSE MONAGHAN SMILED AS SHE HEARD THE Skype call coming through on her laptop.

'Hi, Jeannie,' she called out while waving to her sister.

'Hi, sweetie! How are you?' Jeannie chirped back.

Born as identical twins, they'd looked incredibly alike until recently. Seeing as Jeannie was married to Dr Nick Marx, plastic surgeon to the beautiful people of LA, there were a few details of her face that didn't quite match Rose's any longer.

'Oh dear Lord, what happened to your eyes?' Rose asked, peering closer at the screen and scrunching her face. 'Wow, that looks sore. What on earth have you done now?'

'Nick did a quick eye-lift for me,' Jeannie said with a flippant wave of her hand. 'The bruising will go down in a couple of days. It's not sore. It was literally an in-and-out quick fix.'

'You look like you've been battered with a lump hammer,' Rose said, wincing. 'It looks seriously painful.'

'He snipped a tiny sliver of skin from my eyelids and sewed me up. It's not a big deal, and it'll make me look younger.'

'You are young. Especially compared to him,' Rose said, failing to hide her contempt for her brother-in-law. 'Doesn't he have enough women to chop up without turning his scalpel on you?'

'Ah, Rose, you're overreacting again, sweetie. Chill! I wanted it done, and if it makes me happy, that's the main thing, right?'

Rose knew she needed to change the subject. Her sister had been having Botox and fillers for the past few years, acting as if it was the same as having a facial at her local salon. She'd had breast augmentation, a nose job and countless other 'minor procedures' involving fat removal or fat injection. Most of the stuff sounded barbaric and quite unnecessary to Rose. Perhaps it was run-of-the-mill in LA, but at home in the Dublin suburb of Pebble Bay, it certainly wasn't.

'I wouldn't Skype Bea looking like that,' Rose said. 'You know how she disapproves of that sort of thing.'

'Too late,' Jeannie sighed. 'I've just been on to her. She wasn't too bad, surprisingly. I got the usual lecture about how I'm beautiful the way I am, yadda, yadda, yadda, but she was working on an order for this new shop she's opening, so she wasn't overly bothered.'

'You're lucky poor Nanny May isn't around to see you,' said Rose sadly.

'Yeah, she'd have had a total meltdown. Bless her, she used to act as if I'd been violated when I told her about my little jobs.'

'Because to her you had been violated. Nanny May didn't understand plastic surgery, especially if it was on one of us. You know she thought we were all beautiful.'

'I know, we were her *little butterflies*,' Jeannie said, taking off Nanny May's voice scarily well. 'Poor Nanny May, I still find it hard to believe she's gone.'

'I know, we all do,' said Rose.

She'd been their nanny from the time Beatrice was born. While their mother and father worked, Nanny May did the school runs, made dinner and helped with homework. She was the one who told them the facts of life and helped them when they had their first period. She was in the front row of every school play alongside their father, and the girls knew she'd kill anyone with her bare hands if they so much as considered hurting them.

She was a feisty little lady. Standing at a mere five feet in height, she commanded respect and usually got it. Her opinions were made known, and while she put her foot down on certain issues, she was wonderful at encouraging the girls to have their say too.

Jeannie had gone home for the funeral, of course. But she hadn't expected to be returning so swiftly. It wasn't strictly necessary for her to attend the will reading, but she badly needed a break, so she let Nick think it was essential for her to be there. Every now and again Jeannie got a pain in her heart that nothing but her sisters could fix, and right now she was feeling that way.

'So tell me again what the plan of action is going to be,' she said as she dotted white cream on the skin around her eyes and winced.

'We've to be at the solicitor's office on Monday afternoon. Mum and Dad are coming from Connemara, so I'm doing a family dinner at Marine Terrace that evening.'

'My flight gets in on Monday morning, so I'll meet you all at the solicitor's office.' Jeannie moved closer to the screen and looked over her shoulder. 'I need to talk to you, Rose.'

'Okay,' she said. 'What's wrong?'

'Not now,' Jeannie said. 'When I see you.'

'Who's at your house? Why are you being so cloak-and-dagger?' Rose asked.

'The housemaid is here someplace.'

'Don't be rude, Jeannie,' Rose said.

'She calls herself the housemaid. What's your problem? Besides, that's got nothing to do with what I need to speak to you about . . .'

'Can't you just tell me?' Rose asked, beginning to feel exasperated with her twin. 'Are you crying? I can't see your face or eyes properly.'

'I'm trying, but nothing is working,' Jeannie said crossly. 'Look, look! I'm making a sad face now. Can you see it?'

'Not really,' Rose said as she leaned in. 'Nope, nothing to show that you're sad. Oh wait, there seems to be a tear sitting in the crust around your eyes.'

'Stop it, Rose. I'm very emotional here.'

Rose stifled a grin. Jeannie was such a drama queen, and she never failed to make her smile. She was guessing her sister's latest issue was about a dress she'd seen or the fact that her husband, Nick, wanted to make the pool bigger. It was never anything hugely taxing, but Rose was looking forward to hearing how Jeannie would tell the story. There'd be arms waving in every direction and a whole lot of expletives. Ali adored her aunt's stories, too, although on more than one occasion Rose had forced her sister to wait until her daughter wasn't in the room. Jeannie's LA lifestyle could be a bit X-rated at times.

The conversation moved to the black-tie fund-raiser ball that Jeannie was attending on Saturday evening. Each year the hospital did a massive night where all the consultants hosted a table. The glitterati came out in force and

Rose knew Jeannie revelled in it all. Rose always felt like the fuddy-duddy boring sister when Jeannie described the amazingly glam events she attended. Rose had one black dress that she wore to pretty much everything. But it did her just fine. Besides, she didn't go to many black-tie parties.

'My gowns arrived this afternoon,' Jeannie said. 'Wait and I'll show you.' She held up a magnificent red mermaid-style dress with a halter neck, bedecked in sparkles. The second one was in the same shade, but it was a fuller ball-gown style with a plunging neckline. While Rose thought they were beautifully glamorous, she wouldn't have the nerve to wear either of them in a million years.

'Wow,' she said in awe. 'You'll be stunning, as always. Why do you need two?'

'I couldn't decide, so I bought both. I'm leaning towards the fishtail one,' Jeannie said, holding it up. She laughed. 'You look horrified, sis! You wouldn't go out in this if I pumped you with drugs, would you?'

'Did I look that bad?' Rose asked with a sheepish grin. 'It's an amazing dress, but you're right, I'd die if I had to wear it. I don't have your figure or your confidence.'

'You could if you'd only come over here and let Nick do a few adjustments.'

'Eh, no thanks. Being pimped isn't exactly on my to-do list right now.'

Ali appeared from her room and padded into the kitchen.

'Hey, how's my favourite fifteen-year-old in the whole entire world?' Jeannie said, beaming at her.

'Hi, Jeannie,' Ali said with a lacklustre wave.

'Seriously! Is that it? Where's the enthusiasm? Hey, look at my dress.' Jeannie held it up again.

'Oh my God, that's sick! Can I have it when you're bored with it?'

'Yes, of course! This one and about another ten that you've got your eye on, my darling.'

'Yes! Thanks, Auntie Jeannie!' Ali grinned and peered into the computer screen. 'What the hell happened to your face?'

'My face will be fine in a couple of days. It's called maintenance. You don't need to know any of this stuff yet. You have taut, young, blemish-free skin and I hate you for it.' She poked her tongue out at Ali, making her laugh.

Jeannie launched into a spiel about the new line of Kardashian lipsticks, which Ali lapped up like a kitten.

'It's selling out in the stores here, but I've ordered you some. I'll FedEx them as soon as they arrive. I don't think they'll get here before I leave for Ireland. Oh, and I have three or four dresses I'll bring for you as well. I've worn them twice, so I'm totally done with them.'

'Awesome,' said Ali.

'Okay, we're going to say goodbye,' Rose said. 'It's time for a bit of supper. Chat to you soon. Let us know how the ball goes.'

'I'll give you a quick call so you can see my make-up before I go.'

'I hope you're having someone do your face,' Ali said. 'And I hope they have some sort of magic wand to cover those black eyes.'

'I'll look just fine,' Jeannie said defensively.

As they closed the laptop, Rose felt she ought to explain

to Ali that it wasn't necessary to interfere with one's features.

'Your aunt only does it because she's married to a scalpel-happy surgeon. But I don't think women should feel pressurised into altering their appearance.'

'I hear you,' Ali said, looking bored. This was the only facial expression Rose got to see these days, like every word out of her mouth was utterly tedious. 'But I'd do the same thing in Jeannie's position. In fact, I'll be flying over to Uncle Nick as soon as any of my face droops or my body begins to go south, as Jeannie so delicately puts it.'

'Why?' Rose asked, looking upset. 'You're beautiful the way you are. Why would you want to look plastic? There's too much emphasis on looks these days. Women should be judged by their attitude and achievements and how they treat others. Not by how smooth their skin is.'

Ali rolled her eyes. Rose knew she was preaching to deaf ears. Her daughter was as fickle as her sister and at times it really bothered Rose.

'I don't want you to grow up thinking the world will treat you better if you spend time and money on your looks.'

'Mum, whether you like it or not, the fact of the matter is that women *are* judged on their looks. Every day. Besides,' Ali perched on a high stool and looked out at the rolling Irish Sea, 'I love make-up and hairstyles and fashion. It's fun! I'm going to make a fortune as a make-up artist to the stars when I leave school.'

Rose didn't want to argue with her daughter, again. At the moment it seemed that was all they did. If Ali wanted to chat about lipstick with Jeannie and it made her happy, then so be it. But Rose wasn't going to allow her to be a make-up artist. Not when she was a straight-A student.

Rose suddenly caught herself, she'd always told Ali that she could do anything she wanted. But that was a whole other day's argument.

As she whisked up eggs and milk to make some scrambled eggs, Rose tried to concentrate on looking forward to Jeannie's visit and the family meal they'd all share in a few days' time.

'Hurry up if you want a lift, Ali,' Martin said as he breezed into the kitchen.

'Eh, I'm making scrambled eggs and smoked salmon for us,' Rose said. 'I've made you toast with that grainy bread you like as well. And I've a nice bottle of red I thought we might share.'

Her husband didn't even raise his eyes to look at her. He was staring at his phone, as usual, tapping away. It made Rose's blood boil.

'I've a meeting with those Italian people about getting the agency for that furniture line in the very bright colours,' Martin said as Ali rushed off to find her shoes and coat. 'I'm taking them to dinner in the French place in Pebble Bay. Have to be there in twenty minutes.'

'Well then, where the hell is Ali going?' Rose asked.

Martin glanced at her. 'She's heading out with Ross for a couple of hours. She asked and I said that was fine.'

'But I've made food now,' Rose said, feeling stung. 'Why didn't you tell me? I would've liked to go too. I like to be involved as well, you know. Besides, I don't think that range will sell. Irish people aren't that crazy about the thought of a bright orange sofa or a lime-green leather armchair. Don't do any deals until I see the stuff, okay?'

'Rose, leave me to worry about this end of things. You keep going here with Ali . . . and whatever you do.' He swooped to kiss her absently on the cheek, as he always did, then turned away.

'Bye, Mum, I'm meeting Ross,' Ali said as she followed Martin towards the door.

'Who is Ross?'

'This new guy I'm seeing. We're having something to eat and going to the cinema.'

'I didn't give you permission,' Rose said crossly.

Ali rolled her eyes at her mother and Martin smiled. 'Dad did,' she said, slamming the door shut behind her.

Rose felt like crying as she stared at the saucepan of scrambled eggs and the six slices of brown toast she'd laid out on three plates, with smoked salmon garnished with fresh dill. Sighing, she knew she needed to accept the fact that she'd be eating alone yet again.

Chapter 3

JEANNIE WALKED OUT OF HER HOME OFFICE AND into her porcelain-tiled white kitchen. While her sister and niece were getting ready for their evening meal, she was starting her day. LA was eight hours behind Dublin and that time difference was crippling when she visited home, which she tried to do four times a year.

The sound of the door buzzer made her look into one of the many small screens that were dotted around the house for viewing the gate. She squinted and then winced as her eyes watered. Spotting the squat bubblegum-pink beautician's van, she pressed the button to let Nina inside the property. Her face was stinging from the cream she'd dabbed on and she was feeling a bit sorry for herself. Nick was gone to work and had called out that he'd be late again this evening.

She knew she shouldn't complain. They had one of the most magnificent homes in the area, while Nick was charming and gorgeous and made rakes of money and treated her like a princess. What more could she ask for? She was the envy of half the county, and every time they went out, men ogled her as women tittered at Nick.

She'd come to LA from Ireland almost twenty years ago with two pals as an eagerly optimistic and boundlessly enthusiastic nineteen-year-old au pair planning a summer of sun and fun and not much else. Although she'd grown up in a leafy suburb and was certainly not a country girl, Jeannie had never known a place like LA. When the summer ended, she'd secured a job and slotted into everyday life, vowing to become a native.

She'd connected with Nick while she was waitressing in a café near the hospital. It was love through the steam of his cappuccino, and she swiftly swept him off his feet. The fact that he was a newly appointed plastic surgeon and she was a barista never felt like an issue between them. Her confidence, quick wit and joie de vivre was a combination that beguiled him from the start. The cattier women in the locality liked to snigger behind manicured hands that it was purely a physical attraction. 'The man would make his fortune if he could make any of the ladies in LA look like her.' But most of them knew that kind of natural exquisiteness couldn't be bought, nor could it be carved with a scalpel.

They'd dated, danced and fallen hopelessly in love. By the time she was twenty-two, Jeannie was Mrs Nick Marx and played the role beautifully. Growing up with her father's family interiors business meant that home styling came naturally to her. Quite in spite of herself, she carved out a nice little niche business putting finishing touches to the magnificent homes of LA.

'You decorate the houses and I'll create the dollies to sit in them,' Nick liked to say.

'As long as you never introduce me as an interior designer, you're safe,' she warned.

Jeannie would never have Rose's patience for transforming entire spaces with clever colour. Instead, she could sweep into a room and know that a plush sea-green

lamb's-wool rug would enhance a living room. Or a metic-
ulously sourced French boudoir-style sleigh bed would
change that master suite from tack to class. Or a series
of mismatched chairs in acid colours would look a thousand times more chic than a five-seater leather sofa. She
had no store filled with finance-draining stock, nor did
she work regular hours, but somehow she managed to
pull in a tidy profit from her work.

From the word go, they'd agreed that an open marriage
would suit them best. Well, Jeannie had told Nick so and
he'd agreed, knowing it was the only way he could hope
to hold onto her. In the hospital and on the board, Nick
was king. At home, she wore the trousers, and very much
decided when she might take them off too.

Jeannie was a clever girl. She'd known from the moment
they'd started dating that she'd have to play a good tactical
game if she were to hold onto him. After all, he could have
any girl in LA. From what she'd heard, at one point, he
pretty much had, too. She listened to the whispers and
titters each time he took her to an event and came to realise
that the only way she would keep hold of Dr Nick Marx
was by staying one step ahead of him.

She'd teased and flirted with him long before she'd
allowed him into her bed. The first time they'd had sex
was after the first annual fund-raiser ball, just like the one
they were attending tonight. She'd spent every last cent
she owned on her dress, hair and make-up.

'You've dazzled tonight,' he'd whispered into her ear.
'Let's get out of here.'

He'd taken her to his apartment and they'd undressed
each other from the doorway. She'd wanted him just as
much as he clearly wanted her. The sex was hot, fast and

energetic. She'd stayed over for the first time. But instead of staying in his arms the next morning, much as she'd longed to, she'd risen early and said she needed to get home.

'Won't you stay a while longer?'

'I've got to go. People to see, things to do. Call me.'

And he had. Twice that day and three times that evening until she eventually called him back.

'Hey, sorry to have missed you. I was working on a new venture I'm trying to get off the ground.' Part of that was true. She did want to start a new venture. But she hadn't the time or the funding. Instead, she'd sat by the phone, chewing her nail extensions, hoping she was doing the right thing by pretending to be unavailable.

'Come to dinner with me tonight,' he'd begged.

She'd wanted nothing more. 'I can't,' she'd said, sounding hesitant. 'I have a date.'

'Oh.' His voice dropped like a stone.

'I'm sorry, it was arranged ages ago. I didn't know we were going to . . .'

'No, of course not. So how about tomorrow night? Or the night after?'

'Tomorrow sounds good,' she'd said with a smile.

They'd had a great evening and ended up in his bed again. Afterwards, as she lay in his arms, he'd let his guard down.

'I think I'm finished with sowing my wild oats,' he'd joked. 'You probably have every second guy in the café asking you out. I wish you weren't so young. I'm guessing I don't stand a chance at keeping you for myself, right?'

He'd looked so vulnerable, and for a moment she'd almost caved.

'I'm kind of at a point in my life where I want to have fun, meet different guys and see what's out there. I'm too young to be tied down.'

All the same, they'd continued to date. She made it clear that she wasn't prepared to be with him exclusively, a fact that drove him wild with desire. She swiftly learned that this was her most powerful tool for keeping him wanting her.

Any time she made out that she was having hot sex with another guy, he retaliated by taking her to an amazing restaurant or the hippest new bar, where he'd have a table reserved with the finest champagne on tap.

When Arthur, a stunning French boy, started working at the café and showed a huge interest in her, Nick had taken her to Zach's, the most exclusive Michelin-starred restaurant in LA. He hung on her every word and after dessert he produced a diamond necklace.

'What's this for?' she asked, as she tried not to hyper-ventilate.

'So you can think of me at all times.' He fastened it around her neck and kissed her.

'Nick, it's beautiful, but I don't know if I can accept it,' she said.

'Please!' he begged. 'I want to spoil you.'

She excused herself and walked to the ladies' room, hoping to goodness that she looked calmer than she felt. Once inside, she rushed to the mirror and stared at the round diamond on the white gold chain. She'd never owned anything so beautiful or expensive.

Knowing she couldn't keep stringing him along, she made up her mind to stop with the shenanigans when he took her totally by surprise. When she returned to the table at the restaurant, he seemed to have it all worked out.

'I have a proposition for you,' he'd said. 'I understand the stage you're at. I'm fifteen years older than you. But I can't bear the thought of losing you. So I want you to hear me out.'

'Okay.'

'I want you to sleep with whoever you like, have fun and do what you need to do. But marry me. Have it so that you always come back to me. Then someday, when you're ready, you'll hopefully want to stop messing about and I'll be there.'

She was utterly flabbergasted by his idea. Did she want to be married at twenty-two? Did she want to bother at all if she was still going to have to act as if she didn't really care? Did she love him enough to marry him? A million thoughts zoomed around her head.

'Aren't you going to say anything?' he asked.

'Let's get out of here,' she replied.

Nick paid the bill, hailed a cab and they went back to his apartment, where they made wild, passionate love, even better than any time before.

'So,' he said afterwards, resting on his elbow and staring at her. 'I have to know. Will you marry me and we can have an open relationship until you're ready to settle down with me?'

'Yes,' she heard her own voice saying.

The wedding was low key; it happened so swiftly that nobody from home, bar Rose, even attended. She was so unsure of everything at that point, but he never knew it.

She learned to keep him on his toes by dangling younger men with groping hands in front of him. It drove him wild with desire, and after a while she began to enjoy the whole arrangement. Her confidence grew and she actually became the woman she'd only been pretending to be.

For the past twenty years she'd strutted about, blonde curls tumbling, with a figure to die for, and had quite simply had her cake and eaten it too. But at the end of her last lust-crazed six-week liaison, with a lean, tanned personal trainer who was twenty-two but looked sixteen, Jeannie had suddenly felt differently. Work was busier than she'd ever planned, her sessions in the gym were becoming a chore and she had begun to feel jaded by her lifestyle. She found it difficult to get up in the morning and was so tired she had to pull over on more than one occasion to have a quick doze in the car. She attended her doctor and was astonished and horrified to find out that she was pregnant.

Something had clicked inside Jeannie and she knew it was time to either bring Nick along with her and be a proper family, or get divorced. Perhaps it was a throwback to her Irish upbringing and a country that didn't allow divorce, but the idea of walking away from her marriage without knowing she'd given it her best shot wasn't her style. Maybe it was age creeping up on her – she'd be thirty-nine next birthday – ugh, so horribly close to forty – but she had a not entirely welcome feeling that it was time she grew up.

More than that, she'd developed a new feeling called guilt. She had no idea who the father of this baby was. There were three possibilities – Johnny from the gym, Marco from the Italian restaurant, or Nick.

If Rose or Beatrice or, God forbid, her parents knew about their open marriage, they would curl up and die on the spot. She could almost hear their mother saying, 'You weren't raised to behave in such a dreadful manner. Find a man who wants you and nobody else. This is outrageous!'

Nanny May would've brandished her wooden spoon at both of them and threatened them with the devil.

But Jeannie knew deep down that she was the problem, not Nick. She was barely eating and was stressed to the hilt, so she hadn't put on weight, but she reckoned she was about five months along, although she honestly wasn't sure. All she did know was that she was running out of time. Soon her belly would swell so big that no matter what she did, the world, including her husband, would know she was pregnant.

'Hey, Nina,' she said, pulling the oversized panelled front door open. Waving to the two gardeners, she ushered the beautician inside. 'Wow, it's hot out there today.'

'Tell me about it,' Nina said. 'The air con is bust in my van and I honestly thought I might melt while I was stuck in the traffic.'

'Have a cool drink,' Jeannie said, grabbing a bottle of diet soda from the fridge. She poured them both a tall glassful while Nina set up her nail station.

'You're having a full body-spray tan today as well, am I right?'

'Yes please,' said Jeannie. 'And do you think you'll be able to cover this on Saturday for the ball?' she asked, circling her finger around her eyes.

'Cover what?' Nina said, winking. 'You'll be stunning as always, my lovely. Now sit.'

Nina was from Russia, but had been working in LA for a decade. Apart from her genuine skills as a beautician, Jeannie adored her because she was a fellow foreigner and, most importantly, she didn't gossip. While she revelled in being a socialite, Jeannie wasn't comfortable with the whole town knowing her intimate business. Especially when some of it involved other women's husbands! She'd learned to keep people at a distance. LA wasn't like Ireland. At least, it wasn't like Pebble Bay where she, Rose and Beatrice had been raised. The community spirit was certainly alive and well in LA, but Jeannie knew that ninety per cent of it was superficial. She couldn't deal with the whole church farce either. So many of her neighbours were staunch church-goers who turned up every Sunday dressed as if they were going to a cocktail party, throwing cash at the latest fund while simultaneously back-stabbing one another at every turn.

While she had an endless supply of ladies-who-lunched to hang out with and could fill her enormous living room with hand-gesturing, champagne-quaffing fashionistas at the drop of a hat, Jeannie knew that none of them really had her back. The fact that she earned her own money was a bone of contention for some of the more shallow women she knew. Her best frenemy, Brittany, the wife of an ortho-paedic surgeon friend of Nick's, always had something to say about Jeannie's job.

'My Rodger would never let me work. He thinks I'm far too precious.'

Jeannie would just smile and nod. Her Rodger was a naughty boy and certainly didn't keep to himself. He and Jeannie had gone through a couple of months where they'd met in hotel rooms and had wild sex. He was good in bed, but outside of it Jeannie found him rather repulsive after a while. He was far too big-headed, and although she knew she was just as much to blame as he was, she figured he was a shit, so she'd stopped meeting him and ignored him when they were out. He got the message, but she knew for a fact that he was carrying on with other women still. All the while he encouraged and indulged his wife's 'precious' behaviour. He picked up the bills for her shopping and listened to her whining about her knee, her shoulder and whatever else was wrong that day.

Jeannie didn't do precious, and she most certainly wasn't going to put herself in a position where she was at any man's beck and call.

'Always have your running-away money,' her mother used to say. It was one of the only pieces of maternal advice Jeannie had stuck to rigidly.

'So,' Nina said as Jeannie sat opposite her and held out her hands to be manicured. 'What colour will you wear to the ball?'

Jeannie pointed to the crimson bejewelled ball gown that was hanging on the back of the door leading into the office.

'Nice,' Nina said, nodding. 'I thought you were going for the tight fishtail style?'

'Yes, I was originally, but I ordered both and now I think I prefer this for a change,' she lied. Jeannie's style was always tight, to make the most of her incredible figure. But she was terrified that someone would notice her belly and ask questions. The ball gown had cost a fortune and it had a plunging neckline, so it would show off her pumped-up breasts. She zoned back in on Nina, who was chatting away happily, unaware of Jeannie's inner turmoil.

'I have the perfect colour. It's called Red Carpet. No imagination used up creating that name, eh?'

As Nina began to file her nails and tease back her cuticles, Jeannie led the conversation. Once they got through the usual pleasantries, where Jeannie asked about Nina's good-for-nothing out-of-work husband and her two young sons, who were as wild as Vikings, Nina asked Jeannie how she was doing.

'I'm okay,' said Jeannie with a heavy sigh.

Nina continued with her work so that there was no other sound except the gentle sawing of the nail file for a few minutes.

'I told Nick I'm tired of all the bullshit,' Jeannie said.

'Good girl.' Nina nodded.

'You're never going to believe what he came back with.'

'Try me,' Nina said, without moving a facial muscle. 'Give me your other hand, darling.'

Jeannie did as she was bid and sat chewing her lip.

'So tell me already,' Nina exploded.

'Yeah, so he went all soppy on me and cried, telling me he was scared I was going to ask him for a divorce.'

'But you didn't, right?' Nina looked down her slender nose at Jeannie.

'No. I love him, Nina. That wasn't the idea.'

'So what happened? I can see that you are addled. Not like you. Normally you are this high-energy girl. You are bossy and clicking your fingers. Today, you are like a wet rag. What's happened?'

'He wants us to start a family,' Jeannie said.

'And why do you make it sound like he's asking something insane?'

Jeannie pouted and looked for a moment as if she might cry.

'Hey.' Nina dropped her voice by four octaves and eyeballed her. 'It's me you're talking to now.'

'I'm already pregnant, Nina.'

'What?'

'I think I'm nearly five months along.' Her voice cracked and she began to sob, covering her face with her hands.

'You're destroying your shellac and you're scrunching your face,' Nina said. 'Now tell me all about it and try to remain calm. There's no good in getting yourself so crazy.'

'It's all a disaster,' Jeannie said. 'The baby could be Nick's or two others'. I haven't the foggiest, but worse than that, how am I going to do this, Nina? Being a mother is the type of thing Rosie's good at.' She was pensive for a moment. 'Beatrice doesn't have kids, but I reckon she would even be brilliant at it as well. She's so organised and would be able to get into the swing of being a mother, just like a project. But I can't do it. I'm not good at anything apart from ordering accessories online from Paris and Milan. Or buying ridiculously expensive dresses that no longer fit.'

'If you're so unsure of the whole thing, why don't you get rid of it?' Nina asked as she pulled Jeannie's hands back onto the table so she could continue with the manicure.

'Oh no,' said Jeannie, looking horrified. 'I couldn't do that. I guess it's ingrained in me that once I'm pregnant, I'm to go ahead with having the child. There's still no abortion in Ireland.'

'No way!' Nina said in astonishment. 'That's crazy! What about young girls who get pregnant, or rape victims? Surely there are exceptions to the rule?'

'Nope,' said Jeannie. 'For the record, I don't agree with not having the choice. But when I was faced with it myself, I couldn't consider it.'

'Why didn't you tell me sooner?' Nina asked kindly. 'I

knew you were in odd form, but I didn't know why. You've been in turmoil for months, my poor darling. Did you at least tell your sisters when you were home for the funeral?'

'God, no!' Jeannie said. 'They'd be so overexcited about it, they'd drive me crazy.'

So much of her and Nick's life was surrounded by fluff, and she knew she needed more sustenance. But being a mother was something she'd successfully avoided until now. She wasn't at all convinced it was the sort of sustenance that would save her.

'Nina, I haven't even told Nick. So you have to promise me you won't say a word.'

'Hey, my lips are sealed,' she said zipping her lips with her fingers. 'I know it's not my business, but why were you having unprotected sex, darling?'

'I know, I know,' Jeannie said, looking cross. 'I'm beating myself up each and every day for being so stupid.'

'So this child will be Nick's and Caucasian or someone else's and dark-skinned – those are the choices?'

Jeannie nodded miserably. It wasn't a simple case of having the baby and burying her doubts over its paternity. Johnny was African American, Marco was Italian, while Nick was white American. It would be plainly obvious if the baby wasn't his.

Admitting to Nina she was pregnant wasn't going the way she'd hoped. Nina got carried away, dishing out details of her two sons' births, until Jeannie held up her hands.

'Please, I'm squeamish, and totally against hearing gory stories. Can we pretend I didn't mention it after all?'

Nina changed the subject quickly; she knew well enough to keep quiet when asked.

Jeannie chatted about nothing much as Nina finished her

nails and then sprayed her with tan. As she stood naked apart from the disposable knickers, the soft rounding of her tummy was quite obvious, but Nina didn't comment. Promising to return on Saturday afternoon to do Jeannie's make-up for the ball, she waved and then sped out the gate.

Jeannie walked into the office and logged on to the computer to see when the Italian pony-print chair she'd ordered was being delivered. It was a one-off piece for a local high court judge to give his wife for her birthday, and Jeannie couldn't wait to see it.

With shaking hands, she typed in a word she had never used before and hit the search engine.

Pregnancy.

Her eyes bulged as she read some of the basic information. Flashbacks of the unprotected sex she'd enjoyed taunted her. She knew she should've used condoms, especially with her lovers, but she had regular tests, and she'd assumed the pill would cover her for pregnancy. She might have forgotten to take one or two at times, but she'd never been exactly brilliant at remembering to do stuff that required her attention every single day. The situation was ironic, really. So many couples needed thousands of dollars of IVF to conceive these days. Bitchy Brittany never stopped telling her that most women's eggs were fried beyond use past the age of thirty-five.

'I had to have our kids one after the other, bang, bang, bang. I'd happily have stopped at one. But you know what it's like. We gotta hang onto our husbands. He wanted three and I couldn't survive if I had to work.'

Taking some deep breaths, Jeannie calmed her quickening pulse as she tracked her furniture order and printed the tickets for her flight home.

Hearing Nanny May's will would be such a sad occasion. They all missed her terribly and this would be like a line in the sand. The end of her and everything she stood for. She hadn't had many possessions as far as Jeannie was aware, so none of them was expecting anything material. But Nanny May had never been about things or money; she was love and principles and, in many ways, the linchpin of their family. It could never be the same without her. Wiping a tear from her cheek, Jeannie went to the dressing room to pack a bag.

She wanted to hug Ali and spend time with Rose and Beatrice. The new bridal shop looked like a dream place and the flat above was totally darling and Beatrice's pride and joy. So she wanted to show her interest. She had no idea how Beatrice was doing it. This new store, although it was a gift from their parents, clocked her total up to six. Already she was like a blue-arsed fly tearing from one premises to the next. But that was Bea. Always busy and always in charge.

Jeannie opened another diet soda and sat back, thinking about how she'd spend her time in Ireland. She had convinced Nick that going for a few weeks made sense, so she'd have time to do what she pleased. She might even take a trip to the back end of nowhere and visit her parents. She knew her dad would fuss over her and her mother would . . . Well, her mother would do what she always did and try hard to tolerate her. And that would be fine, too. The feeling was mutual.

Maybe a bit of quality time with Ali would tip her in the right direction for being a mom. Perhaps this mothering instinct thing was contagious and she could channel some from her twin.

As she walked out of the office and towards their home gym, Jeannie passed her four-thousand-dollar gown for the ball, fingering the hand beading longingly. This type of thing would be out once her body was battered by pregnancy, so she might as well enjoy the fund-raiser. This time next year she'd probably be attending in a duvet cover caught up imaginatively with a sparkly belt to disguise her mummy tummy.

With the music pumping, she started up her treadmill as she simultaneously compiled a mental list of the things she'd need to buy to take home as gifts. She always arrived laden with cool stuff that the girls couldn't get in Ireland. That'd be something fun to concentrate on. Better than nappies or bottles or screaming in the middle of the night. Or her husband's face if he knew the truth.

Chapter 4

BEATRICE PUT HER BREAKFAST THINGS IN THE dishwasher and rushed to brush her teeth. It was an hour and a half before the new shop was due to open, but she'd taken in a delivery of Pnina Tornai wedding gowns late the night before. She was the only Irish agent for the stunning range of dresses, and brides flocked from near and far to buy them.

She'd stayed late last night and divided the order between her six stores. A courier was due in fifteen minutes to collect and dispatch them. She was blessed to have managers in the other shops who were as passionate as she was about the wedding business. She gave them great freedom with how the windows were dressed, and although she was spending the lion's share of her time at the new shop, she was careful to show her face in the other five regularly and unannounced. She paid generously and praised her staff, but she was a tough cookie to work for and expected nothing but the highest level of commitment. So this morning the managers would be open extra early to take in the new gowns and get them onto the shop floors and into the window well before the first customer arrived.

Her ever-reliable assistant Isobelle would be there before nine. She'd worked with Beatrice the longest, since her first shop opened in fact. She was like clockwork, and the most cheerful lady imaginable. In her late fifties, she had worked in bridal boutiques all her life and was utterly tuned into her job. The brides loved her, and so did Beatrice.

Since moving to the new premises, Beatrice felt her life had surged forward in the most exciting way. She'd started her first wedding boutique six years ago. Ironically, she'd opened the doors of that first shop within a week of ending her marriage to Davy Moore. The distraction had been welcome, and it couldn't have been timed better in her opinion.

'I can't understand you, Beatrice,' Martha had said. 'You've let the most eligible man in town go and here you are, knee deep in wedding paraphernalia without shedding a tear. I don't know what's gone wrong here. Maria Moore is on the phone begging me to talk sense into you. So I promised I would do just that.'

Beatrice had hung up feeling dreadful. Her mother got on her high horse about things at the best of times, but clearly Beatrice's failing marriage was in danger of sending her over the edge altogether. To say that Martha had been very excited about her relationship with Davy from their first date was putting it mildly.

'Hold onto Davy Moore, he's from good stock and he's perfect husband material. Just imagine, I could deliver your babies at home. You wouldn't need to go to the hospital at all if you didn't feel like it.'

'Mum, I've been on one date with him. Don't you think you're getting too far ahead of yourself there? Calm down!' Beatrice had laughed.

But her relationship with Davy had progressed very

swiftly. Between Martha and Maria, Davy's equally pushy mother, they'd had them marched up the aisle and into a suitable house while filling out application forms for schools for the two-point-four children that Martha would deliver.

'Tell Mum to back off and leave you alone,' Rose had urged her. 'She's losing the run of herself.'

'You're lucky that you and Martin are made for one another. She did the same thing to you.'

'Yes, but I guess I was happy about it,' Rose agreed. 'She has Nanny May running about like her slave. You'd swear it was her own wedding she was planning, not yours.'

They hadn't even returned from their honeymoon when Beatrice knew she'd made a grave mistake. As the months passed, she became more and more unhappy. Davy didn't know what to do to help her and she hadn't the words to tell him.

'Come to the doctor with me,' he'd begged. 'Perhaps you have depression. Lots of people suffer and don't get help.'

'I'm fine,' she'd said. But really she wasn't. She felt empty inside, and she knew she needed to divorce Davy.

With a heavy heart she'd told him what he already knew. Their marriage wasn't working and she wanted to leave him.

'You stay where you are,' he'd said. 'I'll go to Australia. It's what I'd planned and then we got together and I changed my mind . . . but if we can't be together, I'll go . . .' He'd looked at her, willing her to beg him to stay. But she didn't. She couldn't. She was ashamed of herself, but she simply didn't love him. No amount of talking with her parents and in-laws would change her mind.

Everyone bar her was astonished when Davy announced that he was emigrating to Australia. Guilty wasn't the word for how she'd felt, making him go alone. But she simply couldn't do it. He'd held out hope right until the last moment.

'Maybe if you come with me and we're away from everything, you'll feel differently?' The pleading in his pale hazel eyes had broken her heart.

'Davy, you're one of the most amazing people I've ever had the privilege of knowing. You deserve someone who adores you as much as . . .'

'. . . as I adore you,' he'd finished, his eyes filling with tears.

'I'm sorry,' she'd whispered miserably for what must've been the hundredth time. 'I can't make myself love you. I tried. I thought it would come when we were married . . .'

They'd stayed in touch for the first while, but after that things had drifted. She wasn't at all surprised when divorce papers arrived. Although it was what she wanted, and also needed so she could move on, Beatrice still cried herself to sleep for a week afterwards. She hated herself for hurting Davy and wished she'd had the guts to call a halt to their relationship well before the wedding.

It was a hard lesson, but she vowed she wouldn't make such a monumental mistake again. As a result, she'd become the uber-organised person she was today.

If only her marriage had been as successful as her shops. Bridal Belles, even though she'd opened at the height of a global recession, had soared. Once she'd secured the agency for a number of exclusive lines of gowns, everything had fallen into place work-wise. That first shop had thrived, leading her to open four more in as many months. With a bank loan and a large investment from her doting dad, she'd expanded and quickly become the go-to boutique for brides across Dublin. Her shops were featured in glossy magazines and newspapers all the time. She had celebrities vying for her dresses as the business went from strength to strength.

When her parents retired last year and went to live in Connemara, each of the girls was given something substantial to help with everyday life. Beatrice was handed the keys to a brand-new premises in the heart of Pebble Bay village, with an upstairs flat.

The location was prime, and as a result she saw an immediate rise in sales. She loved her work and threw everything into it. She never felt lonely when she had Ned, her beloved little dog, by her side. Ned was a true character and the customers loved him. Beatrice had chosen him from an array of pups at the rescue centre ten years previously and they'd been firm friends ever since. He was mostly a terrier and had the softest brown ears, like little teardrops of velvet. Beatrice wasn't sure who enjoyed the petting and cuddles more, her or Ned. Most days he sat in his bed behind the counter until it was time to go on a visit to another shop or upstairs to the flat.

This morning, because Beatrice was so busy with the stock-take, Ned was acting up. He dropped one of his toys onto a dress, which he knew was naughty.

'If that hadn't plastic over it, you'd be in big trouble, mister,' she said, scooping him up and kissing him. He wriggled until he was resting with his head on her shoulder. He shuddered and made a little delighted noise. 'I can't sit and snuggle with you at the moment, Ned,' she said.

'Please be a good boy and sit and watch. I'll give you a chewy stick.'

He took the chew and sat back in his bed. She was certain he was smiling.

The gowns she was opening were nothing short of works of art. The beading and lace were so beautifully appointed; none of the other designs she carried was like them.

The appointment book was full for today, and Beatrice knew that once the first bride-to-be arrived at nine, it would be back-to-back with fittings. Once upon a time she'd allowed walk-ins, but now she was so busy it had to be strictly appointment only, with the door locked for the less forward-thinking brides who hadn't thought to book in. The other five stores had the same policy, so it meant she could keep a better eye on exactly who was coming in and out the doors.

Since her parents had gone to Connemara, the pressure had been taken off Beatrice in so many ways. For a start, she had Sunday afternoons to herself now. Before their move, she'd met her parents at mass and gone for lunch either to their home or to a restaurant. Sunday had always been Nanny May's day off and they'd never infringed upon that. As Jeannie was in LA and Rose didn't believe in any of the Catholic 'mumbo-jumbo', Bea had fallen into a routine with her parents.

'I wouldn't waste my Sundays festering in a church. Just tell Mum and Dad you've got a life to live,' Jeannie scoffed.

Beatrice sighed as she thought of Jeannie in LA. Perhaps she'd had the right idea, flying the nest. She was always her own person and it kind of suited her personality to do something wild. As children they'd be put in the same outfit for mass and Sunday lunch. Jeannie would have to do something to look different. Whether it was a bow in her hair or a pair of bright red tights, she'd somehow manage to bend the rules, which would inevitably start an argument with their mother.

Beatrice beavered away in the stockroom and got through a massive amount. The showroom was cleared and the stockroom was all sorted by the time the clock struck nine.

Isobelle arrived, much to Ned's delight, and almost immediately so too did their first appointment of the day. While Isobelle dealt with the blushing bride-to-be and her entourage of three, Beatrice saw to a lady who was there for her final fitting. She used the expert services of a wonderful lady from Moldova called Alina to do her fittings. She took the dresses, protected in carefully zipped covers, and worked her magic, returning them in quick succession. Most of the time her adjustments were bang on, but if there was anything else required, Alina did it with good grace. She had four girls working under her and they were all equally brilliant. Bridal Belles provided them with most of their work, and as a result, Alina would always oblige if there was an emergency fitting required.

'I hope this fits today,' said the girl Beatrice was dealing with. She had lost a ton of weight and Beatrice was glad that her big day was next week.

'You just keep shrinking on me. I can barely keep up with you.'

Mercifully, the dress was perfect and Beatrice took the final payment and made sure the correct veil and headdress were included.

'Have a wonderful day,' she said as she waved the girl

off. 'If you think of it, send me a picture to put on our wall of love!'

The wall had been featured in magazine articles and was quite something to behold. Almost all their brides had sent a picture, and Beatrice pinned them all to the wall. Each of the shops had them and they were a lovely, novel idea that had taken off.

The day's post brought two more pictures. She showed them to Isobelle before adding them.

How ironic, she sighed, that she would never be up on that wall. She had many photographs from her wedding to Davy, but they didn't belong up there among those people who had gone into their marriages full of hope and mutual love. She'd lied to both herself and Davy. As a result, she had resigned herself to being alone. After all, that was what she deserved.

Today, more than others, her heart felt heavy. For a brief moment she allowed herself to wallow in sadness. She and Davy were seven years married today. She wondered where he was and how life was treating him. She hoped he was as gorgeous and successful and full of life as he'd been before she'd broken his heart. So many times over the years she'd been tempted to look him up on Facebook. But she'd watched some friends doing it and it became a sort of obsession to track their exes. It inevitably prolonged the agony of being apart, and in turn they'd have to almost wean themselves off Facebook. She'd decided they both needed a clean break, so she'd resisted attempting to send a friend request. He had too, so it seemed best for both of them.

'I'll never love anyone the way I love you,' he'd said as he walked away for the last time. She wanted that bittersweet line to be their final and parting conversation. Not a false and forced pretend-ship on Facebook.

The doorbell rang. Pulling a tissue from her pocket, she wiped the rogue tear that had escaped, plastered on a smile and rushed to open the door for the next bride.

'Dad! What are you doing here?'

'I thought you might be feeling a bit blue with the day that it is.' He took Beatrice in his arms and patted her back just like he'd done when she was a small child. Beatrice sniffed and tried desperately not to lose it.

'There, there. The feeling will pass, my pet. You know it will. These anniversaries are difficult. I should know. I get a lump in my throat every year on my parents' anniversaries, and they're both dead a long time. So I can sort of imagine how hard it is for you. A failed marriage is like a death really.'

'Oh Dad, you're so kind. I can't begin to compare my mess of a marriage to you losing your parents.'

'Both involved a whole lot of emotion that we've no control over. So in my mind, they are comparable.'

'The whole marriage thing is hard, isn't it?' Beatrice said. 'I know our situations are very different. You adore Mum, whereas I couldn't love Davy, much as I tried. But I've never felt the urge to try again. I feel that if I keep to myself, it'll be easier. I'm minding my heart this way,' she said with a watery smile. 'I'll stick to Ned and my TV to keep me company! That way I'm protected.'

'It doesn't mean you don't have sadness in your heart, darling.'

Not for the first time, Bea thanked her lucky stars she had her dad in her life. The twins used to tease her when they were younger that she was the apple of their daddy's eye. But there was more than a grain of truth in their jibes. Perhaps it was because she was the firstborn. But she and Jim had a special bond that went far deeper than her relationship with Martha.

If she was worried, happy, sad or scared, it was Jim she turned to. He usually had an answer for her, too. On days like today, when he'd driven all the way from Connemara to let her know that he was by her side, she literally couldn't thank him enough.

'You remembered,' she said as they hugged again.

'How could I forget?' he said with a sad smile. 'I was giving away my firstborn child to that man.'

'Didn't you like him at all?' she asked as she wiped her face with a tissue and tried her best to smile.

'I liked him well enough. But I can't say I'd have liked it even if he were Tom Cruise. Whoever he was, he was taking my girl and that made me jealous as could be. It wasn't personal on his part. I just love you so much I couldn't bear the thought of losing you.'

'But you could never lose me, Dad. I'd be lost without you, no matter who you had to hand me over to.'

They chatted for a few minutes until the next bride arrived. Jim took a bouncy and delighted Ned for a walk and Beatrice handed him the keys to the flat upstairs. He could access it from a separate entrance outside rather than traipsing through the shop.

Beatrice marvelled at him. How did he know the right moment to appear with a warm hug and the words she needed to hear? And he'd taken Ned out. He called him his furry grandson, a title that always made Beatrice grin from ear to ear.

Clicking into professional mode, Beatrice felt able to face

the rest of her day. She also knew she'd get by through absorbing yet another woman's joy as she shopped for the most important day of her life.

She ought to be thankful for all the great things in her life, she admonished herself. Forcing a smile, she chatted to her customer, anxious to hear her excited story of how she'd got engaged and what had led her to Bridal Belles today.

Chapter 5

MARTHA BENT DOWN TO TIE HER GOLF SHOES. SHE was attempting to convince herself that a round of golf would do her good. It was a bit windy, but the air was so clear and she knew it would get her circulation going.

Jim was already in Dublin. He'd just called to say he was with that flea-bitten creature that Beatrice treated like a surrogate child. The thought of her eldest daughter in that flat with the dog, working her fingers to the bone, rushing from one shop to another, made Martha shudder. It wasn't the way she'd had it planned for her. Why couldn't she have grinned and borne it with Davy? The perfect life had been right there in her lap.

They probably would've had children by now. So Beatrice wouldn't have felt the need to open all those shops. She could've had one shop . . . and they would've had the help of a nanny, no doubt. The whole concept of throwing away her life and opting for this awful prison was beyond her.

Jim had insisted on driving up at cockcrow this morning to spend a bit of time in Dublin before the reading of Nanny May's will, next Monday. She couldn't for the life of her work out why he had to be there for the whole weekend. She wasn't going. What was the point? She'd been terribly fond of the woman, of course. She was almost part of the family really. When she thought about it, Nanny May had afforded her a lot of freedom. So she was more than thankful for that. But she didn't feel the need to go tearing to Dublin to sit in a stuffy solicitor's office and hear a piece of paper being read aloud. Jim could tell her what was said. That was enough.

She headed towards the golf club. A couple they knew vaguely from Dublin had made the move to the area and she wanted to make them feel welcome. As she gazed out at the divine view, with a sea so calm it looked like glass, she thought yet again of the letters. She wished she hadn't pocketed them now. She'd no idea why she had. It was almost as if she hadn't wanted Nanny May to have the last say. She was always the one the children had run to. She was even the one Jim had run to. She recalled a row they'd had one lunchtime.

The twins couldn't have been more than a few months old. They were sitting in high chairs, those exquisite ones she'd ordered from Harrods long before it was fashionable to do so. They were matching wooden-framed chairs with rosebud oilcloth covering, and a chair in the same design for Beatrice.

Nanny May was feeding the twins from a spoon while Beatrice was struggling to feed herself.

'Wouldn't it be less messy if you fed Beatrice too, Nanny May? There's going to be pasta on the roof at this stage.' She'd smiled as she said it. She most certainly hadn't been rude. But Jim had verbally attacked her.

'I think Nanny May is encouraging Bea to feed herself, which might be messy to begin with, but how else will she learn? For a woman who works with babies all day, you astonish me at times with how impatient you can be.'

'There won't be so much as a smudge of bolognese sauce to be found when you return, Martha,' Nanny May said evenly.

'Now thank God for that,' said Jim, his voice dripping with sarcasm.

'And nobody will die,' Nanny May added. She and Jim chuckled and Martha had left the house feeling like an outsider. She'd blazed with anger, only calming when she pulled up at Linda Caulfield's house, where she was nicely in labour.

Today, for some reason, she was reminded of that sense of being left out. Those blooming letters were still stuffed into the inside zip pocket of her handbag. She should chuck them in the nearest bin. But a curious part of her had thought she might steam them open. After all, they were addressed to *her* daughters. Whether or not she could teach them to eat spaghetti successfully, she was still the one who had given birth to them. So in a roundabout way, those letters were hers too.

She was a bit irritated that Jim had gone shooting off to Dublin today, leaving her to welcome the Malones alone. But she knew first-hand that making this move wasn't as easy as it might seem. She'd been struggling with it. Although they'd known many of the people in the area, having visited their holiday home for two decades, it was a different thing upping sticks and moving here permanently.

The bright green colour of her little Smart car never failed to make her smile. Right now, addled and irritated, she lurched her head forward to glimpse the bonnet. It was a gas! Her Dublin friends all thought she was a total looper when she'd first bought it.

'You're not really taking it in that colour, are you, Martha?' said Mary Crowe. 'They'll certainly see you coming from the other side of the bay!'

'Good enough for them,' she'd said, proud as a peahen. 'Ballyshaden won't know what's hit it!'

When they'd lived in Dublin, she'd driven a gorgeous Mercedes bought for her by Jim. But down here, while they still had Jim's plush car, all she needed was a little runaround for times like today when she wasn't with him.

Ali called it her 'super-green snot mobile' on account of its colour, which made her roll around laughing. In turn, Martha would laugh too. That child had the most infectious laugh she'd ever heard.

'But I feel as if I'm in a huge car until I get out,' Martha reasoned.

Jeannie latched onto Ali's nickname, as did Beatrice, so the poor little car was never referred to as anything but the super-green snot mobile. The girls all found the name really funny, so she played along. But in truth, she wasn't that keen on it. She certainly didn't want the locals picking up on it. She wasn't fond of feeling belittled. Even if it was only through her car.

As she hurtled around the winding bends of their road and onto the main road for the golf club, Martha felt as if she were almost flying. The little car hugged the bends and was so easy to manoeuvre.

The scenery on both sides was breathtaking. To her left, through the hedge, she could see golfers happily whacking balls. To her right there was rippling azure water with gulls dive-bombing for fish.

She was caught totally unawares when she came upon a car stopped by the side of the road. There appeared to be a young woman waving her down. Pulling to a halt, she climbed out and rushed to her.

'Oh, thank God you're here,' the woman said, huffing and puffing. 'I was on my way to work. I'm not due for three weeks. I . . .' Another contraction silenced her as she leaned her hands on the roof of the car beside the open door. 'Aaagh, I think the baby is coming. I'm not going to make it to Galway hospital on time. It's an hour's drive and I . . . Aaagh.'

'I'm a midwife,' Martha said. 'You've found the right person, my love. Fate has sent me to help you. Everything is going to be okay. I'll just pop to my car and fish out my first-aid kit.' Even though she'd no obvious necessity to carry a large first-aid kit, old habits died hard and Martha had one with her at all times.

'If you want to lie down, get into the back of your car. If you're happier standing, I can deliver your baby here,' she said calmly. 'I'm going to call the ambulance, but I don't think this baby is going to wait for it to get here.'

'Oh no! I don't think I can cope,' the woman gasped. 'I don't want to have my first baby on the side of the road. I don't even know you. I'm so sorry.' She scrunched up her face and her expression told a very experienced Martha all she needed to know.

'Now, lovey, my name is Martha, and I know this isn't ideal, but baby is in charge right now. By the time you've delivered, which won't be long, we'll be firm friends for life.'

'I'm Claire,' said the young woman as another contraction ripped through her. 'I'm so sorry to make you do this . . .'

'Don't apologise, just be a good girl and concentrate on

the job in hand. I'll guide you and we'll have this baby out and into the world in no time.'

Claire did exactly what Martha told her, and moments later she delivered a healthy baby girl onto a pile of coats on the roadside.

By the time the ambulance arrived, Martha had delivered the afterbirth and cut the cord, and both mother and baby were doing fine. She'd wrapped the shocked woman in a blanket and the baby in a towel, and the scene was one of calm serenity.

'If you wouldn't mind bringing them for a check-up, that would be great,' Martha said to the medic. 'The afterbirth is intact, but I'll give it to your colleague for them to check at the hospital.'

'Would you be able to come with me?' Claire asked, looking terrified.

'That won't be possible,' said the paramedic. 'It's too long a journey for all of us to be squashed into the back.'

'You'll be just fine now, Claire. Is there someone I can phone for you?' Martha offered.

'Oh no thank you, Martha. I'll call my husband now. I don't know how to repay you for what you've done.'

'No payment required,' Martha said. 'Odd as it might sound to you, I actually thoroughly enjoyed it. I'm retired, you see. But I miss my work dreadfully.'

'Well we need a midwife like you around these parts,' Claire said, and Martha could see the paramedic nodding in agreement. 'With all the cutbacks, we've ended up with no district nurse either. The new mums have to go to a clinic up in Galway. It's too far, and not ideal if they have other children in school.'

'You have nobody who calls at the homes to check on

mothers and babies?' Martha asked. Claire shook her head.

'Sorry to interrupt your little gossip there, ladies,' said the ambulance driver with a grin. 'But we need to get going. We're really strapped for staff, too. We've another call to get to once we drop Claire in Galway.'

Martha hugged Claire and wished her the very best.

'Wait, I'll give you my phone number, and if you have any trouble with feeding or questions about the baby in the next while, you can call me. I'd be only too delighted to help you.'

'Thank you so much,' Claire said gratefully.

The ambulance sped away and Martha packed up her things. Once the kit was back in her boot, she leaned against the car and stared at the stunning scenery. The air was so clear and it was the most beautiful and peaceful place to live. But until this moment, she hadn't felt at home here.

Midwifery had been her life for so long, and while she wanted to feel content and grateful to be here with the love of her life, it was as if she'd had her right arm cut off since her retirement. She'd have to get used to it and stop being so obstinate, she mused. As Jim said often enough, this was what they'd worked towards. They had plenty of money to enjoy the finer things in life, and now it was their time to do just that.

Her relationship with Jim had been strained since they'd been here, too. She'd been trying to pretend it wasn't, but they'd never spent so much time together. They'd gone from being passing ships in the night to living in each other's pockets. There were days when she drove to the village of Ballyshaden pretending to need groceries, but she actually just needed to be on her own. She'd buy a newspaper and sit in the café, hiding behind it.

She continued on her journey to meet the Malones and play golf, hoping she'd enjoy it a bit more than before.

She played nine holes, and although she did rather well and was complimented by the lady captain on her swing, she was struggling to click with the game. Louise and Mark Malone came off the course exhilarated, while Martha was deflated. She didn't dare to mention the roadside rescue to them until after they'd finished their food. Jim and the girls had drummed it into her that she wasn't to talk about contractions and afterbirth and other gore associated with deliveries while they ate. So she held her tongue until the coffee arrived.

'My goodness, I'd say the young lady was thrilled you came along. Well done!' said Louise, who looked utterly disgusted.

'I enjoyed it,' Martha said wistfully. 'I'm sure the poor girl didn't, and of course the conditions weren't ideal, but it was lovely to be part of a birth once more. It's such a special time in a woman's life.' She went on to tell them how she'd taken coats from Claire's car and went into edited details of delivering the afterbirth.

Mark looked at her and she realised he'd turned a very pale shade of green.

'Too much information?' she asked. He nodded. 'Sorry, forgive me. I forget that others don't find a baby delivery as incredible as I do. My lot at home are the same. I'm not allowed to talk about births while they're eating.'

'I can understand why they have that rule,' said Louise. 'Even though we have three children of our own, Mark didn't attend and I most certainly didn't ask for details. I simply got on with the job in hand and was grateful to be alive afterwards.'

'Oh, I'm so sorry to hear your birthing experience wasn't more enjoyable,' Martha said.

'Enjoyable?' Louise harrumphed. 'It was an endurance test and I managed it three times, but believe me, given the choice, I'd have adopted.' Mark took her hand and kissed it. 'But we got our three fabulous children – one is a solicitor, one is a barrister and the other has a great job in finance,' she continued. 'They're all married off. We like the spouses, and the grandchildren are a hoot when we see them.'

'That sounds lovely for sure,' said Martha, feeling suddenly deflated. She knew she'd have to call one of the girls so she could share her news. Because she had Ali, Rose was quite interested and well able for the detail. But Jeannie was like her dad, with an extra-large dollop of added drama. She and Jim had had a rule for years that they wouldn't take their work home. That worked both ways. Martha found it difficult to muster much excitement for sofas and chairs, so she could appreciate how Jim possibly felt the same way about her job.

Martha apologised once more that Jim wasn't there, then the Malones suggested taking their Irish coffees to the bar. Before she could blink, they were off mingling and chatting to people as if they'd lived there for years. She'd a good mind to tell them that she'd had to be very forceful to get a window table for lunch and now they'd abandoned it without so much as a backward glance. She went to pay the bill and was mollified somewhat to hear that Mark had settled it. Leaving a generous tip, she followed the couple to the bar.

'There you are, Martha,' Louise said, waving her hand high in the air.

Swallowing hard, Martha thought she was seeing things for a moment. But as she approached Louise, she could see that she had a tattoo.

'You have a tattoo,' she said, unable to ignore it.

'Oh yes, when I turned sixty my children gave me a voucher to have it done. It's all the initials wound into a design. Like or loathe?' Louise asked with her head cocked to the side. 'Most people are in one camp or the other. It doesn't bother me. I love it. But I can understand why others think it's preposterous. My sister honestly thought I'd lost my marbles when she saw it. She tells me to put it away.'

Martha forced a laugh and tried to pretend she was cool with it, but really she thought it was a dreadful atrocity to brand yourself like that. A woman of Louise's age and social standing ought to know better.

'I hate to be a party pooper,' she said as the Malones chatted and laughed with anyone who would listen. 'Eh, excuse me, Mark?'

'Oh, Martha, can I get you a drink, love?'

'No thank you, and thank you for lunch as well. That was supposed to be my treat. I'm going to have to leave now.'

'That's a pity. Well, lovely to see you and no doubt we'll see you around here sometime soon. Tell Jim we were asking for him and we'll see him too.'

'Thank you,' she said. 'I will.'

There was no reception on her mobile phone because of the mountain range. But as soon as she got home, Martha phoned Beatrice at the shop to fill her in on the excitement of the roadside birth.

'That sounds incredibly dramatic, Mum,' Beatrice said.

'You're an angel on earth for that girl, you do know that, right? I'd say Claire will never forget you.'

'I just did what any midwife would do,' Martha said proudly.

'I'm sorry to cut you off, but I've another lady arriving in the door this minute for a dress fitting. I'll have to go, Mum. I'll call you as soon as I'm finished this evening, okay? You can tell me more about it.'

'No problem, Beatrice, you go on ahead.'

She dialled Rose's mobile and mercifully she answered. She wasn't the most reliable with her phone and had a habit of leaving it down and forgetting about it. Martha never liked phoning the landline at the shop either. She'd end up having to go through the motions of a pointless conversation with one of the staff, and that didn't appeal to her. Today, Rose informed her she was sitting on a bench having an ice cream, soaking up the sun.

'Pebble Bay is just as good as the French Riviera when the sun shines, Mum. Is it stunning where you are too?'

'Yes, it's gorgeous. I still want you to come and visit us again. The only time you've been here since we've moved, it was wintry and cold. You'll come before the autumn, won't you? You used to love it here when you were little.'

'Yes, Mum, we all loved our summers there. But it's not that easy to up sticks and leave the shop,' she said, clearly making no promises. 'It will also depend on Ali's routine. She has summer exams coming up. Then I'll need to be around while she's on her holidays. It was easier when she was younger. But now I need to try and figure out what she's doing, and more to the point who she's doing it with. Raising a teen isn't easy. We'll organise a trip, though.'

Martha smiled.

'So tell me your news,' Rose said.

'How did you know I had news?' Martha asked.

'Because that's usually why you call.'

Martha launched delightedly into the details, telling her everything.

'Well isn't that a marvel?' Rose said. 'Oh my goodness, you're not going to believe who has just arrived. Dad!' Martha listened as they hugged and Rose screeched a lot. 'This is such a lovely surprise! I'd better go, Mum. Chat to you soon, okay?'

'Yes, dump me for your father as usual,' Martha said. But her comment was lost on Rose, who had already hung up.

Martha stood in the kitchen. It was spotless. She hadn't cooked since lunchtime yesterday because they'd been dining out. She wandered into the living room thinking she could possibly do some dusting in there. The place was like a show house. The bedclothes didn't need changing and there was no ironing. Since Jim wasn't working, he rarely wore a shirt and tie. So she only had a few things to iron now and she did that as she went along.

She had no idea when Jim would get back. Jeannie was coming over from LA, so no doubt she'd want a piece of him too. He could easily stay on beyond Monday, knowing him. Not that it mattered hugely if he was in Dublin or down here. He seemed to have turned into a social butterfly at the golf club. Anyone who bothered with him got his full attention.

'I'm thoroughly enjoying having the time to stop and talk,' he'd said only last week. 'When I'm not in a hurry, I can take all the time in the world!'

He was anxious that she wasn't killing herself either. In fact, he was obsessed with this idea of them both switching off totally.

They ate out more than in, and she knew he was paving the way for her to have an easier time. She was a great reader, and over the last year she'd read every best-seller going. But Martha wasn't great at *chillaxing*, Jim's new buzz word. He was delighted with it and used it whenever possible.

'Just sit with a book and chillax, Martha.'

'I'm going to sit in the garden and chillax, Martha.'

She, on the other hand, liked being around people, and she missed being in a position to help others. Grabbing the phone, she made a spontaneous call to directory enquiries, and moments later she was put through to the nearest health centre, which turned out to be over twenty miles away.

Once she'd explained her situation and how she'd come across Claire that morning, which was met with the praise and exclamations she felt her daughters hadn't given her, the lady seemed very interested in her offer to help.

'There is an opening for a midwife. Lots of women can't travel the hour to Galway hospital for their antenatal checks, so they end up waiting in crowded doctors' surgeries.'

'And some babies don't wait to get to Galway either,' Martha said, reminding her about Claire.

'Oh my goodness, I'd say she was so grateful you came along! She can't be the first woman to need help.'

'It was great timing, for sure,' said Martha. 'How many hours would you require me to do?' she asked, biting her lip. Her heart was beating like a drum as the lady explained that she could call the shots.

'The Ballyshaden area is surprisingly busy, and we've been looking for someone to cover it since old Mrs Markham retired and passed away. She was a dear lady and loved by all.'

'If you don't mind me asking, why hasn't the post been filled to date? Is there something you're not telling me?'

'Well . . .' The woman hesitated. 'The biggest issue is the wage. It's nominal and that's putting it nicely. None of the previous applicants felt it would be worth their while.'

When she heard how much she'd earn, Martha smiled. It wasn't a wage that a young midwife could live on, that was for certain. But she was in the happy position of knowing that she didn't need the money. More than that, the post would be a gift to her. She'd do it for free if they wanted her! She almost said so, but felt she shouldn't sell herself short.

'When can I start?' she asked, feeling butterflies in her tummy.

'Oh goodness, you'll do it?' the lady asked in shock. 'I was fully expecting you to make a polite excuse and hang up just like all the others.'

'I need this job as much as it needs me,' Martha said. 'For my sanity!'

She gave some more details and they came to the agreement that she would start in a week's time. That would give the health board time to fill out her details and make sure she was registered for Ballyshaden. Luckily, she hadn't cancelled her insurance or her membership of the Nurses and Midwives Association. So it appeared that the application could be put through quite easily.

'I know this is a bit irregular,' the lady said after they'd gone through Martha's details, 'but could I possibly give your name out now as the local midwife? There's no one there to help, and I know you're not officially in place until next week, and I know it's a Friday and we're facing into a weekend, but if you didn't mind . . .'

'Not at all,' Martha said, smiling. 'I'm dying to get going, so you can start sending them to me from right this minute. I'm good to go.'

'Really?' the lady said, sounding delighted. 'Well that was actually a leading question because I've got two women looking for home visits. Do you think you could do those – maybe one today and one tomorrow? Look, I know tomorrow's Saturday but it's for the PUK and—'

'I'll do it, no problem,' Martha said, thrilled at the prospect of getting back into the swing of things so quickly. 'Just give me the names and addresses, and I'll set up the appointments.'

'You are truly a godsend,' the lady said. 'An absolute angel.'

Martha laughed. 'No, I'm just a retired midwife itching to become un-retired. It's me who should be thanking you. You've made my day.'

After she hung up, Martha changed out of her good clothes and into one of her rather raggy gardening outfits. She pottered and inhaled the divine clear air. The grass didn't need cutting yet, so she inspected her three flower beds for weeds. The place was shipshape, so there was nothing for her to do. The sun was beginning to set as she sat in a garden chair with a large glass of white wine and watched as it merged with the ocean, creating a spectacular colour display. Sighing happily, she fully appreciated that moments like these were why they'd moved here permanently. It was a beautiful part of the world and she was blessed to be here, but she knew she wasn't quite ready to hang up her Pinard horn.

The only problem was that she wasn't sure how she'd break the news to Jim.

Chapter 6

ALI SAT IN A DAZE ON A KITCHEN STOOL AS HER mother made breakfast.

'I wish you'd stop making pancakes,' she said with a pout. 'My thighs are going to expand to the size of China. Becca says she's only eating fruit and yoghurt in the mornings now. She's doing some new diet with her mum.'

It was at the tip of Rose's tongue to say that Becca's mum was a total airhead who wouldn't know the first thing about nutrition, but she decided not to. Ali was explosive at the best of times lately, and anything she said was shot down with rolling eyes.

'The food I feed you is home-made from scratch, and the last time I looked, none of us needed to lose weight. So maybe we'll go by our rules in our own home, if that's okay with you and Becca?'

Ali thought about that for a moment. Her mum was a totally modern woman. She went on about feminism quite a bit. Not in a burn-your-bra way. More that women could be anything they wanted and that she should 'reach for the stars'. Ali thought it was pretty cool in a way. But sometimes she wondered if her dad wished he had a son, a boy to balance things out. So she would try and talk about rugby with him. She wasn't that keen on it, if she were totally honest. But he loved taking her to international matches and it was always exciting when Ireland scored.

'Okay, ladies,' Martin said, striding into the kitchen. 'I'm going to fly over to the shop. Ali, if you want a lift to school, you need to come now this second.'

With that, Ali dumped her knife and fork onto the plate of half-eaten pancakes, grabbed her bag and left without so much as a backward glance.

Picking up the plates, Rose scraped the food into the bin. A sob caught in her throat as she tried to compose herself. A few pancakes with fresh and expensive berries from the delicatessen was hardly a reason to cry. But she was getting really sick of being walked over. Martin said, 'Jump!' and Ali said, 'How high?' Whereas she was almost invisible – to both of them.

Bespoke Design had been set up by Rose's grandad over eighty years ago. It wasn't just an ordinary furniture shop. They carried all sorts of quirky designers, from Philippe Starck and Ron Arad to traditional lines from Irish craftsmen and women and more regular pieces from companies like Calligaris.

Over the years, Jim Brady had built the business with astonishing passion and flair. Beatrice, Jeannie and Rose had spent many hours of their school holidays working at the extensive store. But it was Rose who had really taken to the business. Her sisters loved the design end, but weren't so interested in the daily grind of running an office. Rose had loved it from the start, every single aspect.

Since Jeannie's departure to LA, Rose and then Martin had become more and more involved in the family business. A year ago, her parents had made the shock announcement that they were moving permanently to the west of Ireland. Jim had been raised there and always vowed he'd return some day.

'We don't want to leave it until we're so old and exhausted that we can't enjoy it. So we're handing the keys and the business over to you.'

Rose recalled lots of whispered conversations between her and her father. Every time Ali walked into the room, they stopped talking.

'What's going on?' Ali asked. 'Why are you treating me like a leper? I'm in this family too, you know.'

Seeing her so hurt had made Rose blurt out all the plans.

'As well as Dad and me taking over the running of Bespoke Design, we're moving into Marine Terrace.'

'Seriously?' Ali shrieked. Marine Terrace was the bomb. She loved going to visit her grandparents and sitting in their kitchen gazing out at the Irish Sea. Unlike most old people's houses, Marine Terrace was done up with the coolest furniture. Her favourite spot was at the corner of the building, where they'd replaced part of the stone wall with a massive piece of tempered glass. The oversized cream leather swivel chair was the perfect thing for curling up on with a hot chocolate and a book while enjoying the view.

'But where will Grandma Martha and Grandad Jim go? Are they taking our house?'

'No, they've revamped the holiday home in Connemara. It's been gutted and turned into a contemporary pad suitable for them to retire to.'

'So we're just going to pack our suitcases and move into Marine Terrace?' Ali said in awe. She already had her own bedroom there. It had a walk-in wardrobe and the most amazing shower room.

'Pretty much,' Martin said.

'Shouldn't we discuss this with Beatrice and Jeannie?' Rose had asked her parents.

'We spoke to both of them,' Jim told her. 'Beatrice has been given the shop with the flat above. We're going to furnish it fully, so she's more than happy. And as for Jeannie . . . she's settled with Nick. They have more money than they can spend in a lifetime. She has no interest in the house or the shop. In fact, her exact words were that she couldn't give a toss if we gave the house to charity. All the same, we've bought her an investment property to rent out. She'll have that as a fallback should she ever need it. But you and Martin have more than earned your stripes.'

'Your father's right,' Martha added. 'You and Martin have worked hard for years at Bespoke Design. Anyone can see that you're the natural choice to take over.'

'But the family home should belong to Jeannie and Beatrice too,' Rose pushed. 'I don't feel right about going ahead with the move unless I discuss it with them first.'

She and Martin called Jeannie, and she assured them that they had her blessing and she didn't hate them. When they called Beatrice, she was so excited about her new shop and flat that she was difficult to talk to.

'I can't wait for you to see it! Dad organised for the most gorgeous fittings all through the shop, and upstairs is a dream! I haven't had the time to bother doing a nice home for myself, being so busy with work. It's fabulous.'

Everything happened so smoothly after that. The removal van arrived and a few of Jim and Martha's favourite pieces, including the bedroom furniture, were removed and taken to Connemara, while Rose and Martin's own things were brought to Marine Terrace. The rest was either sold or given away. Nanny May took quite a few things for her cottage, which surprised them all.

'You didn't strike me as being interested in having this more modern style at your cottage,' Rose commented, 'but it's great that it's going to a good home.'

Martin was a qualified architect, so he was in charge of the refurbishments while Rose stuck to overseeing the business end, along with buying. Having graduated as a mature student with a first-class honours degree in business, she was a force to be reckoned with. Knowing it was up to her to keep the company afloat, and hopefully grow it, she took the responsibility seriously.

Nanny May had stepped in from the time Ali was born, doing all the babysitting and minding that was required.

'I raised you and your two sisters, so one little scrap will be a walk in the park!'

That had gone well for Ali's younger years. But as Nanny May grew older and obviously tired, Martin, in particular, became vocal about whether she should be looking after their daughter.

'Ali needs her mother. Not a sweet but ageing woman. Nanny May was in her prime when she looked after you and your sisters. But there's no real need for you to be working all the time at the shop. You're needed at home.'

Feeling horribly guilty, Rose took a step back from the business. She daren't admit it to anyone, but she found it tough being at home. While Ali was at school she went to her office at the back of the shop. But Martin didn't like the idea.

'Your place is at home. Fair enough if you want to keep up with some bookwork while you're there. But you should be out of here and doing your most important job, raising our daughter.'

Over the years, Rose slowly lost confidence in her own ability and ended up taking more of a step back than she'd ever intended.

It would be wonderful to say that her relationship with Ali was strong and fabulous as a result. But nothing could be further from the truth. Ali resented her and kicked back at her like a punchbag. Martin could do no wrong in his daughter's eyes, and Rose knew they actually sneered at her behind her back. She'd overheard them, and the way Ali disrespected her broke her heart.

'Oh, by the way,' Ali had said only last weekend, 'I'm getting my nose pierced. Becca's coming too and I can't wait.'

'Ali, you're fifteen and you're doing no such thing,' Rose said. 'They'll send you home from school if you do that.'

'No they won't,' Ali said, screwing up her face and looking at Rose as if she was deranged. 'Besides, Dad said I can. He even gave me the money.'

Rose called Martin at the shop.

'Did you tell Ali she could get her nose pierced without discussing it with me first?' she asked, fury boiling through her.

'She said she'd asked you and you'd said yes. Besides, she's a teenager. If getting her nose pierced is the worst thing she does, we'll be doing well. If that's all you're calling me for, I need to go. I'm busy, Rose.'

So Ali went with Becca – who wasn't allowed to have it done – and got a diamond stud in her nose. Rose wanted to sob when she saw it.

Ali liked helping out in the shop from time to time.

There were often deliveries of cool accessories, like lamps and picture frames or pretty twinkly lights for wrapping around her cream sleigh bed.

'If you want to help yourself to stock, you have to work for it,' Rose used to say. So often Ali and Becca would go into the stockroom and unwrap things and put them on the shelves in exchange for something new for their rooms.

But more often than not, Martin would only make them work for an hour before overpaying them with up to one hundred euros' worth of stock. If Rose questioned it, she was shot down. So she gave up on that too.

Ali loved living at Marine Terrace. It was literally five minutes' walk from Pebble Bay village, where all her friends hung out for frappuccinos. Then there was the beach when the weather was nice.

Becca had two younger sisters and an older brother, so she loved staying with Ali. 'It's so calm and quiet here,' she would say. 'Nobody steals your clothes or wrecks your make-up. You've no idea how lucky you are being an only child.'

Ali had admitted to Rose many times that she didn't crave the company of a sibling growing up. Rose had always been quite open about the fact that they hadn't planned for her to be on her own.

'We longed and hoped for another child,' she told Ali sadly. 'But it never happened.' She didn't tell her that it hadn't happened because Martin went completely cold towards her after Ali was born. Rose had never admitted that to anyone.

The thought of Jeannie arriving made Rose's heart sing. Her twin never failed to cheer her up. Even though they'd grown up side by side, she was now like an exotic creature with tales of life in LA, her 'minor procedures' and her amazing clothes. Ali was ecstatic at the thought of her aunt arriving.

'Jeannie is the bomb. She's so funny, and I cannot wait to see what she brings me.'

'Don't be so grabby, Ali. It's not nice. You should be looking forward to spending time with your aunt full stop. Not just so you can see what she buys you.'

'Duh,' Ali said rudely. 'I *am* looking forward to being with her. I'm going to ask if we can go to lunch together.' Rose smiled at the thought. 'Just me and her. It'll be such fun!'

Rose's smile faded as she wondered where it had all gone wrong. Was it normal teenage behaviour? Did all mothers feel wounded by their daughters? Did everyone feel as despised and useless?

Remembering that they had the reading of Nanny May's will to contend with, Rose's heart sank even further. She missed her old ally desperately. In fact, with Bea so busy with the new shop and her dad gone, Rose had never felt so alone.

A ring at the doorbell sent her dragging herself to answer it. Assuming it was someone selling things she didn't want, she opened the door looking pretty glum.

'What kind of a face is that to greet your old dad?'

Rose threw herself into his arms and surprised them both by sobbing like a baby.

'It looks as if I arrived at just the right time,' he said. 'I was in with Bea earlier. Ned and I had a walk then I met up with John Cunningham for a bit of lunch. If I'd known you were having a crisis, I would've come sooner. What's wrong, darling?'

'I'm fine really, Dad,' she said, wiping her tears. 'Just so glad to see you.'

As she made him a cup of tea, Rose knew she'd manage to keep going. Nothing ever seemed as bad when she had her dad. She fobbed him off by saying she was upset about Ali and Martin ganging up on her again. But really, deep down, Rose knew it was a lot more than that. She wasn't happy with her life in general. But she hadn't the foggiest idea how to change it.

Chapter 7

JEANNIE CRADLED A MUG OF GREEN TEA WHILE dabbing at her face. Nick was gone to work and had said he'd meet her at the fund-raiser tonight.

'You're not feeling off at all, are you?' he'd asked as she'd pushed away her breakfast smoothie.

'No. Why?' she'd asked, looking at him oddly.

'No reason,' he said. 'I can't put my finger on it, but you're different lately. You'd tell me if there was something wrong, right?'

'I'd tell you,' she said, smiling and lying right to his face.

'You are amazing.' He leaned over and kissed her. 'See you tonight. I'll wait by the door for you so you're not wandering about in that sexy gown unattached. I see the way Bill Burns looks at your ass.'

She laughed, enjoying the fact that her husband was so right about Bill. He'd jump into bed with her at the drop of a hat, if only she could stomach him! He was the new hotshot on the block at the hospital, and all the women were throwing themselves at him like suicidal mice on traps. Five years ago, Jeannie would probably have made a play for him too. Five months ago she might have, she mused. But it was time to hold back and be thankful for her lot. In fact, she had no idea how much longer she'd have any of this. Looking around at their palatial home, she cringed. If she gave birth to a baby that was undeniably not her husband's, this would all be gone. Nick would rightly hate her and kick her out.

Where would she go? There was no point being at the bottom of the crap pile here in LA. She'd have to go home and raise the child there alone. At least she had that apartment her parents had insisted on buying her. There were tenants to consider, but she'd give them notice and she and the baby could probably camp at Rose's for a while until it came free.

A gazillion thoughts flew around her head. She wandered to the home office and gazed at the plane ticket to Ireland. She couldn't wait to spend time with her sisters and Ali. She put in a Skype call to Rose, hoping to catch her at home.

'Hi, Jeannie!' Rose said, waving. She was sitting on a high stool with a cup of coffee in one hand and a foundation brush in the other. Behind her, Jeannie could just pick out the stunning view of the sea as the sun bounced off the rippling waves, sending wonderful glittery sprays into the air. She'd often sat in that very position herself, allowing the vast wonderment of the ocean to draw her in. While she was lost in its enormity, her own problems always felt somehow less significant. She yearned for that view and the smell of the sea spray when she walked along the beach.

'Wow, I'm astonished!' Rose said. 'You look so much better now. Your eyes have gone down massively.'

'I told you it was only a teeny procedure. So how are things?'

'Great. Dad is here already, which is brilliant. He's gone over to see Beatrice. I think he's taking Ned for a walk.

You know how he likes to feel useful. Then he's meeting one of his cronies to play golf at his old course. Ali's spending the afternoon with some friends in Pebble Bay, so I'm going to the office for a while.'

'Sounds cool.'

'I saw you notice Ali's nose-stud when we were talking. Thanks for not making a deal of it. She did it against my wishes. Although you'll probably think it's wonderful and independent of her.'

'Why did she do it if you didn't want her to?'

'Oh it's not a big deal really.' Rose tried to laugh it off. 'Martin overruled me and made me feel as if I was born in the Dark Ages.'

'Actually, I don't think it's great. That girl needs to listen to you more. I'll give her a piece of my mind when I see her.'

'Thanks, sis,' Rose said, tossing her head. When she did that, Jeannie knew she was holding back tears. She'd never been a fan of Martin's. But in recent years he'd turned into a real asshole. He went over Rose's head with Ali all the time and she could see that he enjoyed playing the two of them off against each other.

'What's your plan?' Rose asked.

'Nina is coming in a couple of hours to do my make-up and hair. It's still really early here, but I couldn't sleep. Before that I'm going to the gym then meeting some of the girls for a detox juice.'

'Sounds disgusting,' said Rose. 'Whatever happened to a cappuccino and a scone?'

'Ugh, too much dairy and carbohydrate in one sitting. My body would combust.'

'I honestly couldn't live like you. I have moments when

I feel like I'll collapse in a heap on the floor if I don't have caffeine. And as for my scone with jam . . . I don't have it that often, but when I do, I thoroughly enjoy it.'

'How's Martin, apart from overruling you?' Jeannie asked through gritted teeth.

'Good, and Nick?'

'Yeah, he's good too.' Both women disliked the other's choice of husband. Rose didn't get Nick. She'd told Jeannie when she'd come for their wedding that she found him garish and showy. For her part, Jeannie found Martin intense, self-centred and unforgivably dull. As a result, their men were one of the only no-go areas between the twins. Both talked to Beatrice about them, so she probably had a better grasp of the truth.

'Martin went off to the shop early today. We got a huge contract last week, to furnish six apartments. Well, actually *I* got the contract. It's for Max Jenkins Junior, the son of the man Dad used to do stuff for? So Martin's really busy with that.'

'Is he giving you and Ali the support you need? Sweetie, I know he's not the most emotional man, so you can lean on me any time.'

'I don't need to lean on anyone,' Rose snapped. 'My husband looks after Ali and me very well, thank you. And he is emotional too. He just doesn't profess it publicly. But that doesn't mean he isn't thinking of us in general.'

'Hey.' Jeannie held her hands up. 'Don't bite my head off. I'm just trying to say I love you and I'm here, that's all.'

'You're not much use over there, now are you?' Rose said, sounding uncharacteristically defeatist.

'I'm coming over,' Jeannie said. 'Give me a chance!

I've booked my flights and I'll be there on Monday morning. I'm coming for a few weeks too. So I can be your helper.'

Rose began to cry. Grabbing a box of tissues, she tried to stop. 'Oh wow, sorry. I'm so glad you're coming, and Ali will be beyond thrilled to spend time with you. She misses Nanny May a lot. That woman was a saint and I'm totally lost without her. But I know Ali would love a bit of craic with you.'

'Well rest assured I will be bringing bucketloads of craic. Ali and I will have a hoot of a time while you slave away in that godforsaken shop. How do you stick it?'

'I enjoy it.' Rose laughed. 'I'm not there half as much as I'd like, actually . . . I just hope Martin has everyone organised to take on this massive contract I just signed.'

'Well you get in there more and make sure of it.'

Rose didn't answer. She knew what would happen. Martin would tell her she should be at home with Ali. The awful thing was that she knew Ali didn't want her near her at the moment. They clashed like saucepan lids and Rose felt she might be better off leaving her alone.

'Hang in there, sis,' Jeannie said. 'I'll be there soon. Dad is with you now too. We'll shoulder one another and it'll be grand.'

Rose laughed out loud at Jeannie's pronunciation of the word 'grand'.

'You've held onto your Irish accent beautifully,' she said, 'but right there you sounded so funny.'

'Ah, top o' the mornin' to ya,' Jeannie said, and they giggled stupidly. She was happy to see her sister laughing through her tears. Jeannie suspected the business might have folded years ago if Martin had been left in charge, but yet again she'd learned to keep her mouth shut. It upset Rose when she gave out about him, and that was certainly not her goal.

'I've no doubt you'll have everything and everyone organised by teatime,' Jeannie said.

'I'll let you go then,' Rose said. 'Enjoy tonight. We'd love to see you all done up. Depending on how late it is, you might have to take a selfie and mail it to us. Ali isn't staying awake that late at the moment. She's got summer exams looming so she's trying to be sensible and eat well and get a bit more sleep. No more watching *Geordie Shore* until midnight.'

'Okay, I'll mail you some photos.'

'Enjoy tonight. Love you.'

'Love you too, Rosie.'

Jeannie felt guilty after they hung up. She should've told Rose she was pregnant. It would have to come out when she got home, and her twin was going to be really hurt that she hadn't shared such catastrophic news with her. But until she told Nick, nobody could know. Nina knew, of course, but that didn't count because she could trust Nina with her life. The CIA could grill Nina all they wanted and they'd get nothing out of her. She knew the value of a well-kept secret.

Feeling antsy and needing to talk some more, Jeannie tried Beatrice on the off chance she mightn't be in one of the shops.

'Well hello there!' Beatrice said as Ned poked his nose right into the camera, causing the screen to become a mess of brown fur.

'Hi, Ned. Hello, puppy!'

Ned turned his head one way and then the other.

'Your auntie Jeannie is talking to you, Ned,' Beatrice said with a smile. 'So how are things?'

'Crap,' said Jeannie honestly. 'I hate my life.'

'Okay, start at the beginning,' Beatrice said. 'I'm about to eat an early dinner because I've an evening appointment coming in a while. So if you don't mind chatting while I do that, I am all ears!'

'Wow, you're seriously busy, aren't you?'

'Tell me about it,' Beatrice said as she sat by the computer and began to eat her chicken stir-fry.

'So I have news,' Jeannie said. 'I'm coming home for the reading of Nanny May's will.'

'So I heard. Dad was here today and he took Ned for a walk. He also told me Mum won't be there for it.'

'Typical,' said Jeannie drily.

They chatted for a bit, but Beatrice was very distracted and Jeannie knew it was a bad time to talk to her older sister. She had her mind on work and that was fair enough. Jeannie would just have to wait until she saw her and then she'd be able to confess that she was a horrible person who loved her husband and didn't want to lose him, but that she couldn't possibly guarantee the baby she was carrying was his.

Realising she wasn't listening to her sister, she tried to concentrate.

'. . . so I reckon Rose will be more grateful than you realise that you're coming over. Good for you!'

'Thanks,' Jeannie said as a wave of fear washed over her. What if she had to keep the baby? She hadn't the first idea of how she was going to be a mother to this child. She wasn't good with babies. They cried when they saw her. The thought of having high chairs and cots and piles of nappies cluttering up the house didn't appeal to her. Maybe she could use the time in Ireland to adjust to the baby thing. After all, she'd always been a great aunt to Ali, right? But she had a sneaking suspicion that she was probably better at sending cool parcels of American sweets, or make-up and clothes.

She wasn't the type to sit in a chair at a child's bedside mopping his or her brow if they were sick. Panic shot through her. Putting her hand on her belly, she wondered if she could stay in Ireland, perhaps someplace that nobody knew her, like the midlands. She could give birth there, have the child put up for adoption and then continue as before. Nick would be none the wiser and it wouldn't matter what colour the baby's skin was . . .

This trip to Ireland wasn't going to be fun from the outset. First there was the sadness of hearing Nanny May's final words and wishes. Then Rose was snowed under at work. So she wasn't going to be up for long chats of support, even if Jeannie did manage to come clean to her. And Ali was studying for her summer exams and hanging out with friends. She wasn't a little girl any more. She wouldn't be happy sitting and playing makeovers with her aunt for more than a few minutes. Beatrice was dressing every bride from Dublin to Kerry and back up to Belfast, while her darling dad would have a nervous breakdown if she told him she was pregnant but wasn't going to keep the child . . .

'Jeannie! Are you listening?'

'What? Sorry, Bea . . . I've so much racing around in my head. I need to get sorted and packed and get ready for tonight. You know me! Always off to the next party and busy with my social life. I guess I'm just anxious about how I'll keep it together for Nanny May's will thing. I'm not great at emotional stuff, as you well know. I'll be a blubbing mess.'

'That's okay. Take a deep breath and you'll be just fine. You've got this, okay?'

'Okay,' Jeannie said, focusing on her sister's nodding face.

'Call me as soon as you land and I'll drop over to Marine Terrace.'

'I will. I love you.'

'And I love you, Jeannie-Beanie! I can't wait to see you. We'll have a great time. Don't be worrying, okay? Ciao!'

Jeannie fleetingly thought of calling her mother in Connemara but decided against it. Besides, she was probably eating out or playing golf. That seemed to be their lives nowadays.

She and her sisters had given their mother six months of living in the middle of nowhere before she'd come running back to Pebble Bay to her 'children'. Each baby Martha delivered was considered one of her children. She talked about them ad nauseam and loved nothing more than when one came to visit. There were drawers filled with thank-you cards from over the years, with each new mother more grateful than the previous one.

It was odd, Jeannie mused, that their mother wasn't great at talking about her actual children. Only the ones she'd delivered.

She thought of her dad. Jim was one of the world's precious gentlemen and always had been. He was the one they went to if Nanny May wasn't there. Not much had changed. He rang her at least once a week and was always interested in what she had to say. 'What have you been doing since we last spoke?' he'd say. Jeannie missed him so much right now and wished she could magic herself to his side. She'd love nothing more than to have a walk along the beach and sit for a coffee afterwards.

Knowing it was probably futile, but simply needing to hear a familiar voice, Jeannie decided to call her mother and dialled the cottage in Connemara after all.

Drat, thought Martha as she hesitated. The phone pealed loudly again. She was just on her way out the door to go to her first appointment. She had called the number supplied by her new employer – the word 'employer' made her smile – and the woman who answered had been extremely relieved that she and her new baby could be seen at home. Martha was anxious to get there. She moved towards the door but then stopped. It occurred to her that it could be a labouring mother on the line. If her number was being given out, every phone call could be important now. Dropping her handbag and medical kit, she rushed to answer.

'Hello, Martha speaking,' she sang out in her most cheerful voice.

'Hi, Mum, it's Jeannie, how are you?'

'Jeannie,' she said, sounding deflated.

'Sorry I'm not someone else. Clearly you're waiting for a more important call.'

'No, not at all,' she said, gathering herself. She looked at her watch. She hadn't much time, and knowing her daughter, she only wanted to talk about dresses or some such waffle. She'd raised all the girls in the same way, but it was beyond her how Jeannie had ended up as nothing more than a trophy wife. She'd been bright at school. The brightest of the three, if the truth be known. But she certainly wasn't making much use of her brain power.

'I won't keep you,' Jeannie was saying. 'You sound like you're in a rush there.'

'I am rather,' Martha said. 'I've got an appointment to get to. Could I call you back, or was there something in particular you needed?'

'I wanted to tell you I'm coming home for the reading of Nanny May's will. I believe you're not going to be there?'

'No, I won't be, I'm afraid. Your father said he'd tell me what was said. I'm a bit surprised that you're flying all the way back for it, though. Isn't that a little extreme?'

'No,' said Jeannie in a voice that was unmistakably sharp.

'Well you can do things at the drop of a hat because you don't work in a job where people are depending on you.'

'Oh yes, totally free and easy and a sponge living off my husband, that's me.'

'Jeannie,' Martha said crisply, 'that is not what I was saying.'

'I won't hold you up,' Jeannie said. 'But I was thinking of coming to visit for a couple of days. In Connemara.'

'Sounds great,' said Martha. 'Let's plan that once the will thing is finished, okay? I'd better run along.'

'Bye, Mum,' Jeannie said.

She had already hung up before Martha could respond. She'd have to speak to Jeannie if and when she visited. She was never too old to be scolded. Her manners were atrocious and she really needed to listen and be less abrasive on the phone. Martha wasn't used to being spoken to like that and she wasn't about to get used to it either. At almost forty, that girl needed to learn respect. Where had she gone wrong?

Feeling a little bit shaken and utterly furious, Martha took her handbag and her medical kit and finally got on her way. As she hurtled towards the address of the new mum she was going to help, she thought of Nanny May and this will reading. No doubt all three of the girls would be in floods of tears. Jim would be treating them like toddlers and Ali would probably be there witnessing the hysteria. That poor child didn't stand a chance stuck in the middle of her girls and their over-the-top emotions.

While she certainly didn't want them having a childhood like hers, she wasn't agreeable to this outward pouring of emotion that was all the rage. She felt it encouraged unnecessary hysteria in some cases and awful hurt in others. This idea of telling people what you really thought wasn't always a good idea, in her opinion.

She felt a bit ill whenever the reading was mentioned because it made her think of the letters. She had no idea what to do with them. And for the life of her she couldn't understand why they were all so excited about it. Sure, Nanny May had been a reliable and constant feature in their lives. But she'd been very well paid to be there. She hadn't appeared at Marine Terrace from Monday to Saturday out of the goodness of her heart. She got a raise each year and Martha paid her for any overtime she incurred. The girls seemed to have her on some sort of pedestal.

If she were honest, Martha hadn't adored the woman. They'd shared a healthy respect for one another, but they'd never had a relationship that went past the necessaries. If there was an issue or something required, such as a school book or shoes, Nanny May would inform her. She'd get the money for the item and it would be sorted. They didn't sit drinking coffee together, nor did they see one another outside of work. So Martha didn't feel it would be fitting for her to attend the woman's will reading. There would probably be family members there and it would seem terribly odd to see her entire clan pitching up. As it was, she was a bit miffed that Jim had gone. She'd told him her feelings on the matter. He'd listened and, after a few moments' silence, had said he still wanted to go. That was his lookout.

Taking several deep breaths and turning on the radio, Martha tried to banish the conversation with Jeannie and those letters from her mind. She moved on instead to how thrilled the local women would be to hear of her appointment. She felt energy coursing through her as she thought of all the good she could do in Ballyshaden. It would be fantastic!

Jeannie wanted to throw her water glass at the wall. Her mother was such a selfish old trog. She always had been and always would be. Her bloody appointment was obviously more important to her than Nanny May's final words. How could she be so callous? Nanny May had enabled her to do exactly as she pleased for years. She'd raised them while their mother swanned around doing anything but care for them. Jeannie had once said that Nanny May should move in and let their mother go and live in the cottage. She'd been sent to her room and told to come out when she was sorry.

'When you're ready to apologise to me, I'll allow you out to play with your sisters.' When the afternoon passed and it came to dinner time and there was still no sign of Jeannie, their father had intervened.

'I'm sure she didn't mean it to come out the way it did. She's a child, Martha. She's only seven years old. She doesn't know what she's saying.'

'I suppose not,' Martha said with a sniff.

Jeannie was sitting on the floor in her bedroom, hugging her knees and fuming. She knew exactly what she was saying. She wished their mother would go and live in the cottage and let Nanny May live with them. If she never saw her mother again, she wouldn't care.

'Will you come and say sorry to your mother?' her dad asked. 'Please, darling. I hate the fighting and I don't want you or your mother to feel sad.'

'Why doesn't she go and live somewhere else?' Jeannie asked as her father scooped her up off the floor and hugged her tightly.

'Because she's your mother and you love her. We all do.'

Jeannie nuzzled into her father's neck and sighed. She loved it when he hugged her. He smelled of his aftershave and the cigars he wasn't supposed to smoke but that she saw him puffing on in the potting shed from time to time.

'Will you say sorry?' he pleaded. She nodded her head, knowing it would stop him from feeling sad.

'I'm sorry, Mum,' she said, with her fingers crossed behind her back. 'I didn't mean to upset you or Dad.'

'Well all right,' said Martha. 'But you mustn't be so rude in the future, you hear?'

'I understand,' Jeannie said, her heart filled with resentment.

Now, more than thirty years later, Jeannie resented Martha just as much, if not more. There was no way she was telling her about her pregnancy. She'd only want to take over and do her holier-than-thou preaching. She'd been awful to poor Rose while she was pregnant with Ali, pointing out what she was doing wrong and bossing her about. Well, Jeannie wasn't going to allow her to interfere this time. If her plan went well, she wouldn't need to worry about any of that. She had an idea in her head.

Maybe she'd take a road trip to one or two of the bigger towns near Connemara and try to figure out some way of having this baby adopted without anyone knowing.

She sat down at her desk and fired up her computer. She went online and tried to find some adoption agencies in Ireland. The information was good, and it became apparent that she'd need to give consent in two stages. The biological father could give consent too, but seeing as she didn't know who he was, but that he was certainly and definitely in America, she hoped she could skip that part. She'd need to see a social worker and give consent to placement for adoption. Then, secondly, consent to the adoption order.

The websites all reiterated that she could change her mind at any point. She could do the first part and then right up until the day of the adoption she could decide not to go ahead.

That seemed dreadfully unfair to the poor couple who were waiting for a baby. All the same, it was going to be in her favour. She didn't have to feel forced into anything. That was good, but in all honesty she felt it would be the best option. Nobody needed to be hurt, her marriage would remain intact and maybe she and Nick would have a baby of their own in better circumstances in a year or so . . .

She'd figure it out once she got there. But meanwhile, she'd need to make sure she was busy all the time while she was in Ireland. She couldn't risk having lots of free time on her hands or she'd go insane.

She walked to the back door and outside. The air was thick and warm so she walked to the pool area and perched on a sun lounger, waiting for her breathing to calm.

She was so on edge lately. Of course, Brittany would tell her to get Xanax. But she didn't want to get into the habit of reaching for drugs to fix everything. Besides, she couldn't take any of that stuff while she was pregnant. She might not want to keep the child, but she certainly wasn't going to damage it.

Just as she was contemplating jumping into the deep end of the pool, the sound of a car horn blasting from the entrance stopped her. Rushing back to the house, she peered into the security monitor and was relieved to see Nina waving. That meant she could stop Skyping people and attempting to take her mind off things. Her head hurt and she wished she could lie down and sleep for a week.

Her heart sank when she saw Viktor, Nina's younger boy, jumping out of the van. He was six or seven, and although he was always instructed to sit in silence, he'd invariably start to misbehave.

'Oh, look who it is,' Jeannie said, wrinkling her nose and crouching down to try and smile at him. He stared back at her with one hand on his hip and the other wrapped around a backpack.

'I'm sorry, darling,' Nina said. 'He will sit with his game machine and make no noise. His papa was supposed to take care of him, but he no come back. I think he went drinking with that idiot brother of his.'

'How lovely,' Jeannie said, raising an eyebrow. 'Would you like a cool drink?'

'Yes please, Miss Jeannie,' said the boy.

She wanted to snarl that she wasn't asking him. She was thinking of his poor overworked mother. But she continued to smile and poured him a soda. She knew she was being horribly impatient, but young children simply didn't do it for her. They irritated her and made her cross. Yet another reason why she ought to put this baby up for adoption. She couldn't face being in a bad mood for the next twenty years.

'Don't give him that glass, Jeannie. It's crystal and I can't afford to pay you if he smashes it. Drink from can please, Viktor,' Nina ordered.

Jeannie put the pretty glass in front of Nina and handed a fresh can to the child. He snatched it and ran to sit on the easy chair in the kitchen. It was more of a sculpture than a chair, if the truth were told, covered in ballet-shoe-pink leather with a thick chrome stand. She'd found it in Paris and couldn't live without it. But it wasn't really for young pups to fling themselves onto wearing dirty trainers. Twitching, she rushed over and scooped the can of cola from his paw-like grasp.

'Don't sit on Aunt Jeannie's pink chair with sticky cola, please.' She turned towards Nina apologetically. 'Would it be okay if we pull over a bar stool? That chair is worth more than my internal organs on the black market. I don't want him to feel bad if he marks it.'

Nina laughed loudly at Jeannie's joke as she pulled a stool over for her son and pointed to him to climb onto it.

'No, Mama! I like it here,' he said.

'Do what you are told, Viktor. That is Aunt Jeannie's special chair and you will upset her. Come, come!' With a swift movement he was pulled to the floor and marched over to where Nina was setting up. She scolded him quickly in Russian as he pouted and stamped his foot. After one more sentence he gave in and did what he was told.

Planting a kiss on his head, Nina joined Jeannie and unpacked the rest of her make-up things. Jeannie wondered how she did that. Moved from shouting at the child to kissing his thick moppy head. She never had an inclination to kiss a child's hair. It just didn't appeal to her.

Normally Jeannie would spill her heart out to Nina. In the past, she'd even told her about her new squeezes and how many times they'd had sex. Nina would wave her hands and scream, saying she didn't want to hear. There were no taboo subjects between them. But today Jeannie knew she couldn't say what was bothering her. Judging by the way Nina was glancing over at her son, there was no way she'd understand.

As a child, when life was too much, Jeannie would sit on the special seat in the kitchen at Marine Terrace and look out at the vast expanse of ocean. She'd stare and stare until she felt like a tiny dot. Soon she'd be there, she thought happily. Maybe she was just homesick. She needed to return to Ireland every few months or she felt as if she wasn't a part of the wonderful unit she and her sisters shared. That was it, she decided. She simply needed some sisterly love.

Her dad would be there, too. She couldn't wait to see him.

For now she had a duty to fulfil. Nick was looking forward to seeing his beautiful wife in her stunning gown as they raised the roof along with funds for a deserving cause. With each of Nina's brushstrokes she felt better. By the time Nina had added the final dusting of powder, her shoulders had loosened.

She waved Nina and Viktor away and slid into her gown. Turning this way and that, she scrutinised her figure. It was lucky she'd ordered the dress a size bigger than usual. She swallowed the lump in her throat. Seeing as the fabric fell in a stunning cascading empire line, all eyes would be on her chest. Nick had done an immaculate job of making her bust more shapely than before, but even he couldn't have created the voluptuous look she was sporting now. The Swarovski crystals twinkled in the fading sunlight, ensuring all eyes would be on her breasts rather than her blossoming stomach, which was perfectly hidden beneath the layers of lace. The ball-gown style meant she didn't look pregnant. Her face wasn't swollen and her arms were still slim. They'd probably all assume she'd had another little enhancement done. She'd have to be ready to look offended should anyone suggest such a thing. She'd need to avoid Brittany. She was as sharp as a flick-knife and would plague her if she suspected anything was going on.

Stepping into her heels, she grabbed her clutch bag and sauntered towards the door in perfect time for her chauffeur-driven ride.

Her entrance to the ball was perfect. She knew the room had inhaled as she'd waltzed over to Nick. They kissed, and he led her to work the room. But by the time they took their seats for dinner, she was deflated once more. Her back ached, her eyes were burning and all she wanted to do was lie down and go to sleep.

Jeannie realised she was no longer happy just being a butterfly. She was oddly disgruntled and that feeling wasn't good. But as Nick winked at her across the table and blew her a kiss, fresh panic crept over her.

Could she go ahead with having this child adopted? What if Nick found out? He'd never forgive her. She could ruin her life and that of the child. How had she ended up in such a mess? She was a total idiot.

Knowing she needed to do something positive today, she turned to the leering creature sitting to her right, who was salivating right down the front of her gown, and tried to be pleasant. As far as she knew he was a big swing at the hospital, so she'd play the good wife, even if it was only for an evening.

Chapter 8

BEATRICE TRIED TO KEEP THE BRIDAL APPOINTMENTS to daytime hours. Otherwise she'd be working around the clock. But some of her brides worked gruelling hours and they simply couldn't make it before evening.

The girl coming tonight was buying a thirty-thousand-euro ensemble, so Beatrice would've welcomed her in the middle of the night if that was what she wanted. The fact that she was marrying the son of one of the most prestigious families in Ireland spurred her on further. Beatrice knew darn well that if Sadie's dresses were admired, she stood to gain a good bit of extra business out of it. Once one high-society girl showed up in her gowns, the others soon followed. It wasn't by fluke that Beatrice was keeping six shops afloat. They were more than afloat too. Each one was doing extremely well. But she couldn't ignore the fact that her newest one, in the heart of Pebble Bay, was wiping the ground with the other five. The clientele in the area were totally different from the women in the city centre or the other suburbs. They saw what they wanted and barely looked at the price tags. They went all out on accessories and veils, not to mention the high-end shoes.

'Hello, Sadie,' she said. 'It's lovely to see you.'

'Hi, Beatrice, thanks so much for seeing me at such an

awkward time on a Saturday night. I'm sure you've lots of social stuff to get to, so I won't keep you.'

'All I'm delaying is sorting my washing, brushing my scruffy little dog and putting on a face mask and a hair treatment while I catch up with *The Late Late Show*.'

'I guess you've had a hard week and you're taking it easy this weekend?'

'It's not exactly rock 'n' roll in my house. It's not even that I'm taking it easy; this is my life. I'm a low-key sort of person. I have moments where I fear I've turned into a rather antisocial and sad creature! But keeping six boutiques going can't be done by burning the candle at both ends.' Beatrice was locked in her own thoughts for a moment. 'Wow, my apologies. I shouldn't waffle at you when you're trying to have your fitting. Forgive me.'

'Gosh, there's nothing to forgive. I envy you,' Sadie said as she walked into the fitting room to slip into her ceremony dress. 'I seem to be going from one drinks party to the next. I have been since my engagement was announced last year. I would love nothing more than a night on the sofa in my pyjamas, with the fire lit and nobody to annoy me.'

'Your husband-to-be is a socialite and there's no denying that!' Beatrice said as she laid out the various accessories Sadie had ordered.

Sadie's engagement had been well documented in the celebrity columns of the magazines. Both bride and groom were from horsey families, with Sadie's owning a world-famous stud and his owning a huge equine training and therapeutic centre. The wedding was being held in a marquee the size of Pebble Bay village, and all the top people from Ireland to Dubai would be in attendance.

'So you're happy with the dress you're changing into for the dancing in the evening?' Beatrice said.

'Yes. I just wanted the ribbon changed from pale pink to cream on the bodice. At least, my mother did.' She rolled her eyes. 'I must apologise for the last time we were here, Beatrice. Her behaviour was awful. She was incredibly rude to you. My mother thinks the world is there to serve her. She's treated like a princess at home and forgets the rest of the planet doesn't love her quite as much as Daddy does.'

'Don't you worry, I didn't even notice,' Beatrice lied. She'd never come as close to decking someone. Mrs Farrell was obnoxiously rude and had clicked her fingers in Beatrice's face, referring to her as 'shop woman'.

'You're so good to pretend you're not offended,' Sadie said. 'If I were you, I'd have turfed us out and told us where to stick our money along with my bloody dresses.'

'Not at all,' Beatrice said as she smiled genuinely at Sadie. 'I'm happy to help you. It's going to be a beautiful wedding and your fiancé is going to die when he sees you!'

Beatrice waited a few moments for Sadie to come out of the fitting room. Normally a bride would put on her dress and come out clutching the untied bodice to the front of her chest, and Beatrice would promptly lace it up.

When there was no sign of Sadie, she called out, 'Are you doing okay in there? Can I help you?'

There was no answer.

'Sadie?' She walked closer and held her ear against the curtain. She thought she heard sniffling.

'Oh no, Sadie, what's wrong?' she asked. 'May I come in?'

'Yes,' she said through sobs.

As Beatrice pulled back the heavy velvet drape, Sadie was standing clutching her bodice, the skirt part barely staying up on her emaciated hips.

'Oh my goodness,' said Beatrice. 'You've lost such a lot of weight.'

'I can't eat,' Sadie said as tears continued to cascade down her cheeks. 'The wedding is drawing closer. The hype is getting to a point where I want to scream. I can't bear it a second longer.'

'Why?' Beatrice asked in shock. 'What's wrong? Don't you want to marry Richard?'

As tears soaked her face, she shook her head silently.

'Oh Sadie,' Beatrice said as she pulled over a chair for the girl to perch on. She grabbed one of the silk mono-grammed dressing gowns provided for brides to wear in between dresses and draped it about her shoulders. Gratefully Sadie shrugged into it and secured it around herself.

'Do you want to talk about it?' Beatrice asked. The dresses had been paid for in full, there was a no-refund policy and quite frankly, Beatrice knew she'd never sell them on. Both were so tiny they could almost be sold as communion dresses. But even so they were now swimming on Sadie's shrinking frame.

'If I tell you, then it'll be real . . . then I'll have to do something about it. I don't know if I can . . . I don't know if I have the courage.'

Beatrice didn't say a word. She left the silence hanging in the air knowing that when she was ready, Sadie would fill it.

'My mother talked about my marrying Richard from the

time we were knee high,' she began. 'His family used to come to our ostentatious garden parties and in return we'd attend his family's ridiculously opulent barbecues.'

'I'd say they were amazing,' Beatrice said wistfully.

'Perhaps they are when you look at them on the glossy pages of a magazine. All the beautiful people wearing the most wonderfully cut clothes by world-renowned designers!'

'Do I fit into that category now?' Beatrice quipped.

Sadie smiled sadly. 'Yes, I suppose you do. Congratulations. I could point that out to Mummy and she could throw a luncheon in your honour.'

'I think I might be busy that day.'

There was another brief pause before Sadie spoke again.

'We were around ten or eleven when Richard tried to kiss me for the first time.'

Beatrice smiled. 'I'd say you were the envy of many little girls who were all too ready to change their pigtails to up-styles to try and catch his eye.'

'You're dead right there. I told my best friend in school, Evie, what had happened and she went into a squealing tailspin and made me tell her over and over again how it had come about.' Her eyes glazed over as she remembered. 'I was at one of those tedious show-off sessions, or luncheons as Mummy calls them, at my house. It was being hosted in the ballroom.'

'You have an actual ballroom in your house?' Beatrice said. Sadie nodded. 'Very cool. Sorry, please continue . . .'

'My mother loved nothing more than a themed event. So this one was a salute to *Charlie and the Chocolate Factory*. The room was bedecked in huge custom-made swirling candy canes and moon-sized lollipops with chains of sweets threaded around the place and fairy lights absolutely everywhere. I was at the chocolate fountain and there was nobody close by. Richard came up behind me and pecked me on the side of the cheek. When I spun around to say something, he was waiting like a great big puckery frog and smacked me one right on the lips in front of Great-Uncle Geoffrey, who responded by choking on a sausage roll. Richard ended up attempting to perform the Heimlich manoeuvre, but couldn't get his skinny pre-teen arms around Geoffrey's fat belly.'

Beatrice laughed as Sadie conceded a watery smile.

'It was panic stations after that. Great-Uncle Geoffrey was turning blue, so my father rushed to his rescue and grabbed him very roughly around the diaphragm, sending the offending piece of food into the chocolate fountain at a hundred miles an hour. I ran away as I heard him struggling to say words like "hoor" and "kissing boys".'

'Hoor?' Beatrice said in surprise.

'Oh yes, Great-Uncle Geoffrey was a potty-mouthed old man. When he drank whiskey, he was like a crab. He'd pinch anyone's bottom, from Granny's to mine!'

'Ew, I can't say I like the sound of him.' Beatrice pondered for a moment. 'You have a way with words. I know you're upset and you're trying to tell me why. But I love your descriptions and you paint such wonderful pictures.'

'Thank you,' Sadie said, visibly relaxing a little.

'So Richard kissed you and you ran away . . .'

'I could bore you and embellish it a lot more, but cutting a long story short, our mothers jumped on the bandwagon and we were paired up for every dinner dance, hunt ball, masquerade ball and any other excuse for a ball that you can think of.'

'It sounds like the life of a Disney princess,' Beatrice admitted.

'It wasn't, believe me. I hated it. All I wanted to do was to write books. Since I could read at the age of three.'

'Three? Wow, you must be very brainy . . .'

'No, I had a nanny who loved reading and I guess she passed that love on to me. At first she'd read to me and I became so impatient for her to turn the pages and hurry up with the story that she sat me on her lap and literally taught me to read. Once I got going, there was no stopping me.'

'So that's why you're so good at conjuring up pictures with words.'

'Thank you,' Sadie said with the first proper smile of the evening. It reached her eyes and made her look even prettier than she had before. Unlike Beatrice's mass of blonde curls, Sadie's hair hung in glossy treacle-hued sections. Her soft brown eyes looked bigger than they should because her face had become so thin. Her frame was so tiny that she looked almost elfin. 'I studied English at university and assumed I would go on to be a world-famous author. I had images of lavish parties that Mummy would, of course, organise. But this time I wouldn't mind quite so much because they'd be book launches.'

'And have you penned your first novel yet?'

She sighed so deeply, Beatrice felt the emotion must've been drawn from her toes.

'I've written three books.'

'That's fantastic! What name did you use and I'll be sure to buy them?'

'They weren't published. I never even got to send them to a publishing house. I made the intensely stupid mistake of allowing Mummy to read them first. She went into an apoplectic fit of rage, yelling and shouting that they were the work of Satan.'

'Why, were they full of sex scenes and bondage?'

'You'd swear they were a step-by-step guide to murdering and cooking my granny,' she said with a grin. 'No, they were books aimed at teenagers. Each one dealt with a different issue that was entwined in a story.'

'What's so wrong about that?' Beatrice asked, looking puzzled.

'Because one of them was entitled *The Girl Next Door*.'

'I don't understand,' Beatrice said. 'Was the girl next door hiding dead bodies in her basement?'

'No, she was a lesbian.'

It took a moment, and finally the penny dropped. Beatrice stared at Sadie as she held her gaze.

'When Mummy read the book and realised how much emotional detail was in the story, she began to question me. Tearfully, I came out and she became the first and only person I have ever told I was gay, until this minute.'

'When was this?' Beatrice asked.

'Ten years ago.'

'So why are you getting married to Richard?'

'Because it's easier,' she said with a sigh. 'I'm thirty-four. Questions are being asked. My parents deal with a lot of people who are very set in their ways. There simply isn't room for them to have an only daughter who is a lesbian. They aren't gunning for a wedding with two brides, sadly.'

Beatrice hugged her and let her cry. There was nothing she could say. Clearly Sadie had made up her mind to go through with this wedding. She was prepared to live a lie because that was expected of her.

'But it's not the 1960s,' Beatrice said, making a last-ditch effort to encourage her. 'I actually feel ill for you that you're walking straight into unhappiness with your eyes wide open. It's a terrible situation.'

'It's not the worst scenario imaginable,' Sadie said, blowing her nose. 'Some women live with violent partners, alcoholics or cruel men. Richard is none of those things. He loves me and will devote his life to making me happy. God bless him, he will never truly succeed, but that's not his fault.'

'I was married,' Beatrice admitted. 'I knew I didn't love him. By the time I admitted it to myself, it was too late.'

'How long ago was this?'

'Seven years now,' Beatrice said. 'So I understand in my own odd way.'

Beatrice had always assumed she'd stay married until her dying day. She'd felt that was the virtuous thing, and the right thing to stand by her Catholic faith. When the divorce papers had arrived a few months after Davy left, she signed them and put them in the postbox feeling as if she'd committed the worst sin imaginable. She'd gone directly to the church, lit a candle and dropped to her knees begging God and Mother Mary to forgive her for what she'd done.

Until tonight, she'd believed she was evil and rotten to the core for breaking her wedding vows. But this girl had made her realise that both she and Davy had a right to happiness. That staying married would've made them miserable. She wouldn't have the shops or any of the other things in her life that had come about once she was single again.

'I hope Davy is happy. I haven't seen or heard from him since he went to Australia,' she said eventually.

'It's not easy, is it?' said Sadie.

'Well, a lot of the time it is,' Beatrice said. 'I make a pretty good living out of it being easy. People love it, in fact. Most of the brides who come in here are excited and delighted to the point of delirium. We're just a pair of miserable cows.'

Once they started laughing, they couldn't stop. Sadie sat in the silken robe, her cheeks streaked with mascara.

'So what are you going to do now?' Beatrice asked, almost afraid of her answer.

'I'm going to pretend I didn't have a total meltdown and tell you my innermost secret and carry on as before. Move along, nothing to see here, thank you very much.'

'Really?' Beatrice asked.

'Really.' Sadie sighed. 'It's gone too far. Half the world's population will arrive in shiny expensive cars wearing the contents of several mink farms draped over every label known to spoilt ladies. I will wear these exquisite dresses and wish with all my heart that someone else was waiting for me at the top of that cathedral aisle . . .'

'Are you in love with someone in particular?'

Sadie hesitated, as if she were deciding whether or not she should say. 'Not right now, but I was.' Her eyes shone with unshed tears as she struggled to hold it together. 'I loved a wonderful woman and she loved me. But when I told her I was going ahead with the wedding, she ended it,' she admitted.

'I'm so sorry,' was all Beatrice could think of saying.

They eventually finished the fitting and Beatrice put the two dresses into special carrier bags that zipped all the way around so as not to crease them.

'Thank you,' Sadie said.

'You're welcome. I aim to please here at Bridal Belles!'

'You've been so kind to me. I sincerely hope you find love again, Beatrice. You deserve to.'

'I hope you do too. I wish you were wearing those stunning gowns for an occasion that made you happy.'

'I'll be okay,' Sadie said. 'Poor little rich girl who can't be pleased about her plush and easy life, eh?'

'I don't think that for one minute,' Beatrice assured her. 'I genuinely wish you could find the courage to be yourself.'

They hugged, and Beatrice waited until she knew Sadie was gone before turning off the lights and going back up to her flat. Ned was thrilled to see her and gave her a hero's welcome, as always. She scooped him up and buried her face in his soft fur.

As she gazed at the letter that was stuck to her fridge with a magnet, the butterflies jumped into action in her tummy.

Monday would be D-Day. She still couldn't quite fathom what she was about to do. One thing was certain, she'd gone too far to back out. Changes were coming, and Beatrice hoped she would be able to cope.

Chapter 9

IN JIM'S ABSENCE, MARTHA WAS AS BUSY AS A BEE. She'd noticed a missed call from him on her mobile on Saturday morning and figured she'd better call him back so he didn't become suspicious.

'Martha, how are you getting on?'

'Fine, and yourself?'

'Good, thanks. It's lovely to see the girls. I've been walking Ned and obviously I'm staying with Rosie, and Jeannie is on her way. She'll be here on Monday.'

'That's good.'

'You can still change your mind, Martha. Are you sure you wouldn't come up? The girls would be delighted to see you.'

Thoughts of Monday immediately made her think of the letters again. For the millionth time she wished she had left them just as she'd found them. Yes, it might have cemented Nanny May in her girls' hearts, but she wouldn't be left feeling like a criminal, at least. She cursed her impulsiveness and resolved to either steam them open or burn them. Jim was still chatting away about the girls and how they could all go for a family dinner together.

'Oh, I think I'll hang on here if it's all the same to you, dear.'

'Okay,' he said. 'You sound busy, what are you doing?'

'Nothing much,' she said. 'Just making a plan for a herb garden. I was chatting to one of the lady golfers and she said she has a very successful one.'

'That sounds great,' Jim said, and they both knew he was feigning interest. 'I won't keep you.'

'Right you are,' she said. 'Take care.'

'I'll tell the girls you send your love, will I?'

'Of course, of course,' she said, hanging up.

She opened her spiral notebook and pulled the pen from within the coiled wire. The lady from the health centre had called again and now on top of the PUK heel-prick test scheduled for today, she had a second house call, for a postnatal check-up.

Although she was glad for the immediate work, she knew it would take a while for the news to spread that she was available. She'd need people to talk to one another, too. Personal recommendations were the best, and although she'd spoken to the local GP, Dr Francis, and he'd promised to point ladies in her direction, Martha was under no illusions. It was going to take time for her to build a little practice here. In a way, that suited her quite nicely. It gave her a bit of time before she'd have to tell Jim.

Attending to these new mothers and their tiny babies made her think back to when her own babies were born. The twins was her tough birth. She'd been utterly wiped out by the time they were both born. She wished to this day that she'd insisted on a Caesarean section. When the midwife, who was a complete klutz – Martha had had to give her instructions – handed her the two girls, all she'd wanted to do was sleep.

'You take them, Jim,' she said, as tears ran down her face.

'Darling, don't cry, you've done an amazing job. Look at them.'

She lied, saying she was overwhelmed by love. In truth, she was beyond exhausted and wanted the two of them taken as far away from her as possible.

Jim cradled them, one in each arm, and crooned to them. They'd chosen their names supposedly together, but she would have agreed to anything.

'This little mite looks like a Jean. What do you think?'

She forced her eyes to stay open for a few minutes longer. 'I think that's beautiful,' she said.

'The other little lady is so serene. She's only a few minutes old, but she's more delicate and calm. What do you think of Rose?'

'Now I love that,' she said, as her eyes fluttered shut.

In those days the midwives took the babies away, only bringing them in to be fed. But because she'd had twins, they were a novelty and everyone wanted to hold them, which Martha didn't mind one bit.

Now, as she got ready to leave the house, Martha decided it was too late to start messing about with the letters. So she left them where they were, telling herself she needed to sort them later that day, for once and for all.

She drove to the first house, where a very unsure and frightened first-time mother was clutching her baby in terror.

'I'm looking for Aisling. Am I in the right place?'

'Yes,' she said, 'come on in. Will this heel-prick test thing hurt him?'

Martha didn't believe in sugar-coating the truth, there was no point, but this was one of the exceptions. Babies needed to have the test on the off chance that they did have PUK. It was a condition that could cause instant brain damage if not dealt with correctly. She couldn't risk the frightened mother deciding not to allow her to perform it.

'No, he won't feel a thing. He'll cry because I'm at him and he doesn't know me.'

She carefully performed the test, puncturing the skin on the baby's foot and squeezing his tiny heel until all the circles on her card were filled with blood.

'That's it, all over and done with. Well done, baba, and well done, Mummy.'

The young woman beamed as Martha put a tiny round plaster on his foot. 'I'm so glad that's over!' she said.

'Ah, it's not easy to hold a crying baby the way you did. You should be very proud of yourself.'

'I don't feel proud,' Aisling said. 'I'm exhausted and cranky and every time I move, my boobs make wet patches on my top. Nobody told me having a baby caused so many places to leak.'

'When you're in the early post-partum stage, your body is desperately trying to heal, feed and bounce back. I have some plastic-backed breast pads,' Martha said, handing some over. 'They stock them in the Ballyshaden pharmacy. It can be good to have a bath with a couple of teaspoons of bread soda dissolved in the water. It helps with the healing process.'

They chatted about a couple more things before Martha stood up to leave.

'I wish you could stay all day,' said Aisling. 'You're a font of knowledge, but you don't make me feel like an idiot. My mother died when I was ten, but my mother-in-law is very much alive and she's full of advice. She delivers it in a militant way and gets cross when I don't do as she says.'

'That can be really hard,' Martha agreed. 'But you need to stand firm. Thank her for her suggestion and tell her you'll absolutely take it on board.' Aisling looked doubtful. 'I wouldn't have been able to say that to my own mother-in-law at first,' Martha admitted. 'When I had my first daughter, my imagination ran wild. I envisaged her having every disease and virus going! So too much knowledge can be a bad thing.'

'Can you come again another day?' Aisling asked.

'I can, of course,' said Martha. 'But you know, it's just struck me talking to you . . . do you think a mother-and-baby morning would be a popular idea? I'd be happy to host it. That way you could meet new mums in a similar position. It's lovely for babies to get out and see one another too.'

'Oh God, I would love it! I could help by telling any of the women I know. You know pregnant women, we end up all knowing each other, so I could drum up interest very quickly, I think, especially as it's so badly needed.'

'I could put up notices in the local shops and ask Dr Francis to push it for me,' Martha said, thinking out loud. Since they'd moved to Ballyshaden she'd noticed just how important community events were. It wasn't the same as living in a city where everything was accessible. But, the locals also tended to make more of an effort to join in. So her gut instinct was that her new venture would grow wings quite quickly too.

'I'd say you could get the community centre for it,' the woman said. 'That's easy to get to and has plenty of parking as well.'

She left with a spring in her step, delighted with her new idea.

Excited to get back into doing what she adored the most, Martha drove straight to the community centre. She hadn't been there before, but it was easy to find and there was a man on reception who was extremely helpful and showed her around. There was a room that looked perfect for small gatherings.

'I don't suppose this room is available any days during the week?' she asked. 'I'm the new midwife and I would like to do some mother and baby classes.' She was about to expand further when the man cut her off.

'It's up to you what you do in the room, love. All I ask is that you pay the rent each week. I can offer you Monday from nine thirty to ten thirty or Wednesday at the same time,' the man said, as he looked up from his computer screen. 'Other than that, it's full. The only reason I have the two times I mentioned is because the girl who taught yoga has moved to Thailand or some such place.'

'I'll take both,' Martha said, knowing it'd be easier to get rid of an hour than to gain one.

She left the centre feeling happier than she'd felt in a long time. She couldn't believe how easy this was turning out to be. It was like it was meant to be. Karma, she thought with a thrilled sigh. But then her brow furrowed as she thought of Jim's reaction. He wasn't going to be pleased. She'd have to expect some negative comments in the beginning but she hoped he would come around eventually. Surely he'd get it when he saw how happy it made her?

Her mobile phone rang and she answered sounding very chirpy.

'Mum? It's Rose. How are you? You sound very pleased.'

'Oh, hello, Rose. Yes, I'm having a great day. The weather is . . . well, it's raining a bit, but the scenery is so stunning that I don't mind.'

'I'm calling to see if you'd consider coming up? Dad would love it and we'll all be here. Jeannie will be here and it would be lovely if we could all be at the will reading.'

'Can you keep a secret from your father?' Martha asked.

'Eh, I suppose so, but I'm not really comfortable about the notion,' Rose said. 'What have you done now?'

Martha giggled and shook her head. 'Oh, you know me too well, Rosie dear. I've just been at the local community centre, organising a mother-and-baby group. There's nothing like that in the area, would you believe.'

'But weren't you supposed to be retired? What happened to leaving all responsibility behind in Pebble Bay?'

'I was bored senseless. Your father loves his golf and he's made oodles of new pals at the club. He's there morning, noon and night. When he's not, he's whisking me off to lunch here or dinner there.' Martha sighed. 'I know I must sound dreadfully mean and spoilt, but it's not for me.'

'Well you need to be happy, Mum.'

'Thank you, darling. That's what I thought. You'll back me up when the truth comes out, won't you? You'll tell Dad that I need to be around my children.'

'Yes, Martha's children have always been the light of your life.'

'Including you and your sisters, not to mention Ali,' she said with a happy giggle.

'So do you think you'll come up at all?' Rose asked.

'No, love. Not at the moment.'

'I'd better go, Mum. Speak to you soon.'

'Aren't you going to wish me luck with my first mother-and-baby talk?'

'The best of luck, Mum. I'm sure it'll be a roaring success. Ballyshaden is blessed to have you.'

Martha hung up feeling as if she'd won the Lotto. She might have known her own girls would be on board with the idea. She dialled Beatrice, wanting to make sure she didn't hear about it from Rose first.

'Hello, darling, have you got two minutes?'

'Yes, Mum. But I'm in the shop and I'm dealing with a client.'

'I won't keep you, I promise. I was on to Rose just now and I told her my news and I wanted you to hear it directly. I'd hate you to think I was going behind your back.'

'In what way?' Beatrice asked, sounding concerned.

'Oh, it's nothing to worry about, love. In fact, it's the opposite.' Martha filled her in and Beatrice, like her sister, seemed ever so pleased for her.

'Thanks for calling, Mum. I have to fly here. I'm glad you're happy.'

Almost bursting with delight, she finally called Jeannie's mobile phone.

'Mum, how are you?'

'Jeannie! I'm really well.' She proceeded to fill her in, explaining that her sisters knew but their father didn't.

'I don't think it's fair to tell us and not Dad,' Jeannie said.

Martha felt fleetingly deflated. Jeannie was always making her feel like that. She'd become very brash, like that dreadful man she was married to. She wasn't sure if it was the way people carried on in America or if it was simply her daughter's obstinate personality, but she was downright rude on occasion. But Martha wasn't going to let Jeannie, or anyone else, rain on her parade today.

'Okay then, darling, I won't keep you.'

'No, Mum, I'm sure you won't. Talk to you again sometime. It's been awesome. Tell Dad, okay?'

'Yes, yes, all in good time,' she said hastily.

Perhaps Jeannie was right. She really should tell Jim. She was just so afraid that he'd try and talk her out of everything. It was by his insistence and wearing her down that she was here in the first place. If she'd had her way, she'd still be in their magnificent home in Pebble Bay and she'd be as busy as ever with all the mums and children who needed her.

Her mobile rang and she saw it was a number she didn't recognise.

'Hello, Martha Brady speaking.'

'Are you the new midwife?' said a panicked man's voice.

'Yes. Yes, I am. How can I help you?'

'Can you come? Right now. It's my daughter. She's having a baby and I don't know what to do. Please, Mrs Brady.'

'Okay, you need to calm down. You're not going to help your daughter if you panic. Tell me where you are and I'll be there as quickly as I can.'

He gave the details and Martha was delighted to tell him that she was close by.

'I'll be there in five minutes. Leave the door open and I'll come in.'

Martha got into her car and set off out of the town. She drove right at the speed limit, hoping the man's daughter could hold on until she got there. She turned onto the narrow road indicated by her satnav and searched for a cottage with a blue door.

To her amazement, it was a large house, two or three times the size of hers. She'd expected a small farmhouse. But this was a beautiful modern house and evidently a lot of money had been spent on it.

She climbed out of her super-green snot mobile and rushed inside. The girl was on the floor in the large living room and she was bearing down.

'Hello, Nurse,' said an older-looking version of the labouring mother. 'Thank you for coming. She's been known to be quick with her babies, but this little one is in a big hurry.'

Martha sanitised her hands and knelt on the floor to talk to the girl.

'So this isn't your first baby, then?'

'No, it's my fifth. It's coming now.' She groaned and squeezed her mother's hand, and sure enough, the baby's head was born. Martha assisted her the rest of the way, and minutes later she was holding a little girl in her arms.

'Congratulations,' Martha said, 'you did an amazing job.'

'Thanks for coming,' the girl said, nodding. 'Fair play to you for being so quick.'

'I'm delighted to help,' she said genuinely.

'What's your name?' the girl asked.

'Martha.'

She looked to her mother, who nodded. 'Grand, so. The child will be named after you.'

'Really?' Martha didn't know what to say. She felt quite emotional and overcome. 'I don't think I've had a baby named after me in all my years . . . I'm thrilled, thank you. I don't even know your name!'

'It's Mary. Mary Shepherd.'

'Well, thank you so much for that, Mary.'

'Mam will see you out.'

Martha packed up her things and hesitated for a moment to see if they'd offer her a cup of tea. She loved sharing a cuppa with the new mum and going over the brilliance of the birth. But it was clear that wasn't happening today. Slightly puzzled, seeing as Mary had named her child after her, she made her way to the front door.

'Will you be staying around here for a while?' asked the older woman.

'Sorry, I didn't catch your name?' Martha said with a smile.

'Mary.'

'Two Marys and two Marthas, how lovely,' she said, trying to lighten the mood.

'So will you?' Mary senior asked.

'Will I be around for a while?' Martha nodded. 'Yes, I hope so. My husband and I retired to a house not far from here. But I missed my job too much so I'm back in the game.'

'Grand, and thanks again. We'll be in touch for the next one.'

'Whoa! Maybe Mary will be happy with five. That's a lot of children to cope with. I had three and it was tough to juggle.'

'I had seven and they were fine. The older ones looked after the younger ones.'

'Seven is a large brood for sure. Is your daughter trying for the same?'

'No,' Mary said, flashing Martha the most dreadful look. 'She's trying for a son, just like I had to. I had six girls before my boy came along. Now our Mary is in the same boat. That's girl number five you just helped into the world. God bless her, she really thought this one might be the boy.'

'But she could have twenty babies and they might all be girls,' Martha said, aghast.

'Try telling her fella that. They need a man to take over the farm and to continue the family name. Her husband is the only son in the family, so the onus is on our Mary to give him a boy.'

'But that's such an old-fashioned way of thinking.'

'You're entitled to your opinion, but that's the way it is. Mary wasn't given this fine house, the car outside the door and all the luxuries she enjoys without a price. See you next time.'

Martha shuffled out the door as it was slammed shut. She drove away with mixed emotions. On the one hand, she was delighted to have a child named after her, but she was genuinely shocked to hear that poor Mary was being pressurised into having so many babies. God help the little girl born today. Martha's heart went out to her. She hoped they would all love her even though she was a girl. Guilt prickled at her.

She herself used to secretly yearn for a son. With the three girls, it was hard not to. But she now realised how lucky she was to be married to Jim. He'd never said she should give him a boy and was always delighted with the girls.

She checked the time on her phone and was thrilled to see four messages enquiring about her mother-and-baby group. Her ladies had obviously been true to their word and started drumming up support already. Martha would have hated to turn up and had just one or two women there, but now she could plan a proper talk, safe in the knowledge that she had at least half-a-dozen interested mothers. Feeling delighted with herself, she decided to pop to the golf club and see if anyone she knew was there. She'd murder one of their toasted ham and cheese sandwiches and a cup of coffee.

When she arrived at the club house, she was informed that the early-morning set were only just beginning to come back in. So she sat up at the bar and ordered her toasted sandwich. She was still waiting when Simon Molloy appeared. He was a former Dublin man, and although she and Jim never socialised with him, they knew of him. He'd made his money in telecommunications. He wasn't what one would describe as demure, and she knew she would end up snarling if she had to talk to him.

'A pint of Guinness, if you please!' he shouted across the empty club house. 'Hello there, Simon Molloy is the name, and you are . . .?'

He held a dark tanned hand out to her. Martha looked down and swore he'd had a manicure. Normally a man like that would make her instantly want to recoil, but he suited the look.

'Hello, I'm Martha Brady. I'm here for a bit of lunch. My husband Jim and I are members and players here.'

'Of course you are. How nice to meet you, Martha. I detect from your accent that you're originally from a different neck of the woods. Have you got a holiday home here or something? This is a lovely spot.'

'No,' she said carefully. 'We've retired here.'

'What line of work were you and your husband in then?'

His pint arrived; he offered her a drink and she declined. 'Cheers, Martha.'

'Cheers,' she said tightly. 'My husband was in interiors and I'm a midwife.'

'Right. Sounds like your old man put you out to work while he got the easy number. I know which one I'd prefer – sitting on a sofa or delivering babies . . . Oh, I think I'll take the sofa.' He roared laughing and only stopped when he realised that Martha was staring at him poker-faced.

'Please forgive me. My wife used to tell me off for being too loud and forward. She died two years ago and I guess I've become a lout again.'

'I'm sorry,' she said, stumbling over the words. She shouldn't make assumptions about people. 'I'm sorry about your wife . . .'

'She was a midwife too. That's why I was making a terrible joke about preferring to stay on the sofa. I know how hard it is. But Florence loved it, so . . .'

He looked so incredibly sad at that moment that Martha had to stop herself from sliding off her bar stool and hugging him. Much as she hated public displays of affection, she felt for this man and for his loss.

'Where did she work? Perhaps I knew her?'

'We lived just outside London. I'm from Dublin originally. I met and married my Florence when we were twenty-one and I came back after she passed away from cancer.'

'So you're on holiday here?'

'No, I found Dublin too cold. It's changed since I grew up there. It's become big and impersonal. I had nobody left, so I ended up down here.'

'Do you live nearby?'

'Yeah, just up the road, within walking distance actually. So I can come and have a pint or play a round of golf.'

'That's a good plan. Do you have family that come and visit?'

'Yes, but they live in London and are working, with smallies in school, so it's not so easy to drop everything and come here.'

'I know,' Martha said. 'We have three daughters and one granddaughter. But they don't come much either. They have their own lives. It's easier for Jim and me to visit them.'

They continued to chat and gravitated towards one another. By the time her sandwich arrived, Martha was sitting beside Simon and they were getting along like long-lost friends.

She ate her sandwich and couldn't remember a time when she had laughed so much. Simon had all sorts of tales involving his wife, and she found him fascinating.

'I'm going to head on my way. I've a few bits to sort out. Nice to meet you, Martha. Don't go too crazy with the auld baby deliveries. Oh, and the best of luck with that mother-and-baby thing, yeah?'

He leaned over and took her hand and kissed it. Normally she'd find that sort of behaviour far too forward, but she was ashamed to admit she liked it.

The bar was beginning to fill up so she decided to make a move too. She wasn't comfortable being there on her own. Jim might hear about it and think badly of her. Or even worse, word might spread that she hung around in bars on her own, thus making her unsuitable to be a local midwife. That wouldn't do.

At home, she ran a bath and tuned in to an interesting documentary on the radio. In the silence of the house she listened intently, enjoying the alone time. By the time she had soaked in the bath and put on some comfy clothes, Martha was tired out. She didn't want to put on the heating, as it was almost summer, but it was very chilly as the rain pelted down outside, so she lit the fire. May was similar to February in these parts, she mused.

She thought of Simon Molloy and how he'd spoken of Florence. Even though he was brash and loud at first, there was no denying he still missed his wife. She'd loved her job too. Martha wondered if they might have become friends if Florence were alive today. She was lucky to have Jim. There were no two ways about it; she had what a lot of people yearned for. Feeling like a heel for shutting Jim out, she dialled her husband's phone.

'Jim,' she said gingerly. 'Can I say something to you and will you promise not to have a fit?'

'Well, that depends,' he said suspiciously. 'Go on then, I'll try.'

'You know how much I loved my work, don't you?'

'Yes, Martha, everyone knows how much you adored your children.'

'Well I've done a little sniffing around and there's a huge gap here for new mothers. They have nowhere to go and nobody to turn to. So I've taken the community centre for an hour, two days a week.'

She could barely breathe and was terrified he'd be annoyed.

'When did this come about?' he asked.

'I've literally finished sorting it today,' she said. 'It wasn't pre-planned. It happened organically and I hope you don't mind. Please don't be angry with me. You weren't here so I had to make the decision.'

He sighed loudly.

'What's wrong?' she asked.

'Nothing . . . actually, there is something . . . I'm hurt that you organised this behind my back. Why didn't you feel you could share your idea with me?'

'I was terrified you'd say no.'

'But I'm not your prison warder. I'm your husband. Since when have I ever told you what to do?'

'I know, but . . . we were supposed to be retiring here . . .'

'Yes, but you're not working. You're doing this a couple of times a week as a nice thing for the community. It sounds as if it might take off and they could run it themselves after a while.'

'Well, they'll need my expertise. I'm kicking it all off with a talk on Monday. A general information speech so they know they're dealing with someone who knows what she's talking about. Then I'll invite them to a regular mother-and-baby group and explain how I'll be there to advise the mums and help with the babies.'

'Yes, of course,' he said tightly. 'So you *are* going back to work essentially.'

'Sort of,' she admitted.

'And if your talk is on Monday, followed by a mother-and-baby class, there's no chance you'll be coming to hear the will being read?'

'No.'

The word hung in the air until Jim clearly decided to fill the silence.

'I got a call from the golf club and I'm delighted to say that Fred Murphy is on my team for the big summer competition now.'

'Oh, that is good news,' she said, even though she

couldn't for the life of her remember who Fred Murphy was. If Jim liked him and thought he was a good catch for his team, then she was delighted. Anything that relieved the awkwardness of the conversation was welcome.

She had a lovely evening watching TV, and even did some of her beloved tapestry work. At ten o'clock she went to bed, taking her phone in case someone called.

It was just as well that Jim wasn't there, seeing as it rang just before six the following morning.

'I'm so sorry . . . Oh God . . . just sorry . . . I know it's a Sunday morning . . . but, oh God . . .'

'Now calm down,' Martha said. 'What's your name?'

'Jilly.'

'Hello Jilly. Is everything okay, love?'

'My waters went at ten o'clock last night and I was having good solid contractions, but now they've stopped. I'm worried sick that the baby will die. I don't know if I should get my husband to bring me straight to the hospital or not. It's over an hour's drive, and we have two children under three already.'

Martha reassured her and said she'd be right over. She dressed quickly, humming as she went, then ate a very quick bowl of cereal, knowing she could be with Jilly for hours.

As she drove away in her car, Martha knew that retirement simply wasn't for her. Not yet, at any rate.

Chapter 10

MARINE TERRACE WAS JUST LIKE OLD TIMES. WITH her dad staying over, the atmosphere was lovely. Rose emerged from the bathroom into the bedroom and had a sudden urge to be physical with Martin. He was still asleep, so she dropped her towel and slid into the bed beside him. Stroking his back, she felt him waking.

His shoulder twitched upwards and he shuddered before sitting up in confusion.

'It's . . . it's you,' he said.

'Who else did you think it was?' she asked with a half-smile.

'Rose, I . . .' He got out of bed and went to the bathroom.

She waited for a few minutes. When he didn't come back out, she walked to the bathroom door and knocked gently.

'Martin, we need to talk.'

'Not this morning. Not right now,' he said. 'You go and get breakfast sorted for everyone and we'll talk properly later, yeah?'

Closing her eyes, she tried to stop the tears. Picking the towel up off the floor, she wrapped it around her naked body and made her way to the dressing room, where she quickly pulled on some clothes. Humiliation was an emotion she'd long since given up feeling. But for some reason she was coming to the end of her tether with Martin. This kind of rejection had gone on for years, but she'd brushed it away, pretending it would pass.

His promise of a chat later on was one of his many lies. The chat wouldn't come about and she'd have to suck it up and keep the emotions she was feeling right now bottled up inside. It was the story of their marriage.

She made her way into the kitchen to find her dad and Ali making pancakes and smoothies with the table set.

'Wow, this looks divine,' she said. 'Ali, I can't believe you're up so early!'

'Grandad woke me,' she said, wrinkling her nose. 'But it's okay. We've been to the shop and bought the papers and the ingredients to make a yummy breakfast.'

'Thank you, Dad,' Rose said, kissing his cheek as he wrapped her in a bear hug.

'I hope it's okay, but I invited Beatrice over too,' he said. His eyes were shining with delight as he continued to flip pancakes. As if on cue, the doorbell sounded and her sister arrived.

'Good morning,' Rose said, smiling. 'How are you today? Are you actually having a day off?'

'I'm planning on a delicious breakfast here and then I will need to scoot off and do a few things, but not too much.'

'I hope you're not pushing yourself too far,' Rose said. Now that she had a chance to look at her older sister properly, she looked odd. Kind of puffy around her face and incredibly jumpy.

'Is everything okay?' she whispered.

'Yes, why?' Beatrice asked, looking affronted.

'No reason. I guess you're just tired.'

'That's the way I feel, oddly enough,' she said, slightly snappily. 'But I'm not running a business on my own by taking siestas.'

Martin breezed through the kitchen, barely stopping to say hello to anyone.

'Surely you're not working on a Sunday?' Jim said.

'No rest for the wicked, Jim. I'd love to have a chat and a pancake, they look delicious, but I've a sneaky meeting with someone and it's going to make things easier in the long run.' He tapped the side of his nose and made Jim chortle.

'Ah, you're a tonic, Martin, do you know that? You're always thinking of the business and my girl Rosie.' He looked over at her proudly and Rose knew she needed to produce a winning smile. One that showed just how fortunate she was to be married to this super guy.

He was gone out the front door at the speed of light, before she could even attempt to make conversation with him.

'He's a good 'un, that Martin,' her dad was saying. 'I knew it from the first time you brought him home. He's a steady and reliable type of fellow who knows the right thing to do in most situations.'

'Not all situations,' Rose muttered under her breath.

'Mum?' Ali asked. 'What's wrong with you today? You've the grumpiest puss on your face.'

Rose looked at Ali with a glower that cut her dead. Not today, Ali, she fumed. Don't even consider stirring it and making me look like the villain. Ali was brilliant at that lately. She seemed to get some sort of buzz out of making her feel miserable and stupid. It was either a smart comment or a shrug of one shoulder followed by a toss of her head. Rose had to hand it to her daughter: she was fabulous at making her look like a fool.

'Someone needs a hug,' Ali said, without her usual cheekiness. Rose closed her eyes momentarily and thanked her for not being awful.

'I'm fine,' she managed. 'Now let's sit and eat this feast. The newspapers too! What a treat.'

The conversation flowed, led by Jim, who was quite clearly in his element. As soon as Beatrice stood up to leave, he jumped up too.

'When will you be finished with work? I was going to drop by and take Ned for a walk. I thought we could have a nice quiet dinner together somewhere local. Ali has exams starting tomorrow, so they're tied up. And Jeannie won't be here until tomorrow. So why not?'

'Sure, Dad,' Beatrice said. 'Call over to my place at around six and we'll go for a stroll and then have a bite to eat. If the weather stays fine, we could go to one of the places where you can sit outside in Pebble Bay village.'

'Perfect, I'll look forward to that all day!'

It was on the tip of Rose's tongue to say that she would actually love to go too. That it would be a joy to have a night off cooking meals that ended up in the bin, and that if they were meeting that early, surely Ali could come as well. Yes, her summer exams began tomorrow, but she wasn't sitting her finals in medicine. They were merely end-of-year tests.

Martin would be back whenever suited him, so she wasn't making any provision for him. Especially not after the way he'd behaved earlier – yet again.

But instead of voicing her disappointment, Rose did what she always did and kept her mouth zipped.

'There you go, Mother,' Ali said, throwing her napkin in a ball on her sticky plate. 'Grandad and I did the cooking and shopping, so you can do the washing-up. I'm off to study and I need to talk to Becca about some stuff.'

'Thanks, love,' Jim said, clearly not even noticing that his cheeky pup of a granddaughter was treating her like an unpaid slave. Taking the Sunday papers, he settled himself in the leather seat that overlooked the sea, sighing happily.

Rose's anger melted away. She couldn't think of anyone who deserved to sit and enjoy that view more than her darling father. But as Ali brushed past her, knocking her sideways slightly as she went, Rose had to take a deep breath and count to ten. If she let herself rip, she'd probably grab her daughter by the arm and shake her until she apologised for being such a nasty little cow.

How had her once sweet child turned into this awful demanding horror? Why was nobody else seeing it? Perhaps she was going insane and Ali was being totally normal and she wasn't realising. As she stacked the dishwasher and wiped the sticky pools of maple syrup off the table, Rose allowed tears to fall.

It was time to face facts. She was totally miserable. Her life wasn't turning out the way she'd hoped. She'd given the last few years of her life to Ali, and instead of them becoming special friends with a wonderful understanding of one another, they were like two growling tigresses. It was only a matter of time before she snapped and scratched her daughter's eyes out.

As she took a part of the paper and pretended to read

it, Rose thought of her relationship with her own mother. It was even worse than her own with Ali. Martha was on her own planet. She had no interest in anyone but herself and the babies she delivered. Rose couldn't comprehend how Jim had stayed with her for so long. She was cold and manipulative and did nothing she didn't like.

A wave of grief washed over her as she thought of Nanny May. Ordinarily, she'd be here at a gathering like this, fussing about, helping with the clearing away so Rose wouldn't feel like the hired help. She'd ask her what she had planned for the week and would titter that she was a great girl, managing to keep so many balls in the air.

Right now, Rose didn't feel remotely great. She felt like a failure and a doormat.

Beatrice saw two brides in two separate stores. It was the easiest way of doing it. She didn't open on Sundays officially, but she took appointments if she absolutely had to. One bride was going away to St Lucia in the Caribbean for her wedding and she needed her dress let out at the last minute. She'd come to pick it up on Friday and it hadn't laced up, so Alina had been called in.

'You've become a lot thicker all over,' Alina had said with the tact of a sledgehammer. 'Are you expecting baby, yes?'

The bride had tittered, and Beatrice had sighed with relief that she wasn't clocking Alina over the head with her shoe for being rude.

'We've been trying for a baby for nearly two years. Everyone kept telling us to relax. Easier said than done, I can tell you. So we decided to organise the wedding.'

'And then, bam, you are pregnant!' Alina had finished for her.

'Exactly,' she said with a giggle. 'So while it's annoying for you that I am bursting out of this dress, I'm secretly very happy!'

That final fitting needed to happen today so the bride could, fingers crossed, take her dress on the flight the following day. Alina said she'd be on standby if any disasters happened. Mercifully, the dress laced up and the bride paraded out the door, promising to send a beach wedding photo for the wall of love.

The store she was currently in was her oldest. As she gazed around, Beatrice allowed herself a few minutes of pride. She'd come a long way since this place first opened its doors.

Davy had just gone, her mother hated her, her mother-in-law hated her even more, and she had hated herself the most. The business was meant to get her over a hump until she decided what she wanted to do with her life. Never in a million years had she thought she'd sweep the county, taking over as the go-to bridal destination. Business had become like an addiction for her. The more she pushed herself and the more shops she opened, the better she felt. Because a woman who was as successful as she was had to be a great person, right?

She locked the shop and bid Alina a slightly nervous farewell.

'I really hope the measurements for this next dress are correct, or they'll have my head on a stick.'

She drove twenty minutes across the city to the other shop. The bride for this appointment had been for one fitting only, so it was up to Alina to get it right straight away. She was sixteen and from the travelling community. On that first occasion she'd come with an entourage of seven. They knew what they wanted and were willing to pay for it – in cash. The dress had to stick out so far that the girl looked like a toothpick in the middle of the layers of tulle. Extra skirts were made to create the look she wanted. The bodice was boned and see-through, with enough Swarovski crystals on it to cover twenty ordinary dresses.

'I want to look like the most sparkly princess the world has ever seen,' said the girl. 'My daddy will pay in cash and it don't matter what the price is.'

The veil consisted of two full-length cathedral veils stitched together to create yard after yard of glittering netting in a fabric so fine it looked as if it had been hand-crafted by fairies.

As before, the young bride arrived with her entourage in tow. She was a tiny slip of a thing with talon-long nails, deep mahogany skin, coal-black hair that fell in thick waves to her minute waist, and eyelashes that made her look like Bambi.

'Mary-Johanna, grab that frock and make sure it's what you want,' said one of the women. Beatrice had dealt with many travellers by now. Some of them were wonderfully friendly, wanting to chat and tell her the ins and outs of the wedding, while others, like today's group, were quite plainly in a hurry and had no interest in even making eye contact. Depending on how high up in the community the family were, the venue might have to stay a total secret until the morning of the wedding.

'We get told we can't come to the hotel no more when they catches on that we're travellers,' Mary-Johanna explained. 'So that's why my mammy and the aunties are hassled. They don't mean no harm against you, Beatrice.'

'No offence taken at my end whatsoever,' Beatrice said, holding her hands up high. 'Once you're happy, I'm happy, okay?'

'Okay, thanks, missus.'

Mary-Johanna was ushered to the dressing room, where three women helped her get dressed. Beatrice reiterated that she was there should they need her. Nobody answered, so she stayed quiet. After some shuffling behind the curtain and hushed conversation, the bride-to-be emerged. Standing her on the viewing pedestal, Beatrice had to admit she looked like a little doll. Her beaming smile said it all as the women paced like caged tigers.

'Is that it?' one of them said. 'Can we go? Will I give this one the cash?'

'Aren't you going to tell her she looks beautiful?' Beatrice ventured. 'She's a stunning girl.'

'Ah, that she is,' said the mammy with a grin. 'You're right there, woman. She looks great. Thank you very much. Thank you.' She stuffed a pile of notes into Beatrice's hand. They spilled onto the counter and over the floor.

Bending to pick them up, Beatrice put them into the till, still bunched up.

'Aren't you going to count it to see if I've left you short?' the woman asked, as if challenging her.

'No,' Beatrice said evenly. 'I trust you. And if you haven't paid me properly, that's my own lookout. I'm not going to start a fight with you. My reckoning is that I won't win.'

The woman grinned and then roared laughing.

'You're funny, but you're ballsy,' she said as the others in the group joined in with the hilarity. 'We'll be sending more of the family in your direction. You've made us very welcome and you did exactly what our Mary-Johanna wanted with no question.'

Beatrice folded the veil and packaged the dress as best she could and waved them on their way. There was a sort of innocence about Mary-Johanna that struck her. She was so incredibly young to be getting married. It was customary with the travellers for their women to be young brides. But the sense of community and family was astounding. She was surrounded by people she knew who would mind her and guide her. Their ways were different, but that didn't mean they were wrong.

When she counted the cash, she realised they'd overpaid her by two hundred euros.

Bookwork took up the rest of the afternoon, and Beatrice had to rush home in time to meet Jim. He was waiting with a smile and a hug.

'Hello there, how's my favourite girl?' he asked with a cheeky grin.

'That's not a nice thing to say and you know it,' Beatrice said. But she couldn't help smiling. Her dad had always favoured her. Perhaps because she was the eldest and they'd had lots of precious time together before the twins came along, not to mention when they were babies. Oh, the house had been chaos for a while. Until Nanny May had stepped in and said she'd stay until they were sleeping the night.

During those first few months, Beatrice and Jim would sneak off out for early suppers or even an ice cream. He would put her on his shoulders and take her off to a more serene place, where they would sit and he'd tell her stories about when he was a lad. She had been only two at the time, but Jim often reminded her about how great it had been.

She changed into a tracksuit and they took Ned for a walk along the prom. The rain had passed, making way for the sun to break through. It wasn't that warm just yet, but the bright, lemony light was enough to lift their spirits and lead them into believing there might be a sunny summer ahead.

'I remember you bringing me to that burger joint that used to be in Pebble Bay. The one that was done up in red and white like an American-themed place. The waitresses used to carry the trays high above their heads.'

'And one day you were making a dash for the bathroom and you ran right into the legs of a lady with a laden tray.'

'I got milkshake all down my back and there were chips everywhere.'

'Yes, I had to stop you from eating them!'

They walked a little further and Jim questioned her about the businesses.

'Don't you feel as if you're stretching yourself too thinly, Bea? You never have a minute to yourself. Isn't it hard at times when you realise you're alone?'

'I have Ned,' she said, not in a defensive way. 'I'm fine, Dad, honestly.'

She looked over at him as he gazed out to sea with a half-smile on his face. She adored him and she really wanted to tell him her news. Of all the people she knew in the world, her dad was the one she wanted on her side. But she'd kept things quiet so far. She hesitated as she watched him. His kind face was creased with worry and she knew that telling him, finally being able to talk to someone, was going to serve two purposes. Selfishly, she'd feel better, and secondly, she knew her dad would want to be there with her.

'Dad,' she began. 'There's something I want to tell you. Please don't be cross with me for not saying anything before.'

'I would never be cross with you, darling. What is it?'

Chapter 11

THE FOUNDATION FUND-RAISER WAS A ROARING success. Jeannie did what was expected and talked nicely to the men with the chequebooks. She was the first on the dance floor and the last to leave. She'd found it really easy to pretend to drink and get away with it. She took a glass of champagne for the reception and nursed it; got the waitress to pour a tiny bit of wine into the bottom of her glass and left it there, and nobody was any the wiser.

She'd woken up on the sofa still wearing her dress and fur wrap, clutching her handbag. She'd collapsed there out of sheer exhaustion, but clearly Nick thought she'd passed out drunk.

'Hey, party girl,' he said. 'Thanks for being so great last night.'

'Are you being sarcastic?'

'Nope,' he said, perching on the coffee table. 'You had Dr Benn eating out of your hand. He's impossible to interact with outside the OR, and you turned him into a chatty socialite.'

'He was a bit prickly at first, but once we started talking about the fact that his grandparents were Irish, we were best mates.'

'He's agreed in principle to help me with the clinical trial I've been trying to set up.'

'Really?' Jeannie asked, sitting up.

'This could be a total change of direction for me, Jeannie.' He looked so happy and alive that it made her smile. 'I love being in plastics, but I never intended staying at the same hospital. I have no leeway there and I can't do my own thing. I want to get into the field of life-altering plastic surgery. The feeling I got after I fixed Lauren's face made all the study at med school and late nights of training worthwhile.'

'I know, hun. You were on a high after that girl was finished with her surgeries. You changed her life. Nobody would ever know she'd been involved in such a horrific accident. You were awesome.'

'So it seems that Dr Benn has been awarded funds by the hospital board and he's looking for a way to put them to really good use. He's so interested in my idea that we're meeting this afternoon, along with two of the hospital board members.'

Nick was so animated that Jeannie forgot she was pregnant until she stood up.

'Oh dear,' she said, swaying slightly. 'No, it's not a good plan to stand up so quickly. There's far too much head-rushing going on, not to mention stomach-churning. I think I might be sick. Okay. I'll just lie here and you can take it that I'm really excited and interested in what you're saying, okay?'

He smiled sheepishly. 'This might sound crazy to you, but I kind of feel as if I'm turning into a grown-up.'

'Well, you're hurtling towards fifty-five years of age, so it's probably about time. I, on the other hand, have the mind of a teenager and the body of a very old woman. I don't know if I'm going to survive the day.' She held her head and closed her burning eyes.

'Do you honestly think that I or anyone else could've stopped you last night? You were a woman on a mission. You were having the time of your life.'

'Yes, and I may just be coming to the end of that life. How will I go on a plane in this state?'

'I didn't realise you'd drunk so much. Why don't you change your ticket and go tomorrow, or the next day?'

'I can't. I have to be there for the reading of Nanny May's will. Dad is there too, so I want to be with everyone.'

'Okay, whatever you think,' Nick said. He was staring at her oddly.

'What?' she said.

'I want to talk about something and I don't want you to freak out on me, okay?'

'Okay, I'll try,' she said, groaning on the inside. She hadn't the energy for one of Nick's intense talks. He had a habit of going off at a tangent, telling her his innermost feelings and asking if she'd share hers. She'd got better at it over the years, but right now, this morning, she was in no mood to think of ways of saying she loved him from the bottom of her heart and the inside of her soul, yadda, yadda . . .

'I would like us to think about having a baby. There, I've said it.'

She felt her heartbeat quicken. She couldn't quite fathom whether this was a very strange coincidence or if Nick had guessed her situation. Could Nina have told him?

'I know you're in shock,' he said. 'I don't need an answer right this minute. But will you at least consider the idea?'

'Yes,' she said as her voice caught.

'Take the time to think about it while you're in Ireland. Let the notion sink in and let me know how you feel.'

'Is this make or break for us, Nick?' she asked tiredly.

'No, sweetie,' he said. 'I'm not trying to threaten you. I love you. I just want us to think about having a family, that's all.'

'I hear ya,' she said as she stood and hugged him.

'Oh, Jeannie, can you imagine if I can get into reconstructive surgery and we're blessed with a baby? Our lives couldn't actually be going in a better direction.' He kissed her. 'I missed you in bed last night,' he said, dropping his hand down the front of her dress.

'And I was so exhausted that I couldn't even make it off the sofa,' she said. Of all the things Jeannie loved, sex was at the top of the list. She had more of an appetite than Nick, though that now seemed to have reversed.

'I thought you needed to get to the hospital to get ready for Dr Benn,' she said.

'Yeah, you're right. You'll still be here when I get back, won't you? What time is the taxi coming to take you to the airport?' he asked.

'In forty minutes,' she said with a sigh. 'So as much as I'd love to rip your clothes off . . . you need to go and sort your future and I need to finish packing.'

'Well that's telling me,' he said. 'By the way, I really enjoyed watching you grind up against Bill on the dance floor then seamlessly walk off and leave him nursing a stiffy. He's such an asshole.'

She giggled and held out her hand for him to high-five.

'I'll miss you. You'll call me as soon as you get to Dublin, won't you?'

'Of course,' she said, looking concerned. 'Why are you asking me that?'

'Because I know we're teetering on the edge, Jeannie.

I've known it for a while. I don't want to let you slip through my fingers. Even if I get the funding for my trial and everything begins to get really exciting, it won't make me happy if I don't have you to come home to.'

'You'll have me, Nick. I just need to go home-home for a while and see my sisters and niece.'

'Hey, I'm sure your folks can't wait to see you again too!'

'I know, but how often have they been here in the last twenty years?' she asked.

'Okay, so your parents haven't come, but that's because they were working all the time. Now they're getting used to having free time. They needed to adjust to their new house.'

'I guess,' she said with a shrug.

'We never really encouraged them to come either,' he mused.

'No, we didn't . . . Would it be cool if I ask them to visit?'

'Sure thing. It'd be great.' He looked pensive for a moment. 'We need to include them more going forward, Jeannie. Your mom will be so amazing when we have kids.'

'Hey, let's just slow down for a bit,' she said with a dry laugh. 'We're taking this one step at a time, okay? My mother is not a fluffy little old lady who would sit in a rocking chair singing to our baby.'

'But you're always talking about "Martha's children",' he said fairly. 'Maybe this could be a wonderful opportunity for you and your mom to bond. I could take your dad out on the golf course. We could barbecue out the back and have family time. Why not invite Rose and Ali and Martin and Beatrice too?'

'Thank you,' she said. 'I'll work on all of the above.'

'I want us to turn this place into a family home. It's time, honey.'

'Okay,' she said, hoping her face didn't show how much she was flailing on the inside. 'Good luck at the hospital. I'll call you later.'

Nick drove out the gate looking like the happiest man alive. Jeannie watched him go, tears streaming down her face. Then she pulled out a second suitcase and loaded it with more stuff than she could possibly need. Glittering heels, matching evening bags, unopened make-up palettes, cologne, costume jewellery and a cute Juicy Couture track-suit with a matching tank top with the labels still intact. All of it would make Ali squeal with delight. None of it would be missed by her.

Sighing, she thought of her niece. She had loved Ali since she was a baby. Now she was a teenager, reportedly the most difficult time for getting on with kids, and they were still friends. Jeannie adored her to the point of insanity; no matter how hung-over or tired she was, that girl could never annoy her. But as for Viktor yesterday . . . Ugh, she found him difficult to tolerate, even if he did nothing wrong. Shaking her head, she tried to quash the notion that she was simply a horrible person. Was it a boy/girl thing? she wondered. What if she had a baby boy and hated him? Maybe she was only wired to be able to deal with girls? What if she had two boys, three boys? Oh dear Lord, the sweat was pouring down her back as the taxi arrived. By some miracle, she managed to dress and make herself presentable while the bags were being loaded into the trunk.

Checking that she had her purse, tickets and passport,

she remembered that she needed to look for gifts for Rose and Beatrice. It was fine to give unused stuff to Ali, but her sisters deserved new and well-thought-out things. They'd argue with her – they always did, saying they only wanted to see her and that was their gift – but she liked treating them. Bea had nobody to buy her stuff, and while Rose had Martin, well, he was Martin. Enough said. He'd hardly win Mr Imaginative Gift Giver of the Year.

Sweeping through duty-free a couple of hours later, she spent a small fortune buying both her sisters the season's must-have Fendi shoppers.

'They're not both for me,' she said to the shop assistant. 'My sisters mean the world to me. They'll like them, won't they?'

'Lady, you could buy yourself another dozen sisters if you wanted!' said the sales assistant happily.

Panicking, she added perfume and lipstick collections to the pile. Then, cursing under her breath, she figured she'd better get Martin something as well.

'What do you buy a guy who is totally beige?' she asked. 'It needs to be decent-looking, but not enough to imply I actually like him.' They agreed on bourbon, although she secretly thought he'd be too boring to actually drink it.

'Oh, make it two bottles,' she said, suddenly thinking of her dad. 'And one of those brown Gucci belts. That will look dashing on the golf course.'

The parcels were wrapped and she'd boarded the plane and was ready for take-off when Jeannie remembered her mother. She'd buy her a silk scarf or something equally classy in Brown Thomas before visiting. Closing her eyes, Jeannie knew that no matter what she brought Martha, it wouldn't be quite right. So there was no point in worrying too much.

She lay back against the seat, feeling washed out and exhausted. Delighted to have the long flight ahead, she drifted off to sleep.

Chapter 12

BEATRICE LEFT THE FLAT JUST AFTER SIX IN THE morning. It was Monday, and she had a huge day ahead. The reading of Nanny May's will was later on, but right now she had her own adventure. She knew the traffic in Dublin was likely to keep her waiting. She needed to be on time for her appointment. She'd done everything asked of her and now it was D-Day.

She knew Jeannie would be landing soon and she was really looking forward to seeing her. She wasn't quite sure as to whether or not she'd share her news just yet. She knew her darling dad wouldn't breathe a word, at any rate. She trusted him one hundred per cent.

She pulled up at her destination less than forty minutes later, turned the engine off and sat in the car for a few moments. She was early, but already there were people rushing in and out of the revolving doors to the clinic.

Her dad's car was parked to her right, and now he emerged with a wide smile. Exhaling, she was so relieved he was here. If she'd had to do this alone, it might have been too much.

She'd decided to have a baby around this time last year. She had realised that she was yearning for a child after she'd attended a counsellor for a while.

'You're suffering from depression,' said Deirdre. 'You're mourning the fact that you won't ever be a mother.'

When the words were put to her in such a clear fashion, it made perfect sense. In fact, it was almost a relief to know what was causing her to feel empty and practically dead inside. While she shared nothing of how she was feeling with her sisters, she kept up her sessions with Deirdre for a while and it helped to talk things through. Deirdre also encouraged her to take exercise and make sure she got out and about often.

'The fact that you live alone means that you need to make an effort to join a social club or do things involving others.'

'I see my sister Rose and her family a lot, and I enjoy my tennis club.'

'That's fantastic,' Deirdre said.

At that time her parents had recently gifted her the premises and the flat. It had been fully renovated and each room was more beautiful than the next. There were two bedrooms and a good-sized bathroom to service both. The open-plan kitchen and living room boasted large sash windows; it was quite simply perfect. Yet she was finding it increasingly difficult to muster up enthusiasm each time she walked in. The reason was the spare room. It taunted her. It wasn't that she longed for a flatmate; quite the opposite. She would hate to have a stranger staring at her when she closed the shop doors at night. At her age, she most certainly didn't long for the platonic company of another adult. No, Beatrice wanted a child to put into that spare room.

Once she'd admitted to the yearning, it was as if a magic wand had been waved.

It was Deirdre who told her about the clinic and how it was possible for women to go there for a sperm donation.

'Some women opt for a full embryo. So the egg and sperm are both donated and IVF is used to form a pregnancy. It might be worth contacting them. That way at least you'll know you explored all the options open to you.'

'I know women who've gone abroad and had this done. I didn't realise it was available in Ireland now,' Beatrice admitted.

Pretty much immediately, she had made an appointment to see about having a baby. Crazy as it sounded, that was a possibility. Women like her – single, healthy working women – were able to become mothers!

The people at the clinic were wonderful from the word go. They didn't look at her as if she was a freak. They didn't make her feel as if she were one of life's failures, the way her mother did, and they assured her they would do their best to help her have a baby.

'We will be honest and real with you. We can't guarantee that you will become a mother, but we will use all that is scientifically and medically available to us, which is a lot.'

'I've nothing to lose,' Beatrice said. 'And you're the best chance I have. I'm never going to get pregnant sitting on the sofa after work night after night. I'm not getting any younger, and this way, even if I'm not successful, at least I'll know I tried.'

The counsellors at the clinic urged her to share the plan with somebody.

'Is there a family member or friend who you could have on your side?'

'I'm more comfortable doing this with you people,' she said honestly. 'It's my decision, and while it may seem like a reasonably run-of-the-mill procedure inside these walls, my family and friends would need time to come around.'

'And you don't feel you have that time?' the counsellor asked.

'I don't feel on edge and panicked morning, noon and night,' she said. 'But I can't afford to have anyone by my side who needs their hand held.'

Besides, Beatrice was certain that her family and friends would support her fully should she become pregnant. Unwittingly, her parents were facilitating the entire process, so she felt a sense of their support anyway. Their wonderfully generous gift had done two things for Beatrice. First, the prime site in Pebble Bay had meant a massive increase in footfall and takings. She'd sold five times the number of communion dresses in her first month of trading than she'd ever done in any of the others. She'd had to reorder and take back-stock from any of the fashion houses that would supply her. A new line of eye-wateringly expensive accessories that she'd taken a gamble on were selling so quickly she was wondering if the customers were seeing a different price tag! Secondly, the fact that she wasn't paying rent on a home meant she had the spare cash to spend at the clinic.

She mopped up the information like a sponge and knew very quickly that she wanted to use her own egg and opt for a sperm donation with an option to learn the identity of the father at a later date once she'd had time to think about it.

The injections she'd had over the last few weeks were meant to be hellish. She'd been warned that she might be a hormonal mess, sobbing one minute and yelling the next. But so far she had coped brilliantly. She and Ned had had long, in-depth chats about how they would both need to adjust should a baby come along. She was certain that Ned approved.

In the shop she needed to have her game face on at all times and she would never even consider taking personal issues to work. So that really only left evenings and Sunday mornings for her true mood to shine through, especially if she had a meeting with an addled bride on a Sunday afternoon. As for the crazy mood swings, well, there was nobody bar Ned to shout at, and although she felt uncontrollably tearful on occasions, she couldn't possibly shout at that little brown face.

Beatrice was convinced that she was so eager to have a child of her own that she would've put up with Chinese torture if they had handed her a baby at the end of it.

And now, incredibly, today was implantation day. It was totally surreal.

'It's best to bring someone along with you for support. It'll be a very straightforward procedure physically, but emotionally it can be nice to have some backup.'

She'd been warned that there were no guarantees with this procedure; there was only a twenty to thirty-five per cent chance of it working first time. But Beatrice felt in her heart of hearts that it would. At least, she had right up until this moment. Now all of a sudden she felt overwhelmed and stupid. Why would it work? So many couples tried this for years to no avail. What made her so special?

Knowing she wasn't helping herself by getting into a state, she got out of the car. Her dad walked over and took her in his arms. He didn't say a word. He didn't need to. Just having him there, making her feel like his little girl once more, was all she needed.

'Thank you, Dad,' she said as tears spilled from her eyes. He handed her his laundered handkerchief. It was something he'd always carried, and as girls, they'd thought it had magic powers.

'There now,' he would say. 'Wipe your eyes and blow your nose in Daddy's handkerchief and everything will be all right.'

As soon as they did that, he'd follow it with a hug and some soothing 'there now' words along with pats on the back and they'd be calm. Today, he didn't pick her up, but he did everything else.

'Better?' he asked, looking into her eyes.

She nodded, biting her lip. 'I'm scared,' she said, sounding like a frightened little girl.

'I don't blame you, love, so am I. I really want this to work for you. So we'll close our eyes, take a deep breath and wish with all our hearts that it's going to succeed.'

They did that, and when Beatrice opened her eyes again, they were both smiling.

'That's my girl. Ready?'

She nodded and took the crook of his offered arm and they walked inside.

In reception, she turned to look at her dad, who gave her a thumbs-up and looked as excited as a child in a toyshop, which made her giggle nervously. The building was predominantly glass and the foyer was impressive as it gave a view of all ten floors. The citrus-coloured sofas with funky coffee tables in the shape of oversized fruits looked quirky against the backdrop of green leafy plants. Music played, but instead of the usual pan pipes, it was uplifting jazz. The sound of her heels hitting the hard, sparkly white floor tiles echoed as she approached the desk.

'Hello, Beatrice Moore is my name and I'm here for my implantation.'

The glamorous lady with perfectly coiffed hair and expertly applied make-up and talons of nails looked up and smiled.

'Hello, Beatrice, yes I saw your name on the list for this morning. If you could fill out this consent form and sign it here where the X is, that would be great. Take a seat over there and return it to me as soon as you're done,' she said with a smile.

'Thank you.' Beatrice smiled back and walked over to a bright orange sofa with a lime-coloured and shaped coffee table.

'I feel like I'm sitting in a fruit salad,' Jim said as he sat beside her.

She grinned as she filled out the form. She knew the place would feel more like a hospital once she was taken to one of the many theatres, but right now she could've been in a swanky hotel or cool smoothie bar.

Once the form was completed and signed with a shaky hand, Beatrice gave it back. The woman thanked her but kept their conversation to a minimum. She noticed how carefully all the employees chose their words. They didn't commit in any way nor did they give false hope or get too excited. It was professional, yet they showed enough warmth to make sure the ladies or couples didn't feel as if they were on a conveyor belt.

A couple walked in as she took her orange seat once more. It was nice to have someone else to look at as they sat on an acid-green sofa with a round orange table. She longed to scoot over and bombard them with questions. Was it their first attempt? Had they children at home? How long did it take to work for them? But most of all she wanted to know if it was going to work for her. Nobody could answer that, sadly. Only time would tell.

Just as she felt she might need to start rocking to control her nerves, Jim spoke.

'Those people probably think I'm your partner. It's all the rage now, you know. Men my age going off with young ones.'

'No offence, Dad, but I don't think I could settle with an older man.'

'None taken. I agree with you. I wouldn't be able to shack up with someone the same age as one of you. It's a concept that baffles me. Look at our Jeannie. Isn't her fellow a good few years older?'

'Yeah, fifteen as far as I remember. But it doesn't seem as odd somehow. I suppose it's because I'm used to seeing him on Skype and he's very cheerful and positive, so his age doesn't seem to come into it.'

Her name was called and she hesitated.

'The next part is very clinical,' she leaned in and whispered. 'It involves stirrups. Would you wait here for me?'

'I'm not afraid of stirrups, just for the record. Don't forget I've heard stories about births that would curl most people's toenails. I can stay at your head or even face the other direction and hold your hand.'

'Bless you, Dad,' she said. 'You're my hero. But I'd be more comfortable if you're here to hug me afterwards.'

'Well, I've an endless supply of hugs. So I'll be here. I have my newspaper, my coffee and some sort of odd-looking thing that the hippy woman in the shop advised me is good for me, so I'll be nipping over there to buy a chocolate croissant instead!'

As she walked away, Beatrice turned to wave at her dad, who was beaming from ear to ear. She loved him dearly for coming to mind her. It felt so good to have him there. The tears wouldn't stop falling as she struggled to compose herself.

The nurse led her to the procedure rooms, which were familiar by now so she wasn't as nervous as she'd expected to be. She was simply an emotional wreck.

Once inside the small theatre, she was in no doubt that this was indeed a medical place. There were no novelty sofas or cool pieces in here. Just an examination table complete with stirrups and an overhead manoeuvrable flying saucer of a light. The team were buzzing around like bees, setting up the equipment trolley for the doctor.

'Hey, love, what's the matter?' a nurse asked. 'Are you okay to go ahead?'

She nodded and explained that she'd only told her dear dad at the last minute and how grateful she was that he was there to support her.

She was calm, and had wiped her face and blown her nose by the time the door flew open again and the doctor was in the theatre. With his cap and gown and a mask dangling around his neck, he meant business.

'Good morning, Beatrice, I am Dr Jonathon Barlow and I'll be performing your implantation today.'

'Hello,' she said, shaking his hand.

'I need to run through our schedule and make sure you understand exactly what's going to happen. Is that okay with you?'

'Yes.'

'So you have four embryos available to you,' said Dr Barlow as he scanned her chart. She nodded. 'We will implant two today. Do you understand the implications?'

'Yes,' she said, sounding shaky and scared. 'I could have one baby or two babies or, if it doesn't work, I'll have no babies.'

'Correct,' he said as a nurse took her hand. 'You know that the odds are between twenty and thirty-five per cent that you will become pregnant?'

She nodded again.

'Okay, Beatrice, if you would go with the nurse and I need you to remove the bottom half of your clothing and put on the hospital gown, with the ties to the rear. Once you've done that, I'll be ready to go.'

She went behind the curtain and did as she was asked. Walking gingerly towards the examination table, she knew the next few minutes wouldn't be pleasant, but she also knew it would be over quickly.

The same nurse attached herself to Beatrice's side.

'I'm Jenny and I'll stay here all the time, okay?'

'Thank you,' Beatrice said, wanting to hug the woman.

'After the egg retrieval and the injections and all the other stuff you've been through, this will be a doddle.'

Beatrice nodded. For the first time in this entire process, she really wished she'd told her mother what was happening. As she turned her head away from Jenny, so she wouldn't see her tears, she wondered if Martha might have come along. She hadn't told her because she wasn't sure of how she'd react. Would she click into midwife mode and want to help her in a medical way? Would she understand why Beatrice was even doing this?

No, Beatrice knew she'd made the right decision. It was best that she hadn't told her mother. This way, she couldn't try to talk her out of it or tell her what she was doing was morally wrong. She'd battled with guilt in the beginning. She'd spent many long hours on bended knee, praying and begging for a sign that she was doing the right thing. She'd gone to the church one Sunday afternoon and prayed to Mother Mary, asking her to guide her.

The following morning, as she'd bent down to unlock the shutter covering the new shop window, she'd found a tiny white baby's mitten. Naturally her mother would scoff and say that somebody had simply dropped it. But Beatrice took it as her sign. She'd picked up the mitten and brought it inside the shop, taking a moment to thank Mother Mary for answering her prayers.

She'd come to the conclusion that this was her last chance to be a mother. If God didn't want that to happen, the procedure wouldn't succeed. She had two possible chances with the embryos she'd created. Two were being used today and two would be frozen for use at a later stage if nothing happened.

If a pregnancy resulted – and that was a big 'if' – she would tell her mum quite quickly. She couldn't expect her dad to keep the secret for her indefinitely. Mind you, the situation wouldn't affect them too much seeing as they were all the way across the country in Connemara.

In fairness to her dad, he came up to visit regularly, but her mother was a different story. Beatrice knew that her mother loved nothing more than a pregnant woman, and she hoped she'd be pleased for her.

The doctor approached the examination table and it was all systems go. There was lots of hustle and bustle along with bright spotlights. She'd got used to having her feet in stirrups. The first time it happened she honestly thought she'd die of shame. But now she'd do it out in the car park if it meant she'd have a baby in nine months' time. She barely had time to think and certainly hadn't got around to feeling uncomfortable when Dr Barlow spoke again.

'That's it, done and dusted. Well done and thank you for being so still. I wish you the very best.'

'Oh, thank you,' she said in surprise as Dr Barlow rushed out with the team in his wake. Jenny patted her arm and Beatrice realised she was still holding her hand.

'Thanks, Jenny. You've been so kind.'

'Not at all,' said Jenny. 'I'm delighted to be here with you.' She helped her to release her feet from the rather high stirrups. 'I'll bring you a cup of tea and some toast and let you rest there for an hour, and then you're free to go home. Is there anyone you'd like me to inform?'

'Yes, my dad is out in the waiting area. Maybe you'd tell him I've to wait an hour and say that I understand totally if he wants to scoot off and I'll see him later.'

Jenny smiled and left the room. As soon as she came back, she had a message from Jim.

'Your dad's exact words were that he was staying put, but thanks for thinking of him.'

Beatrice smiled. That was just like Jim, polite but to the point.

'I've heard mixed reports . . . well, I've been looking online,' she admitted. 'Some people say that at this stage I should go for bed rest for a few days and others say mild exercise is a good plan.'

'Our advice here at the clinic is to take it easy for the next couple of days. No heavy lifting or vigorous exercise.'

'I feel as if I want to stay in bed for nine months in the hopes of making a baby.'

'I understand,' Jenny said. 'I got into IVF nursing after the birth of my first child.'

'Did you have IVF each time you had a baby?'

'Yes, and it took us five rounds but we ended up with two wonderful children as a result. So well worth it.'

'And you changed career afterwards?'

'Not entirely. I was nursing in a large city hospital in Limerick and my husband was offered a promotion in Dublin, so I decided to take the bull by the horns and apply here.'

'Well I'm certainly glad you did. You've been so kind to me and I really appreciate it.'

'My pleasure. Now, let me get you that tea and toast.'

It was still only just after nine o'clock in the morning when Beatrice walked out of the clinic. Seeing Jim and having him hug her again turned on the tears like a tap. He patted her back and waited for her to calm down. He had a second clean handkerchief, which made her laugh.

'How many did you bring?'

'A few,' he said with a grin.

Once she assured him she was perfectly fine to go back to the shop on her own, he walked to his car and drove away.

She marvelled at her dad. He was the kindest, most accepting man she knew. Selfishly, she wished he'd come back from Connemara. Life just wasn't the same without him nearby.

She was technically pregnant now, which felt exhilarating and terrifying in equal measure. Walking to her own car, she jumped when her mobile phone rang.

'Hello, Rose,' she said as tears flowed yet again. She'd

no idea why she was crying, but the sound of her sister's voice had set her off.

'Sorry to bother you so early, I know you're probably up to your eyes at one of the shops, but I was wondering if you'd like to drop over for dinner this evening? Jeannie and Dad will be here and I thought it might be nice for us all to be together after the will reading. I didn't want you buying dinner, and it's always nice to know the plan in advance.'

'Yes, you're right, I would've bought something.' Knowing she sounded dreadful, she tried to cut Rose off. 'I'm going to go now, I'm in the middle of something. See you at the solicitor's later on, yeah?' she managed.

'Have you got a cold?'

'No, I've had a sneezing fit and I'm a bit croaky,' she fibbed.

'Okay, well we can firm it up later on, but let's plan that you'll drop over when you're finished at the shop. I'm not in work today, so I'll be here.'

'Can I bring anything?' Beatrice asked, trying to sound less emotional.

'Not a thing. I'm just going to do steaks and chips with a glass of wine.'

'I'll bring a bottle,' Beatrice said. It suddenly occurred to her that she wouldn't be able to drink.

'Don't bring your car. We'll have a couple of drinks and celebrate Nanny May.'

'Okay, sounds great,' she said.

Rose was gone and Beatrice felt lonelier than ever.

In her car, she allowed herself twenty minutes of sobbing before mopping her eyes and opening the window to cool her burning cheeks. She drove home and went directly to the flat without even looking into the shop to see how things were. She'd never done that before and she didn't care.

Once home, she climbed into bed feeling utterly washed out. She lay on her back with her hands on her tummy, hoping at least one if not both foetuses might like it in there and decide to stay.

Ned climbed onto the bed and looked at her with pleading eyes. She rarely let him up near her face, but right now she couldn't think of anything better than hugging him. With a contented little sigh, he snuggled into her and they both fell asleep.

Chapter 13

MARTHA HAD FLASKS OF HOT WATER SET UP, WITH a Kilner jar of tea and one of coffee plus a sugar bowl, milk jug and plates of home-made biscuits. It was a nice focus for the mothers to make a cuppa and offer one to someone they didn't know. Meanwhile, there were a few toys and some soft surface matting for toddlers and small children to use.

'I thought we might have a chat about subjects that worry or interest you during pregnancy,' she said. 'If you can all take a seat, that'd be super. Toddlers are welcome to run around and play.'

She had set the chairs in a semicircle, so once the ladies were seated, she stood in front of them.

'Today I thought we'd kick off by discussing nutrition during pregnancy, especially morning sickness.'

Martha could do these little speeches in her sleep. But it never grew old because of her audience. She knew the best type of support was peer-to-peer. So all she'd need to do was deliver a bit of clinical research and that would kick off a discussion where the ladies could share little golden nuggets of advice.

'I find eating a slice of toast the minute I wake up works for me. It's as if my body forgets to feel sick.'

'I swear by toasted almonds for nausea and heartburn,' said another.

Martha shrugged her shoulders and rubbed her hands together in delight. They really were a great group of women and she knew she was going to enjoy working with them.

'I have some business cards in the holder by the door. Please take one and make sure to call on me if you need help with a medical issue or especially a pregnancy question.'

'Sorry, Nurse Brady, but do you deliver babies at the women's homes if they would like that option?' asked a heavily pregnant woman.

'Please call me Martha, and yes, I do,' she said with a smile. 'That used to be very popular when I first trained, which wasn't yesterday or the day before,' she joked. 'But it's coming back because of hospital overcrowding. I am almost finished registering to do home births in this area, so if you can all kindly hold off until the end of this week or the beginning of the next, I'll be ready!' There was a ripple of laughter; the women were all clearly beginning to relax. 'But if you can't hold on, don't worry, I'll be there. I'm a registered member of the Nurses and Midwives Association, so the local health centre has approved me to perform home births if there is no other option.'

Martha was mingling with the mothers who were still there having tea and coffee. They were complimenting her on everything from her talk to the delicious cookies. It was just like the old times and she was lapping up every second of it.

'There's nothing quite like home-baked goodies,' she said. 'Not that mothers with new babies have time for that sort of thing. So I'm thrilled to give you all a well-deserved little treat.'

The women said they'd learned more in twenty minutes of listening to Martha than they could've imagined.

'I'm thrilled you found it useful,' she said. 'I do hope you'll come again and bring your friends. From here on in it will be less formal. More of a mingling and chatting to me and one another.'

'You're fantastic,' said a woman with a tiny baby who couldn't have been more than a week old.

'Oh, you are kind,' Martha gushed. 'Yes, come on in, you're more than welcome,' she called out to a hesitant young woman pushing a buggy with a toddler inside.

'Dr Francis told me about you. I'm expecting again and he said I should show my face.'

'And I'm so glad you did. I'm Martha.' She extended her hand. 'Do you know any of the mums who are here?'

'No, I can't say I do,' she said, looking around anxiously.

'Not to worry, many of my mothers are in the same boat. Come along and let me introduce you to some of them.'

Martha had forgotten just how isolating it could be in the countryside. When the girls were small they used to meet more Dublin families than local ones while they were on holiday here. Many of the locals kept their heads down and didn't really look to speak to them. But she'd always assumed that was because they were blow-ins. Now it was becoming apparent that the locals preferred to socialise in families, which was wonderful many years ago before so many people migrated to cities and different countries.

'It's easier when the babies grow up a bit and start school,' said one of the more chatty mums. 'But before my

Patrick started, I was on my own. Now that I'm expecting number four, I still like the idea of having somewhere to come and chat about pregnancy. Each one is different and I can't tell you how tired I am this time.'

The women left smiling and chatting, happy in the knowledge that Martha would be there again on Wednesday.

Her mobile rang just as she finished putting her flasks and things into the boot of the super-green snot mobile.

'Is that Martha? Are you the midwife?'

'Yes, dear, how can I help you?'

'My cousin was at your talk there this morning in the community centre; she's told me you're terrible nice.'

'That's kind of her,' Martha said. Experience taught her to stay quiet and there'd be more chance of this terrified-sounding woman telling her what was wrong.

'I need help. I'm in labour, but it's not going the way the others did. I'm forbidden to go to the hospital. My husband thinks they're full of bugs that no antibiotics can kill and that I'd be putting the baby's health at risk.'

'Where exactly are you?'

The woman gave the address and luckily there was a house name so Martha was able to pin it on her map function on the phone as they chatted.

'I have you,' she said. 'I'll be there in ten minutes. Can you tell me your full name, please, love?'

'It's Geraldine Conneeley.'

'Thank you, Geraldine, I'm hanging up now and I'll be with you in a few minutes.'

Martha's phone tuned into the Bluetooth setting, and using her hands-free kit, she phoned the doctor's surgery to check whether they had any history for Geraldine.

'She's only been here once,' Dr Francis said. 'But she has

six or seven children as far as I know. Her husband is a strange man. He doesn't believe in doctors or hospitals. His mother was a great woman for herbal remedies and lots of folks used to go to her.'

'Okay, thanks for the heads-up and I'll keep you posted.'

When Martha pulled up at the house, one of the ladies she recognised from this morning's group appeared at the front door.

'Thanks for coming, Martha. I'm Elisabeth and I was at your talk just now.'

'Hello, dear,' she said. 'It's lovely to see you again.' She grabbed her medical bag and rushed into the house behind Elisabeth.

The dark living-room-cum-kitchen was like a zoo. Small children and older ones were lolling about in the dreadful mess as Geraldine buzzed about making lunch. Every now and again she'd call out and hold her belly.

Martha watched the scene for a few moments before clapping her hands and sending the children out the back, where she promised them they'd get lunch and anyone who was good would get a lollipop. Old habits died hard and she still carried a jar of them with her.

'Elisabeth, would you be a dear and sort out the lunch while I have a look at Geraldine?'

'No problem at all,' she said, glowering at Geraldine. 'I've been telling her to let me but she wouldn't.'

'I can make a few sandwiches, Elisabeth. I'm not gone soft, you know.'

'There's nothing soft about allowing your cousin to help while you're in labour,' Martha said.

'She's as fussy,' Geraldine said as another pain gripped her.

'All the more reason to let her help you. Is there a bed where I can examine you and see what's going on?'

Geraldine led her to a back room where there was nothing much more than a bed. It was dingy and in need of refurbishment and smelled of damp.

Martha opened her bag and rooted around to find her headlight.

'Don't mind me putting this on! I'll look like a miner, I know, but it's the best thing for being able to see.'

As Geraldine had another huge contraction, Martha could see exactly what was happening.

'The baby's head is too big to pass out,' she said. 'I'm going to have to perform an episiotomy. That's where I make a cut so the opening in your vagina is larger. Baby's head is right there, looking to be born.'

'Do whatever you want, just get it out,' Geraldine said, as she tried to breathe through the pain.

'I'll give you a shot of local anaesthetic to numb the area first.'

Martha knew that she wasn't going to get much talk from Geraldine – she was in too much pain and too frightened – but she was incredibly relieved that the woman had called her. This baby had been stuck for a while and needed to get out right now.

She administered the local anaesthetic and made the cut. Moments later the baby was born.

'Thank you, Nurse,' said Geraldine as some colour returned to her pasty face. 'You've been so kind. I was afraid I was going to die. Is my baby okay?'

'He seems fine,' said Martha as she cut the cord and rubbed him with a towel. He began to pink up nicely and let out a very loud roar. They both laughed with relief.

'It would be advisable for you and baby to go in an ambulance to the hospital for a proper check-up,' Martha said.

'Why?' Geraldine asked. 'Aren't you good at your job?'

'Well I'd like to think I am by now,' Martha said.

'Then there's no reason for me to go to hospital, is there?'

Martha finished stitching Geraldine and made her promise to either come to the clinic next week or allow her to do a home visit.

'Elisabeth says you have lots of knowledge and that you can tell stories, and that you make it real easy for mammies to come with little children too.'

'I'll even make you a cup of coffee or tea if you come along.'

'I'd like that,' Geraldine said. But her brow furrowed. 'I'd have to see what Joseph thinks, though. He's my husband.'

'See what Joseph thinks of what?'

They turned to see a large looming man dressed in workman's trousers and a dark loose-knit sweater all covered in hay.

'Joseph! We have another son. This is Nurse Martha. She came and helped me.'

'I'm sorry to barge into your home, Joseph. Your wife called me because she rightly knew there was something wrong with her and the baby.'

'Martha had to cut me to let the baby out,' Geraldine said.

'Your wife and baby could've been in serious danger if she hadn't called.'

Martha looked at Joseph, fully expecting him to get

annoyed, but instead he crumpled, putting his shovel-like hands over his eyes and sobbing. After a few moments, he rubbed his face roughly and thanked Martha profusely for being so good to Geraldine.

'I was raised to have a fear of hospitals and doctors,' he said. 'My mam was a healer. She used herbal remedies that her mother used. We never saw a doctor all our lives and I thought that was a good thing.'

'Well in lots of ways it probably is,' said Martha kindly. 'How amazing was your mother that she raised a family and acted as a doctor? Women were truly exceptional back then.'

'She was wonderful,' Geraldine said from the bed. 'She knew so much and we miss her, don't we, Joseph?'

He nodded. 'We need to move with the times, though, Geraldine,' he said. 'We get letters from the children's school, you know. They ask us to let the children have injections to stop them getting things like the measles. But we're too afraid to do it.'

'How about I bring you some information on the injections and go through it with you?' Martha said. 'How many children do you have?'

'This little fella brings us up to eight,' Geraldine said.

'Good Lord! That's a fine brood indeed. Geraldine, you look fantastic. I can't believe you cope with so many.'

Geraldine grinned, looking proud. 'And our Elisabeth in there, she's only on number two and you'd swear she had ten!'

'Not every woman can cope like you,' Martha said as she patted Geraldine's leg. 'Now, let's get you cleaned up and maybe the children would like to meet their little brother.'

'This is only our second son,' said Joseph. 'So he'll be spoiled by the girls.'

Martha helped Geraldine with the afterbirth and changed the bedclothes while she had a shower.

The house was simple in many ways. There weren't many mod cons and the only television was a small old-fashioned one in the shape of a box in the corner. She didn't reckon it was the hub of the home like so many she'd been in.

As she was handed a cup of tea with a thick slice of the most delectable fruit cake she'd ever tasted, all the children came swarming in. Geraldine appeared in her dressing gown and slippers, cradling the baby. There was a round of applause and great whooping cheers as he was welcomed.

There was no doubt in Martha's mind that the heart of this home was the kitchen and the lovely people in it.

She left them arguing about what the baby should be called.

'There's nothing wrong with Conor, and so what if it's after Conor McGregor. He's my hero.'

'I think he looks like a Dwayne,' one of the girls said.

'You and your Dwayne Johnson poster. We're not calling him that!'

Martha was brought to the car by Joseph, who insisted on carrying her bag.

'I can't thank you enough for saving Geraldine and the baby, whatever the poor child ends up being called.' They laughed and Martha offered him her hand to shake. He pulled her into a great bear hug. 'Drop in if you're passing, won't you?' he said.

'I will, of course. I'm dying to hear what his name is!'

As she drove home, Martha couldn't wipe the smile

from her face. She dialled Beatrice's number, knowing she'd love to hear about her latest escapade. God bless her, she was on her own in that flat with nothing but that little yappy dog for company. She'd be delighted to hear today's story.

Martha was quite disgruntled when the call went to voicemail. She tried Rose instead. She didn't usually have as much time to listen. She fussed endlessly with Ali and that took up her entire life. Rose needed to get back into the shop more and stop with the helpless housewife routine, she thought crossly.

Rose's mobile went directly to voicemail as well. She couldn't phone Jim; he wouldn't be pleased that she was delivering again.

She worried about the girls still. She probably always would. But Martha knew she'd done a good job of raising them because they were independent and didn't come running to her every five minutes. That was the right way to have them. There was nothing worse than adults who'd been so overprotected as children that they couldn't conduct their lives as grown-ups.

That, she feared, was how Ali was headed. Rose was there at her beck and call. She never left the child alone.

She dialled Jeannie's mobile, but it was turned off. She'd be exhausted after the long flight and was possibly having a sleep. That was understandable, but it honestly didn't suit Martha. She wanted to tell her story and let everyone know what a hero she was.

It was nice for Jeannie to come and stay at the house with Rose, she mused. Twins were a strange thing. They had such a strong bond from the womb and it was never quite broken. Really, Beatrice was like the odd one out when they were growing up. She must've felt left out at times.

Still, Beatrice had Jim. How he adored that girl. He thought Martha didn't notice over the years, but he used to take Beatrice on walks, bring her to the ice-cream parlour and even sneak to the cinema with her. They had a wonderful bond that was still as strong today.

Martha suddenly remembered the reading of Nanny May's will. Ah, that was where they all were. That was why nobody was available to hear her tale.

A moment of guilt washed over her as she remembered what Nanny May had done for her. She'd facilitated her career really. She'd stayed at home and done the motherly thing with the girls.

The guilt was swiftly replaced by anger. The woman used to get on her nerves, but could she say it to anyone? Oh no, Nanny May was a living saint according to her girls and Jim. She could do no wrong.

Martha smarted as she thought of the day she'd returned from a conference in Milan with Jim. She'd accompanied him, as she did on the more pleasing junkets. They'd take an extra day or two and have a little break together.

Nanny May had moved into the house and was minding the girls. It was just before they broke up for the summer holidays. Martha had bought them the most delectably beautiful dresses with matching sandals and she was excited about giving them. They were getting out of the car and the three girls burst forth from the front door to greet them. Jim did his usual and tossed them in the air, kissing and hugging them. Martha held out the bags containing the clothes, telling them she had a lovely surprise for them. Somewhere in the midst of the horseplay with Jim, Jeannie fell and her knee spurted with blood.

Martha dropped the bag and rushed to help her. But Jeannie pushed her hands away and ran to Nanny May, crying and bawling and telling her what had happened.

'There now,' said Nanny May. 'I think your daddy was a bit too excited about seeing you.'

'I was si-sighted about seeing my daddy,' said Jeannie, tripping on her words.

'Never mind, come with me and we'll find a plaster and your knee will be better in no time,' said Nanny May as she picked her up and took her inside.

'Poor Jeannie,' said Rose, tearing in to help.

'Oh no!' said Beatrice. 'It's okay, Jeannie-Beanie, we're all going to mind you.'

'Aren't they sweet the way they look out for one another?' said Jim.

All Martha could do was look at the designer clothes and sandals strewn on the pathway like rags. Anger boiled inside her. How dare that woman! It was one thing for her to give a helping hand, but it was quite another for her to step on Martha's toes like this.

She marched into the kitchen where Jeannie was sitting on the counter having a plaster put on her knee.

'Thank you, Nanny May,' said Jeannie. 'I love you, Nanny May,' she added, wrapping her arms like spaghetti around the woman's neck.

'I'll leave your new dresses and things on the table. When you feel like looking at them, perhaps you'd come and let me know whether or not you like them.'

The girls looked at their mother in shock as she flung the bag onto the kitchen table and marched to her bedroom.

A short while later, they appeared in the bedroom dressed identically in their new clothes.

'Thank you for our dresses,' they chorused.

'You're welcome,' she said. 'Now take them off and we'll wear them to mass on Sunday.'

They filed out of the room and she could hear Nanny May instructing them to be careful of the things.

Martha had spent the rest of the day in her room. It wasn't a lie when she'd said she had a headache and couldn't see anyone. But it had taken her until that evening to calm down and quash her anger. She couldn't tell Jim that she was furious that her own children favoured Nanny May over her. He'd answer by saying that she could cut her hours at work. There was no chance of her doing that. She shuddered at the very thought of it. Yet she didn't like being made to look like a fool. She needed Nanny May so she could have her freedom, but there was no chance she'd let her make a mockery of her like that again.

The blasted letters were still in her drawer at the cottage. She hoped they weren't referred to in the will this morning or she'd be rightly bunched. Sighing deeply, she knew it was time to either get rid of them or hand them over. She'd have to come up with a reason for holding them this long. She could lie and say that Nanny May had entrusted her with them and they were only to be given once the will was read. Who would know she was lying? Yes, that was feasible. The idea made her feel better.

In fact, the world seemed like a better place now that she knew she was going to be needed once more. Martha wasn't ready to sit back and do nothing. She had so much to give and so many people who genuinely wanted to avail themselves of her knowledge. If Jim wanted to spend his days playing golf, so be it. She was glad for him that he'd found happiness, but the arrangement simply wasn't working for her, and she needed to confess and get on with things.

As soon as Jim returned from Pebble Bay, she was going to tell him about her new business. After all, life was precious. She certainly wasn't going to waste hers sitting around or swinging a stick and chasing a small white ball.

Chapter 14

BEATRICE WAS THE LAST TO PULL UP OUTSIDE THE solicitor's office. The early-afternoon sunshine had been obliterated by diagonal rain. She spotted Jeannie with a bright pink umbrella. They dashed inside and Jeannie was able to hug her sister properly.

'How are you?' Beatrice asked.

'I'm good, a bit jet-lagged and a bit dazed, to be honest. I'm looking forward to getting this part over with and then I can rest and catch up with you all.'

Jim gave her a discreet wink as he walked towards her and embraced her. 'And how are you today, my darling?' he asked, squeezing her tightly.

She smiled at him. 'Oh, you know, Dad, same old, same old, how about you?'

'I've been having a lovely morning pottering about,' said Jim.

'How's the new store?' Jeannie asked Beatrice. 'Is it still going down a bomb?'

'Totally,' said Beatrice. 'I had no idea quite how much the brides around here are willing to pay. It means I'll do a totally different order for next season.'

'That's exciting,' said Rose.

'Would you like to come in, please?' said the solicitor. They filed into the room and took a seat each, waiting expectantly.

'Good morning. I'm Timothy Kearney and I've been given the job of finalising the affairs of May Denis today.' He looked around the room. 'Are we still waiting for someone?' he asked. 'We're one short.'

They all looked at one another and Jeannie made a face.

'I'm afraid my wife can't join us today,' Jim said, his cheeks colouring a little.

'Oh, I see,' Timothy said, frowning. 'That's unfortunate. I will ensure she is informed of what transpires here.' He jotted a note and then sat down and joined his hands together.

'Your friend, May Denis, left a short will, so I won't take up much of your time. I must first, however, apprise you of an unusual situation with regard to Miss Denis's final wishes.'

'Unusual?' Jim said. 'What do you mean?'

Timothy cleared his throat and looked uncomfortable.

'The first stipulation of Miss Denis's will regards private letters she wanted to give to each of you four.'

The girls looked at each other.

'Fantastic,' Beatrice said. 'Nanny May really was a legend. Even from the grave she's managed to surprise us and make us feel special. I can't wait to read mine.'

'Well that's the problem,' Timothy said. 'You see, the letters cannot be located. We have searched every nook and cranny of Miss Denis's cottage, but to no avail. And they were never sent to us for safe keeping. The will was only written in recent weeks when she got the news about her heart. I'm terribly sorry.'

'But . . . I mean . . . she must have written them,' Jim said, looking angry. 'They have to be there somewhere. And what news about her heart?'

'I can assure you, Mr Brady, we have searched every-where. And we will continue to do so. But I'm afraid we don't have the letters for you today. I'm truly sorry about that.'

'I feel like crying,' Jeannie said, and promptly sobbed openly. 'I can't believe she did something so special and we can't have them.'

'Nanny May was a second mother to my girls,' Jim said. 'Those letters are deeply important to us. I can't believe she was sick and didn't tell us.'

'I do understand,' Timothy said, nodding solemnly. 'Every effort has been made, and will continue to be made. I'll contact you the moment they turn up. I'm dogged about continuing to search for them because I believe she did write them – she told me so herself when she was here. In fact, she became very emotional when she told me about them. She did mention that they weren't quite finished, which was why she didn't bring them along that day. So they exist, in part at least.'

'The poor darling,' said Beatrice as she too began to sob. 'Why didn't she let us look after her while she was ill?'

'It was the least we could've done for her after everything she did for us,' said Rose. She looked up at Timothy. 'Our mother has never had time for our family, hence her absence here today. Nanny May stepped in and nurtured us and made us feel loved and cherished.'

'She was the most selfless person I've ever met,' said Jeannie. Tears continued to roll down her frozen face, and a delicate sniffle confirmed that she was indeed crying.

Timothy looked from one to the other of them, then continued. 'If I may, I would like to turn to the issue of

Miss Denis's savings and how she wishes them to be distributed.'

'Hang on a moment,' Beatrice said suddenly. 'You said to the four of us. Does that mean there's no letter for our mother?'

Timothy consulted the paperwork in front of him. 'It says here, in the will that Miss Denis prepared a month prior to her death: "I wish to leave four letters, which must be delivered in person to Jim, Beatrice, Jeannie and Rose Brady. Please ensure this wish is carried out."'

Beatrice looked at the others. 'I wonder why there's no letter for Mum.'

'Well,' Jeannie said, 'you could hardly say Mum felt the same way about Nanny May as we did, could you? I'm not sure *Martha* would want a letter from her. She'd probably burn it without reading it.' Jeannie's voice was fuelled with anger as she said her mother's name.

There was an awkward silence, during which Timothy cleared his throat again and looked even more uncomfortable.

'Shall I proceed?' he asked quietly.

'Yes, of course, sorry,' Jim said. 'Please continue.'

Timothy began. '"The last will and testament of May Denis. I wish to leave my pale pink suite to Miss Ali Monaghan as she loved it so. Please keep it in storage until she has a place of her own. I also bequeath a sum of twenty thousand euros that she will inherit when she turns twenty-one."'

'Twenty thousand euros,' Rose said in shock. 'I didn't think she had that amount. And the pink suite. Oh, I can't believe she left it to Ali. It's the prettiest and most gorgeous thing. She'll be utterly delighted. And it's worth another twenty thousand euros at least. It's only a few months old, as you know . . .' She stopped as the penny dropped. 'I tried in vain to get her to go with a cheaper option. We have one that's not as expensive, but she insisted on the Shrewsbury collection. Now I understand why.'

Timothy cleared his throat once more and continued.

'"I also want her to have the bedroom suite, including the wardrobe."'

'She's giving her incredible forever pieces,' said Rose, tears falling down her cheeks. 'And enough money to put a deposit on a flat. She's such a darling.'

'"For my three girls, there is nothing I can give you that would show how much I loved each one of you. You were the daughters I never had. I purchased three identical sets of jewellery last year. Diamond studs with a round matching pendant. I hope that you'll enjoy wearing them. After all, diamonds are a girl's best friend!"'

Timothy presented the sisters with a small black box each.

'"I am also leaving you twenty thousand euros each. I hope you will use it to buy something special.

'"To Beatrice I am leaving my dinner service. You were the one who helped me build it by buying a plate for Christmas or a sugar bowl for my birthday. I have ensured it's complete. I hope it serves you well and that it is used for many entertaining evenings with loved ones."'

Beatrice took a tissue from the box Timothy was offering. She adored the porcelain dinner service with its pale-pastel pattern. It would be a joy to use and she'd treasure it.

'"To Rose I would like to leave my rose-detailed pendant. I can think of nothing more fitting. I hope you will wear it and think of me."'

'Oh my goodness,' said Rose as she blew her nose. 'I always assumed that was costume jewellery. But now that we're hearing about how much money Nanny May had, I'm wondering if it's real.'

'I can confirm that it is indeed real. It's worth upwards of ten thousand euros and is an original Chanel design,' Timothy said.

The women looked from one to another in total amazement. They never would have believed that Nanny May was as wealthy as this or that she owned such extravagant pieces.

'This proves how much she adored you girls,' said Jim as he stared into space.

'Yes, we really were lucky to have her,' said Beatrice. 'She wasn't with us for the money, that's for sure.'

'"For Jeannie, my little firecracker! Oh, how you brought colour to the household! I want you to have my 'Gingerbread House' painting, as you called it. It's an original Cora Fallon, so don't put it near the front door in case it gets swiped."'

They all laughed, delighted to have something to lighten the mood.

'Wow,' said Jeannie. 'I can't believe how generous she's being.'

'If it's okay with you, I'd like to finish reading,' said Timothy.

'Of course,' said Jim.

'"Last, but by no means least, Jim."'

The girls all turned to look at him. He was sitting in between Rose and Beatrice, so he grasped both their hands.

'"The letter will tell you all you need to know. But it's only right and proper to let you know that I am leaving my cottage to you. Over the years, you helped me with each and every room. If I so much as mentioned that I needed an item, you would bring it home from work the following day."'

Jim nodded and smiled.

'"Perhaps you will change the place to suit your taste. A lot of the furniture has gone to the girls, so you may need to replace it. I've got a funny feeling you'll know where to go for that!

'"The letters to each one of you let you know exactly how I felt about you. All that's left for me to say is thank you. Thank you for letting me into your lives. Thank you for letting me love you and cherish you. Thank you for being the very heartbeat of my life.

'"I chose not to tell you I was ill. I didn't want to frighten you. I also wanted our last few weeks together to be just the way things always had been.

'"I will watch over each one of you. Until we meet again, I send you love and light.

'"Nanny May."'

There wasn't a dry eye in the room as Timothy handed them each a copy of the will. Knowing he had other clients waiting, they left promptly, arranging to meet up at a regular haunt for a late lunch.

'Do you want to come in my car, Dad?' Beatrice asked.

'Yes, Bea, that'd be great. See you all there,' he said.

As soon as they sat into the car, it was as if the pin had been pulled from a bomb.

'Where the hell are those letters?' Jim exploded angrily. 'Someone has stolen them. Swiped them, knowing they're addressed to us.'

'It's really odd for sure,' said Beatrice. She could feel the fury emanating off her father, and she didn't know what to say. She'd never seen him like this before. He was always so self-possessed and calm. It was clear how much Nanny May's letter meant to him. She drove carefully, trying to make light conversation to distract him.

Finally, they pulled up outside the restaurant and she found a parking space. Jim hopped out quickly and strode up the path. Beatrice sent a text to pay for her parking, then followed him inside, where the others were waiting.

They were given a lovely round table at the back of the restaurant, which was perfect. They'd be able to talk without the whole of Pebble Bay knowing their business. Once they'd ordered and their drinks had arrived, Jim led the conversation, still fizzing with anger.

'Who would do such a thing? We need to backtrack and think of who was in the house that day.'

'None of us have them, so it was someone outside the family. What about the police? That guy who came in and made phone calls to the ambulance and stuff?' said Rose. 'Perhaps they have them at the station?'

'Good idea!' said Jim. 'I'll call them right now.'

Jim had all the emergency services' numbers in his phone and got through to Pebble Bay police station swiftly. After a bit of passing from one person to another, he was eventually connected to a man called Ciaran.

'Yes, I met you there that day, Mr Brady. It was unspeakably sad. You all loved her dearly. That was obvious. How can I help you?'

Jim explained, and Ciaran said he wished he had the letters but he didn't, nor had he seen them that day.

'Never mind,' said Jim. 'Thanks for your help, and if anything springs to mind, you have my number now.'

'Yes, I do,' said Ciaran. Jim knew he wouldn't hear from him again.

'Let's ring Mum and ask her who else was in the house. She's good at remembering details like that.'

'Well I'm not ringing her,' Jeannie said. 'She can go and swing as far as I'm concerned. Did you see Timothy's face when we said she wasn't coming to the reading? She's such a selfish cow. She suits herself and doesn't bother with anyone unless they're in labour.'

'It would've been lovely if she'd come,' said Rose, trying to be diplomatic. 'After all Nanny May has done for us over the years, she should've been there.'

'Why didn't you tell her to come, Dad?' Jeannie asked. 'I mean, didn't you ask why she wasn't bothering?'

'Nope,' said Jim. 'She's a grown woman, Jeannie. I can't tell her what to do.'

'So if I'd said I wasn't coming, you'd have said nothing?'

'I might have asked *why* you weren't coming,' he admitted. 'Maybe it's different because you're my daughter, so we have a different relationship.'

'Yeah, uh-huh, we have a relationship that's not screwed up. You're kind to me and I try to be the same back.'

Jim looked into the middle distance as he dialled Martha's number and waited for her to answer.

'Hello, Jim!' she chirped.

'Hi Martha. I'm here with the girls in a restaurant and we've been to Timothy to hear Nanny May's will being read.'

'Oh yes. How was it, dear? Was it terribly sad? Are the girls all sobbing? No doubt they are. Nanny May always encouraged that sort of behaviour.'

Jim paused for a moment. His wife's lack of empathy

and the absence of any sign of mourning for a woman who was part of their family infuriated him.

'Jim?' she said. 'Are you still there?'

'Martha, the girls and I are finding Nanny May's passing extremely difficult. So I would really appreciate it if you could show a bit of compassion.'

'I'm very upset too. I just show it in a different way.'

'Right,' said Jim. 'So something has come to light during the reading of the will.'

'Okay,' she said, as her heart began to quicken its pace.

'It seems Nanny May wrote each of our three girls and me a letter. But the letters are nowhere to be found.'

'Gosh,' said Martha. She thanked her lucky stars that she wasn't on Skype. Feeling as if she might vomit, she grasped the steering wheel of the car, waiting to hear what Jim would say next.

'I need you to make a list of all the people you saw at the house when you found Nanny May.'

'Why?'

'We need to establish who was there so we can get to the bottom of this.'

'But what are you planning on doing, Jim? Accusing people of stealing a bunch of letters? That's not going to work. Besides, there were lots of people in and out, from the police to the paramedics. Anyone could've picked them up.'

'And done what?' Jim said. 'Tossed them in the bin?'

'Yes, that could've happened.'

'Not if they were addressed to us.'

Martha had a sudden brainwave. She'd let the dust settle, then in a couple of weeks she'd visit Pebble Bay, go to the cottage and deposit the letters in a drawer or somewhere

where they wouldn't be found easily. Then she'd go to Rose's and suggest they do a search and, Eureka, she'd produce them from their hiding place. She'd be the hero of the hour and the blasted letters would be nothing to do with her any longer.

Delighted with her plan, she heaved a sigh of relief. Why hadn't she thought of this before?

She would have the final say. Not Nanny May.

Chapter 15

ONCE THE FOOD ARRIVED AND NORMAL CONVER-
sation resumed, Jim calmed down somewhat. Beatrice was
watching him carefully, and she could see that slowly his
shoulders dropped and he looked more tired than angry.
She reached over and took his hand, smiling at him. He
gave her a small smile in return.

'You okay, Dad?' she said quietly.

He nodded. 'Fine. It's just been an incredibly frustrating
day, starting off with your mother not bothering to come,
and now the letters . . .'

'I wonder what Nanny May wrote in those letters,' Rose
said. 'We all had such different relationships with her. I'd
be fascinated to read mine.'

'Totally,' said Jeannie. 'I couldn't get away with anything
with her. She'd be on Skype giving me that disapproving
look if I tried to do anything too radical.'

'Yes,' said Rose with a smile. 'Remember when you
tried to go for a cheekbone job last year? You really
wanted to do it, but there was no way she was going to
allow it.'

'What's all this?' Jim asked, looking astonished.

'Eh, thanks, Rosie,' said Jeannie. 'Yeah, I wanted a cheekbone job and Nanny May got wind of the fact and all hell
broke loose. She rang me, then Skyped me, and told me

in no uncertain terms that she would never forgive me if I went ahead with it.'

'Didn't she say that it was barbaric and you weren't to destroy your beautiful face?' said Rose.

'Yup,' said Jeannie.

'And she finished by saying that she'd have to get on a plane and nurse you herself if you did it. She was terrified of flying,' said Beatrice. 'So she would've killed you.'

'I forgot how frightened she was of flying,' said Jim, smiling and shaking his head. 'Do you remember her accompanying us to London for a weekend?'

'Oh, that was the time we saw the stage version of *Cats*,' said Beatrice. 'It was Christmas time and the lights on Oxford Street were magical.'

'Nanny May bought a mug in Harrods,' said Jeannie. 'She point-blank refused to buy anything else, saying that if she didn't need something, there was no need to waste money on it. Until she saw the teddy bears with knitted jumpers with "Harrods" and the year on the front and *insisted* we should all have one.'

'I argued with her to the point of violence!' Jim laughed. 'I didn't want her spending her money on you three and said I was more than happy to pay for them. I swear I feared for my life. She threatened to swing at me with her handbag!'

The girls laughed at the image. Nanny May was a tiny lady, but she was as feisty as they came.

'I wouldn't have liked to cross her,' said Beatrice. 'When she made up her mind about something, that was it. There was no compromise and no changing the situation.'

'I think one of the things I loved her for the most was her bribery over our outfits,' said Jeannie.

'What do you mean?' said Jim.

Jeannie looked at Beatrice and nodded that she should tell him.

'You know the way Mum used to make us wear those hideous clothes, all matching and ferociously expensive?'

'Yes,' said Jim. 'Believe me, I tried to argue for you all, telling her that you should be allowed to pick your own clothes. You were far too old to be shoved into velvet dresses with white collars, but Martha wouldn't listen.'

'Nanny May tried to reason with her too,' said Beatrice. 'But when we knew there was no changing her mind, Nanny did a point system with us. Each time we had to wear the matching dresses, she'd award us points.'

'Points meant prizes!' said Jeannie and Rose together as they giggled. 'We'd get something really cool, like a hair crimper or a Lolo ball or dangly earrings from Top Shop.'

'I don't remember you having things like that,' Jim said.

'We hid them at Nanny May's house,' said Jeannie. 'Her spare room was like the coolest playroom imaginable. There was a dressing table with a magnifying mirror and make-up. And hair stuff so we could style our hair before parties.'

'So we'd leave Marine Terrace in whatever hideous thing Mum had last purchased for the price of a small car,' said Rose. 'And we'd stop off at Nanny May's and change and do our hair and make-up.'

'The thrill of it all was astounding,' said Beatrice. 'Nanny May used to sit in the kitchen saying out loud that we were dreadful people to lie to our mother. Just knowing we could possibly get caught out was brilliant.'

'Did Martha ever catch you?' Jim asked. 'I don't reckon she did. I would've remembered it.'

'No,' said Rose. 'The closest we came to being sussed was one time when I had the wrong-coloured tights on when I got home. But we managed to convince Mum that I'd had them on all along.'

'I had no idea that Nanny May did any of this,' said Jim. 'She was a godsend in so many ways.'

Beatrice cleared her throat and pinged her water glass with a teaspoon.

'Ooh, excellent,' said Jeannie. 'An announcement!'

'Is it?' Rose asked.

Jim took Bea's hand and nodded at her, as if giving her the final push to tell her sisters.

'So, as you know, I couldn't make my marriage work. Davy wasn't for me and since then I haven't found anyone worth sharing my life with.'

Bit by bit, Beatrice told her sisters what she'd decided and what she'd done.

'So right now, this minute, you're pregnant?' said Rose.

Beatrice nodded as tears spilled down her face.

'Hey,' said Rose. 'Don't cry. It's going to be fine. Now that you've told me, I can help you. Have you told Mum?' Beatrice shook her head. 'I don't blame you,' said Rose. 'She was an awful cow to me when I was expecting Ali.'

'Was she?' said Jim. 'I thought you two were quite close during that time.'

'No. She bossed me around, and no matter what I did, she was there ready to criticise me and tell me I was doing everything wrong. She made me feel like the worst mother in the world.'

'Well I don't need that and I won't put up with it either,' said Beatrice. 'I'm older than you were, so I guess I can cope with telling her to bog off more easily.'

As the sisters chatted, Jim sat back and watched them. They really did not have much time for their mother, a fact that shocked him. He knew they weren't close. Of course he did. But he'd chosen to ignore the fact that she had treated them with such indifference. Guilt washed over him as he realised that he should have stepped in. Martha was a very complex woman, but that wasn't the girls' fault.

'Hey, Dad, did you hear me?' Rose said.

'Sorry, I was miles away.'

'We were saying that you're right, we should pop over to Nanny May's house in a while and have another look for those letters. They're of no interest to anyone else, so we reckon they're still there somewhere.'

'Yes, good plan. I need to say something,' he said suddenly. 'I've sat and listened to you talk about Nanny May and your mother. I want to apologise.' He struggled with the lump in his throat. 'I should've stepped in. I'm sorry that you had such a dreadful childhood.'

'Dad,' Beatrice said, 'please don't think we had a horrible childhood. That's not true, is it, girls?' The other two shook their heads. 'All we were doing was reminiscing and remembering Nanny May and how kind and lovely she was.'

'That doesn't mean we had a bad time,' Jeannie said. 'Mum is a difficult woman and Nanny May balanced her, that's all.'

By the time they'd finished lunch, they were all pretty exhausted. Rose and Jeannie couldn't stop hugging Beatrice, who said she needed to go home and lie down.

'How about we leave searching the cottage until tomorrow?' Jim suggested. His daughters nodded in agreement.

'Will we all convene again at Marine Terrace at seven this evening?' Rose said. 'Beatrice needs a rest, and I've to go to work for a while.'

'I'm going to take a nap too,' said Jeannie. 'My body doesn't know what day it is, let alone what time it is.'

'I've a loose arrangement with Trevor to have a coffee and a walk along the prom, so I'll give him a buzz now,' said Jim.

They all said their goodbyes and headed off in different directions. As Beatrice pulled her car away from the kerb, she watched her dad walk towards the sea. She had to swallow back her tears. He looked so dejected. Her heart swelled with love for him and she promised herself that she'd mind him now as well as he had always minded her.

By seven o'clock, everyone was hungry again, but not in the best of form.

'I think we're all wrung out after today,' said Jeannie.

'I slept for most of the afternoon and I feel as if I'm still exhausted,' said Beatrice. 'Let's hope that's a good sign.'

'It sounds about right,' said Jeannie, as she swiftly covered up by saying that she'd heard the early stages of pregnancy were exhausting.

'Does this mean you've been looking into the idea?' Rose asked her.

'Well, Nick is keen to start a family at some point soon,' she said. She told them about his idea to open a new clinic for reconstruction rather than cosmetic surgery.

'He needs the funding from the hospital and he was meeting yesterday with some of the people who could make it happen.'

'Wow, I hope it works out for him,' said Rose.

She cleared up and loaded the dishwasher while Ali went to bed. Jeannie said she'd climb in beside her for a few minutes before heading to her own bed. Rose could hear the two of them giggling – no doubt Jeannie was entertaining Ali with stories that were totally unsuitable, but that was why she loved her so much!

Rose sighed happily as she blew out the candles around the kitchen. She'd enjoyed every second of this evening. Hearing Jeannie's infectious laugh once more was balm for her soul, and she was delighted for Beatrice. She knew her older sister would be a wonderful mother and she had fingers, toes and everything else crossed that this IVF would work out. Beatrice had explained that she had another bite of the cherry if this round wasn't successful.

Rose knew another couple who'd tried IVF. They'd had six or seven rounds and it didn't take. The last she'd heard they'd adopted a little boy from Russia. So while she was happy that Beatrice was trying for a baby, she was worried for her. She was glad she'd reached out and told their dad, though. They had a lovely bond and she was relieved Beatrice hadn't felt she should go alone when push came to shove.

'Hey, watch, this is how you move your booty,' she heard Jeannie shouting from Ali's bedroom, followed by a thudding noise that sounded like Ali had rolled off the bed, she was laughing so hard.

Jeannie *was* like a firecracker! Rose had forgotten what a blast of fresh air her twin was. Her presence was strong and like a rainbow of colour. She too would make a great mother, she mused, but in a totally different way from Beatrice.

That Nick guy she was married to was about as shallow as a saucer of milk, so she hoped he really was thinking of having a baby. She sincerely hoped Jeannie wasn't wasting the best years of her life with a man who wasn't worthy of her.

Jeannie would hopefully spend a couple of weeks with them. Rose was determined to have some deep chats with her twin. While her life in LA seemed to be going well and she had a good thing going with her business, money wasn't everything. What would her future hold if she ended up divorced and alone? Rose was quite frankly staggered that the marriage had lasted this long. But she honestly wasn't sure Jeannie was thinking ahead enough.

Rose had long since given up expecting Martha to be the perfect mother. But she hoped she would step up to the plate for Beatrice now all the same. She'd need all the support she could get. Yes, Rose would try and orchestrate a bit of involvement from their mother. She might suggest a little weekly email with advice or something that would keep them in contact regularly. A part of Rose still felt hurt at the lack of affection Martha had shown when she was pregnant with Ali. Yes, she'd been full of unasked-for advice and criticisms, but she hadn't been exactly supportive. She didn't want that for Beatrice.

Chapter 16

AS JEANNIE SANK INTO THE HUGE BED IN ROSIE'S spare room, her body ached. She was always tired after the journey from LA to home, but tonight she was floored. It was so good to be back home with her sisters and Ali. It was a relief that drippy Martin was away on business. Rose had seemed surprised when she'd got a text to say he'd had to leave suddenly for an impromptu meeting somewhere, but Jeannie didn't care. She was really pleased to have Rose to herself. Their dad was such a sweetie and she was thrilled he was there. Especially this morning with Bea. Wowzers! She couldn't believe that Beatrice was possibly having a baby. She had so much admiration for her older sister. Jeannie knew, when Bea had told them about the process, that there was no way she'd ever have that courage. And to do it all alone? Not a hope. Her sister really was an amazing woman.

Jeannie had always wondered why Bea's marriage to Chocolate Balls hadn't worked. She'd called Davy that because she'd thought he was so self-absorbed and in love with himself that he'd eat himself if he were made of chocolate. Beatrice always swatted her and told her not to say it, but it made her laugh nonetheless. Needless to say, Davy thought it was fabulous and loved her saying it.

Now that it had transpired that Beatrice was seeing a

shrink, Jeannie felt as if she'd let her down big time. Rose should've seen it and reported the situation to her. Why hadn't they noticed their big sister was in such turmoil?

As she lay with her hands above her head, the magnitude of what she had going on hit her. There was no way she could tell anyone she was pregnant. Imagine if Beatrice's pregnancy didn't work out. What then? Could she put her hand up and say, 'Ooh, by the way, I've got one cooking in here and I'm not in the least bit interested in it, so do you want it?'

Would it be like years ago when she had clothes that Bea wanted so they'd swap?

Babies weren't really that easy to give away, mind you. As she'd surfed the internet on her phone, Jeannie had realised there was an awful lot involved with putting a child up for adoption. She'd jumped from one website to the next, but each one of them wanted to involve social workers and counsellors and a whole pile of nosy people who would probably make her feel like the nastiest person on the planet.

She looked around the room. It was totally evident that this was Rose's house now as opposed to her parents'. She was glad Rose had made it her own. It was so different from Jeannie's highly polished home back in LA, with its marble flooring throughout and the minimalist style. This house was pretty modern, especially in comparison to the way it had been when they were growing up. This had always been the spare room, and back then it had probably been quite musty and forgotten. But Rose had done a wonderful job with it, making it far more homely. The pictures on the walls, the bedside lights with their quirky coloured shades, the brightly coloured towels in the bathroom and the tiny posies of garden flowers on the bedside lockers all screamed of Rose's style. Jeannie had forgotten how wonderfully comforting that was.

Her thoughts moved to Nick. She loved him, really loved him. She felt ashamed of how she'd behaved during the course of their marriage thus far, and in turn how she'd let him treat her. She hoped they could start over. She didn't feel her heart wanted someone else. She didn't look at her suitcase spilling onto the floor here and wonder what it would be like to leave him for good. In fact, the thought of that left her cold. But it was time to want more and to make that happen.

She wasn't at all sure that she'd be able to be a mother, though. When she watched Beatrice talking about holding a baby in her arms, it was as if she were already feeling that warm little bundle. All Jeannie could think of was getting rid of her bundle.

She wondered what her parents' house in Connemara looked like now. She'd like to visit and see for herself. She had so little contact with Martha that it would be weird to go on her own. Perhaps Beatrice would come with her. Rose would probably be stuck here on account of Ali's school exams.

She thought of Martha. She was a strange woman in so many ways. She'd get up in the middle of the night and drive for hours to help a stranger, and yet she had three pretty darn amazing daughters, none of whom she had a decent relationship with.

Their dad was a dear man. Always thrilled to hear her voice and genuinely eager to know how she was. She could hear him smiling down the phone when she called. It had been wonderful to spend time with him today. He was loving every second of being retired and quite clearly it was suiting him perfectly. But she wasn't surprised to hear their mother was slowly sliding back into her job. After all, it was the true love of her life and they all knew it.

She texted Nick, letting him know she missed him and loved him. He rang immediately.

'How's everything going?' he asked. 'Are the girls over the moon to see you?'

'Over the moon,' she confirmed. She told him about Beatrice and how emotional the day had been. He asked about Ali and Rose, then told her that he was fully committed to putting his heart and soul into making things work between them.

'We'll make beautiful babies, and if they're not, I'll ensure they are by the time they're twenty-one.'

Jeannie giggled uncontrollably. 'You're a wicked man, that's a terrible thing to say. Don't all people love their children unconditionally?'

'Sure, but that doesn't mean they don't know if their kid is pug ugly.'

She laughed again, but as Nick took off on a tangent, wondering what their children might look like, she felt nothing but fear. Her hand rested on the mound of her tummy as he chatted happily. God bless him, she thought, he hadn't a clue about what she'd done.

'They should have your hair,' he was saying. 'Blonde curls are always beautiful. And your mouth. You've got a pout that's the envy of half of LA, and it's nothing to do with my scalpel.'

'They need your eyes, dancing and blue as the August sky,' she said, hoping she didn't sound as terrified as she felt.

'No matter what, they'll be ours and we're gonna love them so much,' Nick said. 'I'm so excited about this, Jeannie.'

She nodded as tears slid down her cheeks. 'Okay, so I'd better try and get some sleep while I can.'

'You do that, baby girl. I'll talk to you tomorrow.'

'Talk to you then.'

'Oh, and tell your sisters and Ali I say hi and that they're to come to LA, won't you? The more I think about it, the more I realise that we need to bring your family into our lives more.'

'I know. But they have a lot going on just now. We need to wait for Bea to find out if she's pregnant. But I promise I'll mention it.'

'It could be the best time for us to step in, honey. Bring them here to relax. They can lie by the pool, get Nina to come and do stuff for them. Take Ali to the outlets shopping . . . What do you say? How about we gift them some flights? I can book them. You just give me the dates.'

'I will,' she said. 'Give me a few days to figure out what would work, yeah?'

'Sure.' He hesitated for a moment. 'I honestly thought I was losing you, Jeannie. There's been a shift in you lately. I'm only trying to stay with you, honey.'

'I know, and I love you for that. We're good. We're tight. Night, sweetheart, love you.'

'I love you more.'

She hung up and cried again. By the time she'd blown her nose and splashed cold water on her face, it was late. She climbed back into bed and finally slept.

* * *

Rose knew she needed to get to bed. She wasn't a great sleeper at the best of times, but she needed a few hours so she could get up and make breakfast in the morning. It would be fantastic to have everyone around the table. She'd told Beatrice to come over whenever she liked.

'I don't want you feeling left out because you're the only one not staying here.'

'I'm not seven years old and crying because I wasn't invited to the birthday party,' Beatrice had said.

'I know. But your hormones are probably all over the shop and I want you here with us. It's such a treat for all of us to be together.'

'Except Mum,' Beatrice had said.

'Oh, yeah. Well, she's shown us all how little she wants to be involved, hasn't she? Poor Nanny May deserved more from her today. Mum's behaviour is disgraceful. She's the first one to talk about decorum and manners, and now look at her! Showing herself up.'

With the others gone and the house finally silent, Rose stared out at the dark inky water and wondered what the future would hold for each of them. She closed her eyes and said a silent prayer that Beatrice would carry a child to full term. Her admiration for her knew no bounds and she deserved a baby. Jeannie was such a wonderful addition to their lives. She hoped she'd stay for a few weeks so they could hang out properly. Even though she'd lived away from home for years, Rose still missed her sorely. And for herself? She hoped things would change, and that she would find the fulfilment in her life that had been missing for so long.

She was quietly philosophical as she walked into her bedroom. She'd brushed her teeth and changed into her nightie before she spotted the note on her pillow. For one crazy second, she wondered if it were Nanny May's letter. Filled with excitement, she snatched it up.

As the words seeped into her head, her heart stopped and her blood ran cold.

Chapter 17

THE FOLLOWING MORNING, JEANNIE WAS FEELING rotten. The pitiful sight of her lying listlessly on the sofa made Rose feel utterly useless.

'What can I do for you?' Jim asked. 'Is it food poisoning? Did you eat something dodgy on the plane, perhaps?'

'Nah, I'll be fine. It's probably just really bad jet lag. I slept fitfully last night. Ignore me.'

'Look at the stack of waffles and fruit,' said Jim.

'And the coffee is fresh in the plunger pot, though if you prefer the Nespresso capsules there's a machine over there. I . . .' Rose caught her breath and gave a tiny yelp.

'Hey, are you okay?' Jeannie asked.

'Yup,' she said, waving her hand. 'I'm totally fine. I just wish I had more time to sit and eat with you guys. But I have a really busy morning. I'll be here in the afternoon if anyone wants to do something.'

'You go on ahead and we'll find anything we don't have. Although looking at this feast, I reckon you've thought of pretty much everything.'

Rose took a mug of black coffee and swallowed too much, burning her throat. She yelped again and had to run to the sink for some cold water. She added it to her coffee and drank some more. Unable to stomach any food, she walked to the coffee pot again. She picked it up and put it back down.

'Rosie, what in the name of God are you doing? You're like a lunatic,' Jeannie said. 'Can I help you?'

'No, not at all,' she said. 'I'll be fine in a minute. I'm hassled about this morning, that's all. We have a huge contract teetering on the edge. If we get it, it'll mean a bonus for everyone involved.'

'Sounds great,' said Jim. 'Can I come and do anything? After all, I've been there and done that. It wouldn't bother me to step in and help.'

'Thanks, Dad,' she said. 'You're a darling to offer, but I'll be fine. I'll head off now and see you all later.'

'Your bag, Mum!' said Ali.

'Oh, shoot. Thanks,' she said as she grabbed it and left.

Jeannie dragged herself up off the sofa and padded over to the chair at the window and curled up, drinking in the view. As she knew it would, the vast ocean expanse calmed her, giving her the push she needed to make a few calls. She arranged to meet up with Meghan and Sam, her two friends from school. Meghan said she'd book a restaurant in Pebble Bay and they'd see her there for lunch.

Ali went off to study, while Jim was popping over to walk Ned for Beatrice before heading to his old golf course to play a round with his friend Trevor. He'd already been on to the solicitor's office, but they had informed him another search was being conducted that morning for the letters and had asked them all not to visit the cottage just yet, until that search was concluded. Meanwhile, Jeannie called the cottage in Connemara and got no answer, so tried her mum's mobile.

'Hey, Mum, how are you?'

'Hello, dear. I'm on my way to do a home visit. It's a bit of a damp day here, but what's new?' She laughed. 'Are you ensconced at Rose's?'

'Yes, very happily ensconced in the sea-view chair,' she replied. 'So I'm thinking of planning a visit. When suits you best?'

'Oh, that's wonderful news. It really is. I'll look forward to it greatly. I can collect you from the train if you let me know when you're coming. Or maybe you'd come with Jim. He's always driving here, there and everywhere. I'm ridiculously busy most of the time, but I'll sort something for you.'

'Thanks, Mum. I'll figure out the best time to come. I'm here for a couple of weeks, so we'll find a few days that work.'

'Talk to Jim about it. He's the best for arrangements, and the fact that he's there with you means you can figure it out together.'

'What do you make of this conundrum with Nanny May's letters?' Jeannie asked. 'I cannot fathom who took them or where they've ended up. It was a pity you didn't make it to the reading of her will.'

'I know. It *was* a pity, but I was busy. What can I say? It simply didn't work out for me.'

'Do you ever stop and think of other people?' Jeannie said.

'All the time,' said Martha curtly. 'I spend my time running from Billy to Jack helping other women. Earlier today I was with a woman who would've died and so would her twins had I not been there. The first one was breech so I had to—'

'Mum!' Jeannie shouted, interrupting her. 'I don't care.

I'm not interested in other people. What I care about first and foremost is our family. Rose, Bea, Dad and until now, Nanny May.' She knew she was shouting, which would antagonise her mother.

'Don't shout at me, Jeannie. You know I can't bear it.'

'You are astonishing,' Jeannie said in a quiet voice. 'I hope the strangers whose lives you burst into are there when you need them. I hope you have a good core group of people you can count on. I certainly do. They're called family.'

'Oh dear, you really are in a stinking mood,' said Martha. 'Now please don't hate me, but I need to go!'

'You go, Mum.'

'Bye for now, Jeannie, and I'm thrilled to bits that you're coming. I'm looking forward to hearing all your news. Especially if you have more stories of wealthy people behaving badly, I do love listening to those. Now, that dreadful woman Dorothy is approaching. I'd better talk to her. Goodbye, dear.'

'Bye, Mum,' Jeannie said, feeling truly outraged. They'd known Larry and Dorothy for years. They seemed like a perfectly nice couple. Larry and her father golfed together and the women tolerated one another as a result. Well, if the truth were told, Dorothy was perfectly lovely to Martha, who was catty and difficult in return. It was a pity they didn't get on better. But poor Dorothy was a very old-fashioned kind of woman who literally lived for her husband. They'd never had children and that was probably why Martha disliked her so much.

'We have nothing in common. She has no children, no grandchildren and no interest or knowledge of what it is I do.'

Jeannie always suspected that Martha looked down her nose at Dorothy and made the poor woman feel inferior.

'She's a gibbering mess. It's impossible to have a conversation with her. All she talks about is Larry . . . "I do this for Larry . . . I do that for Larry . . . " We were out in a restaurant, and during conversation with the other couple she was asked what she did for a living, to which she replied that she "looks after Larry". What kind of numbskull thing is that to say? How can she hold her head up high and say things like that in this day and age? Women the world over are taking control and trying to ensure equal pay with men, and then this joke of a woman is proudly shouting that her entire life revolves around her husband.'

Suffice it to say that Dorothy had never been forgiven for that comment and in Martha's head she was a total write-off. Jeannie wondered if things were any better now that they were all retired. Dorothy was from good stock and when her parents passed away she'd inherited a very large house with three acres of land just outside Ballyshaden village, with an uninterrupted view of the sea. Bespoke Design had been commissioned to give the place an overhaul, and according to Rose, it was out of this world.

Still, Jeannie mused, she would know all the dynamics when she went to visit. She knew that getting upset or annoyed with their mother was futile. She'd never been any different and she didn't exactly have a favourite. As Jeannie had pointed out many times, she despised them all equally!

Usually she and her sisters could laugh about it, especially now that they were older.

'Nah, she hates me more because I made a mess of my marriage,' Beatrice said.

'I think she hates me the most because I live with a loud Yank who brandishes a scalpel for a living,' joked Jeannie.

'Ah, but I am loathed more than both of you put together because I produced the only grandchild and she's another bloody girl,' said Rose.

The three sisters always knew they could find a softer side in their father. But he'd been at work all the time while they were children and he generally didn't understand half of what was happening. Neither did Martha, and she never bothered to ask Nanny May what was going on. Jim did his best, and Sunday mornings were sacred when they were growing up. After mass, the girls would go with their dad to buy the Sunday papers, and Jim would allow them to choose whatever they wanted from the sweets stand.

As she thought about it now, Jeannie wondered why they'd never had any kind of a ritual with Martha the way they'd had with their dad. There were no clear memories involving their mother, in fact. None that were heartwarming or fun, at least. There were rules, for sure. Tons of them that needed to be obeyed or there would be another boring lecture.

'I'm not annoyed with you, Jeannie. I'm disappointed. I wish you'd thought about your actions more. I wish you'd considered the outcome.'

After years of listening to the same speech, all three girls could recite it word for word and it flew right over their blonde curly heads. Nanny May was the one they went to if they were hurt, sick or sad.

The day she'd started her period, Jeannie was well prepared. Nanny May had sat and read 'the book' to her and Rose. Jeannie had roared laughing at the sex part, while Rose looked stricken and a pale shade of green.

Rose had beaten her to it and got her period a couple of weeks before. Jeannie didn't remember being shocked or traumatised when it happened to her. Instead, she was just a bit cross that she'd got hers second.

'Your little bodies are doing what nature intended,' said Nanny May. 'But it's not a competition.'

'I think I need a bra now,' said Jeannie. 'Can we go and get one?'

Nanny May hugged her and stroked her hair. 'If you'd like to, then I think we could do that.'

So Nanny May had taken them to the department store that had been built at the edge of Pebble Bay. The fact that Jeannie's chest was as flat as a pancake was immaterial. They found one that looked as if it had been made for an elf, and Jeannie sauntered into the changing room.

Rose hung about at the side of the shop, looking mortified.

'Would you like a bra too, pet?' Nanny May asked.

'Only if I don't have to try it on,' Rose whispered.

'All right, darling. When we know Jeannie's size, we'll get you one too.'

'You won't say out loud that it's for me, will you?' she asked, looking terrified.

'No, I won't say a word. I'll just select one and tell the shop lady to put it in the bag. Is there one you like?'

Rose nodded and whispered that she'd love the one with tiny rosebuds all over it.

Jeannie came out swinging her chosen bra, which was black with lace detail. Nanny May instructed her to go and look for a pair of slippers, telling her she needed new ones.

'I'll meet you over there,' she said, using the time to select the bra for Rose and pay for it without Jeannie knowing.

Once they got home, it was obvious what had happened.

'But why didn't you come in the changing room with me?' Jeannie asked.

Rose shrugged her shoulders, looking as if she'd die first rather than let the whole shop know her intimate business. Not much had changed over the years. Rose was still a motherly sort, whereas Jeannie was the party girl.

It suddenly occurred to Jeannie what she'd do if she absolutely had to be a mother. She'd get help, obviously. What was the point in spending half her life stooped over a poopy nappy? They could hire a lovely, sturdy, motherly type to do that. Preferably one with several hairy face-moles and a problem with bottom gas so she wouldn't feel like she was playing second fiddle to an out-of-work model.

She could feel sweat beading at her brow. She couldn't think about being pregnant or having a baby right now. Nope, that was a whole other day's thinking. The adoption idea seemed to be rightly complex and she wasn't going to be able to do that without anyone noticing. She'd have a proper think later on this evening.

Right now she needed to get herself together or she'd be late for lunch.

Dragging her large hard-shelled make-up case over to the dressing table, she pulled the sides down to reveal the layers of carefully sorted cosmetics.

'Oh, I think I've died and gone to heaven. That is the coolest thing!' Ali said as she swooped into the room. 'Mum has a tiny grubby washbag with the same five things that she's had since I was born.'

'Your mother doesn't have as much time on her hands as I do. Besides, she was always the more pragmatic twin. Why aren't you at school?'

'I don't have an exam this morning, so I'm headed in shortly for the afternoon one. Were you always the crazy girlie one?' Ali asked as she lay back against the pillows, chewing her nails in concentration.

'Yes, and stop doing that to your hands. If you destroy your nails, you'll regret it. When was the last time you had a proper manicure?'

'Eh, like, never,' Ali scoffed. 'I'm fifteen, way too young for that sort of thing in Mum's eyes.'

'Um,' Jeannie said. 'I'll clear it with Rosie first, but I can see a spa day looming.'

'No arguments from my end,' Ali said, yawning. 'Just give me a few days to do these stupid exams and I'll be right there with you. There's a gorgeous place a few doors down from Auntie Bea's place that I've been longing to try.'

'Okay, I'll speak to Rose and let's see if we can all go. A Brady girl pamper day! It would be divine for your mum and darling Bea, too.'

Ali beamed as she studied every move Jeannie made. 'That stuff is so gorgeous. It's the most subtle shimmer but it lifts your eyes brilliantly,' she said.

'Isn't it the bomb?' Jeannie said with a smile. 'Take it any time you need it.'

'Thanks, but I think I'd need a bucket of that stuff to stick my entire head into.'

Ali watched as she examined the corner of her eye. 'Auntie Jeannie, do you honestly think you needed all that surgery? I mean, Mum is obviously the same age, and I think she looks beautiful just as she is.'

'Do you think I don't look beautiful any more?' Jeannie asked, swinging around to face her.

'I'm only trying to get my head around it. I'm struggling to understand why you want to go to the hospital for sore stuff when you're pretty as you are.'

'It doesn't hurt that much.'

'Liar.'

Jeannie smiled. 'I probably wouldn't do any of it if I had you there to keep me in line.'

'Doesn't Nick tell you that you're beautiful the way you are?' Ali asked.

'Of course. He adores me and treats me like a princess, no matter what I do. That's the way it should be, kid. I've been lucky with the men in my life. First my dad, now Nick.'

'My dad is amazing too,' said Ali. 'He's the best when it comes to going out or buying stuff. Mum tends to say no, whereas Dad goes over her head and says yes. It's brilliant,' she said with a little giggle.

'Where's he gone this time?' Jeannie asked.

'I dunno,' said Ali. 'He goes on trips quite a lot. I'll call him in a while and see what he's up to. He always lets me have stuff from the duty-free, too. There's a new eyeshadow palette I want, so I'm going to ask him for it. Katie and Sarah are going to be *so* jealous! I get amazing stuff from you, too. So I'm a lucky girl. But Dad is the bomb.'

'Yeah, did you ever hear that phrase that the only man you can trust is your daddy? Well you keep that in here,' Jeannie said, thudding her chest.

'That's sweet. I like that,' said Ali.

'Your mum is a darling too, you know.'

'Yeah, I know,' said Ali. 'But we seem to clash a lot.

Mum is pretty serious. She over-thinks most stuff and in the end I feel as if she's kind of ruining the fun.'

'She'd never want to do that,' said Jeannie. 'She just loves you so much that she wants to protect you.'

'Yeah, I suppose so,' said Ali. She suddenly looked bored with the whole thing. 'I think I'm going to ask Grandad if he'd like to go to the burger place tomorrow. He's never been and he can't get his head around guacamole on a burger!'

'If you're doing that, I think I'm going to see if Rosie and Bea will come to the bistro with me.'

'Nice plan,' said Ali as she texted Jim. 'That's a goer, so I'll book it online.'

Jeannie texted her sisters too, and both were delighted with the idea.

Tomorrow, with just the three of them there, Jeannie might open up to the girls. It was getting to the point where she needed to talk before she exploded.

Chapter 18

THE FOLLOWING EVENING, THERE WAS GREAT excitement at Marine Terrace. Ali had spent the best part of two hours doing her hair and make-up.

'Grandad is going to be delighted with his date,' said Jeannie. 'I'm loving the way you've used that sparkly eyeliner. You're seriously good at make-up.'

'Thanks, Auntie Jeannie,' said Ali, beaming. 'Want me to do yours?'

'Sure,' said Jeannie. She closed her eyes and Ali set to work. Like a butterfly landing and swooping, her niece worked her magic, using a palette Jeannie had bought and never bothered to use.

'This stuff is fab and we can't get any of this line here. They do one tiny one that Dad got me in the duty-free, but it's pretty crap. It doesn't have the darker shades for doing the smoky eye.'

'I'll take your word for it,' said Jeannie. 'My problem is that I have this amazing girl who comes to my home and does everything from waxing to hair and make-up. So any time I go out, I just call Nina and she works her magic.'

'Well, while you're here, if you want make-up at any stage, let me know and I'll do it.'

A few minutes later Ali said she was finished, and

Jeannie stood up from her bed where she'd been sitting and looked in the bedroom mirror.

'Good job, baby girl! You could seriously charge people for this. Have a little sideline and make some cash.'

Ali laughed and hugged her, saying she needed to go and meet Jim.

'Have fun, sweetie, and thanks again,' Jeannie said.

Ali shouted a goodbye to Rose and the front door banged. Jeannie pondered for a moment. Ali hadn't hugged or kissed Rose goodbye. They didn't really chat much or get involved with one another. Figuring it was none of her business, she parked the thoughts.

She tried on two pairs of trousers, but neither was going to zip. Cursing under her breath, she pulled a maxi dress from the wardrobe and draped it over her head. It was cut on the bias, with lots of tiny pleats. It was also lined, so it was very forgiving. Her arms were still as toned as ever, but as she ran her hand over her tummy, it was decidedly rounder. She had no idea how far along she was. Her periods tended to be erratic at the best of times. But she figured she was around five or six months. She remembered Rosie saying that she barely showed until quite late on. She didn't put on much more than a stone in weight either.

'I'm waiting for this massive big tummy that my friends seem to have,' Rose had said. 'I almost think they don't believe I'm pregnant.'

'Get your scan printed on a T-shirt!' Jeannie had said, and they'd both laughed.

'Rosie-Posie!' Jeannie called now, as she grabbed one of her favourite handbags. She was having a Fendi moment where she loved everything they did. Remembering the bags she'd bought in duty-free, she grabbed them and put them into a plastic carrier. She'd give them to the girls when they got to the restaurant.

Feeling nervous, she thought about whether she'd tell her sisters about her pregnancy. Time was running out in several ways. Firstly, she was going to start showing. But secondly, she'd need to put a plan in place. She longed for a bit of support. She knew they'd help advise her. She wasn't sure she could continue to do this alone.

'Hi!' Rose said, appearing in the bedroom doorway. 'Ready to rock 'n' roll? I'd prefer us to be there a little early rather than leaving Bea on her own.'

'Totally,' said Jeannie. 'Let's go.'

Jeannie wanted to tell Rose she looked great, but she couldn't. Her twin looked exhausted and her face was pinched with stress. Assuming she was feeling the pressure from this big contract at the shop, she made a mental note to try and take her away, even for one night to a spa, where they could chill and relax.

'Well, look at you!' said Rose. 'You'd know you don't live in Pebble Bay any longer. You're like a movie star, Jeannie. Those wedges are fab, and as for your handbag, uh, it's utterly divine.'

'Glad you like it, and it's your daughter we have to thank for my look tonight. She's seriously good at doing make-up. I mean, she's talented.'

'She spends enough time doing it,' said Rose, rolling her eyes. 'No matter how many times I tell her to stop wasting her time and put the effort into her schoolwork, she doesn't listen.'

'She's a fifteen-year-old girl, Rosie. Most of them are into the same thing. She's experimenting with her looks and trying to find who she is. We did the same thing.'

'Yes, except we had maybe four colours between us and we hadn't a clue.'

'There you go! Now the kids go to YouTube and there are tutorials on how to do each look. It's so exciting. Okay, let's move.'

They left the house and meandered towards the bistro. The air was still warm, but Jeannie was glad of her wrap all the same.

'Not quite LA temperatures,' said Rose. The sea was glistening to their right and the clear, salty air was delicious in comparison to the mugginess Jeannie had got used to. They met a couple of people that Rose knew, both of whom exclaimed that they hadn't known she had a twin. Rose kept the chat to a minimum, saying they were meeting someone and they were late.

They got to the bistro just as Beatrice came around the corner.

'You're always early,' said Jeannie with a giggle. 'We honestly thought we'd get here before you tonight!'

'You know me with timekeeping,' she said as they hugged hello.

The bistro was almost full with an array of punters, everyone from young couples to families with bored-looking teenagers. Their table was inside a little booth, and Rose explained that they could connect their phones and play their own music.

'Ali loves it here, but I find it a trial because she booms out music and I can't hear myself think! In fact, the last time we came here we ended up having a dreadful row, and herself and Martin pretty much ganged up on me yet again.'

'Does that happen much?' Jeannie asked, with her head cocked to the side.

'What, the arguments or the ganging-up?'

'Both,' said Beatrice.

The waitress came and gave them menus and called out the specials, then offered to take a drinks order.

'Will we get a bottle of Prosecco to kick things off?' Rose asked.

'Well I can't drink,' said Beatrice, 'but you girls go right ahead. I'll have a cranberry juice, please.'

'I'm off alcohol at the moment,' said Jeannie. 'It's a diet I've been following. Nick is getting really bored with me! I'll have a large bottle of sparkling water.'

Rose ordered a glass of Prosecco.

'So,' Jeannie said, 'getting back to Ali. Have things been this bad between you guys for long?'

'Oh no, it's nothing really. Just the usual teen stuff. Martin has always been closer to her than I have . . . There's not a lot I can do about that. I did everything I could to try and make us more of a team. I mean, I look at her friend Katie and her mum. They go shopping and for little trips away together. I've suggested doing a spa weekend and she instantly wanted Martin to come too.'

'That's tough, honey,' said Jeannie. She put her hand over Rose's. Perhaps it was the fact that Jeannie had quite literally reached out, but suddenly Rose couldn't hold back any longer. Once she began to cry, the floodgates opened.

'Hey,' said Beatrice. She was closer to her on the curved sofa of the booth so she pulled her into her arms. 'It'll be okay. Lots of teenagers go through a stage of not getting on with one parent. You hear about it all the time.'

'It's not just that,' Rose blubbed. 'It's Martin . . .'

'What about him?' Jeannie said, barely hiding her dislike for the man.

'He's . . . he's left us.'

'Whaaat?' Jeannie yelled, before clamping her hand over her mouth. 'When did he leave? I *had* noticed he wasn't there . . .'

'He went two days ago and left me a note saying he didn't love me and couldn't live a lie any longer. He said he only stayed this long for Ali, but he'd still be there for her.'

'What a shithead,' said Jeannie as Rose sobbed into Beatrice's chest.

'Darling, don't worry,' said Bea. 'It's all going to be okay. We're here and we're going to be here no matter what.'

'Too right,' said Jeannie. 'Oh, Jeez Louise, I want to kill him. I always thought he was a snake. What a weak asshole to tell you in a note. It's only a step up from a text message.'

'It's pretty cowardly all right,' said Beatrice. 'But it doesn't matter how he did it. The facts remain and you need to just try and look after yourself and Ali.'

'How are you going to tell her?' Jeannie asked. 'Oh, maybe you could write a Post-it note and leave it on her bedroom door?'

'Jeannie,' Beatrice said sternly. 'You're not helping with comments like that.'

'Sorry,' she said, looking like a petulant child. 'I'm just so angry with him. How could he do that to you after seventeen years of marriage and God knows how long before? How could he do that to Ali? Where has he gone?'

'I've no idea,' said Rose as her tears began to dry up. She didn't want other diners staring at her.

'Why didn't you tell me before?' said Jeannie. 'I can't believe you went through the motions for two whole days and didn't say anything. No wonder you were behaving so oddly. Darling, you can't do this on your own and you don't need to.'

'I think I was in shock,' Rose said. 'Now that it's sinking in, I feel like killing him. But that's only the minor part of the issue. The major part is Ali.' Tears choked her as she tried to remain calm, but the hours of holding back had to come out in some way. 'She adores him. Idolises him. She's going to blame me. I just know it. She'll think I drove him away.'

'Well, then you need to make sure she understands that the whole thing is a massive shock for you too,' said Jeannie. 'He's not going to lay the blame at your feet.'

Once she'd had a good cry, Rose felt so much better. It was as if she'd spilled the poison and it was running away from her in a horrible dark river. Jeannie and Bea were incredible. Jeannie said she was in no hurry to go back to America and Beatrice was definitely staying put.

'If I'm lucky enough, I'll be pregnant and you're going to be my first port of call. You and Ali. So we can be our own little family and watch out for one another.'

'I'll be here for a while . . .' Jeannie paused. Rose was wiping her eyes and thanking Beatrice for the tissue. Should she tell them? She looked from one to the other and bottled it.

'You'll be here for a while and what?' Beatrice said.

'And I'll come back as often as I can. I've had a chat with Nick about this. He wants me to see my family more, so I will. He totally supports me no matter what I come up with.'

'I wish you'd told me you were having difficulties,' Beatrice said quietly to Rose. 'I would have been there for you long before now.'

Rose nodded. 'I'm not so good at talking about stuff, or asking for help.'

'It's really important we be there for each other,' Jeannie said seriously. 'We're kind of into the second half of life. This is the part that we have full control over. So it's up to us to make a massive attempt to avoid fucking it up . . . Gosh, it feels good to curse,' she said with a satisfied grin on her face. 'I can't say anything like that to my friends in the States.'

Rose laughed. 'Well, I'm not crazy about bad language, but if that helps you feel free, you can curse like a sailor for thirty seconds when we Skype! But cursing aside, I guess you're right,' she said. 'So can we please make a pact? That we will tell each other things from here on in – no matter how big or small?'

'Aye, aye to that,' Jeannie said, saluting her.

'I agree completely,' Beatrice said with a smile.

'Thank you,' Rose said, wiping her face with a napkin. 'I love you both so much. I'd be utterly lost without you.'

'We've managed so far by sticking together, even if we have kept stuff from one another, and we'll get through this too,' Jeannie said.

'But we'll miss having Nanny May to help, won't we?' Beatrice said sadly. 'She'd be great in this situation.'

Rose smiled. 'Definitely. She'd have given Martin a right piece of her mind, then moved in with me and Ali to keep us on the straight and narrow.'

Silence prevailed as each thought about all they had lost with Nanny May's passing. It was at moments like this that they really understood how much she had done for them all their lives.

'Let's raise a glass to the woman who brought us up,' said Jeannie, picking up her sparkling water.

Rose and Beatrice tearfully picked up their glasses and they clinked.

'To Nanny May!' they chorused.

Chapter 19

ISOBELLE, BEATRICE'S ASSISTANT, WAS IN TEARS AT the other end of the phone as she hiccuped that she'd just vomited.

'I thought I'd be okay. I felt rotten this morning, but I'm so sick. I can't stay, Beatrice.'

'Don't worry,' Beatrice said, as she began to gather her bits and pieces. 'I'll be right there. Lock up and go on home, lovey. I'll be there in five minutes. I'm just over at Marine Terrace with my sister. Don't you give the shop a second thought.'

'Okay, there's nobody due for twenty minutes.'

'All right, you head home and I hope you feel better soon.' She hung up and bit her lip. 'That was Isobelle; she's got a vomiting bug by the sounds of it.'

'I'm free, so why don't I make myself useful?' Jeannie offered. 'I'm dying to see your place anyway.'

They got to the shop, where there was a faint smell of disinfectant. Jeannie looked over at Beatrice and poked her tongue out, wrinkling her nose.

'Poor Isobelle,' she said. 'You wait here. I'm going to do a quick zip around with a disinfectant spray. If you are pregnant, you can't afford to come down with a bug.' It did occur to her that she should be equally careful, but she couldn't go there.

'No, and we don't need a scene like in *Bridesmaids*, with girls crouching down having cramping incidents in my dresses!'

Jeannie grabbed a spray and ran a cloth under the hot tap. She quickly cleaned every surface, from the door handles to the bathroom. Beatrice opened the windows and lit scented candles to keep the place smelling citrusy.

By the time the next appointment arrived, Jeannie was scanning rails and making mental notes.

'Can you find me a notebook?' she asked.

'Why?'

'I'm stepping in. Lord only knows how long poor Isobelle will be gone. She can't even contemplate coming near you until she's totally better.'

'Oh, I can't manage without Isobelle!' Beatrice said, looking stricken. 'I'm so busy, Jeannie.'

'You have me! I'm not in a hurry to go anywhere. Mum and Dad won't mind if I see them this week, next week, or the week after that. Nick has said I've to take as long as I like. I can learn quickly and I won't be shy about asking you questions.'

'But you're meant to be on holiday.'

'I'm meant to be spending time with you and Rosie and Ali. I'm staying with them, so this will be perfect for us.'

She scanned the glass cabinets, screwing up her eyes against the bright showroom lights.

'Wow, this place is stunning, sis. Your attention to detail is just amazing. These headpieces would sell for ten times the price in LA. Where do you buy them?'

'They're hand-made by a local girl. She has a little shed-style office in her back garden and produces these while her kids are at school.'

'No way! They're out of this world.'

'I think so too. That jewellery collection is a similar story. They're by a couple who fell on hard times during the recession and used their redundancy money to start making pieces out of silver and crystal. They literally sell as soon as I get them on the floor.'

'You should be so proud, Bea. This boutique is wonderful. They all are.'

'Thanks, Jeannie. That means a lot considering you're seeing a lot of high-end places in LA.'

'Let me tell you, you would make a small fortune in my neck of the woods with these products. People have so much money it's a joke. The competition to look good is fierce, and when it comes to society weddings, there are no budgets.'

'It's become pretty insane here too. It's not just the rich and famous either. I see girls dropping ten, twenty, thirty grand on dresses and accessories and I know they'll be paying the credit union for the privilege for decades.'

'Well I'm glad I got married when I was young and that we did it impulsively and to our own style. If I had to do it now, we'd need a five-hundred-seater job and I know it wouldn't be fun.'

Jeannie marched off to the other side of the main showroom and flicked through a few more racks, trying to get an idea of what stock Beatrice had. All the while Ned kept a close eye on proceedings.

Within twenty minutes she was fixing her face with a dab of powder and replenishing her lip gloss ready to welcome a party of five, all dressed in matching T-shirts with pink feather boas.

'Ladies! Come with me. Loving the look, this is going to be a dream!'

Beatrice smiled and shook her head, knowing that her sister was going to sell like her life depended on it.

Her own appointment was a shy country girl who had come along alone, having lost her mother the previous year. She was marrying her childhood sweetheart and was using money her mother had left to pay for the incredible bespoke gown she was due to collect. As she brought it out from a stockroom, Beatrice had a fleeting moment of fear. Should she be lying down flat, giving her babies the best chance to settle in her womb? She barely dared to wonder if it was a boy or a girl in there.

She had names she adored. For a boy she liked strong, solid names like Jack or Mark. If she had a girl, she'd thought of Felicity or Daisy. She wasn't a believer in this new wave of androgynous names for children. She loved the thought of a pink-and-lilac-hued room for a baby girl, or she'd seen divine powder-blue fabric with smudgy cream bunnies for a boy. No matter what sex the child was, he or she would be cherished.

'What do you think, Bea?' Jeannie called out. 'Isn't she sublime?'

Beatrice walked over to the main plinth, where the bride was standing in a high-end gown with full accessories and veil. Jeannie had added one of the most expensive headpieces to her side, at the waist.

'I knew the dress needed something else. June is so slight that she needs a bit of definition, so your seamstress can sew this onto a fine silk-gauze belt, right?'

'Yes, of course,' Beatrice said, barely believing the bride would absorb all the cost.

'I know it won't come cheap, but June doesn't want to look like any other bride. Hey, why should she?'

Jeannie added up the total cost and showed the figure to June, who was so swept along by the sales pitch she was almost saying it was too cheap.

'I know it mightn't be the time,' Jeannie continued, tapping her finger against her mouth. 'But have you an idea of what colour you're thinking of for your bridesmaids?'

'I hadn't thought yet,' said June.

'Well, are we all present and correct?'

'Yes,' she said, 'but I didn't think I'd have time today, so we were going to book an appointment for next week.'

'Have I time to show the girls something?' Jeannie said more to herself than them as she flicked through the appointment book on the counter. 'Okay, bear with me. I saw something just before you came in. It's slightly edgy, but I think you girls could pull it off.' She pulled out a roll of silk fabric in a divine shade between sea green and duck-egg blue. There was a matching silk organza, so she brought that too.

'I was thinking of a melange using this colour. Seeing as you are two redheads, a blonde and a brunette, I reckon you'd rock this.' The girls all smiled and nodded.

'I see one jumpsuit, one full-length gown, one cocktail length and for our very petite lady, a bandeau top with a tulle ballet-length skirt.'

Beatrice jumped on the moment and produced one of each style in a pale pink.

'These are the samples of the styles; I carry them in navy and pink for trying on.'

The women dashed into the changing cubicles, giggling and shouting across to one another.

Twenty minutes later, they had that sale too. With

deposits paid for everything, the group left in a wake of excitement.

'You're good,' Beatrice said, shaking her head in awe. 'Would you ever consider opening a store in LA? You're a natural, and you have such a quick eye for knowing what suits. I've been at this game for years and I don't think I could've done what you just did.'

'Of course you could. You do it all the time!'

Beatrice hugged her, and that was pretty much the only contact they had until the door closed for the evening.

'I'm pooped,' said Jeannie as she flopped onto a couch. 'You need more than one person in here with you. Can you afford it?'

'Yes, and I've kind of been ignoring it, but you're right. I don't suppose you'd like to move home and join me?' Beatrice raised an eyebrow.

They locked up and made their way upstairs to the flat, where Beatrice made a beeline for the bathroom. For the first time all day she allowed herself to think of the pregnancy. As she pulled down her underwear, she was almost afraid to look.

There was no show or bleeding, so there was nothing to say it wasn't working.

Jeannie was so impressed with the flat. Ned looked like he was showing her around as he walked from room to room.

'It's so much lovelier in reality. FaceTime doesn't do it justice,' she said. 'I'm loving the nod to the window seat at Marine Terrace, too.'

'It's not quite as salubrious, but it's essentially the same view!'

'It certainly is. I'm so glad you've got this set-up. The spare room is perfect for your baby, too.'

'I have so many ideas, but obviously I need to wait and see if the IVF works and if there will be a baby at all.' Jeannie hugged her. 'And then if it does . . .' She took a deep shuddering breath. 'If it does, I think I'll find out the sex so I can have the room decorated to suit.'

'So you're not raising the child as androgynous then? Or going for a safe colour like lemon or pale green so as not to step on the toes of those who believe in gender neutrality?'

'Definitely not. Each to their own, but I'm going old school. If it's a boy, I'm thinking boats or bunnies and navy and white and Hamptons style, and for a girl I'd go for all-out pinks and lilacs and cream.'

'Good for you,' Jeannie said. 'I agree. Funny that we both like the idea of strong girlie or boyish decor. We're probably very out of vogue, you know?'

'I couldn't give a fiddler's,' said Beatrice. 'It's almost illegal to like pink if you're a girl these days. I see it all the time with brides coming in. Some of them want their bridesmaids in pink and are apologetic about it.'

'Yeah, as if liking the colour pink or tulle or frills makes us weaker as women! What a load of crap.'

'Totally,' Beatrice said.

'So how are you feeling now?' Jeannie asked, nodding at her tummy.

'I'm still not bleeding, so that's all I can hope for at this point.'

As the sun went behind a great big angry grey mass of cloud, it began to rain. Lightly at first and then hammering against the windows, making them almost curl towards one another.

'Ugh, on evenings like this I feel like crawling into bed,' said Beatrice.

'Ooh, let's do that,' Jeannie said, rushing into the master bedroom, kicking off her shoes and jumping in. Giggling like schoolgirls, they snuggled in and listened to the therapeutic rhythm of the rain.

Ned appeared and Jeannie pointed at him. 'Not a hope, doggy. Not in the bed.'

Beatrice giggled. 'Aw, poor Ned. I do let him in sometimes, and he hates the rain. It scares him.'

'He's a dog, Beatrice. Not a person. If you have a baby, you'll need to make sure he doesn't get jealous and eat its face off.'

'Oh stop!' Beatrice said. 'Ned would never do anything like that!' He climbed onto the bed and sat over on Beatrice's side. Jeannie clearly didn't mind that much, because she let it go.

'This is so nice,' she said after a few minutes. 'Do you remember that time when all three of us were sick with chickenpox? It literally rained for the week. Nanny May went to the chemist to get that awful pink goo to put on the spots.'

'Calamine lotion,' Beatrice said wistfully. 'She dotted it on every single spot on each one of us, bless her.'

'She was incredible, wasn't she?' Jeannie said. 'She did far more for us than our own mother did.'

'I know Mum loved us,' Beatrice said fairly. 'But she would never have taken the time to dot a thousand spots with a cotton bud of pink lotion.'

'She was always flying about and headed for the next crowning baby. I think it became like an addiction for her. She couldn't get enough of newborn babies and mothers.'

'I wonder if she'll want to mind us when our times come?' Beatrice asked.

'What do you mean, *us*?' said Jeannie, as her mouth went dry. 'I love the way you're so sure we'll both be mothers. I know it's your greatest wish, but I'm not so sure I'll ever feel the way you do.' Spiking with paranoia, she looked over at her sister, who had her eyes shut and was clearly enjoying relaxing. She forced herself to be calm; there was no way her sister knew she was pregnant, right?

'I don't doubt we'll both be mums. In fact, I can picture us both holding babies,' Bea said dreamily.

Jeannie curled in towards Beatrice just like she used to. She was always the most emotional in every way. Rose coped quietly while the whole world knew of Jeannie's turmoil and, in turn, her affection.

They talked about the IVF process and Beatrice was pleasantly surprised by how much Jeannie knew.

'I sort of wish I'd told you sooner,' she said. 'I don't think I knew how to, though. Growing up in a house where babies were born most days, I guess it made me feel I should either do it the usual route or not at all.'

'I think you did the right thing by not telling Mum. She'd do what she always does and find fault. She'd knock the air out of a hot-air balloon with her cutting comments at times. But I wish you'd told me and Rose.'

'I wish I had too,' Beatrice agreed. 'I know I'm repeating what we already said, but it can't be emphasised enough . . . Can we make a pact to be more open from here on? We've got one another, so why not lean in?'

Jeannie looked at Bea as she gazed at the ceiling. This was her moment. They were being honest. She really should tell her she was pregnant.

But how could she? The news wasn't fabulously exciting

and wonderful. She didn't even know if she'd keep the child. And what if Beatrice's IVF didn't work? She let the moment go, figuring she might never have to tell her sister about this baby. If her plans went well, she'd conceal the pregnancy, have the child adopted and nobody would be any the wiser. She'd already decided this afternoon that she was going to tell Nick she needed to stay in Ireland for a couple of months to help Beatrice with the shops. After that, she'd have to figure something out when the time came. One step at a time, she mused.

They chatted about Davy and men in general, and Jeannie told her sister how much she still adored Nick.

'I'm glad you do. I'm glad your life is what you want. Because if it's not, you'd be so gratefully welcomed back here.'

'I know, and thank you for saying that,' Jeannie said. 'I was actually thinking of staying around for a while.'

'Are you considering living back here?' Beatrice looked excited for a moment.

'Not really, I like my life. Love it, in fact. If I could shift you, Dad and Rosie and Ali to my house in LA, I'd be complete. But I think I'd like to hang around for a few months, if that's okay by everyone.'

Beatrice snuggled into her shoulder. 'That is truly okay.'

Back in Marine Terrace, Rose was pacing nervously, waiting for Ali to come home. Jim had left to return to Connemara, so the house was horribly quiet. Ali had finished the last of her exams, and she was probably on a high. Rose knew she needed to tell her about Martin, even if it was going to burst her bubble.

Right on time, Ali flew in the door.

'OMG, it's nasty out there. I should've accepted your

offer of a lift. We went for a hot chocolate, but nobody wanted to hang around considering how vile the weather is. I'm going to have a shower and then I'm heading to Katie's before going to the gig. It's going to be so cool.'

'Ali,' Rose said, in a voice that could barely be heard.

'What, Mum? Don't tell me I can't go to the gig. I've bought my ticket. We discussed this last week. Dad said I can stay until the end because I'm coming home with a few people. Katie and Lauren are staying here tonight.'

'I don't want to discuss you going to the gig,' Rose said. 'I need you to sit down for a minute, love.'

'What's going on?' Ali asked, suddenly realising that there might be an issue.

'It's your dad . . . I'm afraid he's left us.'

'What? Are you deranged? Dad wouldn't do that. What have you done? Why has he gone? When did he go?'

As Rose explained about the note, tears flowed from her eyes. 'I'm sorry, sweetheart. I don't know what else to say to you.'

'Oh my God, this is just fabulous. You've clearly caused this. What have you done? It's obviously your fault, because Dad wouldn't leave me. He loves me. We have, like, the best relationship going.'

'Ali, please . . .'

'Don't touch me. This is totally down to you. If you hadn't been a crap wife, he'd have stayed.'

'Ali, that's not fair. It's not my fault that Dad has chosen to—'

'He wouldn't choose to leave me. Not a hope in hell. So this is totally down to you. You're always annoying him and asking him stuff about the shop and going on and on about work. I'd say he couldn't stick another minute with you driving him insane. I'm gonna find him and see where he's living and go there.'

'Ali, don't say that,' Rose choked.

'I hate you. I've always hated you. You're the most old-fashioned, boring person. All you want to do is ruin my fun. You haven't a clue about anything cool. Look at Auntie Jeannie! She's like the coolest person ever. How can you two be, like, twins? It's totally insane.' Tears rolled down Ali's cheeks as her arms flailed.

'Please come and sit down and let's talk about this . . .'

'No way! I'm never sitting anywhere with you again.' With that, she flung open the front door and ran out into the lashing rain.

Rose collapsed into a chair. She truly felt as if she might die of a broken heart. It was one thing knowing that Martin didn't love her. She'd have to work through that in her head. But hearing Ali speaking so harshly to her was quite another. Had she and Martin planned this? Was Rose going to be left alone? How had her daughter built up so much anger towards her?

With her fingers fumbling on the buttons, Rose dialled Ali's mobile. It went straight to voicemail.

'Ali, please come home. Please come back and let's talk about things. I love you so much.'

Next she tried Beatrice's new shop, knowing both her sisters were there.

'Bea, it's Ali . . . she's gone. I told her about Martin, and she went ballistic and ran off into the rain. She could be anywhere.'

'I assume she's not answering her mobile?'

'No. Oh, Bea, what will I do? She really hates me . . . she said such horrible things to me.'

'She's a teenager. She's supposed to say horrible things to you. It's in the unwritten contract that comes with being a mother. She doesn't mean any of it, I promise you.'

Rose continued to sob.

'It's okay,' said Beatrice. 'I have an idea. I'll finish locking up – we were literally about to leave and come over when you called. Jeannie will be with you in a few, and I'll follow, okay?'

'Okay,' Rose parroted. 'See you soon.'

What felt like ten years later, there was a knock on the door. Rose flew to answer it and she and Jeannie fell into one another's arms.

Her mobile rang and she fumbled in her pocket, hoping it was Ali. Instead it was Beatrice, but she had good news.

'I've found her. She's at Becca's house.'

'Oh, thank God. Why didn't I think of that? Well done, Bea.'

'It's okay, you're stressed to the hilt, so don't worry about that. I'm going over there to speak to her. Lucy said she can stay over. She'll make sure they don't go out.'

Rose hung up and cried again.

'She's at Becca's, and Becca's mum has promised to keep them in tonight. Oh, bloody hell, how am I going to manage her without Martin?'

'One step at a time. One day at a time. There's no easy way of doing this.'

For the next hour the twins sat and shared a pot of tea and a large bar of chocolate.

'Uh, why does chocolate taste so good with sea salt and caramel inside? Why does it taste so good full stop?' said Rose.

'It's medicinal,' said Jeannie. 'So that means it has zero calories.'

Beatrice arrived and Jeannie and Rose practically pulled her in half as they hugged her and begged for information.

Ali was still very angry and hadn't wanted to speak to Beatrice at first. If it weren't for Lucy, she wouldn't have spoken to her at all.

'I don't want to see you either,' she screamed at Beatrice. 'You're as much of a cow as Mum. I hate her and I don't want anything to do with any of you assholes.'

'Okay,' Lucy said gently. 'I understand that you're upset. But you cannot stay in this house if you speak to anyone like that.'

Ali looked shamefaced.

'Give Beatrice ten minutes,' Lucy said. 'That's all I ask of you. After that, you can go to Becca's room. You can stay over if you like.'

'Yes please,' said Ali.

'But you have to be polite. I don't need the younger ones hearing you and joining in.'

'I'm sorry, Lucy,' Ali said. 'Sorry, Auntie Bea.'

As it turned out, Beatrice had stayed almost an hour, during which time she had explained how upset Rose was and how she'd never do anything to hurt Ali. She had also reiterated that, sadly, Martin was the bad guy in this scenario.

'I said I knew how close they were,' she told Jeannie and Rose. 'But that Martin had chosen to leave. She knows it's not your fault, but she's so incredibly hurt and she adores her father, so she wanted to blame someone else.'

Rose and Jeannie listened as Beatrice finished off by saying that Lucy had promised to call if anything was said or done that she felt Rose ought to know.

'She's a lovely woman.'

'Yes, she certainly is,' said Rose. 'Ali and Becca have been best pals since the age of three and are a good combination. Ali's fiery, while Becca is calmer and quieter.'

'She sounds like the right person for Ali to be with right now,' said Jeannie. 'A bit like how it's best we have our darling Bea here with us. I'm too feisty and all I want to do is hunt Martin down and have him killed slowly and painfully.'

'Whereas I reckon it might be better if we take stock of what's happening,' Beatrice said. 'We know Ali is safe. So Rose is the priority.'

'Did you tell Dad before he left?' Jeannie asked.

'No,' Rose said. 'He needed to get back to Connemara and I didn't want him fretting. And also, I know that if I'd told him, I'd have been a sobbing mess.'

'Well, fear not,' said Beatrice. 'You've got us and we're going to mind you.'

'Yes, we are,' said Jeannie as she hugged her twin close.

Chapter 20

THE CAPTAIN'S PRIZE WAS THE MOST COVETED AT the golf club. Jim was back from Dublin and eager to join in with the build-up. Each June, the whole community of Ballyshaden looked forward to the dinner-dance. It had been decided several years previously to open the event to non-members. It was the biggest fund-raiser for the club and the whole parish was buzzing in anticipation.

Lots of Martha's new mothers were attending with their husbands, making up tables of farmers, shop-owners, cousins, and couples who simply wanted a good night out.

The marquee people had come from Galway city, and this year, for the first time ever, two of the largest size were required.

'They've joined them together to make the most magnificent ballroom imaginable,' Jim reported. 'There'll be four full buffet tables and four bars to ensure the queues aren't like last year.'

'We missed it because of that stupid thing in the Mansion House. Thank goodness we're not tied to the shop any longer,' Martha said.

'That *stupid thing* was a European Business Awards ceremony and I won a prize, if you recall,' Jim said with a half-smile. 'I wonder if Rose and Martin will be nominated in the coming years. I'd love to see them getting recognition in their own right. It would prove that they are worthy and not just stepping into my shoes.'

'The fact of the matter is that you raised a little chick, and once it was a golden goose, you handed it over to them. Nothing will change that. It's your baby, your hard work and your success, Jim.'

'In that case, you could argue that I did the same. My father started the business.'

'Yes, but it wasn't pulling the profits you got. Our girls were all given the best and have never known hardship. I sincerely hope they appreciate how lucky they are.'

'They're fantastic women, each one of them,' Jim said wistfully. 'They're strong and determined and we've never worried that they're sitting back and doing nothing with their lives. I'm glad we could give them a nice upbringing. But I certainly don't think they take any of it for granted.'

'You were always such a softie with them,' she said, hugging him. 'Between you and Nanny May, they could easily have ended up like those dreadful precious socialites I loathe to see in the backs of glossy magazines. You know those wannabes who think life revolves around parties and looking in the mirror? Although Jeannie is dangerously close to being that shallow.'

'I wouldn't call her shallow, love. You're being unreasonably harsh there. She's married to a man who makes pucks of money out of the very type you abhor. But Jeannie is no fool. She has her life well sorted.'

Martha bristled at his suggestion that she was being unreasonable. 'I suppose. Either way, they're adults now. They don't need to be hanging onto my apron strings.'

'They wouldn't dream of it,' Jim said drily. 'I think

they've always known you're not exactly the mollycoddling type.'

'Maybe not, but I'd like to think I've been a good role model and that I've raised them to be strong and independent.'

'That you have,' Jim agreed. 'I hate to interrupt you, but we're pushed for time. I can't be late.'

'No, of course not. Nor will you be. Give me five minutes and I'll be with you.'

Martha genuinely only needed five minutes too. Her make-up and hair had been done at the Ballyshaden Beauty Salon, using a token given to her by a grateful young mum.

'I thought you might go and have a little treat ahead of the golf club ball,' the woman had said. 'I took the liberty of booking you in with Olivia. She's the best and I know you'll love her.'

Martha had instantly fallen for Olivia when she'd spotted her delicious round bump.

'When are you due?' she had asked as Olivia ran her hands through Martha's hair at the mirror.

'Three weeks and counting,' said Olivia. 'I feel as if I've been pregnant for years. I can't get at the sink to wash any hair and I feel as if I'm shoving my baby in everyone's face while I do make-up.'

A young girl had washed Martha's hair and handed her back to Olivia, who told Martha all about the hospital service up in Galway and how dreadfully the place was run.

'The waiting times for antenatal appointments are a joke. Last time I sat for almost three hours, then they saw me for five minutes and I was so hassled I forgot the questions I wanted to ask.'

'Well if I can help at any time, just call me,' Martha had said, handing her one of her cards. She'd had to reprint four times, a fact that thrilled her.

'I hear you're a wonder, Martha. The women from all the neighbouring towns and villages are flocking to you. You have such a way with people and the women say you're a font of practical knowledge. Not like the hospital. They've shoved the odd leaflet in my direction, but other than that they haven't the time or energy to stop and talk to me.'

'Oh, that is dreadful, Olivia. Girls need to ask questions, especially with a first baby. It's lovely to hear that the locals are appreciating my services. I'm supposed to be retired. My husband is so involved with the golf club that he doesn't realise half of what I'm doing,' she said with a grin. 'I love it and can't bear the thought of not using my skills.'

'Good for you,' Olivia said as she expertly did her eye make-up, following the best blow-dry Martha could recall.

As Martha changed into her evening gown ready for the dinner-dance, Jim's words were sticking in her mind. He rarely made disparaging comments about her. In fact, over the years he'd been nothing but kind and supportive. There had only been a couple of occasions when he'd exploded, and both were to do with the girls.

Once was many moons ago, when she'd missed the twins' Christmas play. She'd been detained at a birth, but Jim had said he wasn't interested in hearing any excuses. The girls had ignored her for days afterwards. She'd felt uncomfortable in her own home, which was grossly unfair. She hadn't missed the play on purpose. But that mother had needed her.

The second time he'd hit the roof was when she'd disappeared during Rose's wedding. She'd gone to the bathroom just prior to the meal and found a girl in the later stages of labour. Calling for help, she'd just about managed to get her to a bedroom before the baby was born. She had to wait for the ambulance crew to arrive. The girl was alone and spoke very little English. What could she have done? Besides, Rose had an entire room of people to talk to. But Jim had been furious and told her so. Rose had never said a word, so she assumed it hadn't bothered her too much.

Martha helped people and gave advice. She was always available to do what she could. So she wasn't like her own mother one bit. But Jim's remarks earlier had made her feel as if she were. The girls were simply spoilt and poor Jim was a very sweet but rather deluded daddy! His three daughters had him wrapped around their little fingers. Bless him, he had no concept of how women worked. She thought it was a cute set-up really. They pulled the wool over his eyes and he loved it.

But she'd long since stopped questioning her own relationship with the girls. They all got along just fine. There were no arguments or falling-outs. Some of the stories she heard from patients would curl her toes. Mothers and daughters shouting and yelling at one another and refusing to speak for years over silly things . . . Oh some of it was shameful! No, Martha was glad they were civil at all times. That way there was no chance of anything untoward happening.

'Hurry along now!' Jim shouted.

Hurry along . . . hurry along . . . She held her hands over her ears. Those were the very words her mother had used that first time she'd lost her temper. Martha couldn't have been more than five or six. Breathing deeply, she tried to quash the memory. Normally she could do it. She could push the images away and make them seem as if they weren't real. But for some reason this evening they didn't want to go.

A dull ache bubbled from the pit of her stomach, the force of it so strong that it made her catch her breath. She gasped and spun on her heel, praying Jim wouldn't come in. Since moving to the cottage, she'd feared he'd see her like this. The house at Marine Terrace was so much larger, and there was always a bathroom to rush to. Here in the solitude of the countryside, with the cosiness of their quarters, she knew she had to be careful.

Grasping the end of the bed for support, she closed her eyes and inhaled deeply through her nose. Sometimes she could stop the wave this way. But tonight it was too late. The panic took over in great ascending waves from the soles of her feet to the top of her head.

One of many quashed scenes played out in her head, the effect so vivid that she felt as if she were right back there. Once more she was a little girl. Her mother, Agatha, came striding into the bedroom and pulled her backwards by her hair, towards the door.

Martha put her adult hand to the side of her head where the physical pain had once been.

She'd wriggled in an attempt to free herself, making Agatha lurch forward and yank her by her school tie. The movement was so violent it made her choke and splutter. Saliva flew from her mouth as she cried out.

'Don't you dare spit on me, you filthy little monster,' Agatha hissed. 'You've ruined my life. You've taken the love I was meant to have. Your father sees nothing but you. I was the priority before, but now I'll always play second fiddle to you.'

She'd been left with red marks on her neck.

'If your father asks, you will tell him you were bullied by a bigger boy in the playground.'

She'd nodded and agreed. But nothing was ever the same from that day. It was as if a spell had been broken and Martha became nothing more than a punchbag for a woman who despised her.

Her three older brothers were away at boarding school and knew nothing. Martha was too terrified to tell anyone what was happening and truly believed she deserved the treatment. After all, her mother was a lady of high regard. She wore strings of pearls and sang like a lark by the piano after dinner parties. She was poised and serene and as elegant as any of the Chanel models in the magazines.

'You antagonise me, Martha. You bring out the worst in me. I hate myself for having to reprimand you, but it's for your own good. You'll end up in the gutter otherwise. You're out of control and it's my duty as your mother to save you.'

When her father announced that she'd stay at home for secondary school rather than taking up a place at the boarding school in Wicklow with the nuns, she thought she would die. She'd been counting the weeks until she could pack a case and get away.

'But I'm ready to go,' she said, sitting on her father's knee. 'I want to go. I've been listening to tales from the boys for years and I want to experience boarding school too.'

'You're too delicate and shy, Martha. You'd never survive and I don't want to destroy you.'

'But I'll make friends.'

'Besides,' her father kissed her forehead, 'I'd miss you too much. You're my princess. I'd fret without you.'

'But I'd send you letters all the time.'

'That won't be necessary,' said Henry. 'Anyway, your mother is going to need you. We have surprise news. You're going to be a big sister.'

Martha looked to her mother, who was pale and wan. 'Mother?'

'Yes, it's true. So you can stay and help me. We'll need a new nanny, of course. But you will be a great help, I'm sure.'

By the time Agatha was ready to give birth, Martha's dysfunctional relationship with her mother seemed to have plateaued. The pregnancy later in life had left Agatha exhausted and too ill to inflict many beatings. She was in bed a lot, and Martha found it easy to avoid her.

Things changed irrevocably when Martha came home from school one bitingly cold winter's day to find Agatha on the hall floor, writhing around in pain with a pool of blood surrounding her.

'Get help,' her mother screamed. 'Call someone before I die here.' She slumped on the floor and there was a thud as her head hit the tiles.

Martha approached her motionless body and instinct kicked in. She bent down and lifted her mother's skirt. Yelping in fear and shocked to the core by the sight of the baby's head bursting between her mother's legs, she wiped the tears that were blurring her vision and thought back to the book she'd studied. What her mother needed right now was a forceps delivery. Knowing she needed to act immediately, she eased her fingers around the baby's crowning head, cupping her hands to create makeshift forceps, and pulled with all her might.

Groaning noises followed by a loud scream did nothing to deter her as she held on as tightly as she could.

'Push!' she screamed.

'I can't,' her mother yelped as her head thrashed from side to side.

'Stop doing that. Use your energy to get this baby out. Push down into your bottom as hard as you can.'

'I can't, Martha.'

'You can and you will. Now push with all your might.'

With that, Agatha bore down and a miracle happened. There was a gush of warm liquid that seeped up her sleeves, but Martha didn't let go. On the next push the head was born, freeing Martha's hands once more.

'Now do it again and I'll pull the baby out,' she said.

'I want to die,' Agatha said as her head rolled back and she looked as if she were losing consciousness again.

'Mother!' Martha stood and walked to Agatha's head. She crouched onto her hunkers. 'You are going to push this baby out. I'm going to help you. It'll be over soon. You can do it. You've done it before and you'll do it again.'

Agatha nodded, her eyes wild. But mercifully she took direction from her daughter. On the next contraction, Martha pulled the baby free.

Shrugging out of her coat, she settled the child there and rushed to the kitchen to fetch a sharp knife. Doing as Agatha told her, she cut the cord before pulling a blanket from the deep box near the hall door.

'Run and get help,' Agatha rasped.

Martha rushed next door and the neighbour called for an ambulance, but by the time it arrived it was too late for the tiny baby. Born many weeks early, she was clearly malformed and the doctor told them she would never have survived.

'Neither would you,' he added gravely, 'if it weren't for your extraordinary daughter. She acted so bravely and you owe her your life.'

Henry was devastated at the loss of the baby girl, but Martha's heroic deeds elevated her further in his eyes.

Agatha never laid a finger on her after that day. Nor would she look Martha in the eye. But something had changed in the little girl. She realised that she had worth and that she could do something right. When she graduated as a midwife, her mother and father held a beautiful reception at the house. That was where she met Jim. He'd come with her brother and it was love at first sight.

She had never looked back after that. She never spoke of the abuse she'd suffered, the pretence continuing even as she stood at her mother's graveside. She shed some tears and said all the right things to the mourners who came to pay their respects.

Jim knew her as a strong and respected woman who would help anyone who needed her. That was the way she wanted to keep it.

But the fear never left her. It lurked in the corridors of her mind and taunted her at the strangest times. She would've remained childless quite happily. She had no idea of how to be a mother. But Jim assumed they would have children and eventually she knew she would have to oblige. She prayed her first would be a boy. She was so conditioned into believing they were better, easier and more wanted.

Jim adored Beatrice on sight. Martha was afraid to show her too much emotion. What if she, too, was a monster on the inside? What if she carried some gene that made her violent towards her own daughter? So Nanny May saved the day. Martha continued to spread her magic to as many pregnant ladies as she could while keeping a safe distance from Beatrice.

The child didn't seem to notice or mind and the arrangement worked well. She and Jim were inseparable. He took her to the shop on occasion and never seemed to tire of doing things with her. He had no fear of minding her as a toddler, even when she was senseless and darted in all directions. They'd go to the zoo for the whole day with Nanny May, and on Nanny May's day off each Sunday, he'd bring Beatrice to the park or drive with her to the lake at Glendalough, where they'd get ice cream and walk for hours.

When she had realised she was expecting twins, Martha had come close to crumbling and telling Jim she couldn't do it.

'Double trouble!' he'd said in delight. She'd nodded, having to bite her lip to stop the tears. 'Oh my darling, you look positively terrified! Nanny May will still be here and you could raise the entire young population of Pebble Bay with your eyes shut! It's going to be busy but so much fun.'

When he had suggested she give up work for a couple of years, she had quickly put a halt to that idea.

'It's totally out of the question. I can't abandon my mothers. Besides, I need to do it. It's what makes me tick.'

Every day of that pregnancy she had prayed the babies would be boys. At least that way she'd ensure the family name was continued, but more than that, she somehow felt she'd relate to them better. Jim could have Beatrice and she would have two adoring sons. She even had names in her head, George and Harry; they would grow into fine strong young men who would tower over her and accompany her to dinner at the golf club, where people would nod and say what handsome sons she had.

All those hopes were dashed when she gave birth to two more girls. She waited until she was in the room on her own to cry. She felt evil at her own disappointment. After all, it wasn't the babies' fault they'd been born to her.

The twins were a handful from the outset, and most mornings she sat into her car and closed her eyes, taking a moment to rid herself of the feeling of mayhem. Jim revelled in it all and very quickly their roles were assigned. She was the strict parent and he was the pushover. He never actually took her to task over her absences and long hours away from the girls. But she knew there were times when she was on thin ice.

The move to Ballyshaden had seemed like the perfect answer. If she was nearing retirement, why not make it somewhere wonderful? Those first few months were torturous. She'd been denied the one thing that made her tick. But now things were a thousand times better than she'd ever imagined. She felt needed, wanted and respected. The ghosts of the past were further from her mind and she knew that Jim was happy too. He loved the golf club and he and Larry were great buddies.

All she needed to do now was hold it together a little

better. Having weak-minded episodes like the one she'd just experienced was not a good plan. After so many years of successfully shielding Jim from the shame of her past, it would kill her to slip up now.

She quickly clasped her necklace around her throat, then touched up her lipstick in front of the mirror.

Sometimes when waves of guilt hit her, she had to remind herself that her girls had everything they could wish for. They had never been beaten or shouted at. She had never been cruel or nasty. She may have been strict at times, and yes, she'd put her foot down on certain issues, but the girls had enjoyed an idyllic childhood in a wonderful home. So the buck had stopped with her. She had broken the cycle. She only had to spend five minutes in a room with Rose and Ali to know that they were close. In fact, she often thought her daughter was slightly suffocating with the girl. But anything was better than the way she herself had been raised.

There were moments when she had to bite her tongue. Ali was prone to cheeky outbursts towards her mother. While Martha certainly wouldn't have stood for that, she knew it was Rose's way, and at the end of the day it wasn't her business.

As she emerged from the bedroom, she was instantly at ease once more.

'Oh, my, look at you!' Jim exclaimed. 'That is simply stunning.'

'Thank you,' she said, beaming with gratitude. 'Beatrice bought it for me.'

'How well she chose. She knows what suits you, that's for sure. You should send her a photo so she can see the full effect.' He rushed to find his phone so he could do just that. Guiltily, Martha realised she would never have thought of showing Beatrice how lovely the dress looked.

As the phone pinged back instantly, Jim's face lit up. 'She's thrilled and says to tell you how gorgeous you look.'

In a pretty shade of palest blue, the dress brought out her eyes and made her ash-blonde hair gleam. She'd complained a few times about her 'old lady arms', as she called them, so she particularly loved the fact that this dress had elbow-length organza sleeves.

'I saw it and thought of you immediately,' Beatrice had said. 'It's my small way of thanking you for the new shop and flat. I know it doesn't even scratch the surface, but it might remind you of how thrilled I am with everything when you wear it.'

'Thank you, darling,' Martha had said as she'd opened the deep pink velvet box that accompanied it. Inside was the most delicate necklace.

'It's a crystal daisy chain in the same shade of blue. I had it made along with the teardrop earrings. I thought they'd finish the look nicely.' There was a goose-down shoulder wrap in off-white as well.

'You have a good eye, Beatrice, I'll give you that,' Martha had said as she'd fingered the jewellery. 'I love all of it. Thank you.'

Beatrice had beamed. Of the three girls, she had always been the most self-aware. Perhaps it was the fact that she was a singleton and the twins had always had an extra unspoken closeness. Of course, she had Jim and everyone knew how much he adored her. But Martha had honestly thought her eldest was made for life after she'd married Davy Moore. She would never understand why she'd let him go.

The whole business had been a disaster. Martha had hated knowing that they were the cause of the twitching curtains in Pebble Bay for some time.

But that was in the past. Beatrice had made her bed now. If she remained single, that was her lookout. Martha wouldn't make the same mistake twice. She'd found herself knee-deep in that unfortunate relationship, becoming very close to the Moore family, and she was mortified when Beatrice refused to continue with the marriage.

Luckily, Rose had Martin. He was a good, stalwart type of fellow. His family weren't local, so there was no need for her to get involved there. He was a no-nonsense sort and they were rock solid. Rose was the most like her, Martha mused. She coped by being uber-organised and staying busy.

Jeannie was their wild card. She'd always been different from the other two. She had a laugh that was infectious and a personality that was impossible to ignore. Over the years Martha had had to be careful to avoid favouring her. But Jeannie's affectionate and bubbly ways didn't seem to feel the invisible force that held her sisters at arm's length. When she announced she was staying in LA, Martha had sobbed. But nobody would ever know it.

She had always assumed Jeannie would marry one of the O'Callaghans or even the Murphys, both of whom had fine sons who were lawyers and auctioneers. She wanted to see her in a salubrious home, driving a high-end car and being treated like a queen. If she was to believe her daughter – and she'd no reason not to – that was happening in LA. Martha had avoided going over there or getting involved, finding it easier to let her daughter go rather than prolong the pain of missing her.

Now Jeannie was planning to come and visit. The other girls were even talking about joining her. It could work out wonderfully, actually. The local girls were full of questions about them and it was high time they got to see them. Ali was a little beauty too, so it would be wonderful to show her off as well.

The evening was rather balmy following on from a day of torrential rain. Apparently the wet weather had gone towards Dublin, so she assumed the girls were now being drenched.

Jim looked like a young man again as he waited patiently in the living room while she gave her make-up a last look in the mirror.

'I hear there'll be lots of taxis at the club this evening. So one of those can drop us home. We can drive there and leave a car.'

'I need mine,' Martha said immediately. 'I have a special class tomorrow. A little session for ladies having second babies. I'm up to capacity, and if it goes well, I might consider putting on another one next week.'

Jim nodded and looked slightly miffed. 'You've no intention of retiring, have you?' he sighed.

'I tried,' she said as they made their way to his car. 'We're wired differently, Jim. You have your golf. It took over from work and you spend hours playing it. If I had the same interest, you wouldn't be cross.'

'I'm not cross. I just wanted you to feel that you didn't have to tear about. I suppose a part of me worries that I'm not enough for you and that's why you're doing this.'

'You've always been more than enough for me, darling. You know that.'

'Have I?' he asked.

The atmosphere was unbearably awkward all the way to the golf club and Jim was the first to get out of the car. He ran around and opened her door, but he didn't look her in the eye.

There was no time to carry on with the conversation at the moment. As they walked towards the club house, they were greeted by numerous people. Jim knew everyone by name and they were obviously delighted to see him. The place looked just as magnificent as he'd promised. The flower arrangements weren't what Martha herself would order if she'd been paying. They were predominantly star-gazer lilies, with those dreadful orange fronds that stained clothing beyond repair. They clashed with the red table-cloths, a matter that would not have come to pass had she been on the committee. She made a mental note to try and get a little more involved with the club. It would probably mean a lot to Jim.

'Martha!' A group of young women from her classes waved and beckoned her over.

'I'll see you shortly,' Martha said to Jim as she walked over to greet them.

By the time the meal was announced and they sat down with Larry and Dorothy, Martha was feeling quite tipsy.

'How are you, Dorothy?' she asked as they began to eat.

'Fine, thank you. I hear you're delivering babies at a rate of knots. I don't know how you do it. I haven't a minute and it's only me and Larry.'

Martha tried to be charitable and give Dorothy a chance. She knew Jim and Larry were great pals and they were set to receive an award this evening. But much as she tried, she couldn't understand the other woman's mindset. She had nothing to talk about outside of her husband.

'I'm guessing you're a little bit envious of our matching his-and-hers look tonight,' Dorothy said, beaming with excitement. 'We went into Galway city a few weeks back. I don't drive long distances as it makes me nervous. So needless to say, Larry was happy to take me, as I wanted a new top for this very occasion.' She poked her ample bosom out, making Martha want to recoil.

'And lovely it is too,' Martha put in.

'You'll never guess what happened next?' Dorothy paused with her hands splayed at either side of her face. Martha leaned in.

'What happened next, Dorothy?' she asked through gritted teeth.

'The sales assistant let us into a little secret. He told us that they had such a wide range of cummerbunds and dicky bows that he reckoned he could find one for Larry so we'd match!' Her delirious giggles made Martha hope that she'd had far more champagne than she'd realised. 'We took my top to the gents' section and he was correct. So that's how Larry and I match.'

Martha looked across the table and squinted. Sure enough, Larry was trussed into a cough-medicine-pink bow tie, the exact lurid shade of his wife's top.

'Isn't that gas!' Martha said.

The stories continued in a similar vein until Dorothy's great revelation of the evening, which was the new flavours of instant hot chocolate that were now available at the supermarket outside town.

'Now don't go to the smaller one in the centre. They don't have the shelf space of the new one. The parking is free too, which is a bonus. I hate having to root for change, don't you? Although I have my little trolley token.'

'Yes, I have one of those too,' Martha said patiently.

'When you walk in the door, go to the second aisle down and you'll see them beside the tea bags. We've got into the habit of having one after our dinner in the evenings. Larry was only saying last night that he never knows what flavour I'll come up with next!' Dorothy giggled as she listed everything from mint to butterscotch. Martha glazed over, wishing she could swat the other woman like a tick.

The wine began to taste metallic and Martha could feel a headache coming on. Mercifully, the speeches began, followed by the prizegiving. Dorothy cried openly and flung herself around Larry as he and Jim returned to the table with their trophy. Jim agreed to let them keep it in their house, saying that they hadn't really any place special to keep it at the cottage.

'We have a trophy cabinet, and believe me, it will take pride of place,' Dorothy said. 'I'll put it in beside the dog collars, Larry, that'd be fitting, I think.'

Larry patted her leg and nodded.

'Dog collars?' Martha asked in spite of herself.

'Yes,' Dorothy said, taking such a deep breath it was clear it was a struggle for her to speak. 'When our beloved pets pass away, we keep a lock of their fur and their collars in a cabinet. So they know they are not forgotten.'

'Why don't you go the whole hog and have them stuffed, with wheels put under their paws so you can still take them for a walk?' Martha asked.

The rest of the couples at the table sniggered as Dorothy looked confused.

'I don't think you can do that, Martha. But I'd certainly consider it for Juju. She's the cutest little dog and we can't bear to even think of a time when she's not with us.'

The band were tuning and the top tables needed to be rolled away to make way for the dancing. So Martha found herself at the bar with the other uprooted guests. Jim was close by, but all the time engaged in chatter. Martha took the opportunity to people-watch. It might be a little place in the middle of nowhere, but Ballyshaden most certainly wasn't lacking in style. There was a decent community of young people still in the area too. The large IT plant that had been finished last year, just before they'd moved in, had kept lots of people in the locality while drawing some new ones in. This was certainly a lovely place to retire to.

The band kicked off the first hour of the evening by appealing to Martha, Jim and their peers. The sounds of Buddy Holly, Chuck Berry and Elvis filled the marquee. Martha kicked off her shoes and tried to pull Jim onto the dance floor.

'Martha, you should know by now that I don't dance unless I've had far too much whiskey. I haven't reached that point yet.'

'Fair enough. You stay here and pour some whiskey down your throat and I'll dance like nobody's watching,' she said with a giggle.

She was away on her own planet, dancing to Chuck Berry's 'Roll Over Beethoven', when she felt someone taking her hands and starting to jive with her. She opened her eyes to see Simon Molloy smiling at her.

'Simon!' she said and let him take the lead. She looked over anxiously at the bar to see how Jim was taking it. Normally if another man tried to dance with her, he'd appear. But he had his back to her and was clearly stuck in the middle of a conversation with some man she didn't recognise. Sod him, she thought. He wouldn't dance with her and now he was ignoring her.

She threw everything into her dancing.

'You dance like a woman half your age,' said Simon with a chuckle. 'I'm going to have to remove my jacket and take a cold drink. Will you join me?'

She was about to say yes when the tempo changed to a slower song. Jim appeared from nowhere and held out his arm, totally ignoring Simon.

'Excuse my husband's rudeness. This is Simon Molloy, we bumped into one another at the club house.'

'I see, and you figured you'd continue the chat on the dance floor?'

'Apologies if I did the wrong thing by dancing with Martha,' Simon said before walking into the crowd at the bar.

'What was that all about?' Martha asked.

'People will talk, Martha. You are well aware of how quickly they make assumptions.'

'There was no harm intended. His wife died and she was a midwife.'

'I see,' said Jim. 'I didn't mean to be rude to the man. I'm not in the mood for whispers, that's all. I like the fact we can do as we please here. So far that's been the case.'

'Let's just forget about it,' said Martha.

'Agreed,' said Jim, 'and I'll make a point of finding Simon and apologising.' He took her in his arms and they began a slow waltz.

'You're happy enough here, aren't you?' Jim asked her. 'It's doable, right?'

'What, the move?'

'And the fact it's just us,' he said, looking vulnerable.

'Of course, you silly goose,' she laughed. 'Why wouldn't I be satisfied with you?'

'I was never sure that you loved me,' he admitted. 'I always felt we were quite distanced from one another. There's a part of you that I know I will never reach.'

Tears welled in her eyes as she looked at the man who had saved her. Yet all these years, he'd thought the wall she had built was to keep him out.

'I love you more than you will ever realise,' she said honestly. 'I was anxious about becoming redundant. I never want to be the person at the table who talks about flavours of hot chocolate as if it's world news. But working and delivering babies makes me feel worthy.'

'You've nothing to prove any more, though. Why don't you take a step back? Learn to potter. Learn to sit and knit . . .'

'Maybe someday,' she said with a smile.

As they left hand in hand, deciding to give the dance floor over to the younger ones, Martha knew she was incredibly lucky. She'd known what it was like to live in fear and to have someone despise her just for breathing. Jim was her soulmate and she was blessed he was there.

The receptionist at the club offered to call them a taxi. She put her hand over the phone receiver and beckoned for them to come closer.

'If you want an official taxi with the writing on the car and the light-up thing on the roof, you'll be waiting an hour. Or Joseph Michaels is doing a few sneaky sidelines for the night to make a bit of extra cash. He's outside and will spin you home for six euros.'

Jim looked at Martha and grinned.

'Tell Joseph he has a fare.'

They were as giddy as teenagers as Joseph's car slunk around the corner.

'How is it possible to make yourself look guilty while driving?' Martha giggled.

'He's enterprising, I'll give him that,' Jim said. It took all their resolve to hold it together as they sat into the back of the battered Ford Cortina.

'Evening, folks. I took the liberty of laying a few picnic blankets on the seats. I knew you'd be in your finery and you probably don't want Jack Russell hairs stuck to your rear ends.'

The exhaust kicked back and a belch of smoke filled the air. Jim was busy stifling his laugher, so he didn't see the spectacle that stopped Martha's heart. There in the darkness of the car park was Larry, unmistakable in his cough-medicine-pink bow tie, minus his tuxedo jacket, with the full glare of his cummerbund showing. Only it wasn't Dorothy he was kissing. If Martha's eyes weren't deceiving her, it was young Olivia from the beauty salon.

Chapter 21

THE LETTER WAS STILL SCRUNCHED IN A BALL AT the bottom of Rose's bag where she'd left it a couple of days ago.

Work had been hell. The orders for the six apartments were ready for processing, and in Martin's absence she'd had to double-check each one herself. Knowing she couldn't sit and cry or else the contract would be whipped away, she picked up the phone and called two of the staff who were meant to be on days off. Mercifully, Steffy and Cara both obliged. Both were trained to run the shop floor, so it meant Rose could stay in the office and concentrate on the paperwork.

'Nice of your husband to leave you in the lurch,' said Jack, one of their longest-standing carpenters, with a smirk. 'Don't tell me, he's got man flu?'

'He's decided to go away and do a course,' she said, the lie tripping off her tongue frighteningly quickly. 'It was too good an opportunity to miss.'

At the end of business, she told all the staff that Martin wouldn't be back for at least six months. None of them dared question her, but she could tell that they were curious.

She was astonished to see that Martin had done absolutely nothing to progress the contract. She'd put a lot of ideas in place when they made the pitch, but he'd left it all dead in the water. It was a blessing in disguise that he'd gone and she'd stepped in. At least it was still early days and she could pick it up and get it going properly.

On autopilot, she made her way home, stopping to pick up nibbles from the deli.

'Maybe we'll get food delivered from the Thai restaurant tonight as a treat. I'm far too tired to consider cooking. What do you reckon?'

'Fine,' Ali said.

Rose tried to be jolly, but Ali communicated in grunts and eye-rolling.

'Are you hungry?' Rose asked. 'I'm starving, and I'd guess that Auntie Jeannie will be looking for something tasty too.'

She set the table and Ali went off to her room, kicking the door shut. Rose closed her eyes and tried to remain calm. She was getting sick of being treated like a moron all the time. She knew Ali was only fifteen and hadn't the maturity to understand why her father had left them in the lurch. She herself was thirty-eight and was struggling to get a grasp of why he'd done this. But there was a fine line between being emotional and being a little B.

Mercifully, Jeannie arrived with hugs and smiles.

'Do you have any idea how glad I am to see you? I'm on the edge with Ali. She's unbelievably rude and I'm just about to explode.'

'Let's hope that things improve now I'm here. She won't dare be rude if we give her the glower,' said Jeannie. 'She was pretty darn awful this morning. I was just about to grab her and put her in her bedroom. But she's almost as tall as me and I can't interfere.'

'Thank you for being here,' said Rose.

Jeannie said, 'I'll stay as long as you both need me.'

Their takeaway arrived and they ate. Rose pushed her food around her plate and it was clear she needed some adult conversation. Eventually Ali said she was off to her room, and within a few minutes, loud, thudding music boomed out.

'I had to say something to everyone at work. The contract needed to be sorted and there literally wasn't a spare moment. The good news is that they all know now. So I can rely on them to pull together.'

'What did you tell them?'

'That he's gone to do a course and he won't be back for at least six months. They're not stupid, they know he's fecked off. But the news is out, as I said, so tomorrow can be just another day.'

'Can I see the note?' Jeannie asked.

'It's in my bag,' Rose said as she pulled the cork from a bottle of white wine. 'Right now, I need to guzzle some of this.'

Jeannie went and fished it out, then came back to the kitchen and smoothed it out on the counter.

'Jeez, it's hardly an essay considering it's his final farewell.'

Dear Rose,

I have been contemplating this move for some time. I haven't been happy for many years and I don't believe you could possibly be either.

I appreciate that it's not ideal for me to do this while Ali is still young. But there will never be a right time to go, so I'm doing it now.

I am going to London to start a new life. Everything is set up. I have accommodation and a job. I will of course stay in touch as I will always be Ali's father. I will be sharing a house with three others at first so I won't be in a position to have her to stay just yet.

I deserve to find happiness and so do you. So in truth I am doing us both a favour. I know this will come as a shock to you, but once you have time to digest it, I feel you will come to the same conclusion I have. We haven't acted as husband and wife for many years. We are nothing more than friends, and while that is a wonderful thing, it simply isn't enough for me any longer.

I have taken a sum of twenty thousand euros from the business. I have also removed half of the money left over from the sale of our house. Obviously you and Ali will remain at Marine Terrace, so you are gaining in this respect.

I will contact Ali in a few days. She will need time to settle when she hears the news.

I know Jeannie will support you along with Beatrice and your parents. But I hope you can be grown up about this and realise that this is the right move for us both.

Be happy, because you deserve to be. Don't blame yourself. Both of us failed in this marriage, but most of all it was me. I know I've let you down and I will hate myself for ever for that.

We have many years ahead of us. Don't waste yours being bitter or angry about me. Move on, move upwards and be the best version of you possible.

Thank you for the years we spent together. I hope they weren't all bad.

I will be in contact.

Yours truly,

Martin

'They weren't all bad? Is he fucking deranged?' Jeannie yelled. 'What kind of a nutter is he? Well, all I can say is that I take my hat off to him in a way. I never thought he had it in him. I thought he was beige and would never step out of line.'

'There's a bit more to Martin than meets the eye,' Rose said as she drained her wine glass. She filled it up again immediately. 'Help yourself. I know I've the manners of a pig and I'm being like a teenager knocking this wine back, but I need to feel numb.'

Jeannie ignored the wine and was relieved to realise that Rose wasn't monitoring what she was drinking. She simply needed to get very drunk very quickly and no doubt she'd fall into bed.

'What are you going to do?' Jeannie asked.

'Carry on. Be brave and do the right thing by my daughter. Carry the can, be the one who has to do the work, run the house and pretty much pick up the pieces.'

'Nice.' Jeannie nodded. 'Yeah, you're dead right. You've no choice but to knuckle down and get on with it.'

Rose drank more wine and Jeannie listened as she stared straight ahead and described a marriage that sounded about as much fun as a kick in the head. The sex had stopped soon after Ali was born. Martin had attended the birth and told her he was traumatised afterwards. He said he couldn't look at her the same way and that he needed time.

'I tried to speak to him about it and he cut me dead,' Rose said. 'I often asked him if there was someone else.'

'And was there?'

'I tried to tell myself there wasn't, but yes, there was,' Rose admitted.

'Well you can't honestly think that man has been celibate for nearly fifteen years?'

'I know, but it's weird,' Rose said. 'I was shocked when he admitted to it because he never commented on other people. For instance, take Steffy who works at the shop.'

'I haven't met her,' Jeannie said.

'Well I'm sure you will. She's six foot tall, has jet-black hair and the most perfect body, with a washboard stomach and huge boobs.'

'Real or fake?' Jeannie asked.

'As far as I know they're real. But she's not afraid to show them off. She's not slutty or in your face, but there's no denying she has a presence, especially with men.'

'Good for her,' Jeannie said with a nod of approval.

'I asked Martin what he thought of her soon after she started working with us. His answer was that she had sorted the top shelves in the storeroom without a ladder. He actually sat and shook his head, looking impressed.'

'Ah, he was having you on,' Jeannie said. 'You'd have killed him if he'd said she was a firecracker with fabulous tits.'

Rose pondered for a moment before giving Jeannie several other examples of how uninterested Martin was in the opposite sex.

'So you think he's gay, is that it?' Jeannie said, looking as if she finally understood.

'I honestly don't know,' said Rose with a sigh. 'He had no interest in men either, as far as I could see.'

As Rose finished the bottle of wine, Jeannie looked twice as confused as before. She couldn't fathom why Martin had left so suddenly.

'I have to go to bed,' Rose said. 'Sorry, I have so much

work on tomorrow and I'm feeling tired from the wine. I'm probably going to be dying of a hangover. Nighty-night, sweetie.'

'Nighty-night,' Jeannie said, hugging her tightly. 'You don't have to do this on your own. I'm here. We're all here for you, okay?'

'Okay.'

'I love you.'

'Love you too,' Rose said as she stumbled into her room.

Once she was in her bedroom, she finally exhaled. She pulled her clothes off and found a nightdress that would do. Kicking her clothes into a ball in the corner, she fell into bed not even bothering to remove her make-up, which was something she'd never done before.

She knew she should feel desolate and awful without Martin. She should be bawling her eyes out right now, devastated that her marriage was over. But all she felt was relief. The atmosphere was gone. The tension that they were sharing a bed but not having a sexual relationship was finally over. She hadn't realised how trapped she'd felt.

When they'd moved to Marine Terrace, Rose had stupidly thought things might improve. They did in the sense that he started to kiss her again. No unbridled passion, but he'd peck her on the lips when he left for work. Or if she walked into the shop, he'd hug her and kiss her on the cheek. At first that felt strange and she had even caught herself putting her hand up to her face to touch the spot where he'd kissed her.

But they hadn't had an open conversation about the lack of contact for years.

After Ali was born, she'd been perfectly happy to abstain

from sex. That was natural. But when she'd attended her six-week check-up at the hospital and the doctor had asked if she wanted to discuss contraception options, she'd clammed up.

'I have to let you know,' said the gynaecologist, 'that breastfeeding isn't a reliable form of contraception. Many women believe it is, so if you want to avoid another pregnancy right now, you need to take action.' She said she'd be happy to ask Martin to use condoms for the moment. She didn't want to take the pill while breastfeeding, and the thought of a diaphragm didn't appeal.

'Let me know or attend your GP if you change your mind,' said the gynaecologist as he gave her the green light and told her she was in perfect physical health. Her uterus had returned to the normal place and her stitches had healed nicely.

They'd gone to a coffee shop near the hospital. It was a big, bustling place and although it was by no means full, there were plenty of people about.

They took a corner table so Ali's pram could be tucked in beside them.

Rose sat and waited as Martin queued up for their order.

'Now, I know you said you didn't want anything to eat, but the lady was raving about the carrot cake, telling me she'd used her mother's recipe, so I took a slice along with a little square of lemon drizzle cake.'

'Thank you, but I'm really trying to shift the last of the baby tummy. I'm sick of not being able to wear my work skirts. I have so many suits that I can't quite squeeze into but I'm too small for the maternity things.'

'You also said you want to burn them because you can't bear to look at them!' Martin grinned. 'Don't have the cake if you don't want it.' He put his hand over hers. 'If it makes any difference for you to hear it, I think you look great. You're doing so well and you should give yourself a break, Rose.'

'Thanks, love,' she said, welling up. 'That is so nice to hear. I know we haven't "resumed intimacy",' she said, making quotation marks in the air and using a deep voice to hide her embarrassment, 'but now that the six-week check-up is done, I don't see why we shouldn't get back in the saddle, so to speak.'

'Rose!' he gasped, looking around wildly as if she'd just asked him to have sex there and then on the coffee table. 'People will hear you.'

'No they won't,' she said with a laugh. 'They're not within earshot. Besides, who cares? We're not saying anything awful.'

They'd changed the subject and talked about work. Many of their conversations revolved around Bespoke Design, but that never bothered her because it was obviously her dad's passion and they were delighted to be involved. Martin had been in a meeting with Jim the day before and Rose was curious to know how it had gone.

'It was great. Jim has a lot of confidence in me. I'm not used to being championed this much, if I'm honest. He's giving me more and more responsibility and wanted to make sure I'm okay with it.'

She'd been pleased for him and said so. Rose wasn't officially on maternity leave and she'd been bringing baby Ali to work to do the odd thing since she was a few days old. So that day she decided to let Martin go on ahead to the shop while she took a stroll around the clothes shops in Pebble Bay.

He scuttled away and Rose had made her way to the shopping centre on the outskirts of the village.

When it was built, many of the locals thought it would ruin Pebble Bay. But in actual fact it had complemented it. The land had been unused, and apart from the odd influx of travellers' horses from time to time, it was redundant. The shopping centre was two storeys high and housed high-street fashion outlets and a good M&S. It had multi-storey parking too, so it had actually breathed new life into the place.

Pebble Bay's main street still had charm, and people went there either to eat at one of the many restaurants or to find specialist shops, such as Beatrice's bridal boutique or the gorgeous shoe shop, Azur, which carried more unique and special brands than the usual high-street chain store.

Rose was on a mission that day. She wanted to find a set of sexy underwear to surprise Martin that night. She had in mind a bra and pants set with a little teddy-style negligee to go over it. Not wanting to spend a fortune, she hit the high-street shops. In the second one she found exactly what she was looking for. Opting for a soft rose-pink shade, she made sure it was big enough so she wouldn't be oozing out in all the wrong places.

Chancing her arm, she dropped into Liza at Pebble Bay Beauty Boutique and asked if she could possibly fit her in without an appointment for some waxing.

'Can I do it this second?' Liza asked. 'I have a client in ten minutes, but that's all I'd need for a half-leg wax with bikini line.'

'Done!' said Rose, who was crossing her fingers that sleeping baby Ali would give her a few precious minutes more.

A short time later, hair-free and feeling giddy on the inside, Rose made one last stop, in the village off-licence, where she picked out a bottle of pink Moët champagne.

'Are you celebrating something special, Rose?' John asked.

'No, I just thought I'd make a nice dinner for my husband tonight.'

'Good for you,' he said. 'Any day can be a champagne day. You're dead right. Enjoy it!'

At the time, they were in their new home, a town house with a postage stamp of a garden out the back and enough space for one car at the front. But it was theirs and they were delighted with it.

She put the champagne in the fridge, checked the steaks were defrosted and looked in the freezer to make sure there were enough oven chips. She had loads of salad leaves, and a jar of garlicky French dressing would add a bit of flavour.

The afternoon and early evening passed in a jiffy, and by the time Martin walked through the door, the table was set and Ali was fed and happy in a bouncy chair.

'Hi, love,' Rose called out. 'I hope you're hungry. I've an enormous T-bone steak for you!'

'Yum,' he said, as he walked over to tickle Ali's tiny foot.

As Rose presented him with a glass of champagne, he looked confused.

'What's all this about?'

'I'm celebrating life!'

'In your dressing gown at seven o'clock in the evening?'

She raised an eyebrow and smiled. Clinking his glass, she took a deep slug of champagne to give her courage. Then, sucking her stomach in and rounding her shoulders so she was standing up straight, she set her glass on the mantelpiece and pulled her dressing gown open. Slowly she shrugged it off her shoulders and let it slide to the floor. Momentarily she felt like a total fool standing in her underwear with high heels on.

She put her arms around his waist and pulled him towards her, tilting her head to try and kiss him. She planted the kiss on his motionless lips as he stared straight ahead. He didn't flinch or push her away. But he stood like a board.

'Martin?' She smiled nervously. 'Will we go upstairs for a minute?'

'What about the baby?' he asked, looking perplexed.

'She's happy there with her little baby gym.'

'So you're going to abandon our daughter with no supervision while you get your jollies?' He shook his head and looked at her as if she'd lost her mind. 'Besides, I'm not some sort of machine you can put a coin into and expect me to perform.'

'I thought if we had a little champagne and I was looking a bit sexy . . .' She trailed off. 'I thought you might want to . . .'

'I appreciate you've made a massive effort here, Rose. I haven't seen those things before,' he waved his finger around, 'so I'm guessing you bought them. But I'm not in the mood. I've had a long day. Could we do this another time?'

She picked up her dressing gown and pulled it back on. Taking her shoes off one by one, she cradled them in her arms before speaking.

'Do you not love me any more?'

The words hung in the air, floating to the floor like feathers.

'Of course I love you,' he said, setting his champagne glass on the mantelpiece beside hers. 'I just don't think I can make love to you just yet.'

'Because I'm flabby?'

'No,' he laughed. 'Nothing like that. You look just fine. I . . . Rose, the truth of the matter is that I can't banish the image of Ali's head and body coming out of you. I found it horrific. Like something from a horror movie. And I cannot fathom putting myself . . . eh . . . having sex with you . . .'

'But you cut the cord. You held her and cried. You leaned over and kissed me and said I was the most amazing woman in the world. You told me I was a miracle worker and you were in awe of me . . .'

'I was . . . I am . . . I wasn't lying. But I can't banish the image. It looked like there was an alien emerging from your body. For weeks after she was born I had nightmares about it. Now I'm at the point where I am trying to come around to the idea that it's natural.'

'I had no idea,' she whispered. 'I suppose I didn't see any of that because I was the one giving birth. I'm sorry you're so traumatised. Do you think you could have some counselling maybe?'

'I beg your pardon?' he said, looking increasingly annoyed. 'What do you think I'd say? Hello, I'm here because I can't bear to touch my wife after seeing a person being pulled like a slimy extraterrestrial from between her legs.'

Rose knew that having a baby was the most incredible miracle. She also saw it as a privilege. So nothing Martin said was going to change her mind. But she couldn't help feeling uncomfortable that he clearly found her so repulsive.

She finished her champagne, now needing it to steady her nerves, and walked into the kitchen. She heard Martin talking to Ali and said a quick prayer of thanks that he was nice to her at least. He could've decided she was abhorrent and rejected her too.

Their meal wasn't what she'd hoped for. She was still wearing the underwear, which was scratchy and uncomfortable, and she was far too warm in the bulky dressing gown, but there wasn't a chance in hell she was taking it off.

Martin ate hungrily and through a full mouth of steak complimented her cooking.

As he set his knife and fork down, he looked over and noticed her steak was barely touched.

'Are you not hungry?'

'Not really,' she said, staring him directly in the eyes.

'If you're planning on throwing it out anyway, can I have it?'

'Sure.' She pushed the plate across the table. 'Be my guest.'

He demolished her meat too and filled his glass with champagne, glugging more into hers as well. She drank it quickly and sat with her hands in her lap, not sure what she ought to do next.

'I'll wash up, love. Fair is fair,' he said. 'That was a lovely meal and the champagne was delicious.'

He bustled about the kitchen, almost humming, while she stayed in her chair, rooted to the spot by rejection and humiliation. Eventually she pushed her chair back and walked up to their bedroom, where she stepped out of the negligee and peeled off the underwear. Finding a pair of cotton pyjamas, she brought them into the bathroom and locked the door. Not sure what she was supposed to do next, she stared into space and cried.

Feeling like a fool, she cleaned her face and brushed her teeth, wanting to crawl into bed and never come out again.

She could hear Ali crying downstairs. The cries grew louder and louder until she heard a knock on the bathroom door.

'Rose? I think she wants you. Is she due a bottle yet or are you going to breastfeed? I can never remember which one is the bottle feed.'

'It's the ten o'clock feed from the bottle to get her through more of the night,' she said. 'I'll feed her now.'

She unlocked the door and took the sobbing baby from him without speaking. She fed her, changed her nappy and put her in her pyjamas before Martin came looking for them.

'There's an Indiana Jones movie starting and I'm really in the mood for watching it. Why don't you have an early night? I'll take Ali and give her the late-night feed.'

'Thanks,' she said sadly, handing him the wriggling baby. He cooed at her and smiled as Rose stood there.

'Martin, what are we going to do?'

'You're going to bed and I'm watching—'

'I mean, what are we going to do about our marriage?'

'Now that I've said it to you, I'm hoping things improve,' he admitted. 'I've been harbouring it all these weeks. But I feel as if a weight has been lifted from my shoulders.'

Yes, and you've dumped it right onto mine, she thought.

'We need to keep communicating about it,' she said with a sigh. 'You've made me feel terrible tonight. I don't want that to happen again.'

'Hey,' he said, planting a kiss on her forehead. 'Don't feel bad. It's not your fault. I'll have to get over it.'

Agog, she watched him walk off with Ali. She hadn't meant for one second that she felt terrible for making him traumatised. She'd meant that she felt unattractive, ugly and a freak and she quite frankly wanted to punch him.

She went to bed and held her mobile phone in her hands. She longed to call Jeannie or Beatrice. She needed to tell someone what was happening. But she was so mortified, she couldn't put it into words. Hoping it might all seem better the following day, she curled up in bed and fell asleep. It was so long since she'd had alcohol that it knocked her out.

Martin was gone to work when she woke the next morning. Each time she'd attempted to broach the subject after that, he shot her down.

'Leave it, Rose. You're making things worse by going on about it.'

'Not now, Rose, I'll tell you when the time is right.'

'Not that again, let's discuss it later . . .'

Time passed and she gave up trying.

She also stopped reaching her hand over for his. She stopped spooning him at night and she didn't bother kissing him goodbye. His attitude towards her never changed. He was respectful at work, he helped with Ali and when they were in company he was always attentive. Nobody would've guessed there was anything amiss with their marriage. There were times when Rose herself questioned it. She even tried to come around to the notion that most couples were the very same.

But conversations with friends and Jeannie told her the opposite. She recalled one particular day when she met a few of the mothers from Ali's class at school. It was about a year ago. One of the women, who was known for being quite loud and honest to a fault, had leaned in and told the others that she was relieved her husband had gone to Spain to play in a golf tournament for a week.

'It's a corporate thing and Darren goes each year. They're wined and dined and get to use the most magnificent golf course imaginable.'

'Sounds wonderful,' said Rose.

'Well, girls, the best part for me is that I'm off the hook, if you catch my drift?'

'How do you mean?' Rose asked, smiling.

'I adore Darren,' she said. 'God knows, if anything happened to him, I would be lost. But he has the sexual appetite of a man in his twenties. Sometimes I want to lock myself in the spare room and tell him to sort himself out!' She roared laughing and the other women joined in.

'Jeepers, you're hilarious,' one of them said. 'But I have to say I sympathise.'

'Now that we're all having a moment, my hand is up over here too,' said another. 'The older I get, the less I want it. I would be perfectly happy with once a month. It's exhausting and I get so sweaty that a part of me wants to run from the bedroom afterwards and jump into a shower and scrub myself.'

'I hate it when Liam comes in and slobbers all over me with scratchy stubble and I've just put on my eye-wateringly expensive night moisturiser!' They all laughed, including Rose. All eyes were on her so she knew she needed to say something.

'I'm with you girls. I'd happily go to bed in my onesie if I thought I could get away with it!'

'Now that's a subtle hint if ever I heard one!'

Afterwards, as she walked into the shop and spotted Martin chatting to a customer, she felt a rush of anger. Why were they stuck in a sexless marriage? She didn't expect him to perform non-stop, but she had needs and desires and it was perfectly normal to want some form of closeness with her own husband.

'Martin, when you've a minute, I need to speak with you in my office.'

He nodded, and she walked in and shut the door. She wasn't going to let it drop.

She waited twenty minutes, then forty, and he still hadn't appeared. She was in such a state that she couldn't get on with work or pretend she was fine. Calling his mobile, she asked him to come immediately.

He walked in and shut the door, full of apologies, saying he'd been detained on the shop floor. 'So what's up?' he asked, looking hassled and busy.

'Martin, we need to talk about us. Our relationship and the fact that we don't have sex.'

'Bloody hell, Rose,' he hissed. 'Keep your voice down. What if the staff or a customer hears you?'

'I actually don't care,' she said. 'What are we going to do?'

He sat opposite her and reached across the desk and took one of her hands.

'I love you, Rose. We have a good thing going. We have Ali. Not everyone has what we've got. You should be grateful and stop questioning things. It could be a lot worse. I think we do okay.'

'But don't you miss having sex?'

'Not at all,' he said. 'I take care of that.'

Rose stared at him and her blood went cold. 'What does that mean?'

'But I thought . . . I mean, you know by now, right?'

'Know what?' Rose's throat was so tight, she could hardly squeeze the words out.

Martin sighed impatiently. 'Come on, Rose, we're adults. With things as they are at home – which is no one's fault, I hasten to add – well, you know, I have a friend with benefits.'

Rose felt like she'd been punched in the chest. For him to sit there and tell her this, so casually – he was ripping the heart out of her and he didn't even know. He didn't seem to care. She stared at him, unable to speak.

'Sorry,' he said, holding his hands up. 'I presumed you knew. Besides, I figured you and Declan . . .'

'Declan? As in the delivery driver from the furniture warehouse?'

'Well, the two of you always talk for longer than necessary and you make him coffee and he comes up here.'

'So you think I've been shagging a delivery man in my office? He has a child in Ali's year at school and his wife died of cancer three years ago. He comes to me for a coffee some days . . . I wasn't . . . I'm not having a relationship with him.'

'Oh, right.' Martin raised an eyebrow and nodded. 'Fair enough.'

She couldn't quite fathom what she was hearing. Not only was Martin having an affair, but he'd assumed she was having one too – and was even quite happy with the fact.

'There's something really messed up going on here,' she said. 'It can't carry on. I can't live this way . . .'

'Why not? What's changed between today and yesterday?'

Closing her eyes, she told him to get out. She said she'd need to think things through.

Martin walked from the room with the same demeanour as when he'd arrived. He wasn't put out by admitting to having an affair and clearly he didn't think any of it was a big deal.

Rose thought of Ali. She thought of the business and their home life. She thought of her parents and Jeannie and Beatrice. They'd all be disgusted with Martin and furious that he'd been so dishonest.

When she got home that night, everything panned out as usual. Martin and Ali were both happy and she knew that if she wanted things to change, she would have to do something about it herself.

She decided she was going to ask him for a trial separation, but then her parents announced they were moving to Connemara and handing the business over to them, along with the house. In fact, her father told Martin before he told her. She was called into his office to find the two men grinning from ear to ear, with an atmosphere of celebration in the air that was utterly palpable.

'You'll never guess what Jim is offering us, Rose! This is a pinch-me-quick moment. Tell her, Jim, tell her!'

Rose had rarely seen her husband so animated. For his part, her father was so proud, pleased and openly excited about sharing the news that she found herself being swept along.

'Tell me what?' she giggled.

'I'm signing the business over to you and Martin!' The words came tumbling out. Rose perched on a chair alongside her husband and listened open-mouthed as her father let her know the wheels were already in motion.

There were hugs and kisses and Martin picked her up and swung her around. Once he'd thanked her father again, he snatched his keys out of his pocket, tossed them in the air and caught them, saying he was happier than he'd ever imagined possible.

'I need to get to that rebuild in Sandymount village. Sorry to rush away, folks, but I'm guessing it might be appropriate for you two to have a private chat too.'

'There's nothing I want to say that can't be said while you're here,' Jim said. 'But off you go! This is why I'm so happy to be handing my business over to both of you. You adore it, you give it your all and I know you'll take it to the next level.'

So more time passed. The web grew thicker and tighter, and Rose could see no way out. Her life was good in so many ways. She was healthy, she had money and a stunning home, and until recently they were the perfect unit from the outside. But inside the house, Rose could see Martin stepping back, retreating in every way. He was clearly distancing himself slowly. Preparing, she thought bitterly, to walk away for good.

She shuddered as she thought of what her parents were going to say. She couldn't care less about the general public. People separated and got divorced all the time. It was hardly unusual, but she had a feeling her parents would blame her.

Either way, there was now a line drawn in the sand.

It meant she could stop lying and start living again. Ali didn't need this right now. The poor kid was having an awful time. But she'd get her through. Rose would make certain of that. Who knew what the future would hold.

Flinging Martin's pillows on the floor, she moved her

own pillows into the middle of the bed and looked around. She'd get this room done up, she decided. There was a stunning pink and lime-green silk wallpaper in stock at the moment that would look amazing. She was going to start going to the gym too.

In fact, she thought with determination, she was going to start living a whole new life. One where she called the shots and didn't feel as if she were looking over her shoulder or telling lies all the time.

Who knew, maybe she'd even try and have sex at some point again too.

Chapter 22

JEANNIE WAS IN THE SHOWER AFTER A FAIRLY SOLID night's sleep. She was finding the pregnancy thing so difficult. It was becoming harder to hide it too. As the water from the round rainfall shower cascaded down her body, she exhaled happily. She'd love nothing more than a duvet day today.

Luckily the weather was better than she remembered, so she was getting away with wearing her large array of maxi dresses. They were soft and flowy and covered a multitude.

Yawning, she meandered into the kitchen and yelped as Rose came out of her room too. 'Sorry, you gave me a fright.'

'No worries, lovey, how did you sleep?'

'Okay,' she said. 'And you?'

'Yeah, not so great. I'm really sorry. Was I awful last night?'

'No, honey, you could never be awful.'

Rose peeked around Ali's door and screamed. 'Oh Jesus! She's gone. Oh my God, Jeannie. Where is she? She went to bed as usual last night. Where the hell is she? Oh my God, has she run away?'

Rose's face had drained of colour and Jeannie feared she was about to faint.

'Don't worry. Just wait. I'll try Becca's mum. Hopefully she hasn't gone too far.'

They heard the front door open and both ran to the top of the stairs and looked down.

'Hip hip hurray! She's home,' said Ali as she staggered into the hall. 'Let's have an early-morning party. Gin on your cornflakes, anyone? We have both colours. We also have straws, apparently that makes you get drunk quicker.'

Rose was down the stairs just ahead of Jeannie. She stood in front of her daughter, her face white, her hands clutched in tight fists. Jeannie arrived beside her and stared at Ali.

'What's happened?' she asked breathlessly. 'Are you okay?'

Ali burst out laughing and snorted, stumbling into the wall and then over towards Jeannie.

'Par-tay!' she said, punching the air. 'What's wrong, ladies? Too much fun for you? Mum's a boring dry shite, so that's no surprise. But I thought you'd be up for a bit of fun, Auntie Jeannie.' She lurched into the kitchen and perched dangerously on a bar stool, grinning at them and swaying slightly.

Rose looked at Jeannie in shock. 'What am I going to do with her?'

Jeannie reached out and squeezed her arm. 'Can I handle this?' she asked. 'Remember Cassie Smyth's party when we were fourteen?'

'How could I forget?' said Rose. 'You were determined to get blotto drunk.' The penny dropped and she nodded. 'Okay, you're going to speak from experience.'

'Yup.'

Between them, Rose and Jeannie helped a protesting Ali into her bedroom, removed her shoes and swung her around onto her bed.

'Would you make some tea and toast, please?' Jeannie asked Rose.

At first Ali refused to eat or drink anything. She kept falling asleep, but just as Jeannie was about to give up and leave the room, she agreed to take the food and drink for a bit of soakage.

'I'll take it from here,' said Jeannie.

Rose nodded gratefully and left the room.

Instead of giving out or preaching, Jeannie took the attitude of congratulating Ali for managing to do what she'd done.

'Your mother wasn't interested in getting trashed. She was too scared of what would happen. She's one of those people who thinks about the consequences, whereas you and I just go for it. We do whatever the hell we like and feck the rest of them.'

'Yeah,' said Ali. 'Mum is *so* boring she makes me want to shake her.'

'She's one of those people who sits around and waits for her daughter to get home, even if she has work the next day. She does anything she can to make her daughter happy, and no matter what, she'll take the abuse that's hurled at her because she's so terrified of losing her.'

There was silence for a moment before Jeannie stood up and grabbed a packet of make-up wipes. Gently she tried to dab at a scratch on Ali's face. Wincing, Ali snatched the wipe and rubbed at it.

'Sore?' Jeannie asked.

Ali nodded.

'Who were you with last night?' Jeannie asked.

Ali's face coloured a little. 'Friends,' she said defensively.

'Your mum mentioned someone called Ross. Were you with him?'

Ali shrugged and wouldn't meet Jeannie's eye.

'I need you to tell me one thing,' Jeannie said. Ali's head swung around and she stared at her. 'We don't need to tell anyone else. Did you have unprotected sex with him?'

She shook her head.

'There's no judgement here,' Jeannie said, holding her hands up.

'We were too drunk. The cuts on my face are from a fall. I fell in the park. Then he walked off and left me there on my own. I just curled up on a bench. I was so tired. Then I woke up when it got bright and came home.'

'He sounds like a classy type of guy.' Jeannie paused for a bit. 'You know that when you act the way you did, they're the sort you're going to end up with.'

Ali eyed her sullenly, but Jeannie could tell she was listening and taking it in.

'Your mother is beside herself. She can't handle you. She doesn't know what to do. She never did stuff like this. But I did. It didn't end well. The final straw came when I ended up in hospital on New Year's Eve totally blacked out and they had to pump my stomach. I missed the party, I missed my friends, because most of them stopped talking to me. But most of all, I missed being respected. It took me a long time to work that back. For people to stop seeing me as a stupid drunken mess.'

Ali began to cry as Jeannie held her and rocked her.

'You were lucky that boy you were with was too drunk to do anything. You might have ended up back at an apartment where a whole bunch of guys would think Christmas had come, and they wouldn't respect you, darling.'

Ali began to shake as she thought of what could've

happened. Jeannie felt rotten for scaring her. But she was too precious, she didn't want her to be hurt.

She encouraged Ali to have a shower and put on her pyjamas and go to bed for a few hours.

'I've to go to work,' she said. 'But I'll be back later if you want to talk some more.'

'Thank you, Auntie Jeannie,' Ali said, hugging her tightly. 'See you later.'

Calling Beatrice, Jeannie told her she was on her way.

'Rose already called. I heard about Ali. Did you manage to talk some sense into that girl? I'm really starting to get cross with her now. She doesn't think of Rose for one minute.'

'She'll be fine,' Jeannie said. She knew that no matter how long she sat with her, Bea would never understand why Ali was lashing out, using drink and boys. It was likely that she would go to her grave without doing something like that. But Jeannie got it. Unfortunately.

Walking to the shop as quickly as she could, she hadn't time to breathe before her first bride of the day waltzed in, with an entourage of eight people. Jeannie groaned inwardly. Dressed in bright pink onesies, they were clearly here to be entertained.

'Good morning, folks,' she said, mustering up as much enthusiasm as she could find. Her stomach lurched. Grabbing it, she thought she was about to vomit. The sensation passed and she was able to carry on. 'So before we get going, is there a budget you want to stay within?'

'Yeah, four thousand euros,' said Gabby, the bride. 'But if I see something that I really love, we'd have to see what Mammy thinks.'

Mammy was dressed in a onesie too, and to say that

sugar-pink fur wasn't her best look was putting it mildly. She also had a hairband with bunny ears and a rubber nose and whiskers set rammed onto her face.

'What's with the bunny theme?' Jeannie asked. 'Or am I not meant to ask?'

'I used to be a bunny girl,' Gabby said with a giggle.

'What, at the Playboy Mansion?'

'Ah no, just at the strip club in Nassau Street back in the day.'

Right now, Gabby was an outsized bride with hair that was clearly dyed at home and changed on a regular basis. Today it was the colour of an orange highlighter marker, with bottle-green tips. It was dry and fuzzy and yet it still managed to crawl down as far as her ample waist. She had extraordinarily long eyelashes that had clumped in sections, and so many studs in her cheeks and around her lips that she'd give a toolbox a run for its money. Her black lipstick was seriously distracting and Jeannie had to concentrate when she spoke.

'So have you a certain style in mind?'

'Nope,' said Gabby. 'I just want it to be different. Not like the normal run-of-the-mill bride.'

Jeannie was feeling crabby, and it was on the tip of her tongue to say that there was nothing original about her request. That so many brides came in thinking they were really way out there.

'Why can't they just try on gowns and see what suits them instead of trying to make a stupid statement?' she had raged yesterday.

'Just do what you're asked,' hissed Beatrice. 'You're here to sell, not to cause a fight with the brides.'

Jeannie pulled out several gowns in Gabby's size, one of

which was a slightly Gothic-styled ball gown that laced up the back. The skirt was full without being like a cup cake, and it was long enough to be ballet-length on her long legs.

'You could go for a really old-fashioned lacy veil with this, and I have the most astonishing piece that I'm going to show you.' She went to the cabinet and took out a large crystal-encrusted rose in a pale lilac shade. 'What if you had one of these babies made in either blood red or black? Put it on a comb and attach it to the crown of your head with the veil coming out like this.' She bunched the veil so it was literally cascading from the one spot. As it fell, the fabric spread out, showing the pattern of the lace.

'If you're looking to be different,' she added, keeping all sarcasm and nastiness from her voice, 'you could pair it with these.' She pulled out a pair of divine red satin slingbacks with pointy toes. 'That way you'd see the tattoos on your calves and ankles, and if you decided on the rose in red, you could even do your hair with a bit of red and go for a lip in the same colour.'

Much to her astonishment, Gabby looked as if she were about to burst into tears. Her stud-infested lip wobbled, making a slight tinny bell-like noise.

'This is deadly. I've been to two other shops and they put me in things that looked like tablecloths. I looked ginormous and I felt ugly. You get me, and this is just mega.'

Jeannie helped her into the dress, and she turned around and walked out of the dressing room to show the others. A round of applause erupted as a full sofa of pink bunnies banged their paws together, and there were plenty of tears.

Gabby wanted the whole lot. She ordered the rose in red, as suggested, and said she'd make sure the ends of her hair were the same shade of red for the day.

'You've been amazing. I'll be telling my sisters to come here now,' she said.

'That's nice,' said Jeannie as she took her measurements and filled out the order form. 'How many sisters have you?'

'Twelve. Six are getting married this year. So are three of my aunties and four cousins. I'm sending the lot of them to you. What's your name again?'

'Jeannie.'

'Thanks a million,' Gabby said as she hopped back into her onesie and led the other bunnies out.

Jeannie smiled to herself and was about to tell Beatrice about the order when a sharp pain shot through her. It was down low. As in right through her undercarriage. Her stomach went rock hard and she had to run for the bathroom, feeling as if she was going to vomit. Once there, she locked the door and stooped over the bowl. Nothing came. The horrible feeling down below hadn't gone away, though. Sitting on the edge of the toilet, she felt a gush of warm liquid.

Almost bursting into tears she wondered how on earth she could've wet herself. She'd never been a bed-wetter, even as a toddler. In fact, she'd no recollection of ever wetting herself. Then it hit her. Sweet Jesus Christ, is this labour? Jeannie felt a panic rising up from her toes and taking over her whole body. She started to shake, terrified of what was about to happen. She yanked out her phone and dialled 999.

Knowing her sister was about to find out what was going on, she opened the bathroom door and peeked out. Mercifully, there were no customers in the shop.

'Bea,' she said quietly. Too quietly. Beatrice was busy looking through a rail.

'Beatrice,' she said loudly.

Beatrice turned and looked at her. 'Everything okay? Do you need loo roll? I thought I'd sorted that. Silly me.'

'It's not that. I . . . eh . . . there's an ambulance on the way.'

'An ambulance? What on earth . . .'

'Yeah, the thing is, I probably should've told you ages ago . . .'

'Told me what? Oh dear Lord, what's happening to you?'

'I'm sort of pregnant.'

'Sort of pregnant?' Beatrice shrilled. 'How can you be sort of pregnant? You don't have a bump.'

'And I think I'm in labour. And it's too early. Oh God, Beatrice!'

As soon as the sentence was out, total mayhem ensued. Beatrice burst into uncontrollable sobs. She went from crying to yelling to apologising to telling Jeannie that she loved her.

'I'm sorry,' Jeannie cried. 'I know I'm a stupid cow, but I couldn't tell anyone. It's very complicated and I can't actually figure out the best thing to do.'

'Are you insane?' Beatrice shouted. 'The best thing might have been to tell me and Rosie. Oh my God, that night at the bistro where we promised to be honest with one another and lean on one another . . . That was actually you there, right?'

'Yes,' she said emphatically until another contraction hit. 'Holy cow and kick me in the privates with a steel-toed boot. Oh God, this is not funny any more.'

Beatrice was running around, frantically putting things away and getting ready to lock up the shop. The ambulance people burst through the front door with a stretcher.

'Praise the Lord, are you going to knock me out immediately?' Jeannie asked. 'Ow, ow, ow, this is hideous. When does the full anaesthetic thing happen? Get my sister to sign whatever bits of paper you need. I need to be put to sleep.'

They worked speedily and got her into the back of the ambulance, while Beatrice locked up then jumped in beside them. One of the crew told Jeannie she was a great girl.

'I don't want to be a great girl. I've changed my mind and I want to die.'

The man laughed. 'You're not the first to say that and you won't be the last.'

Frantically trying to breathe through the pain, she waited for it to pass before turning on him.

'I'm glad that the fact my body is attempting to pass a whale is entertaining you. I'd like to see you try and do this.'

'Ah, no thanks, love,' he chuckled.

'Riiiight!' she yelled. 'No thanks. Well I happen to feel the same way. People go on about having an experience. So where's Mickey Mouse and Snow White with the happy-clappy music and the lollipops? Because *that's* an experience, not having one half of your body trying to go in the opposite direction to the other. This sucks and I am *never* doing it again.'

'They all say that too,' said the man with a knowing smile. 'You'll be back for number two before you know it.'

'Who are you?' Jeannie fumed. 'Mr Expert on birth?' Another contraction ripped through her and Beatrice grabbed her phone.

'I'm calling Nick,' she said, looking as if she was delighted with herself for being so helpful.

'*No!* He's the last person we're to call.'

'But why . . .'

'Why do you think?' Jeannie said. 'I don't know if it's his. It could be one of three colours. Until it comes out and we see what it looks like, Nick cannot be told.'

'Jesus, Mary and Joseph,' the paramedic said, his eyes wide.

'Jeannie, you're not serious?' Beatrice said. She exchanged a look with the paramedic and shrugged. She knew about as much as he did.

When Jeannie winced with another contraction and shouted a whole array of expletives, the other paramedic, a woman, offered to examine her.

'If you're planning on shoving anything else up there, then the answer is no.'

'Well, it might tell us how far along you are. Baby could be almost born.'

'Okay, good, that would be amazing. Let's go with the almost-born scenario. How do we arrange that?'

'Well, it depends on your body and how much the contractions have done.'

'Does Nick not know anything at all?' Beatrice asked, unable to help herself.

'Nope,' said Jeannie. 'Nothing. He suggested us having a baby together, but I could hardly tell him that I'd gone ahead and done that possibly without him.'

'No,' said Bea. 'He mightn't have loved that idea. So when's your due date?'

'How should I know,' Jeannie said as the paramedic examined her. 'Ouch! Bloody hell, that was harsh. I'm not a massive fan of yours any more. Why did you have to do that?'

'So the good news is you're six centimetres dilated – which means you're definitely in labour. As in it's not a false alarm. Well done, yourself.'

'Six centimetres? I feel like I'm passing a sofa and you're telling me I'm only six centimetres?'

'Relax now. You're contracting nicely, so it might be a swift delivery. We're almost at the hospital now; you'll know more very soon.'

'Okay, great, do they have any kind of a torch that they can shine up my bits and see what colour it is? That would be such a help.'

Beatrice couldn't help giggling, and even the two paramedics hid their smiles as they shook their heads.

'No such thing exists, sorry, love.'

Beatrice fired questions at her like bullets from a machine gun.

'Have you been attending a doctor? Can I call someone for the notes?'

'No,' she said, feeling really stupid.

'I'm sorry, but someone has to say it: you're an idiot. You should've been looking after yourself and this baby, no matter what colour the poor little mite may be. Why didn't you trust one of us to mind you?'

'I was too bloody scared. I know I'm an idiot. I know I'll probably wreck my marriage and you and Rosie will hate me for ever more. But I was so terrified and I figured that if I told nobody, it would go away. But that plan didn't work so well.'

'You've got to try and hold on,' the male paramedic said.

'Typical bloody man,' Jeannie yelled. 'This baby is coming whether you like it or not.' Groaning again as another contraction ripped through her, she bore down and could feel the baby coming out.

'Agh!' she screamed. 'It's coming. It's being born. I can feel it.'

They pulled up at the hospital and she was bumped out of the ambulance and rushed through the corridors to a theatre, where a team was waiting.

'What's the gestation period, please?' asked a man in a gown with gloves and a mask.

'Huh?' Jeannie asked as sweat poured down her face. Another contraction came, the final one as it happened, and the baby slid out.

'How far along were you?' a nurse asked as the baby was whisked away.

'I thought I was maybe nearly six months,' Jeannie said. She began to sob. Beatrice was hugging her and crying too.

'Oh Jeannie, sweetheart, why on earth didn't you tell us? What's going on?'

'I didn't want to when I heard what you've been through. I wanted to wait until you had news either way. It wasn't fair . . .'

'Darling, that's nonsense! I would've been over the moon for you, no matter what.'

'We're just checking your baby now,' the nurse said. 'Being born at this stage isn't ideal, but sometimes that's the way it goes. This little guy seems to be fine but we do need to get him to the hospital to make sure everything is okay,' she added kindly.

They held up the very tiny little boy. His eyes were closed over, and he had a covering of soft downy white hair that looked almost like fluff on his face. He was so small, but so perfect. He also had a slightly bluish tinge. But he was fair skinned – and just then he let out an almighty wail.

'Now I can call Nick,' Jeannie said, smiling in delight. 'Oh God, I'm so happy it's his. So happy.'

'Don't you think he's going to ask why you didn't tell him you were pregnant?' asked Beatrice. 'What are you going to say?'

'Oh shoot, yeah. How about I wanted it to be a surprise?'

'That's a bit much of a surprise, even for you.'

'I didn't know!' Jeannie said, nodding her head vigorously. 'Yes. That's the one I'm sticking to. There was a whole show about this on one of the networks. It was literally all about women who went into labour like I did and, hey presto, they have a baby and they'd no idea it was coming.'

'So for that little boy's entire life you're going to have to lie and pretend you didn't know he was coming?'

'I'd lie to the Pope right now if it got me out of trouble and meant my marriage was okay.'

'But you're asking me to lie too,' Beatrice pointed out.

'Let's just see what happens,' said Jeannie. 'I'll call him. Tell him he's a father and see what comes out of my mouth.'

'That sounds like a great plan,' said Beatrice drily.

Nick's number connected and he answered immediately. 'Hey, sweetheart,' he said warmly. 'How's my beautiful girl today?'

Jeannie hesitated and couldn't speak for a moment.

'I'm good, but there's something I need to tell you . . .'

Chapter 23

ROSE WAS IN THE MAIN OFFICE AT BESPOKE DESIGN. Ali was sleeping off her wild night, and Rose didn't feel like tiptoeing around the house and then facing her hangover, so she'd come to the office for a couple of hours to distract herself from her problems. As she worked through the books, the more she delved into things, the more she realised that Martin had been winging it for months. It was a year since her dad had gone to Connemara and handed everything over to them. It was clear that Martin had been flying by the seat of his pants, with no proper grasp of how to run things.

She sat for two full hours with Susan, the accountant, and was absolutely mortified to realise the hours the poor woman had been working.

'Why on earth didn't you tell me?' Rose asked her as the full extent of Martin's incompetence came to light.

'He said I wasn't to bother you, that it wasn't your lookout.'

'But it's my family company,' Rose said, shaking her head. 'It's not your fault, Susan. I'm not blaming you by any stretch of the imagination, I'm just stunned by his ignorance and his arrogance.'

Rose promised Susan that things were going to improve and that she'd be there full-time from now on.

'I'll stay here overnight if that's what it takes,' she promised. 'We'll get things back on track.'

'You've no idea how relieved I am to hear you say that,' Susan said. 'Myself and some of the other long-term staff were actually considering looking for alternative work. Martin wasn't the nicest boss.'

'And he hadn't a clue, which makes it ten times worse,' Rose finished for her. 'I'm sorry, and I hope we can get things back to how they were.'

'You'll do that with your eyes shut, my girl,' said Susan as she smiled. 'I've known you a long time and you're more than capable. I presumed you'd made the decision to take a step back on purpose.'

'No, I was being totally suppressed,' Rose said with a sigh. 'I'm not afraid to say it, I've had the wool pulled over my eyes, big time.'

With her degree in business and a lifetime of being in and out of the shop with her dad, Rose could run Bespoke Design in her sleep. She had no idea why she'd let Martin push her out. But he'd managed it.

She'd just put the phone down to a supplier in Italy, having confirmed a huge shipment of furniture for the apartments deal, when there was a knock on the office door.

'Sorry to disturb you, Rose,' said Steffy. 'There's a woman called Laura here to see you. She's very agitated and says she's not leaving until she speaks to you.'

'Do you know what it's in connection with?' Rose asked.

A small, round woman with a ruddy complexion and grey hair that she'd pulled back into a neat bun on the back of her head was standing right behind Steffy. She was dressed in a floral-print skirt with a twinset and a cross on a chain.

'It's in connection with a letter I got from Martin,' she said, waving a piece of paper.

Blanching, Rose thanked Steffy and ushered Laura inside, closing the door behind her.

'Take a seat,' she said. 'I don't think we've met. I'm Rose . . .'

'I know exactly who you are. Are you honestly saying you don't know who I am?'

She perched on the edge of the chair and slammed the piece of paper onto the desk. Rose recognised Martin's writing.

'Read it if you like,' Laura said and promptly burst into dramatic sobs.

Rose's blood went cold as she tried to digest the words.

My darling Laura,

We've shared such wonderful times over the past fifteen years. You've been my joy, my fun, my friend and most of all, my lover.

I've come to the conclusion that I cannot continue the way things are. I know I promised that we would be together and I would finally leave Rose. But now that the time has come, I know I need a fresh start.

I love you and I know a part of me will always love you. But years of having to hide our relationship and go behind Rose's back has tainted things for me.

I want to find someone who I can be openly in love with. Can you understand where I'm coming from?

I know you so well. You'll be as angry as a bull for a while, then you'll be heartbroken, and after that I hope you'll realise that I'm doing us both a favour.

Thank you for the years you gave me. Thank you for loving me and I wish you the very best for the years to come.
From the bottom of my heart,
Martin

She handed the note back.

'I got a similar one,' she said. 'Except he didn't really tell me he loved me that much. Nor did he mention you, funnily enough.'

She felt as if all the pieces of the fragmented jigsaw that had been her life were finally falling into place. How could she have been so naive? How had she not seen that Martin was playing away from home all this time? Yes, he'd admitted it to her last year, but she'd thought it was a recent thing. But this, this made much more sense, even if it made her feel stupid and betrayed.

Why had he married her at all? More to the point, why had he stayed so long?

'Did you know about me and Ali from the start?' Rose asked.

'No,' Laura said. 'He only told me he was married about a year after we met.'

'Where did you meet, as a matter of interest?'

'In the Duke's Inn.'

Rose nodded. It was one of the best-known pick-up joints in Dublin.

'How did you feel when you got the note?' she asked, sighing deeply.

'I was stunned,' Laura admitted, 'but not actually that surprised. He was always the one who called the shots. He's a control freak and likes to think he can run the world. He decided where we went, what we did and who we saw. He got quite angry if I deviated from his plans. His excuse was that you would find out. But deep down I knew he was just controlling me because that's the way he is.'

Rose explained that he'd pushed her out of the business and she was slowly uncovering all sorts of messes he'd left behind. 'I reckon we're both better off without him,' she concluded. 'At least you can live your life without having to look over your shoulder all the time.'

'And maybe you'll find a man who doesn't prefer wearing dresses.'

Rose stared at her open-mouthed. For a moment no words would come out. 'He wore dresses?' she managed to ask.

'Oh yes, mostly old-lady ones, brown patterned cross-over jobbies.'

Rose shook her head. 'Well, that's certainly an eye-opener. Christ, he hadn't even decent taste in women's clothing,' she said with a grin. 'I'm sorry you've been left in the lurch. I can't believe I'm saying this to my husband's lover, but you seem like a really lovely person, Laura. You deserve better too.'

'Thank you,' Laura said as she stood to hug her. 'I know I burst in here like a fireball, but I didn't intend to upset you. I just wondered if he'd ever told you the truth, and I thought if he hadn't, then knowing it would make his stupid running-away a bit easier on you. And your daughter maybe.'

'You did the right thing,' Rose said. 'I think it will help both of us to move on if we know everything is out in the open.'

'Rose, I have to say this.' Laura paused. 'You're a beautiful woman. You're clearly very capable and you're so gracious and kind. I hope you find someone wonderful.'

'Oh.' Rose really couldn't say much more. She began to sob and she knew it was purely because Laura had been nice to her.

They chatted for a little longer before Laura left. Rose knew that was the final nail in the coffin as far as Martin was concerned. The shackles were now gone. He had ruled her life silently, and bit by bit she'd lost confidence in herself in so many ways. She was determined she was going to step out of the shadows and show her daughter what a real woman could do.

It was time to take back the life she'd been destined to have. Her father had kept the family company going. More than that, he'd done very well and had bought a wonderful house as a result of his hard work. She wasn't about to allow a snivelling little git like Martin jeopardise that.

Feeling empowered rather than broken and sad, she continued to pick through the finer details of the business.

She was taking a coffee break when her mobile rang. She smiled when she saw the name on the screen.

'Hi, Bea,' she said. 'How are things?'

'Are you sitting down?'

'No, why? Oh please tell me you're okay. What's wrong?'

As the news of Jeannie's baby and the precipitous birth came to light, Rose really did need to take a seat. In astonishment, she listened as Beatrice filled her in on as much detail as she knew.

'But why didn't she tell us?' she asked, as she cried with her sister.

'Honey, there are so many things going on inside her

head right now that I can't even begin to tell you where to start! She's a bit of a mess, Rosie.'

'And here was I thinking my life was a bloody disaster with Martin buggering off. But it seems I have the easier scenario right now. What about Nick?'

'He's on his way,' Beatrice confirmed. 'God help him, I think he'll swim if they can't put him on a flight in the next few minutes. He literally dropped everything. He was so full of concern. He absolutely idolises Jeannie.'

'Wow, it seems we've been putting our faith in the wrong husband all this time.'

'You said it,' Beatrice confirmed drily.

'I'll be there as soon as I can.'

Rose called Steffy and Cara into her office and explained in very basic terms that Jeannie had given birth prematurely and needed her. She'd already sifted through a lot of stuff and had a stack of jobs that would have to be tackled. The pair listened intently as she laid out what needed doing first.

'Leave it with us,' Cara said. 'We have plenty of cover on the shop floor today and it's not as busy as we'd antici- pated, so Steffy and I could actually help out with some of the bigger contracts.'

'Are there any part-timers who might like to take on more hours?' Rose asked.

'I can think of three,' said Steffy.

'Good. Contact them and see if you can get them on board. We're going to need to pull together. But right now, this minute, my sister needs me.'

'Don't worry, nothing is going to collapse this afternoon or this evening,' Steffy said sensibly.

'And if it does, we'll fix it,' said Cara.

'Thank you, both of you,' she said.

As she rushed out the door, she dialled Ali's mobile number, hoping she'd pick up. She'd probably be feeling really horrible when she did, but Rose didn't want her to miss this.

'Hello,' Ali said, sounding sulky.

'Hi, love,' Rose said, ignoring her tone. 'So this is as crazy as it comes, but your aunt Jeannie had a baby boy a while ago.'

'She what?'

'You heard me,' said Rose, laughing. 'I'm going to the hospital to see them. Will I swing by and pick you up?'

'Is this some sort of crazy prank?' Ali said suspiciously.

'Not at all, it's apparently true. I'm as shocked as you are.'

She collected Ali, and although they didn't talk much on the way, things weren't quite as strained.

When they arrived at the hospital, she circled the area for a parking space. Like a vulture, she zoned in on a car that looked like it was leaving. Crawling over to hover, she thanked the heavens when it began to pull out. Much to her annoyance, it stopped as it was halfway out of the space. She honked her horn and was mortified when the driver jumped out and approached her. She rolled down the window, looking sheepish.

'Sorry for being so rude. My sister just gave birth prematurely and I'm in a heap.'

'That's okay, love,' said the woman. 'I only wanted to pass on the parking ticket. It has hours left on it!'

'Thank you, thank you, thank you,' Rose said, making the woman laugh.

'Hope the baby is okay.'

Rose reversed into the space, Ali shoved the ticket on the windscreen and they ran across the road and into the hospital at a speed Usain Bolt would have been proud of. She texted Beatrice to say she was there, and her sister pinged back instantly saying she'd come and get her at the reception desk. Apparently they needed a special pass to get into the neonatal care unit and only immediate family were permitted.

They hugged hello and Beatrice led them through a set of double doors that sprang open when she used the pass from around her neck.

'I haven't been allowed to see the baby yet,' she said. 'But they've let me sit with Jeannie.'

As they entered the room, a team of doctors were surrounding the bed. The head doctor, whose name tag announced him as Dr Cronin, stopped talking momentarily as he spotted the two blonde curly-haired women who looked exactly like the one in the hospital bed.

'My twin and older sister and niece,' Jeannie said needlessly.

'Are you happy for me to continue?' Dr Cronin said.

'Yes please,' Jeannie said, looking terrified.

'So your son has been checked over by our team. We reckon he was probably closer to thirty-six weeks than you thought. His breathing is great. He's a strong little man and we won't need to hold onto him.'

He gave a few more details and they filed out, leaving Jeannie looking delighted and excited.

'Darling, why didn't you tell me?' Rose asked, stricken.

'I couldn't tell anyone,' Jeannie said. 'I couldn't get my head around it. I wasn't sure I wanted it . . . I even . . .' She looked from one face to another and bit her lip.

'Go on, we won't judge you,' said Beatrice.

But Jeannie couldn't tell her that she'd even considered putting the baby up for adoption. Ali was standing there. She'd think she was a horrible cow if she said that.

'I just didn't know how to tell you when I came back and heard about everything Bea's been through to try and get pregnant,' she said, taking Beatrice's hand. 'How could I say that I already was? It would've been so insensitive of me . . .'

'No it wouldn't,' Beatrice said. 'Gosh, what must you think of me that you worried about telling me some of the most astonishing news of your life?'

'I didn't want to hurt you, that was all.'

'Oh Jeannie, you are the most sensitive and astonishing woman, do you know that?' Bea said. 'Firstly you're in helping at the shop, and then all the while you're concealing your pregnancy to save my feelings.'

The baby was brought in and each of the women got to hold him. Jeannie decided she wanted to speak to Nick before they named him.

After a while, a nurse came and said that Jeannie and the baby needed to get some rest. Rose and Beatrice promised to come back later with some pyjamas and a washbag.

As she lay in the room, finally on her own with her baby, Jeannie couldn't quite fathom all that had happened. Nick was on his way. Until then, she would try to sleep. She'd need her energy for the next few days. Putting her hand into the cradle, tears streamed down her face as the baby wrapped his tiny fingers around hers.

Right there and then, Jeannie knew that she would walk through fire for her son. She was in love like she'd never known before, and it felt wonderful.

Chapter 24

JIM WASN'T IN THE BEST OF FORM. IN FACT HE'D been downright difficult since the night of the dinner-dance. It wasn't Martha's fault that she'd spotted Larry in a compromising position. Maybe she shouldn't have told Jim what she'd seen, but she had been so shocked she couldn't hold it in.

'Don't tell me any more,' Jim fumed. 'If you did see him with that girl, it's none of our business. God knows it's the last thing Dorothy needs at this stage of her life. Surely Larry wouldn't be that stupid.'

The only thing that was keeping him going was the news that the entire family was coming to visit soon. There were no definite dates yet, but the promise of a forthcoming visit was enough to make Jim glow with happiness. Even Jeannie's American husband was coming. They said they were bringing a surprise for them, and Jim was constantly throwing out suggestions as to what it could be. Martha thought he was being foolish. It was probably some souvenir of LA that would end up in the bin. But it would be nice to show them around and she was looking forward to taking them to the golf club for dinner. She'd sent a text to them formally inviting them as their guests on whatever night they chose. She'd put in brackets that the dress code was jacket and tie for the men and that the ladies should go all out.

Martha thought for a moment and had to stop herself from getting angry. Having produced three daughters, she had a single grandchild. It was a bit of a dismal show really, but something that was both out of her control and none of her business. Jeannie didn't appear to have any maternal instincts and Martha didn't suppose the American fellow was wildly paternal or sensitive. Anyone who could chop people up for a living had to be slightly cold on the inside.

When she'd worked her stint at the hospital during her training, she'd developed a healthy respect for the surgeons. After all, many of them saved lives. But unlike most of her colleagues, she had zero interest in netting one of them. She didn't need to go home to talk shop nor did she want a man who was capable of cutting flesh and drinking a mug of coffee ten minutes later.

No, she'd chosen well with Jim. He was everything she'd hoped for and more. He respected her and to this day he'd treated her kindly and with love and affection.

Jim had taught her about warmth. At first she'd found his gentle embrace startling. She wasn't used to being touched. He liked to hold her hand when they walked, a gesture she now adored. He used to cause a bit of a traffic jam on the footpath in Pebble Bay when the girls were little. He'd insist they all held hands and they'd often end up like a wall of giggles, zigzagging through the other pedestrians.

Jim was like a child knowing his family were on the way to visit.

He wanted them all to stay at the cottage but there simply wasn't room, so Martha had taken it upon herself to book them into the hotel. It would work out best in the long run, Martha mused. She was so busy at this stage that she'd only fret wondering who had eaten breakfast and whether or not they were comfortable. Her kitchen would be pulled asunder, the hot press would end up in a tangle and her calm and order would be disrupted. She'd no doubt the girls would be more comfortable at the hotel. They could turban as many towels around their heads as they liked and transfer fake tan onto those sheets, and nobody would mind.

She'd host a dinner, or maybe a late lunch. That way they would feel they'd been included in the cottage without her having to stop her life.

She honestly hoped Jeannie was going to behave. She had always been on the wrong side of cheeky and she hoped she'd grown out of it by now. Still, living in America wouldn't have helped. Martha didn't have direct experience of LA, but she'd made her mind up that it was a showy place filled with vain and brash people who had more money than sense.

She was looking forward to seeing Martin. He was more along the lines of what she liked. He was quiet and courteous and never demanded to be the centre of attention. He'd be immaculately dressed too and wouldn't drink too much, make too much noise or cause a stir. He was also a decent golfer and would accompany Jim for an afternoon.

Martha knew the locals would be impressed with her girls. She wouldn't be in a position to tell them what to do or how to behave, but she hoped at this point that they wouldn't let her down.

Her mobile phone rang; it was an unknown number.

'Hello, Midwife Martha speaking!'

'Martha? It's Olivia. From the salon in town.'

'Ah yes, Olivia,' she said, trying to hide her distaste. 'What can I do for you?'

'I was wondering if I could possibly sign up for a home birth? I mentioned to you that I wasn't happy with the service up at the hospital. Well, I was there again this morning and I really hate the thought of giving birth there. It's like a conveyor belt.'

'I see,' said Martha. She hated to turn any girl away, especially a first-time mother. Really it was none of her business who the father of Olivia's child was, though a voice in the back of her head was yelling that Jim was going to be apoplectic when he heard she was looking after this floozy.

'All right,' she said. 'Can you get your files and I'll come and see you?'

'I have them here. Oh thank you, Martha. I'm so relieved,' Olivia said and began to cry.

'There, there,' Martha soothed. 'There's no need to upset yourself. It's not good for you or baby. Let me fetch my appointment book and I'll see when I can fit you in.' She leafed through the pages and decided she could drop in the following morning. They made the arrangement and hung up. Knowing it would cause uproar, Martha decided to use her patient confidentiality clause. She wouldn't say anything to Jim and the argument would be avoided.

Humming to herself, she got her things together and headed to the community centre. By now her groups were well publicised and they were always packed. The women had decided among themselves that it would be nice to bring some baked goods. So there was always a lovely selection of tasty treats. Bit by bit people had donated toys and equipment as well, and there was an informal exchange service in operation. Everything from Moses baskets to buggies and car seats came and went. Martha was the main voice in the room and she made a little speech each week, concentrating on a different aspect of pregnancy, birth and then motherhood. The women swapped stories and helped one another. The atmosphere was wonderful and it made Martha's heart sing to know that she'd been the catalyst for it.

The day flew, and as she pulled up at the golf club just after six o'clock, Martha was ravenous. She'd survived on tea and biscuits all day and was ready for their early-bird dinner.

She noticed a missed call from Beatrice and another from Rose, but she was far too exhausted to listen to them rattling on about the fun they were having together. She was a little jealous of how well the girls got on, especially when she wasn't included in the banter.

At least this evening it would be just the two of them, which suited her perfectly. She'd done enough talking and humouring of people for one day and was relieved that Jim would want to fill her in on his day of golf.

The bar was unusually busy for midweek and her heart plummeted like a stone when she saw Jim waving for her to join him with none other than Larry and Dorothy.

'Good evening, folks,' she said, hoping the other couple were having a swift drink to keep Jim company and then heading off.

'Martha! How lovely to see you,' Dorothy said. 'I hope you don't mind but Jim mentioned you were eating here and I haven't the wherewithal to cook this evening so we asked James in reservations if we could join you.'

'I told them you'd be delighted,' Jim boomed as he stooped to kiss her. 'I couldn't call you because my damn mobile phone died earlier. I mustn't have plugged it in properly last night. Don't mind us being rude for a minute; I need to find out what happened at the end of a story here.' To her disgust, he leaned in and listened to Larry as if he were imparting the winning lottery numbers.

'Thank goodness you arrived,' Dorothy said, rolling her eyes. 'I've been listening to the ins and outs of today's golf with the visiting team from Limerick. I'm bored to distraction!'

Martha was fuming as she made light conversation with Dorothy. For something to say, she told her about the girls coming and how they were hosting a dinner here at the club.

'Oh, that'll be so lovely for you and Jim,' Dorothy said, her eyes shining. 'I envy you. The emptiness of not having a child never quite leaves, you know?'

Martha's heart went out to the other woman. She could be a bit senseless at times, almost naive, but there was no badness in her.

'Did you ever try to adopt or anything?'

'Yes,' Dorothy said with a sigh. 'We came really close to getting a child. A little girl. Everything was organised but the mother changed her mind at the last moment. I was Lily's mother for two weeks,' she said as tears filled her eyes. 'There was a two-week cooling-off period. I never dreamed for a second that she'd be taken from me . . .'

'Oh Dorothy, I'm ever so sorry,' Martha said. 'I had no idea.'

'I never wanted to run the risk of having my heart broken like that again. I felt it was safer to leave things the way they were. Larry is a brilliant man. I realised he was enough. He's my world and that's different from what I once imagined, but what we have isn't that usual, especially these days. So many couples don't make it.'

Martha opened her mouth, ready to tell Dorothy that Larry wasn't quite as squeaky clean or honest as she imagined, but she couldn't be the one to rip the bottom from this woman's world. Guilt wrangled with pity as she thought of what might be the right thing to do. If it were her, she'd want to know the truth.

Should she risk ruining this poor woman's retirement years? But at the same time, she couldn't allow the village to sneer behind her back. She didn't deserve that. Either way, this wasn't the time or the place. She'd sleep on it and decide in the morning.

They had a pleasant meal, just the four of them. Martha found there were actually lots of things to chat about. She never realised, for instance, that Dorothy was running a local knitting group.

'Yes, I take the community centre on Tuesday evenings. It used to be ladies of our vintage and older, but lately I have younger women too. Knitting has become very trendy again.'

'I must come and join you some Tuesday,' Martha said. 'If you have space, of course.'

'I'd love you to,' Dorothy said, smiling warmly. Martha was glad she'd never let the side down and shown her contempt for this woman. She made a little vow to try and be more accepting of others. Perhaps, she mused, she could be a bit closed-minded.

By the time they were ready to leave the club, the rain was lashing down in sheets. Martha had been so distracted by remorse that she hadn't drunk more than a single glass of wine over dinner, so she insisted on driving.

'I'll drop you both home and we'll go on to our house,' she said.

As they trundled up the road and turned into Dorothy and Larry's house, she saw the place with fresh eyes. The garden was like something from a fairy tale. There were split levels with pretty rockeries, stunningly placed rhododendron bushes and several seating areas that took in various views.

They'd been there at drinks parties and for dinner several times, but Martha had never allowed herself to appreciate it.

'The place looks wonderful,' she said. 'Even in this rain.'

'You must come with the girls and their husbands,' Dorothy said immediately. 'I would be thrilled if you think you could fit us in.'

'Thank you,' Martha said. 'The girls would love that.'

'I'll call you tomorrow and we'll put a date and time in the diary and that way it will happen,' said Dorothy firmly.

There was silence in the car as they drove back towards the cottage. Jim seemed lost in his own thoughts and Martha was itching to discuss Larry's indiscretion.

'What'll I do?' she asked as they pulled up at home. 'Should I tell Dorothy what I saw?'

'I don't know,' Jim said, rubbing his face roughly. 'I can't fathom why Larry would do such a thing. It simply doesn't add up. He showed no remorse or guilt this evening. He and Dorothy are the same as always . . . I don't understand.'

'I think I need to tell her,' Martha said with a sigh. 'I don't want her to be made a fool of. She doesn't deserve that. But at the same time, they've got that lovely home and all she has is Larry . . .'

Jim nodded. 'I agree. All she has is him, but if he's not being honest with her and we're knowingly not telling her . . . We're meant to be her friends.'

'Let's sleep on it and decide what to do in the morning.'

They dashed into the cottage and Jim set about lighting the stove. Even though it was supposed to be summer, the west of Ireland could be pretty darn chilly.

'We'll cosy up and have a nice cup of tea,' Martha said as she put on her nightdress and dressing gown. They weren't avid television watchers and decided to play a game of chess. They were getting to the crux of it when Martha's mobile phone rang.

'Ignore it!' Jim said. 'You can't disappear chatting and leave me in the lurch.'

She giggled and looked at the screen to see who it was. Not recognising the number, she answered.

'Hello, Midwife Martha speaking, how may I help you?'

'Martha? It's me, Olivia. I've only had a few pains, but my waters have just gone and I swear I can feel the baby's head. Please help me!'

'Okay, Olivia, I need you to try and remain calm. When you say you can feel baby's head, do you mean that the pressure pushing down is that strong?'

'No, I'm touching it with my fingers. I can feel it.'

'Okay,' Martha said. 'I'm getting into my car and driving to you, but the odds are that baby is going to be out before I get there.'

'Not if I can help it,' Olivia said. Her scream let Martha know that the next contraction was having a profound effect. She snatched her bag, blew a kiss to Jim and jumped into the car.

Her phone clicked on to hands-free and she was able to guide Olivia, who was doing a fabulous job.

When she pulled up at the salon, she let herself in the side door, which Olivia had left on the latch. She raced up the stairs and into a beautifully bright flat, decorated in various shades of yellow. It made it seem as if the sun were shining in spite of the dreary weather.

'I'm here,' she said as she rushed to Olivia's aid. She was just in time to see her baby boy being born. 'Well done, you clever girl,' she said. Olivia was half laughing and half crying as she gazed down at the little baby on the floor.

'I think I'll need a new rug,' she said. 'It's a boy! Wow, I thought it was going to be a girl for some reason.'

Martha nearly yelped out loud as she looked down and examined the child a little further. He had a shock of spiky jet-black hair, his skin was extremely sallow and when she gazed into his eyes she could see quite plainly that he was Filipino.

'He's beautiful!' she said as relief washed over her. 'Where is Daddy from then?'

'Oh, didn't you know?' Olivia said. 'He's from the Philippines. He's back there at the moment, as a matter of fact. He went to see his ailing mother and she sadly died last week. He's coming home tomorrow morning. He's going to be so surprised to know he has a son already!'

Martha delivered the afterbirth and helped Olivia into the shower before filling out all the necessary paperwork. It was very late by the time she was getting ready to leave.

'I don't like you being here alone,' she said. 'So I've made up my mind. You're coming home with me. Just until your husband returns.'

'Oh no, there's no need,' Olivia said, but Martha could see that she was greatly relieved.

A short while later, they were all tucked into the car and motoring towards the cottage. Martha knew she ought to say something about the kiss. Before she walked in the door and had to see Jim, before she had to call poor Dorothy, and before she self-combusted.

But this woman had just given birth. Clearly the child wasn't Larry's, and she was apparently happily married, even if her husband was halfway across the world. Instinct told her to stay quiet.

The rain was coming down in sheets, so she asked Olivia to stay put while she asked Jim for help. Dashing into the cottage, she filled him in as best she could and asked him to help move the mother and child into the spare room.

'And he's definitely Filipino?' Jim said.

'Yes,' Martha said. 'So we need to tread carefully here, Jim. Now I'm beginning to wonder if I'd had a bit too much to drink. Maybe I have it all wrong?'

'Let's hope so,' he said. 'Let's get this girl in and make her comfortable.'

All was quiet in the spare room until about five o'clock in the morning. Martha woke to the sound of the baby crying and Olivia attempting to soothe him. Knocking on the door, she padded in and helped her position him on her breast.

'Good girl,' she said with a smile. 'You're doing a fantastic job.' Olivia looked simultaneously exhausted and exhilarated as she stared back at Martha with bleary eyes. 'Did you get any sleep?'

'Not a wink,' she said with a grin. 'I couldn't stop looking at him. I can't believe he's here. I can't believe he's ours. We never thought this day would come . . .'

Martha sat on the edge of the large double bed and waited.

'Isko, that's my husband, he never lost faith. He's quite spiritual, and over the past few years as we tried and tried to get pregnant and nothing happened, he kept telling me that God would send us a child if that was what we deserved.'

'Lots of couples have difficulty,' Martha said. 'It's meant to be the most natural thing in the world and yet it can be such a trial.'

'I'd given up hope, if I'm honest,' Olivia said. 'I couldn't spend any more time living on my nerves, hoping that month would be the one . . . praying every week at mass that I would be worthy enough to be a mam. Then the tide turned. I opened my salon, Isko took on a new client for his landscape gardening business and a miracle happened.'

'How so?' Martha asked.

'If I tell you, please can you promise not to say it around the village? I made a vow that we would be discreet . . . Also you have a connection with the people in my story.'

Martha's mind was whirring. She was certain she'd seen Larry kissing this young woman. Yet the child was clearly of Filipino descent. It didn't add up.

'Your good friends, Larry and Dorothy,' Olivia said.

'Yes.'

'They have been sponsoring couples for over twenty years.'

'How do you mean?'

'They don't have children of their own, as you know. So many years ago they decided to set up a fund in Galway.

There's a fertility clinic close to the city centre. It's not attached to the hospital and they do private practice. But it costs a lot. In excess of ten thousand euros to be exact.'

Martha was agog.

'Each year Larry and Dorothy donate the money to a couple to help them have a baby. This year they chose Isko and me. Dorothy and Isko clicked the first time they met. He's been working with her in the garden, and during the course of one of their many conversations, he told her of our heartache at being unable to afford IVF.'

'So they paid?' Martha said.

'Yes. Normally they don't have much contact with the beneficiaries – they leave it up to the couple as to whether or not they stay in touch. In our case they've been nothing short of incredible. They're going to be honorary grand-parents!'

'Really?' Martha asked, as she felt a weight lifting from her heart.

'Well, Isko's family are in the Philippines and my parents are both dead. I have a sister who lives in Dublin and one in New York. So we're on our own. We couldn't ask for kinder or more wonderful people in our lives. I feel a bit guilty saying it, but I am closer to Larry than I ever was to my own father. He was a gruff man whose main focus in life was drinking pints and playing darts. Any man can be a father, but it takes a really special guy to be a dad,' she said. 'He and Dorothy have been wonderful.'

'But they never told us,' Martha said. 'I know Jim doesn't know a thing.'

'They insisted on keeping the whole thing quiet until the baby was born. They said they wanted us to be sure that they should be involved going forward.'

'Wow,' said Martha. 'I had no idea.' She bit her lip and closed her eyes for a moment. 'I saw you with Larry on the night of the captain's ball. You were outside as we were leaving. I . . .' She hesitated. 'I thought the two of you were kissing. I got the wrong end of the stick and this past while Jim and I thought you were having an affair.'

'Oh, seriously?' Olivia burst out laughing. 'I probably was kissing him,' she said with a smile. 'But not in the way that you suspected. Oh dear! I'm so sorry you've been faced with that conundrum.'

'I was actually going to call poor Dorothy tomorrow and tell her,' Martha said. 'Oh my goodness, you have no idea how relieved I am that you're not sleeping with Larry!'

'Just wait until they hear!' Olivia said. 'Or should we not tell them?'

'Maybe it would be best left unsaid. It was such a horrible thought that I don't want to say it out loud. Have you told them about this little fellow?'

'Yes, I called them last night as soon as you went to bed. I've sent through pictures and they've been so wonderful. They didn't ask to come and see him. They left it for me to invite them. With your permission, I'd like them to come and collect me. I'm going to stay with them for a couple of weeks. Dorothy is going to help me.'

'Oh, that's wonderful news. I couldn't be happier for all of you.'

Martha slipped out of the room and told a very relieved Jim what was going on.

'That's fantastic news,' he said, beaming from the bed. 'I honestly thought I didn't know my friend. I couldn't fathom how he was being so two-faced. He speaks about

Dorothy with such love and respect, it simply didn't make sense.'

Later, Martha set about making scones and setting the kitchen table. By the time a very excited-looking Larry and Dorothy arrived, the cottage was filled with the warming aromas of baking and freshly ground coffee.

'Come in and we'll have a little celebratory breakfast before you go!'

She led them up the stairs to where Olivia was waiting proudly with her son. Giving them some privacy, Martha said she'd see them in the kitchen.

She was surprised when Dorothy appeared first and by herself.

'Larry is putting Olivia's things in the car,' she said. 'I believe you got the wrong end of the stick.'

Martha blushed, wishing Olivia hadn't told her.

'I was going to speak to you about it today,' she said. 'I wasn't prepared to have you made a fool of.'

'Thank you,' Dorothy said, reaching her arms out. When Martha didn't flinch, she hugged her. 'I've often felt a little intimidated by you. I felt you didn't like me that much. There were so many times when I wanted to tell you about our little programme. But you being a midwife and all that . . . I wasn't sure you'd approve.'

'Approve? Dorothy, you and Larry have made miracles happen for no personal gain. I think you're the most generous and amazing human beings. You've given the gift of a child to how many couples?'

'Six,' she said. 'Six babies have been born. Sadly not all our beneficiaries managed to have a child.'

Martha indicated for her to sit down. Putting the large cafetière on the table, she added the basket of warm scones.

'I'm sorry if I was intimidating. I try hard not to be.'

That was true. Martha knew she had a tendency to be very matter-of-fact about things. She also knew that she could be downright cold at times. She knew because she could see and hear her mother in herself. Any time she noticed, she tried hard to change. She didn't want to be like her in any way.

'I'm glad you'll have some contact with Olivia and Isko and the baby. You deserve to. I think it's fantastic, and if there's anything I can do, call me at any time, won't you?'

'I won't interfere and I won't step on any toes, but thank you. I'll certainly keep that in mind.'

As the others joined them, the mood was jovial.

'Martha and Jim's girls are coming to visit,' Dorothy told Olivia. 'It would be lovely for everyone to meet. Perhaps you might bring the baby and Isko?' She looked at her hopefully, and Olivia promptly burst into tears. 'Oh no! I'm sorry, you don't have to.'

'No,' she said through great big sobs. 'I would love that! You guys are the family we thought we'd never have. This little bundle of joy is the child we wouldn't have had. We owe you so much and yet you want to give more.'

Martha knew she was sharing an incredible moment as her kitchen was filled with life and hope.

Chapter 25

BEATRICE HAD DECIDED TO GO HOME WITH ROSE once they'd dropped Jeannie's things off at the hospital. They had sat up and talked about Jeannie and the baby and how they hoped Nick would forgive her for not telling him about it. They were still talking about it at breakfast, trying to digest how her life had changed irrevocably in the last twenty-four hours.

'I thought she had it all sorted,' Rose said. 'I knew my life was a total disaster, but I honestly thought she had it figured out.'

'Me too,' said Beatrice. 'You just never know, do you? She said she wanted to tell us both when she got here, but she couldn't in case it upset me.'

'How are you?' Rose asked, her face filled with concern. 'Did you sleep last night?'

'Yes, astonishingly. I was exhausted actually.'

They were still talking as Ali sauntered into the kitchen, dressed in one of Jeannie's black-tie gowns with full make-up and her hair pinned up.

'It is I, Queen Ali, here to visit you.' She swept around the kitchen counter and posed like a model before going back to the bedroom.

'Rose, she's a scream,' Beatrice whispered. 'She certainly hasn't inherited any of our hang-ups, that's for sure.'

'I vowed when she was born that she wouldn't grow up feeling as if she wasn't good enough. I know we all have moments of that thanks to Mum.'

'Moments?' Beatrice said. 'I think I've been running from myself for years.'

'I've never had much confidence,' Rose said. 'I think I slotted myself into the big sister role and didn't think I was much else.'

'We need to try and change the way we think,' Rose said. 'Especially if you're going to be a mother. You don't want that baby having issues with confidence.'

'No, you're right.'

'I hope I've broken the cycle,' Rose said. 'Although I might have forgotten about myself a bit along the way. I don't know why I put up with Martin and my farce of a marriage for so long.'

'We need to sit and talk about it properly,' Beatrice said. 'But you can't do it in front of Ali.'

They finished breakfast and cleared up as the conversation flowed. Ali was sitting on the sofa watching TV, and they tested the water to see if she was listening.

'I'd say that's the wrong thing, what do you think, Ali?' Beatrice said, waiting to see if she'd answer. When she didn't even flinch and stayed in a TV daze and a world of her own, her phone lighting up constantly with text messages, the women decided it was safe to chat.

'So how are you coping?' Beatrice asked Rose. 'Have you heard from Martin today?'

'No, and to be honest I don't have anything to say to him right now. I need to get my head straight, lick my wounds and eventually scrape myself off the floor. I just need a bit of time.'

They talked about logistics for the next few days.

'I've so much work to do, it's scary,' Rose said. 'I thought yesterday that I mightn't cope with the business, but it's actually a blessing. I'll get my teeth into it and that way I have some hope of staying sane. I want to get in to see Jeannie and I'm sure you do too. There's no point in us going at the same time.'

They called Jeannie, who sounded utterly exhausted. She was in isolation as they were worried she had an infection. Nobody bar her next of kin was allowed in, so that was that. Nick was due to land in the next couple of hours, and would go straight to the hospital. Jeannie said she'd let them know as soon as she was allowed visitors. Meanwhile, she told them, very bossily, they were to go to work.

'You both have empires to run. I'm in the best hands here.'

Ali went off to school, and Rose and Beatrice decided to have one more coffee before they headed into the day.

'Had you an inkling Martin might leave?' Beatrice asked. 'It's just you never mentioned any problems. I feel as if I've let you down so badly. I'm sorry, Rose.'

'Hey,' Rose said. 'You have nothing to apologise for. Things have been really weird between us for a long time. We haven't had sex since Ali was born.'

'What?' Beatrice yelled, then clapped her hand over her mouth. 'Are you serious? But why? Didn't you want to, or was it him?'

Rose told her the whole sorry tale. Everything from the humiliation of having to face his rejection to the latest revelation of Laura paying her a visit.

'But he's gone to London without her,' she was quick to add. 'He's starting again.'

'How lovely for him,' Beatrice said. 'But honey, why did you stay in the marriage for so long?'

There was a pause as she waited to hear. Rose was clearly searching for the right words to explain. Beatrice was utterly flummoxed that she'd missed such a massive problem right under her nose. Obviously she couldn't be expected to know the details of her sister's sex life, but it had never occurred to her for one minute that their marriage was anything out of the ordinary.

'I didn't think I deserved any more,' Rose said eventually in a small voice. 'I honestly felt I was faring quite well. We had Ali and then Dad signed the business over . . . followed by this place . . . I felt guilty that you and Jeannie seemed to get less.'

'Obviously I can't speak for Jeannie, but as far as I know, neither of us has ever felt hard done by. We were pleased for you and Martin.'

There was a pause before Rose spoke again.

'Look at the three of us. You married someone you didn't love. Not only that, you didn't even fancy him. I had a sexless marriage. Now we have Jeannie giving birth to a child and for some weird reason she didn't tell anyone.'

They were drawn to the door by the sound of Ned barking. They'd let him out into the garden to do his business and he'd been happily pottering since. Beatrice let him in and picked him up, hugging and kissing him.

'How's my little baby boy?' she crooned.

Rose looked at her. 'How are things human-baby-wise? When will you know?'

'Five more days,' Beatrice said with a nervous smile.

'No rumblings either way yet, so I'm taking it as a good sign.'

Knowing they both had loads to do, they set off for work. Rose towards Bespoke Design and Beatrice to her newest shop.

Beatrice really was baffled by the revelations about Rose and Martin's platonic farce of a relationship. Rose was beautiful. She turned heads everywhere she went. She could have any man if she put her heart and soul into it, yet she'd allowed Martin to undermine her and keep her like a prisoner for all this time.

An image of their mother flashed into her mind. Fury filled her like hot lava from the inside. Martha was the reason they were all so emotionally challenged. She had a lot to answer for, Beatrice thought angrily. Their father had done his best over the years, but Martha was one complex woman. She was willing to give herself to a stranger at the drop of a hat, but she had never been there for her daughters.

Nanny May had been, though. That poor woman had done everything for them. Now that she thought about it, Nanny May had probably done the Santa Claus shopping and bought their birthday gifts. The only thing their mother did was buy them fancy outfits that they didn't want to wear. She'd come home from places like Milan or Paris, when their dad was at trade fairs buying furniture, with bags of clothes that they hated. Beatrice recalled one Christmas in particular when she was shoehorned into a bottle-green velvet dress with a white satin collar. She'd started her period the week before and the soft flowing fabric came to well above her knees. Overtly conscious of anyone seeing her knickers, she looked at the short dress in horror. There were white wool tights and Mary-Jane shoes to match.

'Couldn't I have something different?' she pleaded. 'The twins will look cute. People can smile at them. I want to blend in.'

'Nonsense,' Martha said. 'You always get dressed properly for Christmas and this year won't be any different. Besides, the things can't be taken back. I'm hardly going to fly to Paris just to suit you. The dresses are designer ones and they cost a fortune. You're behaving like an ungrateful brat and I don't appreciate that.'

She wanted to die when they were marched off to mass on Christmas Day, just the way her mother wanted, paraded into the church with Martha walking behind them.

'Stand up straight, Beatrice,' her mother hissed as she fixed the flat bow that pulled her long blonde curls over to one side.

She was thirteen, and all she wanted was a pair of snow-washed jeans, mismatched Converse runner boots and a sweatshirt from Benetton, the coolest shop at the time.

The twins were a couple of years younger and were oblivious to her pain. The worst moment of all came when she walked past Jacinta O'Meara. Jacinta and her older sister were the coolest girls in school. As the Brady girls waited in the aisle for an elderly lady to waddle her way into a pew, many of those present regarded them with appreciative smiles, but Jacinta and her sister took one look at poor Beatrice and dissolved into giggles, elbowing one another. Beatrice glanced over and drank in their outfits. In stone-washed denim jeans with black polo-neck belly tops, they were like something from *Top of the Pops*. Jacinta had fingerless lace gloves and neon-green nail polish, with leather strings wrapped around her wrists. She too had a bow in her hair, but hers was black lace tied in a floppy, haphazard way that suggested she'd fallen out the door with no time to make it look neat. Her liquid eyeliner created the perfect feline flick and her mouth was slicked with Constance Carroll cherry lip gloss. Beatrice had asked for some in her stocking, but Martha hadn't allowed it.

'Looking hot,' she sneered at Beatrice, who veered between wanting to punch Jacinta's powdered face and wanting to curl into a ball and die.

All during mass she could feel Jacinta's mocking expression from several pews back. She tried to sit out communion, but her mother gave her the look that told her she needn't choose the church to make a stance.

Afterwards she ran home, not caring if she got into trouble. She hid behind the garden wall and waited in the cold for the others to get there. The twins thought it was the funniest thing and kept asking her why she'd run away.

Her father opened the front door and led her inside, asking her to sit at the kitchen table and talk to him. His face was filled with concern as she sobbed and then launched herself at him. But when Martha came around the corner and into the house, the mood changed.

'Don't ever do that again,' she said. 'You have no idea how good you have it, Beatrice. There are children in this very community who have nothing. They're born into a different world, through no fault of their own, and they haven't a hope.'

'She's upset,' Jim said, hugging her again. 'Maybe we need to let her make some more choices. It's Christmas Day. I want my girls to be happy.'

Martha insisted they sit in their dresses until dinner was

over. By then the damage was done. Thinking about it now, Beatrice was grateful that there was no social media in those days. If it were now, there'd be humiliating photos on Instagram for all the world to see. At least all that remained of that time was her own embarrassment and humiliation.

But that day had marked a defining moment for Beatrice. She realised, without a shadow of doubt, that her mother cared more about what other people thought than about how her daughters felt.

The clothes battle lessened purely because Martha was too busy to notice. Jim gave Beatrice an allowance and she took a weekend job at a newsagent's. With her own money she was able to buy the things she really wanted. But it was clear that Martha had washed her hands of her after that incident. There was no fighting or nastiness, just a sense that she was overlooked by her mother.

She and her dad grew increasingly close and she knew she could tell him anything. For that she would be eternally grateful.

Nothing changed much until Davy showed an interest in her. From the word go, she had no feelings towards him. Rose thought he was divine-looking, Jeannie thought he was a brilliant catch and pretty much everyone thought it was a match made in heaven. Everyone but her . . .

He treated her like gold dust. He showed her off proudly to his friends and she was suddenly elevated to a level that Jacinta could only wish for. It made her smile to herself when the girls she'd longed to know in school suddenly came out of the woodwork and were eager to meet her for coffee or invite her to lunch.

She went. Of course she did. After all, that was what

she'd craved for so many years. But the mindless chatter and the constant competition wore her down very quickly. She was in her early twenties and working for a high-end clothing boutique, having finished a business course in college. Some of her friends were single and the panic they carried was insane.

'If I don't meet someone soon, I'm going to have to go and live in London,' Mary-Jane admitted. 'There are slim pickings here in Pebble Bay and even Mum is dropping hints about spreading my wings. What if I end up on my own?'

Perhaps it was because she was with Davy, but Beatrice couldn't understand the mad rush to be part of a couple. As her friends slowly dropped like flies, off into wedded wonderland, in spite of herself she got swept along with them.

For the first time in her life, she was the centre of her mother's world. Martha and Davy's mum, Maria, went into overdrive. The wedding was stunning and Beatrice felt truly beautiful. That had never happened before. Before she left Marine Terrace in the vintage Rolls-Royce with her beloved father, she looked at herself in the full-length mirror. The bride who stared back at her filled her with pride. Her professionally applied make-up and her carefully teased hair piled loosely on the top of her head made her look like someone she didn't know. Her dress was a magnificent work of art: a silk sheath with a V-neckline adorned with a layer of shimmering hand-made lace. The tiny beads and crystals twinkled as she moved and the pooling train followed on behind as if it were made of liquid. Her veil was a show-stopper in that it trailed almost the full length of the church with the same intricate bead detailing.

The outfit had cost so much she'd wanted to step away from it, but Martha had insisted on paying, telling her she was worth it.

Beatrice loved her wedding day. It was everything she'd dreamed of, mostly because her mother had her back. Each time they locked gazes, Martha let her know how happy and proud she was.

On honeymoon, she knew she'd made a grave mistake. Davy couldn't have been more attentive. In fact, he wanted to make love and hold her hand 24/7. Even sitting on the sun lounger while at the beach he'd reach for her. The hotel staff smiled indulgently at them as they walked, with his arm always draped around her shoulder.

He was witty, funny and very good looking in a pretty, boy-band sort of way. But much as she tried, Beatrice couldn't make herself love him.

By the second week of their honeymoon, she was locking herself in the bathroom just to get away from him.

'Holiday belly troubles,' she'd lied. Sitting on the closed toilet seat was preferable to having him all over her.

Davy wanted a brood of children. He said he'd provide for her and that she didn't need to work unless she wanted to. They had a stunning home to return to in Pebble Bay and the scene was set for the perfect happy-ever-after.

He asked her to stop taking the pill once they returned to Ireland. She agreed, and as far as Davy knew, they were officially trying for a baby. She felt like a criminal for going to a women's health clinic out of town to get a new prescription. She kept the pills in a shoebox at the back of the wardrobe, and each time she took one, she sank further into herself.

Eventually, less than a year after they were married, as

her mother and Maria were revving up and wanting to organise an anniversary party, Beatrice came clean to Davy.

'But I thought you were happy? Did I treat you badly and make you feel unloved?' he asked with tears in his eyes. 'Beatrice, I'll do anything to keep you.'

She shook her head and told him it was nothing he'd done wrong nor was there anything he could do; that she'd tried to make herself love him but it wasn't going to happen.

'You deserve more,' she said.

He'd asked for a bit of time so he could process things. Two weeks later, he came to her and said he was moving to Australia. He couldn't live in Pebble Bay and not be her husband and he knew his parents wouldn't take it well.

'They believe in the sanctity of marriage and it's going to shock them to the core that we're splitting up.'

That was an understatement. Maria went crazy and told Beatrice that she'd made her bed and she was to lie in it. She forbade them to separate and told Beatrice that the matter was never to be spoken about again.

Martha added her own twopence worth and told Beatrice to have a baby.

'Have three or four or five, even. Have so many that you don't have time to sit questioning your feelings. Things will tick along after that. You'll get used to Davy and he will become a habit that you won't want to break.'

'No, Mum,' Beatrice said. 'I can't live a lie, and now that it's out in the open, it can't be taken back.'

'Oh yes it can,' Martha said, her eyes blazing. 'It hasn't been announced in the newspaper. You and Davy will heal the hurt and you will show the world what a wonderful family you are.'

As she put her hand on her belly now, Beatrice wondered

if her mother's next words were a prediction of what was to come.

'You were punching above your weight, Beatrice. I can't believe you've thrown it all away. I hope you're ready to be on your own from here on in.'

Those were the final words on the subject. Martha never asked her about her feelings after that. Beatrice started the shop and built a life that was on her terms. She'd been on a few dates. Just drinks or a dinner out. She'd met one guy called Harry whom she'd liked. He had a job when they first started going out but he'd chucked it in, saying it was taking up too much of his time. He began to call to the shop at odd times of the day, and Beatrice knew that if she wanted to be with him, she'd also have to carry him.

She didn't love him enough to do that, and felt deep down that she deserved better.

She opened a second shop, then a third, fourth and fifth. Business was booming, but nobody else had come along. Time had elapsed and she'd had to consider her options.

She'd joined a dating agency after two utter disasters involving Tinder. But nobody made her feel alive. None of the men made her feel better when she was with them, nor did she particularly fancy them.

'What's wrong with me?' she'd asked Jeannie a few months back. 'Should I simply settle? Is there no such thing as true love and is it not meant to feel amazing?'

'There is such a thing,' Jeannie told her, 'and you deserve to find it.'

The counsellor had hit the nail on the head with regards to the baby situation. She'd do her best to sort that and then she'd look for someone.

* * *

Beatrice woke several times in the night. Her mind was racing and she was finding it almost impossible to relax. She got up and made chamomile tea, but nothing helped. By dawn she had given up the notion of sleep and opted for a shower. Using her precious Jo Malone shower gel, she inhaled the grapefruit-scented steam and allowed the deliciousness to awaken her senses.

Unable to eat much, she forced a few spoonfuls of porridge in before walking down the stairs to the shop. At least if she could do something constructive she'd feel less useless.

She was knee-deep in communion dresses when there was a faint rapping at the door. Puzzled, she wondered if it might be one of the assistants arriving enthusiastically early. Peering out, she saw an agitated-looking man with dark curly hair, shaved at the sides. He was tall and well-built and looked extremely respectable. He was dressed in dark indigo jeans with boating shoes and no socks, and his short-sleeved white shirt showed an even tan.

He squinted as he spotted her and waved slightly awkwardly.

'Hi,' he said. 'Sorry to disturb you. I actually wasn't expecting to find anyone here . . .'

She pulled the door open, suddenly thinking it might be a foolish idea. Pebble Bay village hadn't woken up yet; even the bakery was still closed. This man could be an attacker and she was about to let him inside.

'Can I help?' she asked. He didn't lurch forward or even attempt to step any closer to her, so she relaxed a little.

'This is really embarrassing,' he said, pulling his fingers through his hair. 'I'm here to return two dresses. That is . . . I wanted to know if you might take them back? I don't want a refund. They're paid for, but they won't be used now, sadly.'

'Oh?'

'Yes. You see, the issue is that our wedding . . . my wedding that was due to take place soon . . . eh, tomorrow, as a matter of fact, is now no longer . . .' He walked away, then turned around and came back. Tears were spilling down his cheeks as he tried in vain to stop them and wipe them away.

'Are you Richard Blakely?' she asked in astonishment. 'You're the man Sadie Farrell was due to marry?'

'Yes,' he said, looking haunted. 'I have Sadie's dresses in my car. She came to me last night and told me she can't marry me. It's finished and she asked me to take the dresses back. We'd like them donated to another girl. Someone who would love them and can't quite manage to pay . . .'

'I think you'd better come in.'

Beatrice stood to the side and Richard walked in.

Chapter 26

JEANNIE HAD FINALLY ALLOWED ONE OF THE nurses to take the baby so she could have a shower.

'You'll watch him properly, won't you?' she asked, looking genuinely worried.

'I do this all the time, it's my job,' the nurse said. 'Now I understand that you feel as if he's the only baby in the universe, and to you he absolutely is, but I promise you he'll still be here when you get out of the shower.'

'Yes. You're right. Good point and very well put. I like you. You're direct and you instil confidence in me.'

The nurse smiled and watched as Jeannie made a second and then a third attempt to walk away from the sleeping baby.

'I'm going this time.'

When she stood into the shower and the warm water ran over her, she felt wonderful. Rose had packed her washbag and overnight bag with stuff she'd never have thought she'd need. Starting with tiny matching citrus shampoo and conditioner and shower gel that had been swiped from a hotel. Inhaling the uplifting scent along with the steam, she felt rejuvenated.

In the bag she found a packet of small flying saucers that were plastic on one side and soft on the other. As she took one out to cleanse her face, she noticed the label on the packet: *Plastic-backed breast pads.* Just as she was about to toss them back in the bag, she looked down and realised her breasts were crying all of their own accord. Pulling a bra out, she yelped. It had hooks and clips and side windows. Although Rose had obviously tried to choose a pretty one – the manufacturers had put some random bit of white lace where they could – it was still functional rather than beautiful. She shoved a breast pad through each window and put it on.

As she was pulling up the tent-sized knickers, her breath caught at the sight of her tummy. It looked like a balloon a few days after a birthday party, a little bit saggy and very sad. The knickers covered it: result! All of it was beginning to make sense. Most of her body parts were going to weep and leak. She'd better ask the nurse about it before Nick arrived. Would it go on for long? As in weeks, months, years? Would her body ever look normal again? And as for the downstairs department . . . Would it ever go back to its original shape, or would there be a hole the size of a bowling ball there indefinitely?

Rose had brought her pretty cotton pyjamas with a matching dressing gown. When she put them on, she felt like a million dollars. How could a simple thing like being clean in new pyjamas with the correct items of absorption feel so amazing?

Shuffling out of the bathroom, she smiled at the nurse and asked her about the leaking issue.

'No, pet, that'll stop in the next few weeks. Every woman is different, but in general—'

'Eh, pardon, the next few *weeks*?' Jeannie interrupted. 'So there's a possibility I could be still spurting from several zones for quite a while then?'

'Ah no, pet, you'll be right as rain well before you know it,' said the nurse as she patted her on the hand. 'Now, this little fella is rooting in my chest for a feed. So would you like to pop back into the bed and we'll get him latched on.'

'Oh, jeepers, no! I'm not breastfeeding. It's bottles all the way here.'

The nurse consulted her chart. 'I'm sure they gave you the rundown on why breast is best?'

Jeannie rolled her eyes. 'Yes, I've heard nothing but that since the moment he came out. But I'm certain I'm for bottles.'

'If that's what you want,' the nurse said, and her tone made it clear it wouldn't be what she would want. 'I'll go get a ready-mixed bottle.'

She went out and came back a minute later with the bottle, which she proceeded to feed to the baby.

Jeannie watched her for a few moments, then she blurted out, 'Can I say something?'

'Yes, pet.'

'It's *my* choice, not yours. I don't want to breastfeed, so would you mind leaving the dirty looks and snooty attitude in the corridor? I've just passed what felt like a whale from a hole that was very badly designed for purpose. So give me a break, yeah?'

'I . . . I wasn't intending to make you feel bad . . .'

'Well you did, you are. Great that we've cleared it up. If you wouldn't mind leaving a note on the door with a boob with a large red cross through it, maybe that'd help your colleagues.'

'That won't be necessary,' said the nurse as she forced a smile.

'Cool,' said Jeannie, 'and thank you for minding my baby. That was the best shower of my life.'

'You're welcome,' said the nurse. 'Much as you might not like to believe me, I am here to help you.'

Jeannie lay back against the pillows and tried to calm down.

'I apologise for my outburst, but you made me feel like a criminal for giving my baby a bottle.'

There was no time for any further discussion as the door opened.

'Nick!' She promptly burst into tears.

'Oh darling, look at you! Look at him! This is the best moment of my life.'

Jeannie grinned and thought how she'd just said the same thing about the shower.

Nick approached the bed and kissed her tenderly on the lips. Pulling a chair over, he perched on it and stared at the baby.

'Oh Jeannie, he's perfect.'

'Isn't he? We make amazing babies, you and me.' Yet again she said a silent prayer that he was Nick's baby. She would never, ever do anything so stupid again, she vowed. 'Want to hold him?'

Nick took him from her and cradled him so tenderly.

'Hello, baby boy. I'm your daddy and I'm gonna make sure you have the most amazing life. Anyone who tries to interfere with that will be . . .'

'Tortured and shot?'

'I was going for a good shouting, but if you'd prefer, we can do the torture and shooting thing.'

They both laughed and the baby jumped and opened his eyes.

'Hi,' Nick said, as tears rolled down his face.

Jeannie began to sob too, which made Nick look up at her.

'You okay, sweetie?'

She nodded. 'I'm so happy.'

'Me too,' he said. 'But I've gotta ask you. Why didn't you tell me?'

'I didn't know,' she said. 'The midwives said it happens all the time.'

'And I hate to mention it, but I assume he's been properly checked out, seeing as you've been drinking alcohol right the way through? It's amazing he was almost six pounds in spite of being early and all.'

'He's totally fine,' she said. 'Can I make a confession?'

He nodded.

'I haven't been drinking. I didn't know what was wrong, but I had some Prosecco a few months back and I vomited for two days.'

'I remember that! You were as sick as a parrot.'

'Since then, any time I even smelled alcohol, I retched. So when we went out to functions I'd take a glass of bubbly and take one sip and that was it. The same with the wine at the table. When you don't say anything, nobody notices.'

'So your body told you and you were already being a mom without even realising!'

'I didn't think of it that way.' She smiled and breathed a sigh of relief that Nick had accepted her story. For the first time she felt her shoulders dropping from her ears, where they'd been firmly placed for months.

'So this little guy needs a name,' said Nick. 'What are you thinking? Jim after your pops or Winston after mine?'

'Eh, no offence to either. But a resounding no.'

They tossed names back and forth and eventually agreed on Austin.

'He looks like an Austin,' said Nick as he puffed out his chest. 'Hello there, meet my son Austin . . . Hey, have you met my son Austin . . . This here is my son Austin.'

Jeannie giggled and lay back against the pillows. As if by magic, the nurse appeared and suggested that she take a nap.

'Maybe Daddy would like to take baby and we'll show you how to wind him and change his nappy?'

'That'd be great,' he said. 'You get some sleep, honey, and us boys are gonna go and learn some cool stuff.'

When he looked over, Jeannie was already asleep.

Chapter 27

MARTIN HAD PHONED THAT MORNING, QUITE OUT of the blue. It was a few days since he'd left, but so much had happened that Rose had genuinely had very little time to think about him. She felt nothing when she heard his voice. Not anger or disgust as she'd expected. Just a kind of numb nothingness that made her want to hang up.

'What do you want?' she asked, sounding bored.

'I was wondering how you are. How is Ali?'

'Fine.' She wasn't giving him an inch.

'Rose, I think we should probably talk.'

'Do you?'

'I think I'd like to come back to Pebble Bay and have a sit-down discussion. I mean, we can't go on the way we were. But it might have been a bad idea for me to walk away.'

'Obviously,' she said drily, 'but you still buggered off.'

'Please don't be like this, Rose,' he said. 'We shouldn't make this any more difficult than it already is.'

'*We*,' she said caustically, 'didn't do anything. You chose to leave. You wrote me a note and bailed.'

There was a pause at the other end of the phone. She actually wondered what he was going to come back with.

'I was confused,' he said. 'But we've both had a little time and it's probably best if we put our heads together and decide what the future should hold. How is that contract going?'

Rose shook her head and smiled. He really had a neck like a jockey's arse thinking he could call the shots and dare to ask her about work as if everything was normal.

'You know I probably should've been devastated when you left,' she said. 'But I wasn't. I'm not. I'm fine. In fact I'm sleeping better and I feel like I have a better handle on what's going on in the business because I'm not having to bounce everything off you. You made a total bags of the business, by the way. For years I figured you were better at handling it than I was. Boy, was I wrong! The staff all hated working with you too.'

'Really?' He sounded utterly defeated.

'You've messed up in so many ways, it's hard to know where to start. But actually you've done me a favour. I'm starting to blossom and I'm loving it. I will never stop you and Ali from seeing one another. But you're not coming back to this house. Why don't you call Laura and see if she'd like to take you back?'

'How did you know about Laura?' he asked, sounding stunned.

'Oh, she dropped by the office and we had a chat. Nice lady. She didn't deserve to be dumped after waiting around for you all this time. You really are a shit, Martin. You need to learn to behave better. I've no sympathy for you if you're feeling you shouldn't have handled things the way you did. I want nothing to do with you and I'll never change my mind. Whatever you organise with Ali is between the two of you. But don't dare set foot in Marine Terrace.'

'What about my things?'

'Text me your address and I'll have them sent.'

She hung up and ignored the phone when it rang again. The sound of the incessant ringing was actually oddly comforting. Knowing he was sweating at the other end, unable to reach her, gave her enough of a kick without having to actually fight with him.

She'd put in a fourteen-hour day yesterday and she was heading to the office for another few hours before their break in Connemara tomorrow.

She was surprised by how excited she felt about going there. She'd need to have the conversation with her parents about why Martin wasn't with them. But she'd cross that bridge when she came to it, and she certainly wasn't going to let it interfere with their time away. She couldn't wait to see her dad again. But then she thought of her mother and knew Martha was going to blame her for Martin's departure. She'd have to be ready for the barbed comments and the insinuation that it was no less than she deserved.

Her heart squeezed inside her chest when she thought of her dad. He'd look worried and hurt on her behalf and he'd want to fix it for her.

Rose closed her eyes and thought of how she'd been at Ali's age. She was quiet and hid behind Jeannie. But she never had proper chats with her mum. She didn't even tell her when she was sick or had a problem. She'd wait for Nanny May to come and she'd call her to a back room and whisper while begging her not to let anyone else know.

She was tired of being that person. Sure, she was successful at work, she had a lovely home and she had her sensational daughter. But she knew the time had come to step out of the shadows. The only person keeping her there was herself. She couldn't blame anyone else. She was nearly forty years old; it was time to take control.

She wasn't busting a gut to meet a man. Oddly, that wasn't high on her agenda at all. What she wanted was something outside of Ali and work to call her own. So she kicked her office door shut and googled the local amenities.

There was an adult education centre at the edge of town and there were plenty of courses running, but she hadn't the first idea of what she wanted to do. Knowing she wanted something gentle and pleasant that wouldn't involve stress or pressure, she gravitated towards cooking and baking. The perfect fit popped up. Tapping her pen against her pursed lips, she dialled the number at the bottom of the page and was a little startled when it was answered instantly.

'I'm enquiring about the Beautiful Baking course,' she said. 'I'm probably too late.'

'You're bang on time,' said the woman. 'If you want it, you'll have the last space.'

'Yes please,' she said before she could change her mind. 'I know it begins next week, but do I need a lot of equipment?'

'We can supply you with an apron and a folder for a small charge, and if you want to purchase any of the items used during the demonstrations, Louise will have them for sale. She owns the baking shop here in Pebble Bay, so she combines her teaching with a few sales.'

'Sounds ideal,' said Rose. 'Can I pay for the apron next week when I come?'

'You can pay for it along with the course fee if that's easier. I can take a credit card over the phone and that way you don't need to mess about with cash. I don't know about you, but I never have any money. I suspect my teenagers clear me out, but I couldn't swear to that in a court of law!' She roared laughing and chatted away as Rose fished her credit card out of her purse. Once she'd paid for everything, she said she'd be there at seven the following Thursday evening. They'd be back from Connemara and it would be something to look forward to.

Putting her head down, she flew through a load of work before venturing onto the shop floor for an hour. It was always worth keeping up with what was going on with the customers. She liked to shake things up by moving stock and putting new things out too. Otherwise people got bored and didn't visit as often. A delivery of things from a recent accessories trade show had arrived and one of the newer girls was putting a window display together.

'That looks gorgeous, Nelly,' she said. 'Thanks for being so creative.'

'This is what I really want to do,' the girl admitted. 'I'm hoping to set up a business with my friend. One where we offer to go into any kind of shop and do the windows on a contract basis. I do two clothes shops and the kitchen shop up the road. They let me go in during the evenings.'

'Well you're doing a brilliant job. I love the section you did with the rugs too. It shows them off so well.'

The young girl was beaming as Rose moved over to speak to Cara, who was finishing loading the van to go on a job.

'I'll be gone for a few days to Connemara. But call any time if you need me,' she said.

'Sure,' Cara replied.

'I'm going to shake things up and repaint the frontage. Nothing major, but I'd like to make my own little stamp.'

Rose felt as if she'd grown a couple of inches in height. The dull ache in her chest was lifting, and for the first time in her life she felt as if she might be capable of doing whatever her heart desired.

She walked into the off-licence and bought a bottle of champagne, along with some wine to take to her parents', then made her way home. Her last stop was the kitchen and bakeware shop. As she let herself in the door at Marine Terrace, she could hear loud and jovial chatter coming from the kitchen.

Nick stood up off the bar stool as she approached. Smiling broadly, he walked towards her, took the groceries and gave her a bear hug.

'How are you today? How's the office? Are you good to go away?'

'Calm it down, Nick! Rosie isn't used to crazy Americans in her kitchen.'

'Hey, I'm sorry. I'm just concerned about you, that's all. I'm so grateful to you for letting us stay here, even with a new baby included in the package.'

'You're more than welcome, Nick. I'm just sorry it's taken so long for you to get here. This should've happened years ago.'

'Hey, Mum,' Ali said as she appeared from her room. 'Is baby Austin awake yet?'

'Not yet, honey,' said Jeannie. 'I'm guessing we'll all know about it when he is.'

Rose jumped into the shower, then pulled on her track-suit and returned to the kitchen.

'Bea! You're here, fantastic.' She hugged her sister hello, then opened the bottle of champagne she'd bought, along with a can of lemonade for Beatrice. With a little giggle, she took the tiny bottle she'd purchased in the baking shop and put a drop in the bottom of each glass.

'So,' she said, carrying the tray of filled glasses over. 'We're going to toast baby Austin and welcome him to the family.'

'It's blue!' Jeannie said as she burst out laughing. 'You're a hoot!'

'Well, blue for a boy, so I figured we could have a blue drink. To Austin!' she said happily.

'To Austin!' they chorused.

'And to Uncle Nick, who is *the* coolest uncle ever. He gave me the new Morphe make-up palette!' Ali said happily.

'Eh, I might have had a little guidance with that one,' he admitted.

'I'm not telling my friends that. They all know about the procedures and surgeries you do, so they already think you're great. Becca's uncle is an accountant who wears the same suit all the time. She suspects he even sleeps in it. He has a ring of dandruff on his jacket and a nervous sniffle.'

'Yup, Uncle Nick wins,' said Jeannie as she hugged him. 'Uh, blue or not, this champagne tastes amazing.'

'I'm glad you're able to drink again,' said Rose with a giggle. 'Otherwise who else can I hang out in bars with?'

'Excuse me, what's wrong with me? I exist,' said Beatrice.

'Of course you do, honey,' Rose said. 'But you're going to be round and pregnant and it puts the men off.'

'So you intend on using my wife as bait?' said Nick.

'That would be about right,' said Rose as they all

laughed. 'I'll give you a few weeks to get back on track and after that I'm forcing you to come out with me.'

'I'll need to get to a point where I don't fall asleep on the bar.'

'Fair enough. For now we'll drink at home instead.'

A little snuffling noise came from the Moses basket and there was almost a riot as they all rushed to see the baby and pick him up.

'Back off,' Jeannie said jokingly. 'He's mine. I grew him and gave birth to him, so I get to hold him. I will display him, however.'

They congregated in the living room, where there was plenty of space for them to sit without crowding him.

Jeannie gave him his bottle and then he lay on her chest facing out with the most contented little face.

'Look at him,' said Rose. 'He's milk drunk.'

His pale blue eyes were drooping a little. His chubby cheeks, which made them all want to squeeze him, were the perfect peachy surround to his full lips. He'd inherited the Brady complexion, which was pale but after a few days in the sun would tan nicely.

'Do you think he'll grow curls?' Ali asked as she sat cross-legged on the floor in front of Jeannie. 'Did I have curls when I was born or was I just fluffy like him?'

'You were a little fuzzball,' said Beatrice. 'I remember us trying to put a bow in your hair for Hilary's wedding.'

'Oh I'd forgotten that,' said Rose. 'It kept sliding out. They didn't have those little headbands back then,'

'Thank God,' said Ali. 'I had some choice outfits judging by the photographs.'

'You were the best-dressed child ever,' said Jeannie. 'We all went mental buying you stuff.'

'And we're going to do it all over again,' said Beatrice. 'Except we have a different flavour to buy for this time. It's so exciting.'

Rose couldn't help feeling bad at how much she'd misjudged Nick over the years. He was warm and funny and there was no doubt that he was besotted by Jeannie. In turn, she was crazy about him. She listened when he spoke and it was clear that they had a really good friendship apart from anything else.

She wondered why she'd taken such a dislike to him years ago. Martin sprang to mind. He'd been like a bull when she'd told him she was going to the wedding. He'd warned her about loud, brash Americans and told her in no uncertain terms that the relationship was a flash in the pan.

'You know what Jeannie is like. She'll be bored with this idiot in no time. Then you'll be too involved and it'll be awkward. Give him short shrift and make it clear that you're there under duress.'

Her mother had added her own bitterness.

'Martin is right, this fellow sounds dreadful. Don't be taken in by him.'

So she'd gone with her hackles up and judged Nick before she'd even met him.

Shame washed over her as she thought of how stand-offish she must've been. She'd actually gone into this man's home and acted as if she was doing him a favour.

Martin may as well have come to the wedding; he was on the phone morning, noon and night making sure she didn't relax or enjoy a single moment. He'd done the same thing when she, Beatrice and Jeannie had gone to a spa for the night last year. It was Jeannie's treat, a matter he'd had issue with too.

'She's able to splash the cash and make you and Beatrice seem like the poor little grovellers.'

'She's not like that, Martin. Anyway, Nick organised it. He made the booking, right down to afternoon tea and the gorgeous treatments we each had.'

'He's gay and he's using your sister as a cover-up,' Martin said. 'I knew there was a reason he was with her and that's it.'

'Why would he be using her as a cover-up?' Rose had fumed. 'If he's gay, he wouldn't be married to her in the first place. He chose nice treatments for us because he's a plastic surgeon so he knows a lot about skin and what women like.'

'Oh, Rose, sometimes I really worry about you,' Martin said. 'You're so gullible and you seriously cannot judge character. It's lucky I'm here to protect you.'

Wow, Rose thought now. He'd certainly been right about her judgement: she'd been completely taken in by him. He'd worn her down and robbed her of her self-belief. Well, her time had come. She was going to make the most of her life from here on in. She had a good business head, a lovely home, a beautiful daughter who tried her patience and pushed her to the limit, but she still loved her to bits and now she had a whole new chapter to begin.

They ended up having an early night. Rose heard Austin crying a couple of times, but not for long.

The following morning, she dashed up to the bakery and got croissants and their delicious cinnamon swirls. She bought a few extra ones to bring for her dad, knowing he'd love them.

Breakfast was a help-yourself affair with a pot of coffee to add to the pastries.

'Okay, we're off,' said Jeannie. 'It's only taken the guts of an hour with about a pint of sweat to figure out how to use the car seat. One of the nurses showed us at the hospital yesterday and made it look so easy, but it's like solving a puzzle. Finally we think it's fitted properly. Austin isn't too bothered, so that's great.'

'See you there and please drive carefully,' Rose said as she hugged Nick.

'Believe me, I'll be going at like two miles per hour!'

The sisters hugged their goodbyes.

Ali appeared and they drove to Beatrice's apartment to pick her up.

Even though the whole reason for going to Connemara was so Jeannie and Nick could introduce Austin, the others had decided to go anyway. Nobody knew when they'd manage it again in the future. Beatrice would have to stay around Dublin for a while, all going well. Rose needed to be at the shop, and Ali wanted to spend the summer holidays with her friends.

Rose said a little prayer that Beatrice would have a happy announcement of her own soon too.

Chapter 28

BEATRICE WAS DOG-TIRED. SHE'D BEEN DOWN IN the shop since five in the morning. Not because she couldn't sleep, but purely because she needed to sort a few orders and leave things ready to go for Isobelle and the new girl, Annemarie.

A message pinged through on her phone. She'd set up a competition on the shop's Facebook page to win Sadie's dresses. After chatting to Richard, they'd agreed that the best policy would be to give the dresses to two different girls. They were a tiny size, so the happy recipients would need to fit them. Beatrice had figured it would narrow the search and mean fewer messages, but she was blown away by how many girls were looking to be chosen.

The names would supposedly go into a hat and two would be pulled randomly to make it fair.

She'd cried like a child as Richard had told her the whole sorry tale. Sadie had dropped over to his place two days before the wedding. As a special gift for her to wear on their wedding day, he'd had a necklace hand-crafted with two intertwining diamond hearts on a white-gold chain. When he gave it to her, it proved to be the final straw, and Sadie simply couldn't pretend a second longer. She'd told him she couldn't marry him and that she was sorry. Then she'd gone to Kerry in the south of Ireland to stay with her brother until the dust settled.

'So it appears the job of unravelling the wedding rests on my shoulders.'

He'd looked so heartbroken and utterly desolate that Beatrice had put her arms around him and rocked him from side to side like a child. He'd been dry-eyed at first. In fact, he'd been taut and tense, but slowly she'd felt his body relax and the soft sound of crying had filled the shop.

She stood away from him and apologised.

'I'm sorry, I don't know why I did that,' she said, cringing. 'I don't normally launch myself at the customers. But then again, most of them are women and that's not my style.'

'Unlike Sadie,' he said. 'That's the issue. She's gay.' He stared at her with such hurt in his eyes. 'So no matter how hard I tried, I could never have made her happy. I think that was part of the attraction with her. I've had my fair share of admirers over the years.' He sighed deeply. 'Many of them just saw a big house, rich parents, fast cars and a glossy-magazine lifestyle. But Sadie was always different. She didn't dissolve into hand-flapping giggles when I walked in. In fact, she made me work to win her over. But I tried so hard. I thought we'd found something special. I really did. Put it this way.' He looked at her. 'I found something wonderful and she felt trapped.'

'I know you're hurt right now,' Beatrice said. 'But it's better that she's called it off before the wedding and the honeymoon and the expectations of a life that isn't going to happen.' She sighed and told him about Davy and how she'd let it go a step further.

'There's never a good time to tell someone you don't love them,' she said sadly. 'I don't think I'll ever forgive myself for not being honest sooner. But I was swept along and I genuinely wanted to love him the way he loved me.'

'Are you gay too?'

'No,' she said. 'But I may as well have been where Davy was concerned. I wasn't attracted to him and there was nothing I could do to change that.'

'Have you met anyone else?' Richard asked her.

He looked like he needed her to say yes and she wished she could, but she simply shook her head, then found herself telling him about the IVF and how she was hoping she could have a child now.

'Wow,' he said. 'And you run this place on your own as well?'

'I love it.'

'So you love something,' he said, and grinned.

'Do I sound like a monster to you?' she asked.

'No,' he said. 'You sound pretty impressive. I think you ought to be admired. You've done so much with your life and you haven't sat about moaning. I'll take a leaf from your book.'

'Oh, you wouldn't want to do that,' she said. 'I'm hardly an example to follow.'

He carried the dresses into the shop. Beatrice put them in the stockroom and he wrote his mobile number on a yellow sticky pad, asking if she might let him know who won them.

'I don't know why, but I'd like to know for certain that they get to attend a wedding, even if it's not mine.'

'I'll call,' she promised. He'd hugged her goodbye and it hadn't felt weird.

She'd put the advert up on the shop's Facebook page immediately, and now there were close to a thousand names on the list. Each one had given a reason for asking for one of the dresses. She couldn't believe how many people were desperate to win. The messages kept coming and she knew it would be impossible to consciously choose just two, so she'd do as she'd promised and put them into a draw.

She typed Richard's number into her phone in case she lost it. The competition would close tomorrow and she'd let him know. That could all be done from Connemara.

She couldn't wait for the time away and was genuinely comfortable about leaving the business for a while. She had a great set of staff covering the stores.

Her bag was packed and she had a lovely dress for dinner at the golf club tomorrow night. She'd ordered a dress for her mum too. She wasn't sure she even liked the things she'd given her in the past, but seeing as there were no outward complaints, she assumed they were okay.

The new one was a shift dress to the knee by a German designer. They were selling really well as mother-of-the-bride pieces as most had matching coats and fascinators. This one was bright pink and the beading was subtle enough to make it wearable. She'd bought her father a new tie from a designer he liked. She knew he'd greet the gift with hugs and thanks enough for both of them.

Also within her luggage were two double packets of pregnancy tests. The clinic had told her they would do a blood test on Tuesday and had insisted she didn't need to use a home-testing kit. But she couldn't help herself.

She didn't feel that different. She wasn't vomiting violently, she couldn't smell things from a ten-mile radius and she wasn't bursting into tears at the drop of a hat. But there were no rules to state that she needed to be doing all of the above.

She'd had no bleeding and that was the main thing that was keeping her hopes alive.

By the time Isobelle arrived to open the shop, Beatrice was ready for bed once again.

'I thought you were going today?' her assistant said. 'Is everything still going ahead?'

'Yes, absolutely, I just needed to fill some orders and leave a few bits out for you.' She showed Isobelle what she meant and then was happy to skip out and freshen up before Rose collected her.

'Are you certain you don't mind having Ned?' she asked Isobelle.

'Of course not. We're going to have a fantastic time, aren't we, Ned?' He wagged his tail from his bed behind the counter. 'See! Now stop fussing and go and have some family time. You need this break. You haven't stopped for a second since you opened here.'

'Thank you,' Beatrice said, hugging the other woman.

She ran up and took a last look around the flat, then brought her suitcase downstairs. Rose was on the roadside with the hazard lights flashing and Ali jumped out of the front seat to help her.

'I'll do it,' Beatrice said. 'You hop back in, and I don't mind sitting in the back.'

'I've got my music,' Ali said, 'and you and Mum will be gossiping. No offence, but I'll be zoning out after about ten minutes.'

Beatrice hugged her niece, who was being good and trying not to pull away from her. She needed to remind herself that Ali was a teenager and she was now the old auntie offering unwelcome hugs and kisses.

They set off on the four-hour drive with everyone in

great spirits. They stopped at Enfield and had a coffee with Nick while Jeannie fed Austin, then piled back into their cars, with Nick teasing Rose that he was going to win the race to get there.

By the time they arrived, Beatrice felt as if they'd put most of the world's problems to rights.

They'd all come together and decided the best thing to do was go to the cottage and surprise their parents with baby Austin.

The arranged time was four o'clock, which had been set by Martha.

'So you'll definitely be there?' Rose had asked her.

'Yes, dear. My goodness, I cannot fathom what is so important that you're setting a stopwatch on my day. I've had both Jeannie and Ali on to me as well.'

'Believe me,' said Rose, 'you'll agree that it's worth being there for.'

'Okay then, see you at four.'

The hotel was quaint, with mismatched furniture and a very homely atmosphere. They decided to treat themselves to afternoon tea. It was served on china and silver cake stands. With three tiers of tiny yet delicious home-made sandwiches and bite-sized cakes, it hit the spot. The pots of tea came with little strainers to catch the rogue leaves.

'Who makes real tea any more?' Beatrice whispered. 'I would be the size of a whale if I stayed here for too long. Even the smoked salmon and cream cheese sandwich bites must be a gazillion calories each.'

'But they're worth it,' Rose said wisely. 'That rule still applies, you know – if something is high in fat and tastes awful, then more fool you. But if it's worth the calories and you savour each morsel, then that's fine.'

They booked a table for nine o'clock that evening.

Beatrice sincerely hoped their mother was going to be welcoming. They were used to her distracted ways and being put last in the line of people vying for her attention. She wondered if Martha would make an effort to be polite to Nick. She held it against him that he was American and seemed to hold him in even lower regard because he'd managed to stick with Jeannie for so long. Martha had been fully sure the marriage would be a flash in the pan.

'I give them six months, a year at most. Neither of them is mature enough to manage a marriage.'

'Nick's in his mid thirties, Mum,' Rose had said. 'We mightn't particularly like him, but Jeannie does and that's the main thing. I most certainly don't wish them any ill. I hope they are happy for the rest of their lives.'

'Oh, come off it, Rose,' Martha had scoffed. 'That's a load of bunkum and we both know it.'

Back then, Rose hadn't been a fan of Nick, but she wasn't going to allow their mother to bitch about her twin's husband. She'd probably say it out and tell Jeannie that she agreed. She was such a shit-stirrer and always had been. She loved nothing more than to see them fighting. Anyway, that was then and this was now. Things were very different, and if Martha tried to so much as imply anything disparaging about Nick, they'd all jump on her immediately.

Their dad was a different story. He was so excited about showing them the cottage.

'I can't wait for you to see it,' he had said. 'It's been totally transformed and it's really wonderful.'

At ten past four, just to be sure Martha would definitely

have returned, they arrived at the cottage. Jeannie ran to Rose's car.

'The super-green snot mobile isn't here.'

'What'll we do?' Jeannie asked as Jim pulled the front door open and was walking towards them.

'Well, Austin's asleep at the moment, so will I leave him in the car for a few minutes and we can take it in turns checking on him?' Jeannie chewed her bottom lip, looking anxious.

Rose knew there was no chance she'd have left Ali in a car on her own when she was only a few days old. So it wasn't fair to ask Jeannie to do it. Besides, if Martha wanted to see him, she could – if and when she turned up.

'No, I'll bring Dad into the cottage and distract him. I think they've made the kitchen and living room all one big room, so I'll talk to him about that and you go into the hallway and call him, ask him to help with something.'

'Mum is a prize bitch,' said Jeannie.

Rose was about to automatically say that wasn't fair. But in truth, she agreed with her sister.

'Don't let her ruin this moment for Dad. He's going to be so thrilled.'

'I know!' Jeannie said as the excitement came back into her face.

Rose ran to her car and filled the other two in on the plan.

'Do you think Grandma's had an accident?' Ali asked.

'Do you know, I very much doubt it,' said Beatrice. 'Don't get me wrong, I hope she hasn't, but I'd say she's just suiting herself as usual.'

Jim was easy to distract as he showed them the main open-plan room of the cottage.

'Here's my sea-viewing chair,' he said as Ali ran to test it out.

'That's pretty fantastic, Grandad. It's just so unspoilt and uninterrupted.'

'Those cheeky seagulls have a habit of swooping at times.'

'How dare they!' said Rose.

'Dad?' called Jeannie.

'Yes, love,' he said, looking back from the sea view.

'Can you come and help me with this, please?'

Jim walked out into the hall.

'Surprise! Come and meet your grandson, Austin!'

'I . . . I . . . don't understand,' he said, stuttering and shaking his head. 'How on earth . . .'

'Let's have that talk later,' said Jeannie. 'I didn't know I was pregnant and I went into labour and, as usually happens after labour, a baby appeared.'

'Oh darling, I'm so delighted for you.' He rushed over and Jeannie hugged him.

'Dad, this is my gorgeous husband, Nick.'

'Well hello, Nick, what a pleasure it is to meet you,' Jim said, shaking his hand and then hugging him. 'I'm so delirious you wouldn't believe it.'

'Me too, sir,' said Nick. 'I've never been on such a long-lasting flight. When I heard the news I couldn't get to her quick enough.'

'I can only imagine,' said Jim. 'Come in, come in! Bring this little man into the living room. Oh Lord, he's gorgeous. You two make very pretty babies. It's such a pity Martha isn't here. I'll call and make sure she's okay.'

He did just that and she picked up on the last ring.

'Hello, Jim,' she said as the sound of plates clattering in the background alerted him.

'Where are you?'

'I'm in the café having a quick coffee and sandwich. I hadn't eaten since eight o'clock this morning.'

'You promised to be here at four for the surprise.'

'Yes, I'm on my way. A few minutes won't matter, surely?'

Jim hung up, because he was terrified of what might come out of his mouth.

'She's on her way and is full of apologies,' he lied.

They looked in every room, complimenting their dad on his choice of colours and design.

'You've kept the wonderful charm of the place but made it so much cosier and more modern.'

'Are you still delighted with the move?' Rose asked. 'A year on, do you still feel it's been the right decision?'

'I play golf to my heart's content. Martha didn't take to it the way I'd hoped,' he said, looking a little disappointed for a moment. 'But she's back doing what she loves. She has groups of women in the community centre and the rest of the time she zooms about in her super-green snot mobile delivering babies or checking on the new mums.'

'Is she working all the time again?' Rose asked.

Jim nodded. 'But it's what she wants. I guess I'm doing what I want, so she should too. She's so good at it as well. People love her and she feels she's doing a service. There was a genuine need for her here in Ballyshaden, so all's well that ends well.'

Beatrice admired their dad. He'd worked so hard for so long, and this was his idea of a happy retirement. Their mother had clearly pushed the barriers away and broken free, leaving him to his own devices. But he loved and respected her enough to let her be who she needed to be. She hoped Martha appreciated him.

They were all upstairs looking out of one of the bedroom windows at the view when Martha's car came up the driveway.

'Will you carry Austin?' Jeannie asked Nick. He took him and cradled him, kissing him on the head.

'Hello? Where is everyone?' Martha asked. They trooped down the stairs, ensuring that Nick was last.

'So this is my husband Nick and my son Austin,' Jeannie said. 'We're leaving now.'

'Why? Are you in a hurry for an appointment?'

'No, Mum, I'm not. You were asked to be here at four o'clock. You couldn't manage to do it. It was probably one of the most important moments in my life. And you just couldn't be here. You chose a sandwich over your grandson.'

'That's not fair! I had no idea you'd had a baby. Where did he come from? I assume he's adopted? You certainly never mentioned being pregnant.'

'She didn't know she was pregnant,' said Rose.

'Please,' Martha said. 'Please, Jeannie, don't go. I'm so very sorry that I went to the café. I hadn't eaten all day. I feel terrible. Please, let's have tea together. Your father has a beautiful table set. And I really want to meet my new grandchild.'

'Please stay,' Jim said, as he wiped tears from his eyes.

'It's okay, Dad,' said Jeannie. 'We'll stay. But let it be known that it's only because you asked us to. Not *her*.'

Martha went to say something and clearly decided against it.

'Come outside, everyone,' said Jim as he tried to regain his composure. 'I think we all need a cup of coffee at the very least.'

Chapter 29

THE PATIO WAS LIKE SOMETHING FROM A MAGA-zine. There was an area for sitting and relaxing, with dark-coloured furniture with large cushions and a matching glass-topped coffee table. Above it was a massive parasol that could swing around to whatever position they wanted.

'That's for the Sunday papers or a good book,' said Jim.

'What about awful books?' Beatrice asked as Jim draped his arm over her shoulder.

'They can be read here, but only for a while, and then they get tossed in the charity pile.'

On the other side of the large square area were sun loungers with soft squashy cushions in a beautiful shade of cornflower blue. Each one had its own parasol and all of them looked out at the sea.

'Wow!' said Ali as she kicked off her shoes and flung herself down on one of them. 'I could sit here for ever.'

'Isn't it wonderful?' said Martha.

The final area housed a cast-iron table with eight matching chairs. The table was set for tea, but it was a bit of a hotch-potch, as Jim had used some of the good cutlery and some of the everyday stuff. He'd also filled a vase with sweet peas, but some of them were tumbling out onto the table. It actually looked better than a perfect arrangement. Over the years, he'd been fantastic at knowing what piece of furniture would fit in what spot; his eye for design was superb. But the attention to detail and more finicky things were usually left to Rose.

'So what's the news with the rest of you then?' Martha asked expectantly.

There was total silence as none of the girls was willing to answer the question.

'Mum and I are going to mind each other and get used to not having Dad around,' Ali said. 'But we'll be fine.'

'That's good, love,' she said. 'But where's Martin got to? Why isn't he around? Has he taken on a contract abroad or something?'

'No, he's gone,' said Rose flatly.

'Where?' Jim asked, looking confused.

'London,' said Ali. 'He's left us.' She pointed and wagged her finger from herself to Rose and back again. 'He and Mum have split and he's busy making a new start without us.'

'Surely not?' Jim looked as if the rug had been pulled from under him.

'I beg your pardon?' Martha looked positively florid in the face with rage. 'How dare he leave when he has responsibilities?'

'It's okay, Mum,' Rose said. 'I'll tell you in detail later, but Ali and I are doing surprisingly well. We still have one another, and Bea is around the corner.'

'We're going to visit Aunt Jeannie and Uncle Nick in LA as well,' Ali said.

'That's all very fine and well, Ali,' said Martha. 'But a week beside a swimming pool won't make up for the fact that your dad has left you in the lurch. To think that I liked him . . . I actually thought you'd done well, Rose, to have a man like him by your side.'

'We both liked him,' said Jim in shock. 'He was a good worker as well. Talented. He always made out that you and Ali were the light of his life. I don't understand.'

'Ali was and still is the light of his life,' Rose said. 'How could she be anything less? But according to Martin, I wasn't enough for him.'

'What did you do wrong, Rose? Why didn't you make more of an effort?' Martha was becoming more and more agitated. 'Clearly you've done something thoughtless and driven him away.'

'I didn't drive him away, Mum. He went of his own accord. I already blame myself, so thanks for adding weight to that.'

'You have no right to blame Rose,' Jeannie said hotly. 'She's amazing and caring and she goes out of her way to make my life as good as it can be. Martin has been having an affair for years. He's not the man you thought he was.'

Martha looked over at Jim, who was sitting quietly at the table. She squared her shoulders and planted a smile on her face.

'That all sounds rather far-fetched. Please tell me it isn't true.' She looked at Rose.

Rose shot a look at Ali, who was sitting with her mouth open and eyes wide. Rose had been careful not to divulge any information about Martin's behaviour, and she could strangle her twin for speaking out of turn. But there was no taking it back now. She'd have to explain it as best she could to Ali later.

'It's all true, I'm sorry, Mum,' she said.

'It's ironic really. I had a notion in my head that Nick

wouldn't stand by Jeannie. I figured because he's an American and a hotshot surgeon that his ego would come first. But here you are and Martin is gone.' It was clear to everyone that she was struggling with her thoughts. 'I was wrong.'

'Wow,' said Beatrice. 'I never thought I'd hear those words coming from your mouth. You were always right. No matter what.'

Martha looked at her with an expression of astonishment in her eyes. 'I don't mean to come across that way. I don't believe I'm always right. In fact, a lot of the time I feel the opposite. I feel like I have something to prove.'

Jim walked over to put his arms around Beatrice and Rose, who were standing next to one another.

'Can we be happy to be together?' he asked. 'Let's use the next couple of days to savour the fact that you're all here. Would that be possible?'

Beatrice told them about dinner at the hotel and they said they'd love to join them.

'You haven't forgotten about tomorrow night and the golf club?' Martha asked. 'We also have an invitation for you to come to Dorothy and Larry's home.' She told them about Olivia and the baby and how they wanted it to be like an inaugural family occasion.

'That's so kind of them,' said Beatrice. 'They've been doing this for years? You just never know what goes on behind closed doors, do you?'

'Indeed,' said Martha. 'It was quite a mystery before the truth came out. I saw Larry kissing Olivia outside the golf club when we were leaving one night. Little did I know it was more of a father–daughter kiss on the cheek than any sort of canoodling.'

'Your mother put two and two together and came up with five,' said Jim with a chuckle.

'It wasn't funny, Jim,' she said. 'I was so upset on Dorothy's behalf.'

'Odd,' said Beatrice. 'I always thought you looked down on Dorothy. You spent time with her under duress, if I'm not mistaken.'

Martha flushed and pulled at the knot of her scarf as if it had suddenly become too tight.

'I'm always polite to everybody, Beatrice. I take offence at you suggesting I'm anything but.'

'I didn't say you were rude,' she said. 'You never seemed to rate her that highly from what I could observe. So it's a pleasant surprise to hear that you are fond of her underneath the frosty exterior.'

'Beatrice, I don't know what's come over you,' Martha said, poker-faced. 'But you seem to be having a bit of a moment there. Are you finding the world a little objectionable today?'

'Not at all,' she said calmly. 'I'm simply saying what I think. There's no law against that. I'm not a teenager any longer. I'm an adult and I speak my mind.'

'That's exactly right,' Jeannie chimed in. 'We can all speak our minds, no holds barred.'

'All right then,' said Jim, clearly wanting to smooth things over. 'Let's make a little itinerary, why don't we?'

'Eh, I think Austin and I are going to take a walk. Can I have the car keys?' Nick said to Jeannie, clearly guessing that his wife was only getting started with talking about how she felt.

'Thank you,' Jeannie whispered.

'Hey, Ali, why don't you come with us?' Nick suggested.

'Love to,' Ali said, looking relieved. 'See you in a bit, Mum.'

'I'll walk out with you,' Beatrice said. 'I want to grab some things from the car.'

She went outside and gathered up her gifts from the boot. She was in two minds now about presenting her mother with the dress. Holding it in the suit carrier, she walked reverently with her arm extended high so it wouldn't trail on the floor.

'Here we are,' she said, rejoining the others on the patio, 'I got this for you, Mum, thinking it might be nice to treat you. But if I'm totally honest, I don't particularly think you deserve it. I've something for you too, Dad. You definitely deserve it.'

'Something for me?' Jim asked, his lovely face crinkling into a smile. As Beatrice kept hold of the hanger holding the dress, his eyes pleaded with her, so she handed it over to Martha.

'I'm hoping you like it, but knowing you, you'll find some sort of fault. As with all my gifts to you, it's given with the best of intentions. All I've ever wanted is your approval. A smidgen of a sign that you feel proud of me or that I've done something you approve of.'

Martha stopped for a moment to compose herself. Unzipping the bag, she peered in.

'Oh, it's a very pretty colour,' she said as one eyebrow shot up. 'I can't say I would've chosen it myself. But it's very nice, I suppose.'

'Take it out,' Rose said. 'Let us see it.'

Martha pulled it from the bag and held it up. Turning it back and forth, she began to nod.

'There's beautiful beadwork on it,' Beatrice said. 'That's

the German label that does the short-style wedding gowns I stock.'

'How are the shops? Have you been busy, or is the new one taking a while to get going?' Martha asked, clearly pleased to have some neutral ground for conversation.

'Gosh, no,' said Beatrice. 'It's so busy, it's incredible. All the stores are, thankfully. Jeannie has been helping me at the new boutique this week. Isobelle was sick and she came to my rescue. She's been brilliant.'

'I was talking to Nick at length last night about the possibility of opening a store in LA,' said Jeannie.

'Really?' Beatrice said. 'I'm so excited for you, honey! We can sit down and go through the suppliers and I'll put you in touch with them. Although you've been such an amazing saleswoman that I'd offer you anything to stay on with me!'

'I can't keep up with you girls,' Jim said. 'You're dead right to seize the day and do something you enjoy. It's wonderful, isn't it, Martha?'

'Yes,' she said. 'I'm happy that you two seem to have found something. Even if Jeannie is hanging on Beatrice's coat-tails.'

'Okay, that's it! Mum, why do you always have to say something nasty?' Beatrice asked. 'You really can sound like a bitter old sow, do you know that? Also, my new boutique has been open for months and this is the first time you've bothered to ask me about it. Doesn't that say something to you? I mean, do you *ever* wonder what any of us are doing? Can you not get past yourself and your utter obsession with other women having babies?'

Martha stared at her, looking utterly distraught. 'Do you really feel that way? My God, you make me sound like my own mother . . . I didn't want to be like my mother,' she said sadly. 'I wanted to be liked. I wanted to be the person who walked through the village and people would wave to me and respect me.'

'You achieved that,' Rose said.

'But it seems I turned my back on you girls while I was doing it.'

'It seems?' Rose said. 'Are you honestly telling us that you weren't aware of how cold you were? If it weren't for Nanny May, we would never have known about motherly affection. You never sat any of us on your lap. You never sat at the side of the bath and watched us play with bubbles. You never read us a bedtime story. You didn't come to sports day at school, Christmas plays . . .'

'We never had a birthday party,' Rose said.

'You didn't say you wanted one,' Martha shot back.

'Yes we did!' Beatrice said. 'Every year we asked for one. We said we'd trade the designer dresses in fancy boxes for a house party with a cake.'

'Girls,' said Jim, 'I think that's enough mud-slinging.'

'We're not slinging mud,' Beatrice said. 'We're stepping out of the shadows and telling Mum what we think. It's not that pleasant, but it needs saying. Besides, it's not our fault this all has to come out. The actions are hers, not ours.'

Martha looked at each of her girls. 'Was I really that bad?'

'No,' said Jeannie. 'You were worse.'

Martha stared straight ahead, looking as if she'd been beaten with a brick. Rose actually felt sorry for her.

'I'm wondering how you came to be so harsh,' she said. 'The baffling thing is how close you and Dad appear to be. He clearly adores you and you adore him, so there has to be some warmth in there. It just needs to be directed at us for a change.'

'Mum?' Beatrice asked. 'What do you think? Can we draw a line in the sand and start over? Where you make an effort and we'll continue to do that.'

'Why would any of you want to stay in touch with me if I'm such an ogre?'

'You're *our* ogre and we're stuck with you,' Rose said. 'We've known you for too long to bother trading you in for a new one.'

Martha grinned. 'I'd like to try and be better,' she said honestly. 'Could we start with dinner tonight?'

'Rome won't be built in one day,' Beatrice said. 'But I don't see why we can't make things better at least.'

'Good,' said Jim. 'Great, in fact. So tonight marks the new wave of my girls being on the same side of the fence.'

'Have you felt as if you were stuck in the middle, Jim?' Martha asked.

He nodded and sighed. 'I tried to talk to you over the years. Don't you recall me asking you to let Beatrice wear those jeans with the patches out to dinner? She wanted to look like Madonna with laces in her hair. You went ballistic.'

'I was scared that the neighbours would think I didn't care. That I'd let her out looking like a scarecrow.'

'Who gives a shit what the neighbours think?' Beatrice raged. 'Why didn't you care about what *we* thought?'

'I . . .' Martha hesitated. 'I was never allowed to have an opinion as a girl. I had no choice about anything and I was never consulted. What I did didn't matter. Nobody noticed either way. I wanted the world to look at me and think I had it all.'

'Great, Mum, but it was at our expense,' Rose said. 'You were like something possessed when it came to etiquette. We were only just short of being marched in a line with books on our heads.'

'Was I that bad?' she asked with a sad sigh. 'Am I still that awful?'

All the women nodded.

'You were feisty from the minute you were born,' Martha said to Jeannie with a smile. 'But I guess you didn't manage to stand up to me quite as well as Ali does. She laughs in my face when I get cross with her.'

'Good for her!' said Jeannie.

'We were around you for longer,' said Rose. 'We learned that it didn't pay to make you cross. If I stood up to you, you'd take it out on Jeannie and that would make my heart hurt.' Rose took her twin's hand and they smiled tenderly at one another.

'Do you know we used to sneak to the tool shed at the very back of the garden and sit on buckets and plot our escape,' Beatrice said. 'I'd tell the twins that I'd steal food and put it in a suitcase and we'd run away.'

'Where did you think of going?' Jim asked, looking delighted with the idea. 'You sound like a live version of an Enid Blyton book!'

'We kind of were,' said Beatrice. 'I used to fantasise that we had an aunt who lived in London or Wales or even Australia. That we'd go on a boat and a train and a plane and land at this imaginary house where there was nothing but fun.'

'There was a swimming pool there with a slide,' Rose said.

'And a room painted brightly and it had all the toys we

weren't allowed to play with, like Care Bears and Barbie dolls.'

'Ooh, we longed for Barbie dolls,' said Rose. 'You said they were tacky.'

'They were and still are,' Martha said with a furrowed brow. 'And she had dreadful clothes. She was an awful creature, she was.'

'But they weren't aimed at you,' said Rose.

Jim sat with his lips sealed and looked at the floor.

'Those dolls caused the biggest argument we ever had,' Martha said, looking over at him. 'I honestly thought we were going to end up divorced.'

'Why? Over a Barbie doll?' Jeannie said. 'Tell us more, please!'

The mood in the room shifted as Martha spoke quietly.

'Jim came home one Christmas Eve with a load of Barbie paraphernalia. A house of some sort, with extra boxes of horrible plastic furniture, along with three dolls. There were outfits for each one in separate boxes too. One outfit was worse than the next. They looked like the sort of thing a call girl would wear.'

'When was that?' Rose asked.

'Oh, you twinnies were only about seven and Beatrice was nine,' Jim said. 'Beatrice wanted the doll from Santa Claus and I figured we wouldn't have many more years of her believing.'

'I lost my reason,' said Martha. 'I wouldn't allow him to put the dolls under the tree. He walked out and sat in the car for hours. I wanted to say sorry and tell him he could put them there, but my stubborn pride stopped me.'

'We found them in the shed a few days after Christmas,'

said Rose, remembering. 'We went there to plan our latest escape.'

'Because of the bears,' said Beatrice.

'What bears?' asked Jim, frowning as he tried to remember.

'I ordered limited-edition Steiff bears,' Martha said. 'One for each of them. I thought they would treasure them and perhaps start collecting them. But when you came home with the Barbie things, I knew I was so far off the mark it was scary. I realised I was just like my mother.'

'So why didn't you have the guts to say so?' Beatrice asked.

'I was wrong no matter what I did as a child. In adulthood, your father never made me feel that way. That night I knew I'd crossed the line. I honestly thought he was going to leave me.'

'Did you consider us at all?' Beatrice asked. 'Did you picture our faces on Christmas morning if we'd found the Barbie things waiting? Did it enter your head that Dad was the one who had listened and you hadn't?'

Martha squirmed and began to wring her hands. 'I was so consumed with Jim and his being annoyed with me that I didn't think any further than that. I began to mull over how ashamed I would be if we got divorced.'

'So we never featured in your thoughts?' Rose asked.

She looked glazed, as if she were far away in her head. Clearly there were a thousand thoughts zooming around in her mind and she simply couldn't put anything into words.

'Mum?' Beatrice said loudly. 'We're trying here. You have to meet us halfway, though. I think you need to see a shrink. You're obviously damaged by your childhood and you still have this dreadful necessity to run, run, run and never stop and never look back. That's bloody exhausting and you'll end up burning yourself out.'

Martha looked over at her and smiled. 'You're a clever woman, Beatrice. All of you are. All of you are incredibly warm and honest too. You get that from Jim, not me.'

'I think it's time we left,' said Beatrice. 'I see Nick and the two dotes back again and it's about to start raining.'

'I give up,' said Jeannie. 'The shell you've created around yourself is far too solid for us to crack. So from here on in, I'll be polite to you. Of course I will. But I would be polite to someone I barely know. It'll stop there. I won't be sending you cute pictures or updates on Austin's progress.'

Martha's mouth twitched slightly when Jeannie said his name. She did that when she didn't approve of something.

'Ah, that's good to know too.'

'What is?' asked Martha.

'You don't approve of his name, do you?'

'No,' she said and flicked a non-existent piece of fluff from her arm. 'I would've preferred if you'd called him after your father, or even my father.'

'We actually discussed that,' said Jeannie. 'But we came to the conclusion that Austin suited him. His second name is James, though,' she added, smiling at her father.

'How lovely,' said Martha.

'I don't care what he's called,' said Jim. 'I'm just delighted he's here.'

Nick and Ali arrived, with Ali pushing the buggy containing a sleeping Austin.

'Well, you'd best be off then,' Martha said, looking as if she'd just had a chat with the ice-cream man.

'You're never going to let any of us in, are you?' Jim asked, as he looked out at the sea.

'Okay, I've had enough of this shrink-type talk. I'm guessing it all began with Nick and Jeannie. Americans love this sort of carry-on. Anyway, let's leave it at that and finalise our arrangement for tonight, shall we?'

'Dad, you know what time we booked the table for,' said Rose. 'I think we should go before someone loses a limb or I end up in prison for murder.'

'Don't be so dramatic, Rose,' Martha said impatiently. 'I'm going to hang up this dress for a good occasion, and we'll be along to see you tonight and we'll all have a lovely evening.'

Chapter 30

NICK AND THE GIRLS CHECKED INTO THE HOTEL with the baby gazing out of his car seat like a little angel. It took Nick three runs to remove all of Austin's stuff from the car.

'How can he have so much clobber when he's so tiny?' Jeannie asked. 'And I packed light.'

'Eh, that's debatable,' said Nick as he smiled and kissed her.

'He's been stuck in there for ages,' said Jeannie. 'I'll take him out and let him have a kick on the floor without his nappy. According to this mothers' website I've signed up to, they love that.'

She put a changing mat on the floor and proceeded to remove the bottom half of Austin's clothing. He didn't do much, so she wasn't sure if the whole idea was for older babies. His little feet felt cold, so she figured it would be best to dress him again. Just as she leaned over him to grab a fresh nappy from his changing bag, an arc of pee flew into the air, hitting her right in the face. Gasping, she yanked her head back, while Nick laughed so hard that Jeannie thought he was going to vomit.

'Oh my God, that was gross!' she said. 'Why doesn't it say in the baby books to beware of boy babies and their ability to pee over half the room at only a few days old?'

She looked over at Nick, who was still laughing. 'Stop it,' she said, attempting to sulk. But after a few seconds she couldn't hold it in any longer and burst out laughing too.

'Now there's a dinner-table story for your mother,' said Nick.

'I dare you,' said Jeannie.

'If you really are daring me, I will accept this challenge and take it on like a man.'

'Bet you cave and she frightens you into silence.'

In the room next door, Rose and Ali were enjoying the treat of being in a hotel.

'I'm going to sleep,' said Ali as she flung herself onto the double bed. 'Ooh, it's like a big marshmallow. Will you wake me when we've half an hour to go?'

Rose needn't have bothered answering because Ali was already asleep. She'd read that teenagers needed more sleep than adults. Well, Ali certainly proved that point

Rose filled the bath and threw in some of the bubble bath the hotel provided. Pulling off her clothes and stepping in, she got a pleasant surprise as she looked down. She'd lost a bit of weight.

Thanks Martin, you complete waste of space, she thought; you're better than any weight-loss programme.

The bubbles were so relaxing that Rose fell asleep, waking as she slid down into the water.

'Mum?' Ali called out. 'Are you okay in there?'

'Yeah, I'm coming now,' she said pulling the plug and standing up to turn the shower on to warm herself up. Stepping out, she dried herself and put on a robe. Just as Ali was about to take a shower, there was a knock on the door.

'Can we come in?' Martha said, with everyone else in tow.

'Sure,' said Ali, looking confused. 'What's going on?'

'None of us knows,' said Jim. 'But Martha wants us all in the same room. Apparently yours is by far the biggest, so can we have our chat in here?'

There were enough chairs and arms of sofas and window seats to make sure everyone had a perch.

Martha waited until they were all seated and quiet.

'Go ahead,' said Jim, encouraging her.

'Okay, so what you all said earlier has made a big impact on me. You probably don't believe me when I say that I never meant to hurt you all the way I have. I wanted to be the opposite of my mother. But it seems I turned into her, bar the violence.'

'Did your mother hit you?' Beatrice asked.

'Yes, on a regular basis. She also verbally abused me, and when she died, I was left feeling as if I didn't matter and wasn't wanted.'

'That sounds familiar,' said Jeannie.

Martha looked over at her. 'I am sorry,' she said carefully. She looked at each of them in turn and said the same thing.

'Will we agree to move on?' Jim said, clearly uncomfortable with the awful atmosphere.

'I haven't finished,' Martha said. 'What I'm about to admit to could possibly terminate my relationship with some or all of you. I understand if that's what you want to do.'

They all looked at one another in dismay.

'I have Nanny May's letters,' she said. There was a collective gasp.

'But . . . but,' Jim spluttered, 'but the solicitor's office wouldn't let us in to look until they'd finished their own search. How did you get permission? And when were you in Dublin? I mean . . .'

He trailed off, unable to comprehend what Martha was saying.

'I found them when I found Nanny May dead,' Martha said. Jim looked as if he'd been slapped, but he said nothing. 'I saw that they were addressed to you girls and Jim and that there wasn't one for me. I was totally consumed with jealousy. I've never been more outraged. So I stole them and hid them and pretended I knew nothing about them.'

There was a stony silence in the room as no one uttered a syllable.

'All I can ask is that you forgive me for what I've done. As I said, I don't blame you if you choose not to.' She sighed deeply. 'If the tables were turned and one of you stole a letter from someone I loved with all my heart, I can't say for definite that I'd forgive you. So I understand whatever way you decide to react.'

She handed out the letters to the girls, then gave Jim his.

'Yours wasn't in an envelope, so I put it into one afterwards. That's why it isn't sealed.'

'Did you read it?' Jim asked.

She paused for a moment. She might as well tell all.

'Yes,' she said and looked at the floor.

'I would have too, if it makes you feel any better,' said Jeannie.

'I'm going to read mine out,' said Rose.

'Good idea,' said Jeannie. 'Will we all do it?'

The girls all agreed. Jim remained silent.

'Don't read yours out, Jim,' said Martha. He nodded.

Dear Rose,

I am guessing you are reading this with your sisters and possibly your parents. I hope that is the case.

From the moment you and your sister graced Marine Terrace there was nothing but fun and laughter. Of the three sisters you are the one I watched with the most worry. You are the quiet one who will always take a step back. You were the one who would take the broken pencil and give your sister the new one. You would help Jeannie with her homework, and take the rap if a coat went missing, insisting it was yours, not your sister's. When trouble came knocking you would share the blame, even though you were in your bed and not out the window at the disco.

You are a wonderful mother to Ali. Nobody can deny that fact. But she is reaching a stage where she needs to be set free a little. You are in danger of stifling her. I know you are doing it with the best will in the world and all you want is for her to know how much you love her. But believe me – she knows.

Your mother set a poor example and you are constantly striving to change that. For all of that I commend you.

Martin is not the man you think he is. I could never say this to your face as in life I felt it wasn't my business. In death I feel it's my duty.

He has slowly pushed you out of the company. He has undermined you and robbed you of your confidence. I have watched how he controls you and calls the shots.

What you have forgotten is that Bespoke Design belongs to the Brady family. He is the blow-in. He is the one who should be grateful to have a stunning home and a wonderful business.

He isn't as competent as he has led you to believe. Please, come out of the shadows and get back to where you belong, running that company, before he runs it into the ground.

Being in Marine Terrace looking after Ali from time to time, I have been able to observe your marriage from the outside. I know you aren't happy. Please, Rose, stand up and fight. Be the strong woman you once were. Don't allow him to turn you into a doormat for a minute longer. There is a world of fun and love out there for you. Don't waste your time on someone who doesn't deserve it.

I love you and I will miss you, but I hope that I can watch over you and see you blossom into the fine, clever and strong woman that you are inside.

You were on the way to being that person when Martin stopped you.

I know the truth can often hurt. So I apologise for landing this on your lap, but I believe you will be able to digest it and take it on board.

Thank you for allowing me to share a part of your life. I will love you and watch over you for ever.

Nanny May x

As Rose finished reading, Ali handed her a tissue.

'How astute was she?' Rose said. 'I can't believe she saw through Martin. She was like a regular Miss Marple.'

They discussed the letter for a while longer until Jeannie said she'd like to go next.

Dear Jeannie,

You were always my fun one. The good-time girl who wasn't afraid to go out and get what she wanted. From the day you ran away, aged four, to 'make more friends' at the swings in the park to the time you bundled onto a plane to LA and carved out a whole new life for yourself, I admired you so much.

Over the years it's been clear that you have enjoyed every second of what life has to offer. Your husband seems to be devoted to you and would bend over backwards to make you happy.

I've noticed a change in you over the past year or so. The fun has become stale, the showmanship is beginning to bore you. You are in danger of spoiling something really great. A successful marriage is a rarity and you don't want to ruin yours.

I feel it in my waters that the time has come for you to return to your roots. Don't be too quick to leave Nick behind. Good men are few and far between. Especially ones who are willing to treat you the way he does.

Your business is at a stalemate, so it's time for you to go back to the drawing board and think again.

It's time to shine, Jeannie. It's time to show that you can be more than a trophy wife with a perfect figure.

For goodness' sake please stop with the plastic surgery. Leave that to Nick and the other fools who are willing to pay him to slice and dice them. You are above all of that.

You've had fun for many years, but I think you want more. If so, it's right there waiting for you. All you've got to do is grab it with both hands.

Opportunities won't fall out of the sky; you need to make them happen. I have full faith in you. You are going to shine brightly like the star that you are. I will watch over you and love you for ever.

Nanny May x

'Wow,' said Jeannie. 'My face is getting it all today. First Austin pees right in it . . .'

'No! Ew,' said Ali as Rose laughed.

'. . . and now I'm drowning in tears.'

'This is pretty rough going,' said Beatrice. 'But what a

wonderful thing that we have Nanny May's letters. Imagine if they really had been lost for ever.'

Jeannie looked over at her mother, unsure if she wanted anything to do with her again. She'd knowingly kept all these letters and gone about her life without a care in the world.

'Did you read our letters too?' she asked.

'No,' said Martha. 'I contemplated steaming them open but couldn't quite do it.'

'How noble of you,' said Jeannie.

'Do you want to read yours, Beatrice?' Rose asked. 'You don't have to just because we did.'

'No, you shared yours, so I'll do the same.' With shaking hands she opened her letter.

Dear Beatrice,

Where do I start? All the other letters were set out in my head with no doubt about what I wanted to say. You, my dear girl, are what I would call the curveball of the family.

All your life you have taken the role of the eldest very seriously. You have shown your sisters a good example and you've always been steady.

The only wobble was Davy.

I could see that you were being bamboozled into that wedding. As usual, you did it in an attempt to please your mother.

I think we all know that you and your dad share a special bond. You hid together when the twins were babies and the house was more mayhem than most would enjoy.

But that bond cost you dearly where your mother was concerned.

Unless something changes dramatically, you are never going to win Martha's approval or affection. The harder you try, the more she will push you away. So my advice would be to cherish your father and find some sort of polite acceptance with your mother.

You are a whirlwind when it comes to business. I recall so clearly how you learned your multiplication tables in the blink of an eye as a little one. Number-crunching and doing deals comes as second nature to you. Much as you probably want to deny it, you are actually quite like your mother in this way. You are both so driven and capable that you make your jobs seem easy.

My only fear for you is that some day you will raise your head and notice that you've left it too late to do the one thing that I believe you would love the most, and that's to be a mother.

I was born with an ability to see into the future. I didn't brandish it, but it hasn't let me down yet.

I know my time is drawing to a close. I know that you will carry on splendidly without me, but I would hate to say goodbye without giving you a little nudge in the right direction.

Be happy, allow yourself to relax a little. You aren't the eldest sister to the entire world and nobody expects you to be. I will watch over you and love you for ever.

Nanny May x

Beatrice looked over at Rose and then at Jeannie as they wiped tears away.

'Well she certainly had each one of us to a T,' said Beatrice.

'If it's all the same to you,' Jim said, 'I'll read mine another time. I wasn't expecting this and I'm struggling here.'

The girls looked over at him in concern.

'A lot of emotion has come out today,' he said. 'I don't think I can deal with any more at the moment.'

They all agreed instantly that their dad's letter was most certainly not their business. Martha looked at the floor. She was the only one in the room who knew its contents.

'I don't know about any of you,' said Rose, 'but I'm far too emotionally exhausted to sit and eat a three-course meal.'

'Let's cancel and get room service,' said Jeannie. 'Then we'll all be ready to have a good day tomorrow.'

'I couldn't sit and pretend everything is fine,' said Rose. 'Too much has been said today.'

'Can I say one more thing?' Jim asked suddenly.

'Sure, Dad, go ahead,' said Beatrice.

'I think we should all acknowledge the fact that your mother had the guts to come here today and admit that she stole the letters. She could've destroyed them and nobody would ever have known the truth.'

There was silence until Rose spoke.

'Mum, you do love us after all,' she said. 'Dad is right. You could've kept those letters hidden and never confessed. That was a really difficult thing to do. So thank you.'

'You're welcome, Rose. I am truly sorry.'

'I know you are.'

Jeannie and Beatrice said nothing, and the silence was deafening.

Jim and Martha left, telling the lady at the reception desk that they were cancelling their table.

'They'll order room service instead,' Jim said.

The journey back to the cottage was a quiet one. Jim longed to read his letter, but he suspected it might contain material that would upset him.

'I'm not sure why I don't want to read my letter out loud,' he said, 'seeing as you already know what it says.'

'You were right not to read it to the girls.'

'Okay.'

Before they reached home, Martha got a call from a lady who lived about ten minutes from the cottage.

'Don't worry yourself, pet. Just breathe through the pains.' She promised she'd be there in about half an hour.

As soon as they got home, she grabbed her bag and car keys and left. Alone in the cottage, Jim ripped the letter open, wondering why on earth his wife had told him not to read it to the girls.

He sat in the comforting silence and read the last words of the other woman he'd shared his life with.

Chapter 31

THE FOLLOWING MORNING THE GIRLS DECIDED TO meet for breakfast, and Rose rang the cottage to invite their parents to join them. Jim said he'd be delighted and Martha said she'd see if she had time.

'What exactly did she say?' Jeannie asked Rose.

'Just what I told you, she'd see if she had time. She hadn't gone through her diary for today yet and she'd either be here or not.'

'Well that's just charming,' said Jeannie. 'At least she's back to her former waspish self. That quiet and meek act didn't suit her last night.'

'She's just selfish and we need to resign ourselves to the fact that she's never going to change one jot. Don't expect anything from her and leave it at that. We don't need her anyway. We have each other and Dad,' said Rose.

'Too true,' said Beatrice. 'Now I don't know about you two, but I'm ordering the full works. I never have time for anything more than a rushed bowl of porridge, so I'm going to read the paper and have a nice pot of tea after my fry-up.'

'That sounds like a lovely idea.'

'Dad!' Beatrice said, jumping up to hug him as he walked into the dining room. 'Mum, you came too. We weren't really expecting you.'

'Yes, but I'm not sure how long I have. I'm in huge demand, you know.'

Jeannie nodded at Beatrice, who shook her head. 'Go on,' she urged.

'What are you two girls at? If you have something to say, spit it out, for goodness' sake,' Martha said, looking smug. She wasn't smug for long as Beatrice filled her in on her IVF.

'You're joking,' she said. 'Please tell me this is some sort of sick and not very funny joke.'

'It's not a joke, Mum,' Beatrice said with calm confidence. 'I am not impressed that you think I would tell you I've had IVF as a joke. Why would I do that? So perhaps you could stop insulting me for just a moment and try and support me instead.'

Martha looked at Jim and guessed by his expression that he already knew.

'So when did you find out about this, then?'

Jim said nothing, just looked over at Beatrice and indicated that she should say what she was comfortable with.

'Dad came with me to the clinic when I had my embryos implanted.'

'Oh, I've heard it all now,' Martha said, throwing her hands in the air dramatically. 'You have zero interest in any story I tell you about my births, and then you'll troop into a clinic and watch your own daughter—'

'I didn't troop anywhere, and I stayed in the foyer. I went as moral support and I was more than delighted to do so,' said Jim. 'Beatrice wasn't telling people about it because she doesn't know if it will work. You know better than any of us how dicey IVF can be.'

'Yes, oddly enough, I would be the one in the family

who knows the most about conceptions and births and yet I'm the last to know about this. Well, thank you, Beatrice. If you intended to make me feel isolated and excluded, you've succeeded.'

'Mum, you're taking this in completely the wrong way.'

'What way would you like me to take it? Say, oh, isn't it wonderful? Well, I simply can't. It's ridiculous that a single woman of your age is attempting to have a baby with no support. Especially when she had a fabulous husband who she tossed aside like a piece of garbage.'

'Not Davy again,' Beatrice groaned. 'I don't need this. Would you for crying out loud let it go? That was years ago; move on, Mum.'

With that, Martha's phone rang in her bag

'Yes, dear . . . yes . . . I think I've an idea where you are. I know you're scared. I'm on my way! Martha is coming, dear.'

She popped her phone back into her bag and stood up.

'Right then, as you heard, I need to go. See you all tonight. Have a nice day, some of us have work to do.'

'Eh, Martha,' Jim said as she began to walk away. 'Have you nothing else to say to Beatrice?'

'Like what?'

'Perhaps that you wish her well. Anything at all rather than hearing about the most important thing to happen to her and then buggering off straight away.'

'I'm not buggering off, as you so crudely put it, Jim. I'm going to work. Is that okay with you?'

'No, Martha, it isn't. But when has that ever stopped you?'

She raised her eyes to heaven and continued to walk away.

'She's a witch and a bitch and a wagon and a total fraud. If only those women knew what a horrible person she is. Rotten to the core,' said Jeannie.

'I'm not going to let her upset me,' said Beatrice. 'I'm finished with that. She'll never change, so we need to build a bridge and get over her.'

Martha pulled over at the side of the road and tried to get her dongle to help boost her Wi-Fi so she could pinpoint exactly where the house was.

Her phone rang again; this time it was a man. He sounded foreign. If she wasn't mistaken, he was Russian. He said his wife was in labour but she was terrified of the hospital as they'd performed lots of tests on her before and she didn't speak very good English so she couldn't understand. She wanted her husband by her side and for someone to come to the house. The hospital said she was far too remote and she'd no choice but to travel.

'You are coming, please, lady?'

'Yes, dear, I'm on my way, but I think I'm lost.'

Martha took down directions and assured him she'd be there as quickly as she could. As the crow flew, the house was ten miles away, but in reality it could take her quite a while. The roads were tiny secondary ones with hairpin bends and poor surfaces.

The journey was arduous. Just as she was certain she was lost, she spotted a house that matched the description.

She knocked on the door and a young man answered, looking terrified.

'I'm Martha, the midwife,' she said. Trying not to be quite as stern as usual, she rushed to the young woman's side.

'I am Katya,' she said as she clenched her teeth. Sweat was covering her face and it was obvious to Martha that she needed to deliver immediately.

'Twins,' she said. Clearly she was unable to speak much English, but she'd picked up enough.

Martha led her to the bed and laid her down so she could examine her. Much to her horror, she could see an arm sticking out of the woman.

Knowing that the baby might be dead already from lack of oxygen, she called an ambulance. She was told in no uncertain terms that they couldn't possibly make it that far. Martha was left with two choices: she either put Katya into her car and drove her to Galway, which could take up to an hour and three quarters, or she delivered these babies here and now.

Katya called out in pain as a contraction hit her.

Martha thanked her lucky stars that she was specially trained in forceps and ventouse suction. She knew she was going to need the forceps in this case. She hooked up her gas and air and put the mask over Katya's face, encouraging her to take long, deep breaths. The poor girl had clearly been bearing down and pushing for a long time.

'No pushing,' Martha said clearly. She made a scrunched-up face and did a pushing type of motion, shaking her head. Katya nodded that she understood.

Martha made her take in as much gas and air as possible. She fell back against the pillows and Martha knew she was as wasted as she could get her. She'd need it, she mused gravely.

Using nothing but gestures, she showed her that she was going to use the forceps to try and turn the child. Her only hope was that the baby was small and would manoeuvre easily. It also depended on the position of baby number two. Having no access to records or scans, she was absolutely shooting in the dark. She'd try for a few minutes, and if nothing happened, she'd have to call for the air ambulance. Otherwise she was risking all three lives.

On the next contraction, while Katya sucked on the gas and air, Martha inserted one side of the forceps.

'Good girl, you're doing so well.' She wasn't lying.

On the next big contraction, she pulled with all her might. To her utter astonishment, there was a shift. The baby turned and Martha could see a head. The child had clearly been lying with its arm above its head. She inserted the second side of the forceps and pulled as if she were dragging a tree from the ground. Swiftly the baby's head was born. Soon after, the body came too. The baby was limp and blue. It was a little girl and Martha was certain she was dead. She grabbed a towel from a pile that the husband had left and rubbed her vigorously, willing her to make a movement. Then, using a bulb syringe, she gently tried to remove the mucus and liquid from the baby's mouth. She was about to give up when there was a slight movement from one of her legs.

'Come on, sweetie, you can do it. Come on,' she said, continuing to rub and syringe alternately. A loud, high-pitched yelp made her jump as the baby moved her head from side to side and balled her fists.

Katya cried out as another contraction took over. Martha called out to the husband.

'Alex, can you come, please?'

He stood by the door but refused to come any further,

so Martha cut the cord, swaddled the little girl in a towel and posted her out the door to her father.

Ten minutes later, with the help of the forceps once more, Katya gave birth to a little boy. Unlike his sister, he came out shouting and yelling and giving out like nobody's business. Katya laughed, even though she was totally wiped out.

'Noisy boy,' she said as Martha nodded and laughed. She swaddled him in a towel too and handed him to his exhausted mother.

Once the babies were cleaned up, Martha changed the bedclothes and helped Katya into the shower. Only when she had a fresh nightdress and make-up on would Katya allow Alex in.

'Congratulations,' Martha said. 'You have a wonderful family.'

They thanked her profusely and gave her everything from home-grown potatoes to a cake made with nuts and honey that looked delicious.

'Can I come and see you again in a couple of days?' Martha asked.

Katya looked to Alex, who nodded.

She tried to explain that the babies would need the heel-prick test, but it was utterly futile. She'd got permission to come back again; that was enough.

As she drove back towards Ballyshaden, Martha had a sudden moment of anger. How dare her family gang up on her and tell her that she was a bad mother? As for Nanny May, circling like a vulture around Jim all these years . . . In truth, she was the one who ought to be furious, not them.

She'd like to see any of them save three lives in one

morning. If they wanted to believe that she had somehow wronged them, they could go and swing. She didn't appreciate being treated like a criminal. She'd keep her distance from now on and surround herself with people who appreciated her.

Chapter 32

WITH ONE THING AND ANOTHER, MARTHA ENDED up spending the whole day on the go. She was utterly exhausted when she got home. Jim was about to get ready for their dinner at the golf club.

'I wasn't sure you'd make it,' he said. 'I'll fly up into the shower and then get out of the bathroom so you can do whatever you feel like doing.'

She made a cup of tea and perched on a kitchen chair. The deliveries never got old. Seeing new life coming into the world and being a part of that was a privilege. The shower stopped and she knew it was her turn to go upstairs. She took the dress that Beatrice had brought. It would be perfect for tonight at the golf club. The design was so pretty and she'd instantly loved it. But instead of saying that, she'd held back and tried to make out that she was undecided. She'd no idea why she'd done it. She hung it reverently on the wardrobe door and looked across at her shoes. There were several pairs that would go nicely with it. She had a shawl that would work around her shoulders as well. Even more pleased with it, she smiled.

Turning, she realised Jim was leaning against the door watching her.

'It's a lovely gift. I got a beautiful silk tie that will look so well with it. We should wear them tonight so Beatrice can see that we appreciate her thought.'

'Yes,' she said. 'I'm going to tell her when we see her this evening that I'm sorry I didn't react the way I wanted. I loved this the second I saw it, but I didn't show it.'

'Why not?'

'I don't know. It's like a little game I play in my head. One where I don't reveal my true feelings to my family. Instead I stay neutral and that way I won't do the wrong thing.' She looked at him. 'But it's not a good game or one that makes any sense. I don't do it with strangers or people having babies. Just our girls.'

Jim took his clothes from the dressing room and went into the bedroom to get dressed. She had a shower and all the while her heart beat faster than usual. There was change in the air. She was terrified he was going to ask her to go.

Once she was dressed and had applied her make-up, she joined him downstairs. He was sitting in his armchair. His hands were clasped and he seemed to be poised and waiting to deliver a speech.

'Jim.' He turned to look at her.

'You look well,' he said with a smile.

She sat on the other armchair and gazed over at him. 'I didn't purposely shut you out,' she said. 'I've always done my best. But I had no idea I was being so awful. Are you going to ask me to leave now?'

He stared across at her and smiled sadly. 'I considered it once. When the girls were very young. But I stayed for them. I knew they needed me. When I found Nanny May, I knew they'd turn out fine in spite of you.'

'But Nanny May came to us by chance. She approached

me in the park and asked if I needed help and told me she was qualified.'

'I orchestrated the whole thing,' he said. 'I knew there was no way you'd agree to hiring her unless you thought it was your idea. The twins were on the way and you were already resentful of Beatrice. I knew something had to be done.'

Martha stared at him, various things clicking into place in her head. 'So all this time you've known she was there because you hired her?'

Jim looked out to sea once again. 'She did the things you couldn't. She cooked, cleaned and did the laundry. That was the part you noticed. But as the girls pointed out, she also looked after them when they were ill, turned up at school plays and cheered them on no matter what they did.'

'She was a good person, there's no doubting that. But we were very generous to her too. She came on every family holiday and spent Christmas, Easter and everything in between with us. Without us, she'd have had nothing.' Martha felt anger welling inside her as she thought of how Nanny May could do no wrong in her family's eyes. 'Over the years that woman must've accumulated a fortune. No wonder she could afford that pretty cottage in a prime position. You insisted on furnishing it too. Not to mention having the men go there to paint and decorate it.'

'Why do you begrudge her a home?'

'I don't. But she did very well out of us, that's all I'm saying.'

Jim moved and sat on the windowsill, with his back to the view. When he glanced over at her, he looked exhausted.

'I've tried, Martha. For over forty years I've tried. You're impossible to love. You won't even let me in on the smallest part of your life. For weeks you've been sneaking about doing your usual, thinking you were pulling the wool over my eyes.'

'I wasn't trying to be devious. I was so bored. I missed my work. I don't know how to function without it. I know I said I'd stop, but I'm simply not ready, Jim. I'm sorry . . . really I am.'

'That's okay,' he said sadly. 'I think we both deserve to be happy, though, don't you?'

'Yes.' Her voice sounded choked.

'So perhaps we need to let each other go. I think we can safely say that retirement hasn't turned out to be what you expected.'

'Well, that's the truth of the matter,' she said.

'So would you let me go?' Jim asked.

'Go where?'

'Back to Pebble Bay.'

'Would you go back to Marine Terrace and live there with Ali and Rose?'

'I know they'd make me welcome, but I have somewhere else.'

'Where?'

He held up Nanny May's letter. 'I thought you'd read it.'

'I did,' Martha admitted, 'but very rapidly, and only that one time.'

'I see,' he said. 'Well, how about I read it to you now, slowly, so you understand everything.'

Martha knew better than to argue. Jim had a determined look on his face and she knew she deserved this. She had stolen the letters after all. So she sat up straight and listened as he read Nanny May's words.

Dear Jim,

As my heart grows weaker and the doctors are telling me they've done all they can, I know it's time to finally speak out. I want to thank you for the years we shared raising Bea, Jeannie and Rose. They were the children I never had. I didn't give birth to them but I loved them just as much as if I had.

All the memories are stored in my heart. The days on the beach, the ice creams as we sat in a row on the rough harbour wall, watching the seagulls ducking and diving.

Each of the girls stole my heart in different ways. They've grown into fine women who I hope will go on to raise the next generation of strong and determined people.

I know they will continue to be wonderful.

And then there was you. You might be aware or perhaps you were so uninterested that it didn't reach your radar. But the truth of the matter is that I have been in love with you all this time. You used to ask if I'd met a nice fellow, someone who would look after me. The answer was that I had indeed met a wonderful man and he was already looking after me, but I couldn't have him. Knowing you loved Martha and that your life revolved around your girls made me hold my silence. I was terrified that you would scoff at me or, even worse, laugh at what a fool I was being.

There were times when I found it difficult to hold my tongue. When Martha upset the girls and in turn you were utterly distraught, I wished I could take you in my arms and tell you it would all be okay.

But that wasn't my place. It wasn't my right.

As I say goodbye I wanted to finally tell you, Jim, it was always you. You were the one, but you were out of bounds. I will miss you the most and I will go on loving you.

Thank you for the memories and the special moments we shared.

Be happy, Jim. If that means changing your circumstances, so be it. Life is precious and it's shorter than you think. Time can suddenly creep up on you. Don't waste what time you have left.

I have left the only thing I own to you. My cottage mightn't be quite what you're accustomed to, but I figured you might appreciate having somewhere you can call home. You see, I don't think your marriage will last once you retire. You and Martha are too different. That was fine when you both worked. But I reckon you will soon see that you are like oil and water.

My home is yours. My heart is too and I will watch over you always.

Love,

May x

'And what's to become of me?' Martha asked, looking aghast.

'I'll give you this cottage. You can continue to dash about, except I won't be in your way. You hate going out for lunch. You can't stand my friends' wives and you resent being asked to do anything you haven't planned yourself. So if you think about it, you would be free.'

There was so much for her to take on board. She needed time to think. Most of all she needed to try and curb her anger, because right now she wanted to go over and shake Jim. How could he sit there so calmly and tell her what to do?

Her mobile phone rang; it was one of her ladies who

was due to have her baby the following week. Automatically she answered it, chirping into the phone.

'Hello, Vanessa. Everything all right, dear? . . . You are . . . How far apart are your contractions? . . . I see. The thing is that I'm meant to be meeting my daughters for dinner. They came down from Dublin to see me.' Jim listened as she told the woman to breathe. She did the breathing with her and promised to be there in ten minutes.

'I need to go to Vanessa,' she said. 'You can tell the girls the situation. I'll follow along to the club and wear the new dress. I shouldn't be too late. But it will give me a chance to get used to our new situation. Get it sorted in my head. By then I'll be able to pretend for the night. We'll do as you suggest. You're right, Jim. This is never going to work.'

As she rushed up the stairs to put on her navy slacks and her white nurse's top, Martha felt a weight lifting from her shoulders. She didn't bother going back into the living room to talk to Jim. What was the point? The game was over and she was about to start doing what she wanted.

When she went outside to get into her own car, she did stop in surprise when she saw that his car was gone. He'd clearly gone on ahead to the golf club. She could imagine the conversation. Stupidly, in the past, she'd assumed they were all in awe of her being so generous to others. Now that she realised how much they resented her, there was no point in wasting her time trying to change their minds. Babies would always need to be born. Mothers would always need help, and when they did, Martha would be there.

Chapter 33

'WE NEED TO SHAKE A LEG,' ROSE SAID WITH A yawn. 'Are you having a shower? It might freshen you up.'

'Why, do I smell?' Ali asked with a glint in her eye.

'Nope, but I'm guessing you'll feel a lot better if you're really clean.' Ali wasn't enthusiastic, so Rose said she'd go first. Ali flicked on the TV and channel-surfed.

'There's, like, six channels here,' she said with a grin. 'How crap is that? I couldn't live without MTV.'

'I'm sure you'd adapt,' Rose said.

She showered and put on a pair of white capri pants with a pretty oversized silk blouse that pulled in at the waist. The sleeves billowed, making her arms look very thin. The large screen-printed dark pink roses were such a gorgeous colour that it made her feel uplifted. The trousers were decidedly loose, which they hadn't been before. She was doing her make-up and rooting in her washbag for a dark pink lipstick when Ali appeared, wrapped in what looked like the contents of the bathroom. One towel around her head, one around her waist and then a bathrobe on top of it.

'Did you leave anything dry?'

'Nope!' she said sunnily.

Rose was humming to herself as she found the lipstick she wanted. In the dressing-table mirror she saw Ali's reflection as she pulled out the contents of the suitcase.

'Damn it,' she said. 'I wanted to wear that tight navy dress.'

'What have you got in there? It looks like half the house to me.'

Rose walked over and they took the things out. Once they were laid on the bed, Ali picked out an outfit immediately.

'Mum,' she said, looking a little shy.

'Yes, love.'

'Don't get offended, but your make-up is a bit . . . well, how can I put it? Dated. Would you let me do it for you?'

'I have done the same thing for donkey's years. Do we have time for you to do it?'

'Even if we're a few minutes late, I think it'd be worth it.'

'Now that's telling me!' Rose said as she laughed.

Ali instructed her to remove what she'd done so she had a blank canvas. Over the next fifteen minutes her daughter transformed her.

'Wow, I love it,' said Rose as she stared at herself in the mirror. 'Thank you so much.'

Ali looked sad for a minute.

'I'm sorry I've been so awful to you lately. It's only since Dad left that I've realised how much you do. You're brilliant in work and at home . . .' She hesitated. 'You're a great mum. Not like Grandma.'

'Thank you, Ali,' she said in surprise. 'That's so nice of you to say.'

'I think we can become a good team, you and me. I'm so hurt and disappointed in Dad. I wouldn't care if I never see him again. He's a total dweeb to just walk out on us without so much as a backward glance. I hate him.'

Her eyes were glassy but she wasn't crying. At that moment, Rose couldn't have felt more proud of her.

Beatrice was standing in the bathroom next door holding the pregnancy test wand. She knew she shouldn't have tried it yet, but she was so excited that she figured it would do no harm to have a quick look at a test.

She'd gone back into the bedroom and got dressed while it processed. Now she picked up the stick with her eyes rammed shut. She was fully sure it was going to contain a little blue line in the bubble window. She was so certain of it that she was already thinking of how she'd drop it into conversation during dinner.

She'd have to start at the beginning really. She'd have to go back in time to the whole Davy debacle and how the marriage was a lie. Her mother would get uppity again and her father would put his large hand over hers and tell her she'd done the right thing. He'd always been so supportive of her decision. From the moment she'd told him, he'd said she was brave and honest.

'You'll end up with a happier life if you stay true to yourself,' he had told her. 'I'm proud of you. I just wish you didn't have to go through such heartache.'

The heat in the bathroom was making her perspire, so she opened her eyes. There was nothing there. The window looked as if it hadn't been accessed at all. Shaking the stick, she tried to make out whether or not it was wet. She sniffed it. Yup, it was wet all right. Yet it was stubbornly without a blue line.

A sound deep in her throat crept upwards and out of her mouth. Dropping to the floor, she sat in a state of shock. She was a couple of days early doing the test, but she'd honestly thought that wouldn't matter. If she were pregnant, surely it would show by now?

Shaking, she pulled herself up off the floor and threw the stick in the bin. She shouldn't have given in and tried to rush things along. Just because it didn't show now didn't mean she wasn't having a baby.

But the test without the blue line was taunting her from the bin. Was this a sign of what was coming on Tuesday? Was she going to end up back at square one? Was she due to be punished for what she'd done to Davy?

She needed to wait and have her blood test at the clinic as planned and take it from there.

She wished she could go to bed and hide under the covers, but she knew it would raise suspicion. Even if she told her family what she'd just done, none of them would truly appreciate what it felt like to see that failed test. They would rightly point out that she was too early in taking it and that she needed to relax.

All the same, she had never felt quite so alone.

A message popped up on her phone. It was letting her know that she had a direct message on Facebook. Clicking onto Messenger, she read it.

Dear Beatrice,

My name is Lily and I was directed to your page by a friend. I know you have a couple of dresses on offer and I thought I would put my name in the pot. I'm guessing I have nothing to lose. I am due to get married in two months' time. It won't be a fancy wedding but a part of me would love to have a pretty dress.

Times haven't been easy for me and my partner.

We lost a child two years ago. Unless you know the pain of having a baby and then having him ripped away again, you won't understand. In fact I hope you don't understand.

Leo had multiple issues from birth and the hospital said he wouldn't make it home, but he did. They said he wouldn't see his first birthday, but he did.

When he took his final breath, I was holding him in my arms. For that I will always be grateful. I was glad that he had his mum when he needed me most.

His dad and I have cried so many tears. We honestly didn't know how to carry on without him. But then a miracle happened. We had another child. A little girl called Daisy. She is perfect in every way and it seems there is a whole new world open to us.

We are getting married in two months, as I said. We have very little money. We live in a modest flat in an area that isn't what I'd call pretty. But it's ours and most of all we have Daisy there too.

Our wedding won't be big. Just our immediate families with lunch in a hotel afterwards. We're looking forward to the day although I know I will wish Leo were there too. He'll be there in spirit.

I wasn't planning on buying a dress. I would rather use the money to do something with Daisy and my husband-to-be.

I am petite in height and width, in fact I buy my jeans in the kids' department. I see that the dresses are described as small, so maybe it will work for me?

Thanks for reading this.
Lily

Beatrice exhaled and wiped the tears from her face. Well there's the kick in the pants I needed, she thought. Replying instantly, she told Lily that she could have whichever of the dresses she preferred. She explained that she would be back at the shop on Wednesday if she'd like to come in and collect it. She gave her the phone number and asked her to speak to Isobelle and make an appointment. Then she sent a quick text to Isobelle telling her who Lily was and asking her to slot her in for an hour.

Isobelle texted back a thumbs-up sign and Lily sent a delirious message thanking her profusely for being so kind.

Putting on her make-up, Beatrice finished getting ready. If ever she'd needed a sign, it was just now. Lily was the perfect reality check. It was too early to take the test. The clinic had given her strict instructions and she'd decided to do her own thing. She had to banish the failed test from her mind or else it would drive her insane.

All was not lost. There was still hope, and she needed to remember that.

She wondered if it might be rude to text Richard to update him on the wedding-dress front. Deciding to bite the bullet, she copied the letter from Lily and pasted it into a text. Once that was sent, she added her own message saying that she'd agreed to give Lily first choice.

He responded instantly, thanking her for sharing the letter.

Good judgement call. I'm delighted that Lily will get one of the dresses. How are you?

She hadn't been expecting any further conversation, but she answered telling him she was in Connemara for a few days with her family and they were off to the golf club for dinner.

He came back instantly saying he loved that area and how envious he was.

What I wouldn't give to escape Dublin now. I've had all the gossip magazines on to me. I never got involved in that stuff. They went through Sadie. But I guess our fiasco is newsworthy for a flash-in-the-pan story.

Beatrice couldn't believe how open Richard was being. He was utterly shattered and hadn't seen the split coming. He'd loved Sadie all his life. He'd even told her he was willing to go ahead with the marriage and turn a blind eye to any extramarital dalliances she might have. Anything but lose her. Beatrice wanted to cry for him.

Her phone pinged again.

If you have time some day, I would love to take you to lunch.

Her heart thudded. Was he asking her out on a date or was he simply looking for someone to spill his heart out to? Either way, it was lovely to be asked.

I'm back tomorrow. I have Lily's fitting on Wednesday morning first thing. Perhaps after that?

Richard responded immediately.

Let's start with coffee? Pebble Bay Café at 11?

See you there ☺

Not quite sure what she'd just arranged, Beatrice knew one thing for certain: she would need a bit of distraction after visiting the clinic for her pregnancy test.

Chapter 34

THE TAXI WAS WAITING AS ROSE AND ALI APPEARED to join Beatrice.

'You look fab!' Beatrice said to Rose. 'I'm guessing your daughter did your make-up?'

'How did you know?'

'I've never seen you perfect the smoky eye.'

'I used the new palette that Uncle Nick brought me. She looks pretty good, doesn't she?'

As they sat into the taxi, Beatrice smiled at Rose. Ali sat in the front, giving them a minute to chat.

'You two seem to be bonding.'

'This trip has been so good for us,' Rose said. 'I thought things were going to go from bad to worse when Martin left. But Ali really seems to have come around. She's very angry with Martin and I can't see her wanting to forgive him any time soon. But we've had a lovely time and she's actually dropped the attitude she used to have with me.'

'I'm so glad for you,' said Beatrice. 'Maybe Martin is right about what he said in his note. Maybe he has done you a favour by leaving.'

They pulled up at the club and as soon as the taxi hurtled off, Ali exploded.

'Thanks, you two!'

'For what?' Rose asked.

'Whispering and gossiping in the back and leaving me to talk to that taxi driver. He was like Daddy Pig from *Peppa Pig*. I couldn't understand a word he was saying.' They were all giggling as they walked into the bar at the club.

Their father was at the bar looking very smart. He was in his best suit and was wearing the lovely tie that Beatrice had given him.

'Where's Mum? Isn't she joining us?' Rose asked.

'No, she's gone to deliver a baby as usual,' Jim said lightly. 'She'll come along afterwards.'

Jeannie and her men arrived. She'd decided to drive because she didn't know how long Austin would last. The baby was wearing a shirt and bow tie, which got him a chorus of 'aahs' as he sat looking like a little Buddha.

'He's so placid,' said Ali. 'If I ever have a baby, I want one like him.'

'You don't need one for a very long time,' said Rose. 'And there are no guarantees.'

'Was I like Austin when I was a baby?'

'No,' they all chorused.

Ali laughed. 'Why, what did I do?'

'You whinged non-stop,' said Beatrice. 'You were the perfect example of why you shouldn't have a baby.'

'You were a little bit of a trial,' said Rose. 'But then you turned into a wonderful girl.'

'Thanks, Mum. I'll sit beside you. Aunt Bea is too mean!'

Jim went around the table taking drinks orders. Rose looked ten years younger and Ali was like the cat that got the cream.

'I did Mum's make-up using that Morphe palette Uncle Nick brought. Doesn't she look amazing?'

'You look fantastic,' Jeannie said. 'I've told you before you could get a little business going, Ali. Do make-up for the other girls when there's a disco on.'

'Always there with a business idea, Jeannie,' said Jim with a grin. 'But you're dead right. You have a talent with make-up, Ali. You should try and make a bit of money doing it.'

'Do I get a cut?' Jeannie asked. 'Seeing as we provided the tools?'

'No, but I will do your make-up for free.'

'Was Mum furious with us?' Rose asked suddenly. 'I'd say she's bucking mad at being taken to task. Is that why she's not here?'

'She is carrying on as before,' Jim said carefully. He looked at the table as if trying to decide something.

'Dad?' Beatrice said. 'Are you okay?'

'I will be,' he said honestly. 'I might as well say it now. Your mother and I are not planning on staying here together. Things have come out in the wash. Our lives are not compatible and I'm going to return to Dublin.'

'Without Mum?' Beatrice asked in shock as she looked from him to the others.

'Yes. Nanny May left me her cottage and I'm going to move in there.'

'No way,' Ali said. 'But what about Grandma? Will she stay here by herself?'

'Yes,' said Jim evenly. 'She spends very little time in the cottage as it is, Ali. All she wants to do is tear around in that awful car of hers delivering babies.'

'That's all she ever wanted to do,' Rose scoffed. 'I don't know why any of us thought she'd change. But don't you love playing golf and being away from the business?'

'I love both, just as you say, but they can be done in Pebble Bay. I miss my life there. I miss you lot, and most of all I've realised that I'm too long in Dublin to settle back down here. This was our holiday place, and much as I have fond memories, it's you girls that I need near me.'

'Well, I'm delighted,' said Ali. 'I miss you so badly. I've nobody to sit on our bench and eat ice cream with, especially in the rain!'

'You two do that?' Beatrice said as tears shone in her eyes.

Ali nodded and giggled. 'And we take off our shoes and socks and see who can last the longest with our feet in the water in the winter.'

'Oh, wow, you guys still do that. Now I feel so homesick,' said Jeannie.

'You're here, you silly goon,' pointed out Jim.

'You know what I mean,' said Jeannie, trying to stop her own tears as she reminisced about so many happy times with her father.

'I've missed you so much, Dad,' Beatrice said. 'I never wanted you to think that you couldn't do what you wanted so I've pretended to be happy that you're here. But it's been awful without you. I'm so glad you do those crazy things with Ali.' She looked at her niece. 'As your auntie Jeannie has just said, your grandad used to do similar things with all of us and we loved it.'

'Do you really miss me that much?' he asked, looking peppery-eyed.

'You bet, Dad. And if everything goes to plan and I get to be a mum, my baby is going to need some sort of a father figure. I can't think of a better one than you.'

'Yes, and I'll have nobody to bounce business stuff off

now that Martin has gone, so while I don't want you even considering coming back to work, would I be able to talk to you from time to time?' Rose asked.

'Any time,' he said, squeezing her hand. 'Beatrice, we can start our Sunday-lunch tradition again if you like. But this time we won't go to mass and we'll go someplace fun and buzzy. A place your mother would call noisy and brash.'

'Now that sounds like a plan!' said Beatrice.

'What about me?' Ali asked, almost bouncing in her seat.

'Well, young lady. We'll have a lot of ice creams to eat to catch up. Some toe-dipping, too. And I reckon you should join us for Sunday lunches any time you're free. But suffice it to say, we will be regular buddies again.'

'Yay,' said Ali as she hugged him tightly.

'I'll be able to catch Jeannie more easily on Skype too. The Wi-Fi down here is so sporadic, we've been missing one another a lot.'

Dinner was surprisingly upbeat. The conversation stayed on the positive aspects of Jim coming back to Pebble Bay. Nobody said much about Martha until towards the end of dessert, when she shocked them all by arriving.

As always, she was perfectly coiffed and looked as if she were stepping out of the house for the first time rather than returning from a birth. She was wearing the gorgeous dress that Beatrice had brought her.

'May I join you?' she asked, looking unsure.

Jim stood up and found a chair from an empty table nearby and put it opposite his at the round table.

'How was the birth?' Beatrice asked politely as the staff fussed over Martha. She told them she'd pass on dinner but that she'd like a pot of tea and a slice of apple tart with cream.

As that was being brought from the kitchen, they all looked at her expectantly, waiting for the usual gushing news that a new little boy or girl had entered the world.

'I don't think anyone really cares about the baby of a stranger, do they?' Martha said. 'You haven't wanted to know for the past forty years and yet it was all I told you.'

There were no arguments. Nobody snatched the opportunity to tell her she was mistaken and it was actually very interesting for them.

'Did you speak to them about our conversation?' she asked Jim evenly.

'I told them that I will return to Pebble Bay while you will remain here,' he said. 'I have agreed to take Rose up on her kind offer to go back to Marine Terrace until I've done a few things with the cottage. I'd like to make a few changes so it feels more like home to me. The solicitor also advised me of a potential problem with damp, so I'll need to get that assessed.'

'I'm sorry that this is happening to you right now. You both must be finding it so tough. But I'd like to say that I think you deserve happiness,' said Beatrice. 'Both of you. Life is short and there's no shame in holding your hands up and saying, hey, this isn't what I want.'

'Bea is right,' Rose said. 'It's easier to say nothing and pretend that things are fine. But what's the point? Both of you should be happy. Dad, I have no doubt you will be. Mum, you need to learn how to be.'

'I think I will be fine, thank you very much, Rose.'

'I think you will be too,' said Beatrice. 'You'll be able to do what you love, which is dashing about delivering babies.

Nobody will get in the way or interfere with you. So it's a win-win situation.'

'But if you happen to feel that you would like a bit of company, we are all willing to come and visit,' Rose said. 'Jeannie might need more notice, but we are only a car journey away.'

'Thank you,' Martha said. 'I appreciate that, Rose. You're a kind and considerate girl. You always were.'

The tea and apple tart arrived and Martha ate quickly. Ali led the conversation, which was mainly about the dresses Jeannie had given her, and how she was going to get invited to as many balls as possible over the coming years. Her banter with Jim meant there were no silences.

Jim signed for the bill, saying the evening was his treat.

'I'm kind of sad,' Beatrice said as a tear ran down her cheek. 'It's going to be a long time before we are all together again. I can't believe you two are actually separating . . .'

'We've been living a lie for a very long time,' Jim said. 'We still respect one another, I think . . .' He looked over at Martha.

'Yes, Jim, we still have respect for one another, of course. Also, we're grown-ups. We're in the winter of our lives. No good will come of tearing each other apart.' Martha sighed. 'So we've decided to say cheerio. I'm delighted with the cottage. I hope you can adapt Nanny May's place to suit you.'

'I will,' he said.

'And what about the neighbours?' Beatrice asked. The neighbours had featured heavily in their lives growing up. What they thought, what they saw and how they perceived the Bradys as a family was of ultimate importance.

'The neighbours will probably have enough gossip to

fuel several pots of tea for a spell,' Martha said. 'That will run its course too. I know this sounds dreadfully shallow of me, but I find country folk less judgemental. I would struggle more if I were still living in Pebble Bay.'

'That's fair enough,' said Rose. 'It's where you grew up and you probably know more people.'

Jeannie had a sudden idea. Nobody knew when they would all be together like this again. She stopped a passing waiter.

'Would you mind taking a photo for me?'

'Sure,' he said. 'Who's going to be in it?'

'All of us,' said Jeannie as she stood up and encouraged Rose, Ali and Martha to stand behind Jim.

'Move in closer,' said the waiter, 'or I can't fit you all in.'

Eventually, after a lot of laughing and messing, they were ready.

'Okay,' said the waiter. 'Say cheese!'

He took a few just to be sure and handed Jeannie back her phone.

'Thank you,' she said. 'You just captured a moment before a load of changes occur.'

'Right,' he said, looking confused as he smiled and moved away.

Chapter 35

MARTHA HAD PLANNED ON DISAPPEARING WHILE Jim left. She thought it would be less awkward and embarrassing and, if the truth were told, less painful. But when it came down to it, she realised that she wanted to face the situation head-on. Nothing was going to change Jim's mind and she knew it was the best decision in the long run.

He'd slept in the spare room, which was fine, albeit completely weird. Martha knew she wouldn't sail through this separation; she'd no doubt the numbness would pass and the pain and anguish would seep through in its place.

She might have guessed her life would turn out this way. Her mother had predicted it, of course.

'You're hard to love, Martha. You always were. You were born with a shell surrounding you.'

She'd never forgotten that conversation, and perhaps she'd lived up to it. Or maybe her mother was right, and she wasn't capable of letting anyone in.

She put in a call to Olivia, who was planning on going to the mother-and-baby morning at the community centre, and asked her if she'd mind opening up and explaining to people that something unavoidable had happened and she'd be there the following Monday as usual. She said to reiterate that the women were welcome to make tea and coffee and offer peer-to-peer support.

Jim looked astonished when she asked if she'd make a pot of coffee before he headed away. He'd been toing and froing to the car since the early hours and it seemed he was almost ready for the off. They hadn't sat and had a long-winded conversation about the imminent split. Instead they'd both taken the polite route, where they acted almost like strangers.

Jim put down the box he was carrying and walked to the kitchen and leaned against a cupboard as she made fresh coffee.

'I don't understand you, Martha,' he said sadly. 'For all our married life I wished you'd do exactly what you're doing now.'

'What, make you a pot of coffee?' she said with a bitter laugh.

'No,' he said evenly. 'Put your work aside and put me first.'

She nodded. She got it. She understood, and she could see where he was coming from. She hadn't realised, of course. For the record, she told him, she hadn't known quite how frenzied she'd been.

'I tried to tell you, Martha. It's not as if I didn't.'

'When?' She knew she sounded like a petulant child and she honestly didn't mean to, but she actually needed examples.

'Do you recall the twins' one and only party with friends, when we went to the cinema? The one in the old place near Pebble Bay that closed down soon after our fiasco?'

'Oh yes, that was a dear old place really.'

'Not when you're stuck there on your own with twenty screaming girls and no movie projector working. You were supposed to arrive with Rice Krispie buns and the cakes.

They were in the boot of your car and nobody could reach you.'

'I was probably delivering a baby. You don't understand, Jim. When nature calls, there's no time to spare.'

'Nanny May saved the day,' Jim said. 'She bought all the blocks of vanilla ice cream from the tiny supermarket next door, stuck them together and emptied packets of Jelly Tots, Smarties and chocolate buttons on top, then dotted it with candles and handed out a pile of plastic spoons. The girls thought it was the coolest cake and they all sat on the floor and gorged on it.'

'Good old Nanny May,' said Martha sourly. 'Was that when you started the affair?'

Jim looked at her and then glanced away. 'We didn't have an affair, Martha. I had no idea she . . . that she felt . . .'

'That she was truly, madly and deeply in love with you? Ah, Jim, you must've known.'

'Soon after that party,' Jim said, 'she had a night out arranged with her sister. The one who lived in Scotland. Both of us were late back from work, so she'd changed from her usual clothes into something more glamorous. I saw her in a totally different light.'

'Did you kiss her?'

'Nope.' Jim didn't flinch as Martha nodded. 'But I wanted to. I couldn't chance having an affair. We gravitated towards one another, but I stopped it. I knew that if it all went pear-shaped, I'd be lost. The girls would be lost. We needed her to stay.'

'Did you love her secretly all that time?'

'Yes and no,' Jim said. 'I didn't really allow myself to go there. But there were moments when I wished we were together.'

'So why did you come here with me? Why keep our marriage going for so long?'

'I felt I owed it to you. After all the years of not really knowing if I loved you or you loved me, I figured the least I could do was try.'

'How generous of you,' she said bitterly. 'You needn't have bothered.' She said it in a matter-of-fact way. 'It wasn't ever going to work between us really.'

'I hoped it might,' Jim said. 'I thought if we were away from everything we knew that somehow a bit of magic might take over. I wanted it to work. I loved the notion that we've been together for so long and that we could rekindle something.'

'I was sick to my stomach when we first came here,' Martha admitted. 'I'd never felt more trapped. I missed my work so badly I could barely breathe. When I delivered that baby on the side of the road that day, it was as if my world had opened up once more.'

'I'm sorry we didn't make it,' Jim said. 'I really do wish you the best.'

'I know you do,' she said with a sigh. 'You're not a bad man, Jim. You're an excellent father and grandfather. You and I are on different pages of different books. We were just too polite to do anything about it until now.'

She poured coffee and they cradled a cup each.

'If there's anything you need . . . for the cottage or anything else . . . I'll look after you financially. You won't go without.'

'Thank you,' she said.

He finished his coffee and put the cup in the dishwasher. Taking a final glance around the cottage, he took her hand.

'I wish you the very best. Please don't be a stranger in Pebble Bay.'

She walked him out to his car and stood waving until he was out of sight.

Hardly a usual scene for a couple that were parting ways after a lifetime together, she mused. But then again, nothing had ever been usual in her life.

Martha glanced at her watch and realised that she could still make it to the community centre for the last ten minutes. She locked up and drove at high speed, knowing that there would be at least one mother who needed her advice.

She was met with a little ripple of applause as the women asked if she was okay. With a smile on her face, she assured them that she was just fine.

There was a discussion about reflux and heartburn in babies. As it happened, Martha had completed a specific course on that very subject not so long ago, so she was able to give them solid information.

When the time was up and the next people to use the hall, the senior citizens' club, began to arrive, she had a brief moment where she wondered if she might feel lonely. As she watched her pregnant women file out, one of the older ladies coming in looked over and smiled at her. Martha smiled back and the woman came to stand beside her.

'You must stay and join us some time,' she said. 'I've been meaning to say that to you. I'm Norah, by the way. You're still terribly busy by the looks of things. But we have outings in the evenings to the theatre and we even do little holidays. We'd love you to join us any time.'

Martha took a leaflet that had a list of names and numbers on it.

'Our committee changes yearly, which means there are always different activities on offer.'

'Thank you,' she said. It was on the tip of her tongue to ask if Norah knew that Jim had left, but she realised there was no way she could know. It was clearly fate or someone watching over her.

'It's very short notice,' Norah said, 'but we have a dinner in Pebble Bay this evening and there'll be a demonstration on flower arranging. Now I know that might sound a bit boring, but we had this lady last year and asked her back. She makes the most extraordinary showpieces from predominantly wild flowers and foliage.'

'Oh, that sounds wonderful,' said Martha. 'Do you know, I think I'll join you!'

'Fantastic,' said Norah. 'I'll take full credit for finding you.'

They swapped phone numbers and Norah gave her the details of the evening's event. There was even a minibus organised to collect and drop home so that she could have a glass of wine if she wanted.

She hadn't made it to her car before her phone rang. Mrs Winston was all in a heap saying her daughter-in-law was in labour and the baby wasn't waiting for anyone. Martha assured her she'd be there in a matter of minutes and took directions, assuring the woman she'd be there to save the day.

The labour was long and hard and she ended up accompanying young Lauren to the hospital, where she had a C-section. Martha stayed with her and said she'd report back to her husband, who was stuck on the farm with the livestock and had no clue his wife was giving birth.

'You're so good to stay with me. I don't know where I'd

be without you,' said Lauren as her teeth chattered in shock.

'I'll stay just as long as you need me,' said Martha.

Lauren was exhausted and after a while said she'd happily sleep. Martha watched over her for a while, then called a taxi to bring her to pick up her car. She waved off the taxi and drove home quickly along the now familiar back roads.

When she reached the cottage, she realised she had fifteen minutes to get ready before the minibus was due to arrive. She jumped into the shower and grabbed a trusty trouser suit, putting a camisole with a line of sparkles around the neck underneath. Her make-up was only just finished when the bus pulled up outside. She hadn't time to feel nervous as she climbed inside.

Norah introduced her to the other five occupants and handed her a child's paper party mug.

'It's Prosecco! Will you have a drop?'

Martha took it with a grin and raised it high. 'Cheers!'

The restaurant wasn't one she and Jim had been to. It was only a step up from a café really, and a bit clattery and noisy. The menu, most of which was served in a basket with fries, was cheap and cheerful. She ordered fish and chips and mushy peas, suddenly realising she was starving.

The evening was fantastic. The flower arrangement master class was incredible, and although Martha knew she'd never be able to recreate any of it, she loved watching it happening. The mood in the room was jovial and the people were so friendly. There were two men in the audience and Norah whispered that neither would be worth taking on.

'They think they're God's gift. There aren't many men

to choose from, so these two have landed in heaven if you ask me!'

'I'm not on the lookout for a man right now,' Martha said. 'I've recently split with my husband and I need to learn how to live without him.'

'Oh, I'm sorry to hear that,' Norah said, and Martha knew she meant it. 'Well, any time you need company, call me. My husband died two years ago and without this group I don't know what I would've done. I understand how it feels to suddenly be alone.'

It was after midnight when Martha turned the key in the door of the cottage. She closed it and clicked the lock across. Flicking on the kettle, she decided she'd have a hot port to send her to sleep.

Jim had always hated opera; he said it was nothing more than glorified shouting. She marched to the stereo system and put on Placido Domingo very loudly, and then turned it up even more. Closing her eyes, she savoured his dulcet tones. She made a stiff hot port and swayed to the music. Knowing she wouldn't be disturbing anyone, she ran a bath with far too many bubbles and turned the music up again. She lit candles, then dropped her clothes on the floor in the bedroom and kicked them across the room, where they landed messily on the chair. Giddy with the freedom of it all, she sank into the bath, inhaling the delicious scent of the bubbles. It occurred to her that she could possibly drown. She was quite tipsy and the warm water was very relaxing.

Did she want to drown? she wondered.

Thinking about it, she knew she didn't at all.

It was past three o'clock in the morning by the time she

eventually turned off the lights and went to bed. She didn't sob. She didn't reach for Jim in the bed and she didn't feel as if her life were ending. Quite the opposite. Martha felt as if a new moon had dawned and she had so much to look forward to. She felt happy for the first time in possibly her whole life.

Chapter 36

WITH THE EVENTS OVER THE LAST WHILE, BEATRICE knew she had no idea what was around the corner in life. Their mother was away with the fairies, but she would be at the other end of the phone should she need her.

It was glorious having Dad back in Pebble Bay. He was like a burst of sunshine and she hadn't realised quite how much she'd missed him until he was there again. He'd started redoing Nanny May's cottage, but being her dad, he was never too busy for her.

He was sitting beside her now as they waited in the clinic for her appointment.

'You're not going alone,' he'd said. 'Not when I can be there. I don't care how old you are, you still need your daddy. I was there last time and I'll be there this time too.'

They would take blood and she could either wait for the hour and a half or they would call her.

'You'll be like a cat on a hot tin roof if you wait at the clinic. Why don't we go for a walk on the beach and have a cappuccino and by then it'll be time.'

So that was the plan, and Beatrice was incredibly grateful for it.

As the phlebotomist took her blood, she literally said a prayer under her breath that it contained the right hormones to say she was pregnant. Once again the doctor on duty told her to avoid home pregnancy tests.

'It's too early to tell and it tends to upset ladies unnecessarily. So let us do the testing for now and you try to stay calm.'

She smiled and agreed, deciding it would be best not to admit she'd already upset herself horribly. So that box was, unfortunately, ticked.

'We'll call you as soon as the result comes back,' said the doctor as they shook hands. Jim stood up and hugged her, helping her into her summer jacket.

'Come on, then, let's get some air and we'll have the result in no time.'

They drove back to Pebble Bay and walked along the beach, passing several people they knew. Jim chatted to each of them while expertly leading Beatrice on ahead before there was any in-depth conversation.

They stopped and bought takeaway cappuccinos and sat on a bench overlooking the beach.

'This is just like old times, isn't it?' Jim said as he held her hand. 'Except this time, instead of being worried about your exam results or whether or not some rogue of a boy will call, we're waiting to know if you'll be a mum.'

'Yeah, it's the same bench but there's quite a jump in importance with this issue, isn't there?'

'If it didn't work this time, you have another go, isn't that right?' Jim asked.

Beatrice assured him she would try again as soon as they allowed her. 'And after that, I'm out of options,' she said.

'Not necessarily,' Jim said. 'What about foreign adoption

or surrogacy? I've heard your mother talking about that. It seems to be more and more popular.'

'Bless you, Dad,' she said, leaning her head against his shoulder. 'This can't be easy for you. In your day the men didn't even go into the births, let alone have to know details of alternative ways of getting pregnant.'

'It's ironic,' he said as he looked out at the view. 'From the time you were teenagers your mother and I feared one of you would come home saying you were pregnant. Ah, it wouldn't have been the end of the world, of course. But it would've changed the path of your lives.'

'We all knew better than to come back to Mum with that kind of news,' Beatrice said.

'And now here we are, hoping and praying that you're going to be a single mum.'

'When you put it like that . . .' Beatrice said with a grin.

Her phone rang. She fumbled with it, almost dropping it off her lap where it was poised and waiting. She looked at the number on the screen.

'It's them,' she said.

'Good luck, love.'

'Hello?'

'Hello, Beatrice, it's Maia, one of the nurses from the clinic.'

'Hi, Maia.' Beatrice could barely breathe.

'So we have your blood results through, Beatrice.'

'Yes?'

'And I'm delighted to tell you that the test shows that you are indeed pregnant.'

'I . . . Really? Are you certain?'

'Yes,' she said happily. 'Obviously it's very early stages. We would like you to come in and see the doctor in a week. I'll send you through an appointment by email if that's okay?'

'Yes, that's brilliant. Thank you, and I'll see the doctor then.'

She hung up and stood up and threw her hands in the air, tossing her head back. 'Yahoo!'

Jim stood up too and pulled her into his arms, and they danced around in a circle, laughing and crying, and didn't care who saw them.

'Will I tell everyone or should I wait?' she asked, chewing the side of her nail.

'Well I think your poor sisters are on tenterhooks and you're not going to get away with not telling them. I'm sure Martha would love to know too.'

She made calls to Jeannie, Rose and Martha, all of whom were thrilled for her.

So much had happened in the past few weeks. Each of their lives had been turned upside down. But crazy as it sounded, she had a feeling things were going to settle and somehow the future would be brighter.

That evening, Rose and Jeannie called over to congratulate Beatrice in person. They sat and had herbal tea and talked about their plans.

'The little cousins are going to have to know each other,' Jeannie said. 'I can come over more. I don't want us to lose touch.'

'We won't,' said Beatrice.

'Oh, Rosie, darling,' Jeannie said. 'Are you feeling broody and left out? Sorry, sweetie.'

'I'm not broody,' she said. 'Thrilled as I am for you two, I couldn't fathom having a baby right now. I'm just envious that you're going to have this wonderful bond. Don't mind me. I'm a horrible cow for even thinking that.'

'You're about as far from horrible as it's possible to be,' Jeannie said, hugging her.

'For sure,' said Beatrice. 'I'll bet you'll be begging me to shut up before long,' she laughed.

'Hey, how was Mum about it?' Rose asked. 'Did she do her I'm-so-calm-that-I-sound-barely-interested voice?'

'No, she actually sounded as if she was having a little sniffle,' said Beatrice. 'I think she was genuinely pleased for me.'

'Wonders will never cease,' said Jeannie. 'I rang her after you did and got the same reaction. She even mentioned coming to visit at some point after the baby is born.'

They chatted for another hour before deciding it was bedtime. Nick and Jim were watching a movie with Ali, and Beatrice said she had a seriously busy day the following day. She said goodnight to everyone and Jim walked her back to her flat. She gave him a tight hug, and he kissed her forehead.

'I'm so very happy for you,' he said.

He stood there while she opened the door and went inside. She felt worn out but exhilarated. The sense of new life was almost intoxicating. She couldn't believe she and Jeannie would have babies within a year of each other; it was the icing on the cake.

She fussed over Ned, then got ready for bed and turned out the lights. Ned shuffled onto her feet, and she let him lie there, enjoying the weight of his warm little body.

As she drifted off to sleep, with a huge smile on her face, she remembered that Lily was coming in tomorrow to pick her free dress. She'd passed on the details of the other entrants and Richard had said he'd tell her his choice when they met for coffee. Given that she chose Lily, she felt it only fair to let Richard have his pick from the rest. It felt good to be helping other women have a wonderful wedding day. Odd as it seemed, she felt it was really helping Richard to get over his own loss.

The following morning, Beatrice met with a very emotional Lily. She chose the ceremony dress and it fitted her like a glove.

'It's like it was made for you,' Beatrice said. 'I'm delighted you'll get to enjoy wearing it.'

'There's no bad omen attached to this dress, is there?' Lily asked anxiously.

'No, there isn't,' said Beatrice. 'The wedding wasn't meant to be and the bride and groom had the sense to see that. It would be a crying shame if it went to waste. It's such a pretty one too.'

Lily had just gone with the dress over her arm when Richard arrived. Looking as if he were embarrassed to be there, he loitered near the door until Beatrice went to say hello.

'I can see you're busy,' he said. 'Are you still free for that coffee?'

'I'm actually finished for the day,' she said. 'I know we said we'd go out for coffee, but I'm pretty tired. So would you like to come in and sit down on the sofa in the main viewing gallery? There's nobody using it. I could do with a cold drink. Can I offer you Prosecco or beer or something soft?'

'I'd kill for a beer,' he said. She grabbed a bottle from the fridge, and poured herself a sparkling water.

'So I made a choice,' Richard said. 'I'd like the second dress to go to Megan, the girl whose father died and the wedding had to be postponed.'

'Wonderful,' Beatrice said, smiling at him. 'I'll text her right now.'

As she did so, Isobelle waved in and said she was off home. Annemarie had gone at lunchtime. Beatrice followed Isobelle out so she could drop the shutters, then came back in and kicked off her shoes.

'Now I can relax for a bit. Wow, I'm pooped. It was non-stop all day.' She told him about Lily and how pretty she looked. She'd taken a photo on her phone, which he said he would like to see.

'I'm glad for her,' he said genuinely.

Beatrice called Richard's choice there and then. After the initial screaming and shouting of excitement down the phone, Megan said she'd be in the following day.

'Job done,' said Beatrice. 'I can see your halo from here.'

Just for something to say, Beatrice told him about Martin. Richard sat and drank his beer, hanging on her every word.

'Jeez, that sounds like a novel. It's insane,' he said. 'She sounds very strong and enterprising, your sister. I hope she makes the company a massive success. You girls have an amazing relationship. That's great.'

Feeling giddy yet oddly nervous, Beatrice said she had some news of her own.

'The IVF worked. I'm pregnant,' she said. Just being able to drop that sentence into conversation was awesome. 'It's the best news I could possibly wish for.'

'Oh my God, that's wonderful,' said Richard. 'You're amazing, Beatrice. You know that, right? I've never met anyone like you. You're dynamic, kind and you've jumped through hoops to be a mother. You blow me away!'

She giggled, and was about to tell him he was being too kind when he leaned in and kissed her, full on the lips. His arm slipped around her waist as he moved towards her further. She pulled away, looking astonished.

'You did hear me say I'm pregnant, right?'

'Yes,' he said. 'And you heard me say I think you're amazing, right?'

She nodded, and when he kissed her a second time, she didn't pull away.

One year later

BEATRICE HELD UP HER DAUGHTER AND ADMIRED her in her christening robe. She'd ended up taking on a whole new line of them when she couldn't find a decent one.

'You're always looking for the next business deal,' said Jim with a chuckle. 'But that's why you're so successful. I'm very proud of you.'

'Thanks, Dad. Will you hold Carla-May while I finish getting dressed?'

Delighted to see her grandad, Carla-May squealed with delight.

'Richard, you need to hurry up or we'll be late,' Beatrice said, knocking on the bathroom door as she ran into the bedroom to grab her jacket and shoes.

'I'm coming!' he said as he appeared, knotting his tie. 'Oh, wowzer, look at you, Carla-May. She's absolutely gorgeous,' he added. 'She's like a little doll.'

'She is, isn't she?' Beatrice said with a happy sigh as she joined them in the kitchen. 'Are we ready to go to the church?'

'I wonder if your mother will turn up,' said Jim as they walked the short distance from Beatrice's flat.

'Well, your guess is as good as mine,' said Beatrice.

Jeannie and Austin were there and she was desperately trying to stop him from running up and down the aisle.

'I need Nick with me,' she moaned. 'I can't keep up with this little guy and I'm as sick as a dog with this pregnancy. I'm so bad that Dr Blake said he wouldn't be surprised if it's twins.'

'Well, they run in the family,' said Rose, hugging her. 'Poor you, I'll mind Austin. You go and sit down.'

'She looks totally green,' said Ali. 'When is Uncle Nick coming over for good? If she is expecting twins, can you imagine what their house will be like? It's already mayhem with just Austin.'

'I think he's coming next week,' said Rose. 'I know it's soon. His new reconstruction clinic opens for business at the end of the month, so it can't be too far away. I don't know how he does it. It was one thing doing nips and tucks, but dealing with accident victims and people who need their bodies rebuilt? I couldn't cope.'

'He's a talented surgeon,' said Ali, 'so I'm glad he's fulfilling his dream.'

'It's great that Richard's trust has given him the funding. They only pick one initiative a year and they went for his before even realising who Nick was.'

The ceremony was almost over when the sound of rushing feet could be heard up the side of the church. Before they even turned around, they all knew it was Martha.

'She's getting earlier,' whispered Jim to Rose. 'Give her another few years and she might actually make a family occasion on time.'

As they gathered with their family and friends in the Pebble Bay Hotel after the ceremony, Beatrice and Richard marvelled at how far they'd come in such a short time.

'This time last year I was heartbroken,' said Richard.

'And I was chewing my fingernails to the quick, hoping against hope that my IVF had worked.'

'Now I couldn't be happier,' said Richard. 'I want Carla-May to grow up calling me Dad.'

'I know, honey, and she will.'

'I'd like to make sure of that,' he said as he dropped to one knee.

'Hey, folks,' Jim said. 'I hate to butt in on your moment, but when you choose to do this in the middle of a party . . .'

'I want the world to hear me, Jim. Beatrice Brady, will you marry me?'

With tears in her eyes, she accepted as Richard produced the most stunning diamond ring.

'Well, I'm ever so glad I managed to make it today,' said Martha. 'You girls have sorted yourselves out rather nicely.'

They gathered around and Jeannie handed each of them a beautiful frame with the photo that the waiter had taken in Ballyshaden.

'That seems like a lifetime ago,' said Martha. 'Although we were all smiling, most of us were hurting on the inside that evening.'

'Things are a lot better now, though,' said Jim as he thanked Jeannie for his photograph. 'How about we ask the waiter to take another one today?'

'We're missing Nick,' said Jeannie as she tried to stop Austin from running around like a lunatic.

'No we're not,' a voice behind her said. 'I'm a little bit jet-lagged, but I'm here.'

'Dada!' said Austin as he ran into Nick's arms.

This time when the waiter took the photo, the smiles were genuine. The Brady family might be scattered from

Connemara to Pebble Bay, but they were all happily living the lives they each wanted to live.

'The only person missing today is Nanny May,' said Martha.

'I wouldn't have thought you'd want her here,' said Rose.

'I've had time to think,' said Martha. 'She afforded me the freedom to be who I wanted to be. Instead of resenting her, I should've appreciated her more.'

'She said in her letters that she'd watch over us,' said Jeannie. 'So I'm sure she can hear you.'

'I don't really believe in that bunkum,' said Martha. 'But if it makes you happy, that's nice.'

The girls grinned. Their mother would never change. She was unbending in her thoughts and actions.

The following day, Beatrice went to lay some of the flowers from the christening on Nanny May's grave. She was about to walk away when she spotted a note sticking out from the side of the gravestone.

Dear Nanny May,

I wanted you to know that I'm sorry for behaving the way I did towards you. Thank you for raising my daughters and helping to shape them into the wonderful women they are today.

I wish I'd realised sooner what a godsend you actually were.

If you truly are watching over us, maybe you'd help Jim find a new woman. I think we both know he deserves that.

Anyway, I just wanted to say thank you. Better late than never, I suppose.

Martha

Beatrice folded it and put it back. She knew it must've taken a lot for their mother to write that. Maybe there was a glimmer of hope that they'd all have a relationship with her at some point. She texted her sisters, telling them that she finally had proof that Martha did think of her own children and not just the ones she'd helped deliver. It was a good feeling. It wasn't quite what they wanted, she knew that, but it was a start. For now, that was good enough.

Acknowledgements

THIS PART ALWAYS GIVES ME THE WILLIES! ARE WE allowed to say willy any more? Probably not . . .

Anyhow, there are literally hundreds of people I'd love to thank and I can't possibly drag you, my reader, through that. So I'm going to try and condense it so you don't fall off you seat or sun lounger or out of bed with boredom.

I have to kick off by thanking my family. Without Mum and Dad I would've been banjaxed this past year. While I was in hospital they seamlessly stepped in and did what was required. They are amazing all the time, but this past year they've been extra special. I love you both with all my heart and I hope next year will be better.

Thanks to my hubby Cian, who has made more hospital dashes than you'd believe. He's packed endless hospital bags and had to listen to me making choking noises at night as my burnt-from-radiotherapy throat made itself known. Thank you for supporting me even while it's been continuously awful. I love you and I hope better times are ahead. I think we deserve it!

Sacha and Kim, our two teenagers, have been outstanding. They've seen more sickness and been through more emotions than most adults have in an entire lifetime. I was so ill at one point that I couldn't even dress myself. Kim was there to help without any fuss. She baked incredible cakes to welcome me home from hospital (several times) and made banners to match. She helped me with online shopping, even ordering stuff in a size that didn't quite fit me but astonishingly fitted her! You're a beautiful girl inside and out and I love you with all my heart.

Sacha, my son, gives the best hugs imaginable. They come in an endless supply and are so gratefully received. His driving skills have improved to a point where I no longer need a tea towel stuffed in my mouth to stop the screams. Only joking. He's a brilliant driver and has brought me anywhere I need to go. He's the most obliging person I know and has done everything to help out at a time when I needed it most. I love you so much and I am so lucky to have you. You aren't just a handsome face, you're also an amazing guy. Any girl who ends up with you will be very lucky. But I hope both of you know that I'll be watching like a hawk and only the most special people will do for either of you. Cue Irish Mammy Syndrome. Yes, it's a real thing and I've got it badly.

Thank you to my brother Tim and his girlfriend Hilary. To the McGraths, my in-laws, and my cousins. To Steffy and Robyn, who are the best sisters I could want. To my aunties and uncles, you are all gems.

Thanks to my agent and friend, Sheila Crowley, who has also shown cancer the door in the past year. Specific thanks to you and Pat for the pillow sprays! Sheila, this book is dedicated to you with so much affection.

Thanks to Marie Robinson for being a constant help, quietly and without fuss. We all love you.

This book wouldn't be on the shelf without two incredible ladies. Ciara Doorley and Sherise Hobbs are my editors. They take my books and polish them up and make them shine. This time, I was a bit broken and they scooped up the pieces of what I'd written and cheerfully kept me afloat, and along with Rachel Pierce, who did the copy-edit, they helped me produce another novel. Thank you, ladies, for your patience, advice and outstanding help.

Thanks also to team Hachette Books Ireland, namely Bernard, Joanna, Breda, Siobhan and Jim. Special thanks must go to Ruth Shern, who brings me to meet the book-sellers. We usually have some sort of accessories. For the Christmas books we had flashing snowman earrings and head boppers. Whatever tack I throw at her, Ruth puts those things on and carries on stoically. I'm not sure what I'll bring for this one, but I'll make sure it's very blingy!

Thanks also to team Headline UK, namely Jo, Helena, Emily and Becky. You all mind me and look after me wonderfully when I visit. You really know how to make me feel special. Between Dublin and London I have such a fabulous group of people at my back.

Thanks to Susie Cronin for your PR skills and kindly delivered help here in Ireland, and I couldn't gloss over the incredible opportunities that Becky Hunter has got me in the UK. Thank you both so much.

I have so many friends who have been there for me over the last very scary and difficult year. I won't name all of them or you will end up dropping off to sleep! But I couldn't possibly finish this acknowledgements section without mentioning a few of them. I'm doing it alphabet-ically, so please don't feel you've been left to near the end because you aren't worthy. You are all equally precious and appreciated: Rachel Allen, Caroline Grace Cassidy, Marian Corson, Teresa Costello, Fiona Costigan, Elaine Crowley, Fiona Cullen, Amanda Ferguson, Elaine Flynn,

Aoife and Emily Kelly, Eve Keogh, Jill Lyons, Julie McGill, Trish McGovern, Suzanne Mackey, Sarah McSharry, Karen Morris, Marie Moynihan, Marie and Laura Robinson, Selina Ross, Chris Upton, Annalea Waddington . . . and I could go on for ever but I really should stop! Anyone I haven't mentioned, I apologise to profusely; it is down to my chemo brain and not your fabulousness.

Three special ladies battled alongside me this year. I wish they didn't have to, but they were strong, brave and determined and I hope they are all done with the cancer lark now. Huge kudos to cancer vixens Emer Shaw, Amanda Cahill and Sheila Crowley. I hated watching you endure the awfulness of this disease. I was so sad and worried when you told me about your diagnoses and now I'm beyond thrilled that you are all on the road to recovery. Did I mention I hate cancer? I want it to leave my precious friends alone from now on, thank you.

Cathy Kelly is the one I go to so I can download. One of us goes first and then the other. After a session of downloading, our hard drives are once again ready for more sh** to be flung at us! Suffice it to say I am surrounded by so many people who care.

Thanks to Aisling Hurley and Sam McGregor of Breast Cancer Ireland for being so supportive and kind. Usually I'm on the fund-raising side of the fence but lately I've been on the patients' side and they are so kind and caring. I'm looking forward to getting back to helping out again. If you'd all like to do me a favour, please download their app that shows you how to check your breasts and gives a little reminder to do so each month. It's available in the app store and it's free.

Thanks to Tom Geraghty and the staff of St Gerard's

School for everything you do for Sacha. With special thanks to Maire Ni Cana for her unbending support and kindness in the background. Thanks also to Brian Moore and the staff of Rathdown School for looking after Kim.

I'm nearly finished! I know you've probably fallen off your chair several lines back, but if you can bear with me for just another few minutes, I want to thank the staff of Blackrock Clinic, my home from home and the place I go to every week to get *fixed*. Dr David Fennelly, Dr Rachel Reddy and the nurses and staff of the Nightingale Unit are my heroes. I am on the floor bowing and thanking each and every one of you. I've said it before and it cannot be said enough, you are all angels on earth and I am beyond grateful to you for keeping me alive. A special hello to Sinead, Johanna and Ella, Riza, Aidan and Robbie.

Massive thanks to Professor John Armstrong and the radiology team at St Vincent's private hospital for the radiotherapy that zapped the massive tumour in my neck. Thanks also to the ambulance crew for taking me to my appointments when I was so weak and ill. I improved daily and I am so grateful to all of you.

My dear readers, those of you who are still awake, I want to tell you how much you light up my life. I get messages and they make my day. It astounds me when anyone takes the time to get in touch. Thank you for reading my stories and buying my books and allowing me to keep doing a job I adore. It's a privilege and an honour and I love it.

To the dedicated booksellers, I hope I'm able to bake you more brownies soon.

Last and by no means least, thank you to Herbie Doodle, our curly blonde loveable ball of fuzz, doggy-do. You make me smile the minute I see you. As for Tom the cat, you're very old and a bit cranky. I can relate to that. You still give little snuggles and I love you for that.

I'm finished!

You can wake up and pretend you were listening all along.

As usual, writing has been my therapy. So I'm going to thank my own novel as well. That's allowed, isn't it?

I wish you happiness and health one and all.

I hope you enjoy *Letters To My Daughters*.

Love and light,

Emma x

Can a rambling Spanish villa hold the key to love?

Remember the promise I made to you at our wedding . . .

Restoring a Spanish villa brings Shelly back to the place she and her husband once loved, fulfilling the promise he made that they would return. But as plans to transform the villa into a romantic wedding venue take shape, Shelly discovers her children may need the move more than she does.

Her son Jake has begun to question the things he values most: his career as a pilot, his relationship with his girlfriend. Could Spain offer him the change he's seeking? Shelly's daughter Leila arrives with a new-born baby in tow, but then hears some startling news she wasn't expecting. As Casa Maria takes its first booking, will it turn out to be more than a romantic promise made all those years ago? Perhaps a second chance at new beginnings?

**Unwrap this captivating story about hope,
love and the special bond between
mothers and daughters.**

Happy Birthday, darling girl . . .

Ever since she can remember, Roisin has
received a birthday card in the post. Signed with
love from the birth mother she has never met.

Brought up by her adoptive parents, Keeley
and Doug, Roisin has wanted for nothing. But on her
thirtieth birthday a letter comes that shakes her world.
For Keeley, who's raised Roisin as her own,
the letter reminds her of a guilty secret she's
been holding for thirty years.

And for Nell, keeping watch in the lighthouse,
the past is a place she rarely goes. Until a young
runaway arrives seeking shelter, and unwraps
the gift of hope for them all . . .

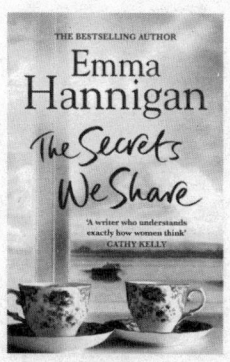

THE BESTSELLING AUTHOR
Emma
Hannigan
The Secrets
We Share
'A writer who understands
exactly how women think'
CATHY KELLY

**Don't miss this beautiful moving story
of heart and home . . .**

Devastated after a tragedy, Nathalie Conway
finds herself on a plane to Ireland. She is on her way
to stay with her grandmother Clara. The grandmother
who, up until now, Nathalie had no idea existed . . .

As Clara awaits her granddaughter's arrival,
she is filled with a new sense of hope. She has
spent the last twenty years praying her son Max
would come back into her life. Perhaps now he
can find a way to forgive her for the past.
And her granddaughter may be the thread to stitch
the pieces of her beloved family back together.

**Uncover the magical secrets of Caracove
in Emma Hannigan's glorious novel**

A little magic is about to come to
sleepy Caracove Bay . . .

Lexie and her husband Sam have spent years lovingly
restoring No. 3 Cashel Square to its former glory.
So imagine Lexie's delight when a stranger knocks
on the door, asking to see the house she was born
in over sixty years ago.

Kathleen is visiting from America, longing to see
her childhood home . . . and longing for distraction
from the grief of losing her husband.

And as Lexie and Sam battle over whether or not to
have a baby and Kathleen struggles with her loss, the
two women realise their unexpected friendship will
touch them in ways neither could have imagined.